Lust,
Love
&
Family Legacies

A Contemporary Tale of Love, Passion and Pain

A Novel

R. Ty Farris

This is a work of fiction. Names, characters, places and incidents portrayed in this production are the product of the author's imagination or are used fictitiously. Any resemblance to actual persons, living or dead, events, and locales is entirely coincidental.

All rights reserved.

Copyright © 2024 by R. Ty Farris
This book contains an excerpt from the short story, *"Richard P. Cannon"* from Book One, **"In the Kingdoms of Black Men,"** from **The Seven Stories Series**, a collection of tales by R. Ty Farris.

Library of Congress Cataloging-In-Publication Data
Farris, R. Ty, author.
Title: Lust, Love & Family Legacies/R. Ty Farris.
Description: First Edition.

Identifiers: LCCN 2023946943
ISBN 979-8-9884348-1-8 (eBook)
ISBN 979-8-9884348-0-1 (Paperback)
ISBN 979-8-9884348-2-5 (Hardcover)

Cover Design by *Le Loup Studios*
The Dauntless Publishing Group LLC Chicago

In Recognition

We all must live through our childhoods. This book is dedicated to those of us still carrying childhood traumas like backpacks into adulthood. Keep on keeping on.

It Takes a Team

During the writing of this novel, encouragement and guidance were offered by several readers who graciously shared their valuable time and insights. Kudos to the collaborative partnership between Immersion XP Publications and The Dauntless Publishing Group for its great work in helping to bring this book to life. The partnership's unwavering commitment provided the foundation for the launching of this novel. Shout outs to both Rodney Hazard for the fantastic book cover design and Megan Sheer for the book's interior design. Many thanks to Ellen Tarlin, copy editor, for proofreading the final manuscript. Her insights are greatly appreciated.

An Independent Publisher
for Independent Authors

Table of Contents

One	1
Two	13
Three	31
Four	37
Five	52
Six	58
Seven	69
Eight	77
Nine	84
Ten	93
Eleven	108
Twelve	117
Thirteen	125
Fourteen	135
Fifteen	147
Sixteen	155
Seventeen	164
Eighteen	175
Nineteen	189
Twenty	201
Twenty-One	220
Twenty-Two	231
Twenty-Three	239
Twenty-Four	251
Twenty-Five	257
Twenty-Six	274
Twenty-Seven	285
Twenty-Eight	296

"You will face many defeats in life,
     but never let yourself be defeated."

– Maya Angelou

One

This weekly outing with Bird, as usual, becomes a journey into their college days and a discussion about women. The lunch fare is tasty and their view of Michigan Avenue adds some street energy to their conversation. After two hours of eating, drinking, and reliving their glorious college days, Marcus checks the time on his cell phone, then says it is time for him to head back to the office. Bird nods but continues his monologue about Myra James. Myra was the unhinged ex who called Marcus out in the middle of the student union some fifteen years ago. Called Marcus out and poured a paper cup of water over his head and the head of Gloria Foster, who was sitting next to him, her head leaning on his shoulder. Bird witnessed Myra's retribution for being dumped and later sought to comfort her behind his friend's back.

"Too much drama," Marcus says. "I guess you found that out."

"She was wounded." Bird shakes his head side to side then says, "Couldn't recover after your treachery."

"I told her it was over two weeks earlier." Spreading his arms wide for emphasis, Marcus adds, "No means no."

"You should have left her sorority sister alone. That got her goat."

"Which is why she came for you. To get me back."

"I know," Bird says. His smirk resembles the same one he displayed when he told Marcus he was dating Myra. "But when she realized you didn't care, it was over before I even learned her class schedule." They both laugh.

The conversation about Myra comes to a sudden stop when Marcus spies an attractive woman walking past the big glass window of the restaurant. Marcus motions for his friend to look. By the time Bird turns his head as instructed, the woman has moved past their line of vision. Bird hunches his shoulders, with arms extended, palms up, and eyes quizzically focused on Marcus, who grabs his briefcase and heads toward the entrance. Bird hustles to follow.

When they make it outside, Marcus sees the woman has stopped and is looking in her bag. His mind struggles for a decision. The midday Chicago sun is bright and hot on this treeless side of Michigan Avenue. His suit is made of a light fabric but doesn't offer much relief, and there's no breeze off Lake Michigan. Perspiration begins to dampen his skin.

He points north and says, "There she is."

"Who?" Bird says.

Marcus turns to face his friend. "The girl in the burgundy outfit. I want to meet her." It's impulsive and ill-advised, Marcus knows, but he's going to do it; he's going after the statuesque woman who has sauntered past.

Bird eyes the woman in burgundy and says, "Nice. But she doesn't look like a woman you can just run upon in the middle of the Loop. She'll think you're up to no good."

"What's my other option? Let her get away?"

Bird grunts, then says, "Won't be the first one."

Marcus nods in agreement but adds, "Something about her. I have to try."

"The only thing at risk is your pride. Shoot your shot," Bird says. "But she's on the move again."

Marcus spins around and strains to see between the weaving torsos and over the top of bobbing heads on the crowded sidewalk. Then he spots her at the corner of Michigan and Adams Street, stopped by a red light.

"I'm taking my shot, pride be damned." Marcus inhales deeply, gives his friend a clenched-fist salute and, with his exposed pride dangling like a leaf in a soft breeze, shifts his feet in her direction and takes off.

He closes the distance between them. Beads of sweat paste the collar of his shirt to his neck. He loosens his tie and frees the top button. He quickens his stride and turns sideways as he slides between slower-moving bodies. Ahead across Adams, she has paused to look in a store window. He cuts down the distance separating them by half. She waves at someone inside then heads back toward him but turns west on Adams.

Marcus turns on Adams, too, but on the other side of the street. He's now parallel to her. Her strides are long, as long as his own. Her bare left leg pushes the limits of the mid-thigh slit in her skirt. His eyes follow her stealthily, and he speeds up when he sees her halted by a red light. His green light lets him cross to her side of the street.

He trots across Adams and steps up on the curb just two feet behind her. He glances furtively around him to see if he's drawn any unwanted attention. Marcus knows the probability of her giving him the time of day is likely nil. Less than nil, and understandably so. Closing in on the next intersection at Adams and Dearborn, she slows, then stops again. Another red light. Marcus has still not come up with a plan of action when he's near enough to touch her. So, he does. He gently places a hand on her left shoulder, the one attached to the arm that holds her purse. She jerks away, whirls around and leans toward him. Her right hand comes within inches of his face. In it is a small metallic container. A single pinpoint hole stares ominously at him.

"Don't, please," he says, throwing up his hands.

The woman's forehead is creased with deep furrows, and her mouth is deformed by a warning pucker while she looks him up and down, keeping the canister poised for action. Many of the passers-by keep moving, while a few stop but stand at a safe distance. A bulky, young Black man, heading in the opposite direction, stops and steps sideways, closer to her. Like a bodyguard, he crosses his arms and glares at Marcus.

"I mistook you for someone else," Marcus says, his voice a low whisper.

She scans him from head to foot again, her eyes pausing at his face, then his expensive tan suit before continuing on down to his well-crafted glistening black shoes and then back up to linger momentarily on his brown leather briefcase. She lowers her weapon.

"From the rear?" she asks.

"I'm sorry," he says, his hands still raised and palms out in surrender.

"Please, put your hands down before people think *I'm* robbing you."

The furrow in her brow and the twist in her lips have disappeared. A slight smile plays at the corners of her mouth now. She turns to the brooding young man standing next to her and graciously thanks him for his concern. He nods, gives a parting sneer at Marcus, and moves on. Onlookers, both the curious and the concerned, also melt away when the young man leaves.

"I didn't mean to startle you," Marcus says as he slowly lowers his hands.

"But you did."

"And I'm truly sorry."

"And who exactly did you think I was?"

"A friend."

"A friend?" the woman says.

"Yes." He's not sure how to exploit this opportunity.

"Your friend is a woman, I presume."

"Yes. Yes, she is." Marcus feels compelled to add, "Her name's Ana. And I'm Marcus. Marcus Gabriel Greene." He holds out his hand, but she ignores it and starts walking away. "I didn't get your name." He hurries to stay next to her.

"It's Ana."

"Really?" His eyes widen in amazement.

"No, not really." She stops walking and faces him. "Okay, you say you made an honest mistake. But I am *not* Ana." She pivots away and starts walking again.

He keeps pace. Optimism colors his words. "May I have your real name so I can apologize more formally?"

She glances sideways at him, keeps walking, and does not respond. Now that he's this close to her, the woman's magnetism is almost overwhelming. She's prettier than his quick glimpses revealed. *Striking* is the only word that comes to mind as he takes in as many details as he can without becoming creepy. That stylish burgundy suit is matched with a pink silk blouse, and showcasing her shapely calves are a pair of white running shoes. The twist in style intrigues him.

"Headed to a modeling job?" Marcus asks, now feeling a sense of urgency. He needs to get her name. He needs to get a phone number. Like a TV pitchman, Marcus feels pressed by his narrow window of opportunity. She continues walking in silence. She's only a couple of inches below his six feet, and her strides are taking her rapidly toward her destination.

"What if I see you again one day? I can't tap you on your shoulder; it's too risky. What am I supposed to do, call you Ana?"

She slows, half turns her head in his direction, hesitates, then tells him, "My name's Teresa. And I doubt that we'll accidentally run into each other again."

"Let's not, accidentally," he says.

"Look, Marcus Gabriel Greene, you're very charming, but I have to get back to work."

He believes her resistance is lessening. "No number?"

"No number."

"My grandfather said a missed opportunity is worse than a failure. Now I know what he meant, Teresa." He offers his hand. She balls her hand and extends it. He follows her lead. They exchange a quick fist bump, a gesture he takes as another straw to be grasped. "You have to be a little curious, so I'll answer your unasked questions. I am not married. I am not involved in a serious relationship. There is no baby's momma drama."

She arches her eyebrows, then says, "Nice to have met you, Mr. Greene." Teresa begins walking away.

His window is beginning to close. Marcus moves quickly to keep pace and says, "It was *not* a mistake."

She stops. "No?"

"It's fate. And how can I…how can we…walk away from something that has been destined to happen?"

Her laugh is unexpected. Its softness pierces the tenuous barrier that separates strangers. Marcus happily joins her. And for a few seconds, they stand on the crowded street corner and share a silly moment.

"I have to go, destiny or not." Teresa's on the move again.

"May I accompany you a little farther?" he asks.

Although she doesn't slow or look his way, Marcus believes her resistance has dissipated, that he's made a connection and that his decision to chase her does feel more like a fateful act than a foolish one. "I feel like if you go your way and me mine, I wouldn't have had a shot even if we met under more conventional circumstances."

"Really?" She glances sideways at him.

"Would I?" he counters.

"Maybe." Teresa's lips press together as if suppressing a smile.

"My heart just skipped a beat," he says, patting his chest for emphasis.

Teresa stops and faces him. "Just what is it that you do?"

Marcus reaches inside his jacket pocket, pulls out a small gold cardholder, slips out a card and extends his hand. Teresa studies it but leaves the card dangling in space. "A lawyer. I should have known." And then she starts walking again.

"Why?" he says, matching her stride for stride.

"You have a way with words."

"Can I consider that a compliment?"

"If you wish."

"And may I ask, what is it that you do?" he says.

He notices her eyebrows arch again, but she doesn't answer. After several blocks, they come to another intersection, and she hesitates, then crosses. Marcus stays by her side as if connected at the hips.

"You don't have an office to go to?" she says.

"After I've gotten your phone number."

"Persistent," she says.

"Enamored."

Teresa attracts her share of obvious attention from men as if Marcus is invisible. She brushes against him as she slants her shoulders to avoid a couple rushing down the center of the sidewalk. Her breasts graze his chest. Her warm breath brushes his face. She doesn't break stride as they cross to the opposite side of the street. And, he notices, she appears cool and undisturbed by the humid July heat, while beads of sweat have now collected under his arms and are rolling downward into his waistband.

They walk until they are next to the city's renowned towering black skyscraper. The glassy structure rises above them like an urban mountain. Teresa slows her pace, steps over to a spot next to the building, and stops. She leans against the smooth surface, appears to study his face, then says, "I'll tell you what. Give me your card, and we'll see what happens." Teresa extends her hand. He lifts his briefcase, opens it, and takes out a pen. He scribbles a number on the back of the card and gives it to her.

"My cell phone number, just in case you miss me at the office." She nods but does not reply. "Please feel free to use it anytime. Day or night."

She looks him in the eyes and says, "I can make it from here. Thanks for the company." She slips the card into her purse.

Marcus moves with her when she turns away, reluctant to be left behind. "Can I get your number, just in case?"

She doesn't seem put off by his refusal to go away. She stops again. "In case of what?"

"In case you lose my card."

Teresa cites the information printed on his business card and then his cell phone number. "Your information won't be lost."

"Good," he says.

"Or discarded. But no guarantees I'll use it. Okay?" Teresa steps closer. "However, Mr. Greene, you've gotten my attention."

All he can do is grin as he stands inches from a kiss.

"I really have to run." She raises her arm and looks at an imaginary watch on her bare wrist for emphasis. "This is where we must part company."

"If I don't hear from you, I'll remember this day for the rest of my life."

Teresa gives a quick wave of her hand. She continues west, leaving him behind. Marcus doesn't follow but stands, with one hand in his pocket and the other gripping the handle of his briefcase, and watches until Teresa has crossed Wacker Drive, then disappeared over the steep rise and out of sight.

* * *

The phone rings three times before Missy answers. "Yes?"
"Try *hello*, at least."
"Hey, boss."
"I'll be there in ten," Marcus tells the administrative assistant, then ends the call and makes another.
"Bull's-eye or blown opportunity?" Bird says.
"I'm a trained sniper. I don't miss."
Bird chuckles, then says, "Her name?"
"Teresa."
"That her real name?" Bird says.
"Yes. I think. Maybe."
"A phone number?" Bird says.
"She took mine."
"Bull's-eye, you say." Bird grunts.
"She's interested," Marcus says, his optimism taking a hit.
"She looks as good as you imagined?"
"Better." Marcus emits an exaggerated sigh.
"My condolences."
"I think it's fifty-fifty," Marcus says.
"She took your info but no promise to call. Am I right? Your odds are more like mine when I play the lottery."
"I took my shot, and we'll see what happens," Marcus says, then disconnects the call. He reaches his office building, and as he pushes through the revolving door, he begins to doubt that he will ever hear from Teresa. She may already have a man. Or even a woman.

Marcus usually gets the woman he goes after. His problem is staying interested after the catch. He knows he's not as afraid of commitment as a few have declared him to be. Nor does he lack passion, although he did suspect that was an issue until his relationship with Ana. He's concluded that he doesn't do well with drama. And all the women he's been with have brought drama of one kind or another: too clingy, too needy, too volatile or too demanding. So, he's always moved on to the next romantic adventure. And if Teresa doesn't happen, there are plenty of other good-looking women in Chicago who won't hesitate to give him a name and a number. And make him promise to call.

* * *

Marcus strolls into his law firm's suite located on the ninth floor of a century-old building and greets Missy, who looks up and beams. He heads straight to his office, grabs the top of the doorframe when he enters, then drops into his brown leather chair and lifts his feet onto the oval table serving as his desk. Directly in front of him is the *Wall Street Journal* with the eye-catching headline, "Spain Wins World Cup in South Africa," and next to it is a stack of folders, all active cases, in a single wire tray. He pulls the tray to him and rifles through the files until he finds the Womack case. It's the biggest divorce case he's ever handled.

His divorce cases fulfill his need to litigate, a need born out of his days on LaSalle Street. Before taking over this law practice, he had been an associate attorney at a major LaSalle Street firm where his practice focused on private equity funds: the paperwork game, as he describes it. Marcus never planned on being an attorney heading up his own law practice, but after his grandfather passed, and after a year of Seleste's cajoling, guilting and begging him to leave his promising and lucrative LaSalle Street career to lead Walker Mitchell Greene & Associates, he resigned.

He opens the file and reads the last Post-it note Seleste has attached to the first document. Seleste, who's been like a godmother to him, is fifty and has worked for the firm since she was twenty-five. He considers her more of a business partner than an employee, and by the time Marcus took over, Seleste was the only employee left after the fifteen lawyers and ten support staff moved on.

Now Seleste, Marcus, and Missy, who is Seleste's goddaughter and serves as Seleste's administrative assistant, constitute the whole staff. The Post-it isn't about the Womack case, though. It's a reminder that he has five other divorce cases where the clients are behind in their payments. He chuckles. Seleste knew he would pull the Womack file just to gloat. The outstanding fees for the five cases total $3,500, and she's marked the amounts in bright red ink.

It's mostly because of Seleste's firm hand that the practice is profitable and allows him to take home $125,000 per annum. That's far less than he could have made on LaSalle Street, but thinking about how he and Seleste have made a go of it makes him proud. Most of the firm's business involves real estate transactions, business formations, and estate matters. Marcus brought in divorce cases in his second year because he got bored doing only the kind of paperwork practice he had left behind on LaSalle Street. Seleste rings his office and tells him that Lucinda Johnson called and said she'd call back in ten minutes.

"I let her know that she has to pay her overdue balance of four hundred dollars, or you'll have to pause her case."

"She needs this to be over," he says.

Seleste chuckles. "That's right. *She* needs it to end. And this is no pro bono case."

"I know," he says, looking at the desk calendar. Seleste has circled the July fifteenth court date for Lucinda and placed a big red question mark next to it.

He stands and strolls over to the two rectangular ceiling-to-floor office windows facing east. Below are rail tracks, two stories above street level, along which elevated trains travel back and forth more than a hundred times a week. Unless he's taking a break from the work and paying attention, Marcus is mostly oblivious to the noisy rumblings from below and the frequent but mild shaking of the building when fully occupied trains roll by. At night, however, he does notice and enjoy the flying sparks caused by metal wheels on metal rails, lighting up his windows like fireworks.

The office building is an historic landmark and has housed the law firm for the past thirty years. Several times a week, whether stepping into the narrow corridor of the building's entrance or standing at one of the narrow windows in his suite, Marcus tells himself he will never relocate. This place is part of his grandfather's legacy. A testament to his grandfather's life.

"Marcus." The intercom startles him out of his reverie. "It's Lucinda Johnson." Before Marcus can respond, Seleste puts the call through. Lucinda's case is one Seleste didn't want him to take because Lucinda couldn't afford his flat rate of $1,000 for a simple divorce with no child custody or property division issues. He convinced Seleste to let him take the case for $600.

"Attorney Greene?" Lucinda says, her voice charging into his office through the phone's speaker.

"How are you?"

"Not too good. I saw him with a bitch old enough to be his momma. He's still my husband. How can he run around with some skank right under my nose?" She pauses, takes in a breath. "I ain't taking that shit off him. Lies wrapped in newspaper with a string, that's all he's given me. That's all he has to offer." Lucinda pauses again to breathe. "Can't keep a job, can't keep his mind off drugs and can't keep his dick in his pants. I put up with him longer than I should have, I know, but I ain't letting him disrespect me like this."

"Because he's a foolish man. Thinks the grass is greener until he's really on the other side of the fence," Marcus tells her.

"Even a blind man can see that bitch ain't greener grass than me. Holding her hand like they were teenagers. Like he used to hold mine." Lucinda's voice cracks with a softer kind of emotion when she makes that last comment.

"You still love him, don't you?" Marcus leans back in his chair and closes his eyes.

"Maybe," she says, her voice just above a whisper.

"You want to slow this process down? Give you two another chance?"

"Chances don't make a difference. They're like free passes to him."

"You think he loves you?" Marcus is the third lawyer Lucinda has hired in the past three years. But this is the closest she's gotten to going through with the divorce.

"I think he doesn't know what he wants, and I'm tired of his cheating. So, I want out, but he can't keep disrespecting me like this while we're still married."

"Then let it go. Let him go. Don't confront him. Okay?"

She remains silent as if digesting his words. He knows she's not crying, though. Lucinda is too tough for that. He can hear traffic in the background. She's calling from her car.

"So, you don't think I need to shoot him?"

"Or run him over with your car."

"Thanks," Lucinda says.

"See you in the morning, bright and early. Okay?"

"I guess it's about to all be over, huh?" Her voice has softened again.

"It's about a new beginning."

"Bye," she says.

Seleste is hard-nosed with his divorce clients, who are mostly women and, Seleste believes, playing him to get a divorce at cut-rate prices. She may be right because he's had to put a few of them in check when they offered to meet him after hours. Still, he gets a rush when he files divorce papers, and it's because his grandfather used to regale Marcus with exaggerated tales of his own experiences litigating.

Marcus laughs when he remembers his grandfather actually calling them *adventures*. This memory of his grandfather also reminds him that his grandfather is dead. Gone. No longer a part of his life. His laughter dissipates and is replaced with a deep sigh.

Two

The stout old man, leaving while she's coming in, shoves the revolving door so hard it propels Teresa into the building's lobby. She turns to give the man an annoyed look, but he's already at the curb, ready to cross the street.

"Now that's what I call rude as hell," she mumbles.

After riding to the eighth floor, she steps off the elevator and sees through her office suite's glass doors that several of the staff are milling about, engaged in animated discussions. Teresa took the morning off to get a manicure, window-shop and buy the number one best-selling novel so far this year. She began reading it over a light lunch taken in a nice restaurant on Michigan Avenue. The commotion she's witnessing now is unexpected. Teresa pushes through the door and asks, "What's up?"

"Something is," Maybelline, the oldest and nosiest employee, tells Teresa. "The board chairman left Mary Ann's office about ten minutes ago, and she told Jamison to tell you to come to her office as soon as you arrive."

Teresa turns without commenting and heads toward the office of her boss. Although board members often meet with Mary Ann in the suite, Teresa is always informed about any planned meeting and is often invited to attend. She sees Jamison, Mary Ann's administrative assistant, motoring her way. His face is taut, although it's usually relaxed and punctuated with a smile.

"Boss lady wants to see you right away," he says.

"What's up?" Teresa asks again just as they reach the executive's office.

"That's Mary Ann's lane." Jamison opens the door, steps to the side and lets Teresa slide past him. Then pulls the door closed as he turns away.

"Am I in trouble?" Teresa says jokingly when she hears the click of the door closing behind her. But, despite having no clue about what could possibly have caused her to be in trouble, Teresa's distrust, mostly kept at bay when it comes to Mary Ann, begins to nip at her self-assurance. Mary Ann *is* white. She *is* Black. That has not been an issue with Mary Ann up to now, but Teresa's years living in a small town in Missouri have taught her that her relations with white people are always subject to unpredictable changes.

"Probably," Mary Ann says, then chuckles.

"What's up?" Teresa says for the third time.

"I'm done here."

"What?" Teresa says and walks over to one of the guest chairs to sit down.

"No need to sit. I'm resigning, effective right now."

"What?" Teresa says again.

"It's your turn. I know you're ready." Mary Ann stands, moves around the desk, trailing her hand along its smooth surface and steps next to Teresa. She's wearing a tailored red jacket with matching pants, a pink blouse with a laced collar and red running shoes. Mary Ann points her index finger, the nail colored pink, for emphasis. Her eyes are direct and unwavering. "By tomorrow, you'll be the new head bitch in charge."

A genuine smile spreads across Mary Ann's narrow face causing wrinkles to gather near the corners of her eyes. Her pallid skin is caked with makeup, but the brown sun splotches can't be hidden. Mary Ann embraces Teresa, a moment no longer than a half-breath, then holds her at arm's length. Mary Ann tugs at her sleeves, then pats and smooths the front of her jacket, then turns away. She goes back behind her desk and picks up her red briefcase and red purse. Teresa doesn't know what to say or do. She just stands and stares in disbelief.

"I know, I know," Mary Ann says. "But you know me. When I make a decision, I'm ready to move. Impatience is my itch that must be scratched. I've informed Jesse already, and he knows what to do. Congratulations."

"Why?" It's the only thought Teresa can express.

"Because you deserve it. You've earned it."

"Why are you leaving?" Teresa says.

"Because it's time. For both of us."

Mary Ann comes back around the desk and hugs Teresa one last time. Outside in the corridor, the rest of the staff have been assembled by Jamison. Mary Ann quietly tells them that life goes on. No questions are asked, and no further explanations are given. She leaves little time for sentiment. There is no proffered opportunity for formal recognition of her years as the chief executive.

There will be no parties or gifts, no plaques and no speeches. She speaks to them of her gratitude for their support and hard work during her tenure and assures them the board will select an able replacement. She shakes each one's hand and kisses each one's cheek. Fifteen minutes later, Mary Ann Sullivan is gone, and her office sits empty and dark.

Now in her own office, Teresa leans back in her chair behind her desk, hands clasped on top of her head, digesting this sudden turn of events. Her boss and only true mentor are no longer her boss and mentor. The reality of Mary Ann's departure strikes Teresa like a hand across the face. It's too sudden, too unexpected. She sighs while staring across at the now silent and vacant corner office. She's feeling a sense of abandonment. Cut off and left alone. Anxious and uncertain. Alone and feeling unprepared to be the head bitch in charge.

Teresa snatches her cell phone from her purse to call Mary Ann, to tell her she wears way too much fucking makeup and the way she handled this is bullshit. Her favorite contacts pop up, and she presses *My Boss*. Teresa stares at the screen. The phone call is on its way. She laughs and disconnects. Teresa knows what Mary Ann will say: don't blink because life is short, and missed opportunities are forever.

Although Mary Ann's voice echoes in Teresa's imagination, it's as real as if Mary Ann is sitting on the other side of the desk. Teresa lifts her head and realizes there are tears forming, clouding her vision. She brushes them away. The phone rings; she recognizes the number and takes a deep breath before answering.

"Has it sunk in yet?" Jesse Wayne Waters, Mary Ann's handpicked Chairman of the Board, is asking.

"It's slowly sinking in, but I had no idea."

"She told me in confidence a month ago," he says.

"Thanks for the warning."

"She made me promise." He chuckles.

"And?"

"I'm sorry, but I owe her, you know."

"I get it. I was just so caught off guard."

"I can imagine," he says.

"She could have given me at least a day's notice."

"She was not going to hold your hand, you know," Jesse says, his alto voice under control.

"I know, I know. Hands are for making shit happen, not for holding."

"Another of her oft-repeated axioms," he says.

"What's next?" Teresa asks.

"We dot our *i*'s and cross our *t*'s. How about six this evening?"

"I should have digested this by then," she says. Jesse chuckles again before disconnecting.

She leans back in her chair again and replays Mary Ann's farewell performance. "What an exit," Teresa says. "I know she already has a landing spot somewhere. She would never subject herself to the winds of fate. As for the rest of us, she only wants to be a memory." Teresa stops talking out loud and lapses into a thoughtful silence. *But she got her ducks in a row. And is taking care of me. And Jesse. Black me and Black Jesse. Mary Ann's idea of a natural team. But can we be that team? I'm not so sure. Jesse is a corporate creation. Too political to be trusted completely. That's his persona, anyway.*

"This is Mary Ann's plan," she says into the air, into the empty space above her. "Not mine. Not Jesse's. A plan with no details for us to follow. At least none for me."

Teresa wonders what Mary Ann's specific instructions were to Jesse. She stands, crosses the corridor to the former exec's corner office, and sits in the leather chair parked behind the huge mahogany desk. She flicks on the small desk lamp and thumbs through a pile of memos stacked to one side. They are copies that need filing. The chair squeaks when she leans back and spins to face the wall behind her. The leather is foam-soft and curves around her like a tender lover's embrace. Sitting in Mary Ann's chair, Teresa tries to imagine how Mary Ann viewed her. Viewed the staff. Viewed Jesse. She closes her eyes.

Minutes pass. Finally, Teresa decides that Mary Ann is authentic. She never professed love for Teresa nor had she acted out of any sense of white guilt. Mary Ann is a fair person and she knows Teresa has earned this opportunity. Teresa takes in a deep breath and allows her mind to fully register what her mentor has done. Mary Ann has made sure that the board won't deny Teresa this opportunity. That's where Jesse comes into play. Her confidence that the position is hers begins to bloom, but it's like that seedling at the front desk: sorely in need of more nourishment. Teresa addresses her imaginary Mary Ann, who is still seated across from her: "I don't trust Jesse like you do. I don't know why I don't, but I don't. Since you set this all up, and I trust your plan, I'll believe. Still, I'm a Missouri girl; I'll hold back just a bit until Jesse shows me."

Teresa frowns, then she laughs softly. "See what your plan has done? Got me delirious and talking to an empty chair."

"You can talk to me. Can I tell you, go girl?"

Teresa flips her eyes open. Toni King has slipped inside the office. Teresa swivels the chair around to face the twenty-seven-year-old woman leaning against the closed door with her arms crossed.

"How long have you been eavesdropping?" Teresa says.

"I just stepped in. Congratulations."

"Oh?"

"Mary Ann told me you're the new boss," Toni says.

"When?"

"On her way out the door."

"Jesse and the board are the only ones who can make that happen." Teresa drums the desk lightly with all ten fingers.

"I'm sure that's all worked out," Toni says.

"You know it's not a done deal until it's a done deal." Teresa's words feed her caution and leave her confidence unattended.

"It's a formality. You've been ordained." Toni's voice, when she laughs, is light and airy. "May I?" she asks, pointing to the guest chair across from Teresa, who sweeps her arms wide as an invitation to sit.

Toni's certainty is reassuring and makes Teresa want to abandon her own wariness, but she can't. Mary Ann's clout might have expired the minute she walked out the door. "It's not smart to take *anything* for granted," she tells Toni.

Toni blinks and unfolds her arms. "You're right," she says. "I want the Associate Director's position *if* it becomes available."

Toni sits erect without touching the back of the chair. Her hands are clasped prayer-like across bonded knees.

"The first in line, huh?"

"I want to be the only one in line." Toni's voice is soft, and her words are measured.

Teresa smiles at her protégé. Toni is smart and ambitious. She also has guts. She's a South Side Chicago girl is how Toni explains her grit. Toni has been Teresa's right hand, like Teresa has been Mary Ann's. "If I get my job, then you've got yours," she tells Toni.

"I won't let you down." Toni rises, hustles around the desk, pulls Teresa to her feet and embraces her. Toni looks sharp in her white silk blouse and black gabardine pants. Her grin is contagious, and Teresa grins, too.

"You know that second job will have to go." Teresa tries to sound firm.

"I know. And I'll only enroll for weekend classes if that's what it takes," Toni says.

"Once you move into my office, all your coworkers become your subordinates. Many won't be happy for you. It won't be all peaches and cream."

Toni laughs. Her wide mouth offers up a perfect set of white teeth.

"Do you think I care? I've been preparing for this opportunity since I came here. I'm ready."

Teresa is not surprised by this hard-edged dimension to Toni's ambition. She witnessed it five years ago when Toni, who'd only been on the job three months, strolled into Mary Ann's office and left with a promotion and a raise. Mary Ann became Toni's biggest cheerleader. When Toni began reporting to Teresa a year later, Teresa replaced Mary Ann as Toni's number-one supporter. A soft touch for strays, Toni said once about herself, then confessed that she was quick to put them out if they couldn't be domesticated. She believes her approach to people is a cross between her empathetic social worker mother and her hard-nosed factory superintendent father. Toni rises to leave. They hug again. Teresa tells her, "Keep this to yourself until everything's official. And try not to look like you just won the lottery."

Toni leaves, pulling the door behind her. Teresa sits back down, props her feet up on the desk, and crosses her legs at the ankles. She closes her eyes again and lets her mind get to work putting together a plan for meeting with Jesse. She should control the agenda. Set her own terms for accepting the position. And what exactly is Jesse authorized to offer her? Mary Ann's salary and benefits?

Mary Ann has always been open with staff about salaries. Even her own. Although it caused some petty jealousies, she insisted that transparency incentivized staff if the criteria for salary levels were clear. Mary Ann was making $100,000. Teresa catches her breath. Six figures. Will the board offer her that? Why wouldn't they? Same responsibilities, then same paycheck. Teresa exhales slowly.

"For a hundred thousand dollars, I'm ready," she says, her voice a soft but excited whisper.

She heads back over to the office where she's spent innumerable hours and days stressing about both the big issues and the minutiae of organizational life. Teresa doesn't look around as she makes her way back across the narrow space. She knows the employees are anxious, but there's nothing to tell them yet. It's now 2:45 in the afternoon and there is much to do but nothing Teresa can do. She isn't the boss, acting or otherwise. Mary Ann's hasty departure left no time for any semblance of a transition.

Watching Mary Ann all these years, her every move, Teresa has always felt she could do a better job. The staff is predominantly Black, and Mary Ann was often offbeat when it came to managing them. Too soft when it came to getting rid of the dead weight. Too undemanding when it came to performance expectations. For the past two years, she even seemed distracted. Less involved. Teresa took over huge chunks of the organization's management and began to secretly lust for Mary Ann's job. Now she's almost there. Then the anxiety, with its thuggish ways, bullies aside her optimism and lets unmoored thoughts get loose in her head. All the unforeseen occurrences, eluding Mary Ann's plan, now stake out real estate in her brain; Jesse gets hit by a car, Jesse slips on some steps and goes into a coma, or Jesse gets whisked away by a UFO. All are leaving her fate in the hands of a lot of old white board members. She knows them all, but they can't be trusted to do the right thing. One Black woman on the board and no Jesse. Teresa groans. And what if Jesse simply says *fuck Mary Ann's plan*.

Teresa dials his cell phone.

"Teresa," he answers on the second ring.

"Hey, just confirming our meeting at six. How are you feeling?"

"Ready to move forward," he says.

She feels silly for making the call. "That's great. Then I'll see you shortly."

Teresa is restless, so she snatches up her purse, hurries through the office along the main corridor and heads for the elevators. A few staff members wave, while others arch their eyebrows as if they deserve to know *something*. She pops her head into Toni's office and announces she is gone for the rest of the day.

* * *

They engage in breezy small talk while they eat. Teresa's baked chicken and veggies go mostly untouched while Jesse devours his filet mignon and smashed potatoes. She scrutinizes him as he eats and talks. He finishes off his main course and leans back in his chair. He points at her partially eaten meal and says, "You don't like your entrée?"

"All these sudden changes, I think, have affected my appetite." Teresa frowns.

"You can have it packaged and take it home for later."

Jesse says this restaurant is his favorite, and Teresa does like the upscale establishment with its wide airy dining area and its rich man's ambiance. The food looks and smells appetizing, too, but her stomach feels unsettled. She knows it's the mounting anxiety in anticipation of *the* discussion. Teresa searches Jesse's face for what she's not sure and wonders how long before it's all over. How much longer before she's gotten confirmation that she is the new exec? His face appears very relaxed without a hint of anxiety, and she hopes her face is equally unrevealing.

"I certainly will, and I'm sure I'll devour it," she replies. "It looks and smells delicious."

"You will love it, I guarantee that." Jesse pauses, cups his chin with his thumb and lays his index finger along his cheek, then says, "I guess we need to get down to business."

"I wish Mary Ann had handled this before she left. She shouldn't have put this on us."

"She knew we would handle this with aplomb," Jesse says. "We are both more than ready to move forward."

His words are potent. Without warning, the elation sweeps through her in unexpected waves. Her face stretches into a grin. Her elation becomes an intense desire to show her appreciation by leaping across the table and slipping her tongue down his throat.

"We are," Teresa says.

Jesse changes his posture and moves his face forward, closing the distance between his and hers. The anticipation has moved up to her chest, making it difficult to breathe. This unexciting man who has failed in the past to cause even a slight uptick in her heart rate is having a profound effect on it now. She feels like a wide-eyed teenager hanging on his every word. He takes his time. He sips from a glass of ice water.

"Teresa Casteel," he says finally, fingertips moving up and down, sliding through the condensation that covers the outside of his glass.

"The board has authorized me to offer you the position of Executive Director of the Chicago Employment Center. Let me add on a personal note that I think you deserve this opportunity."

She sits in silence. She hears his words, and as perfunctory as they sound, they still send a chill up her spine. Teresa hears as well as feels her heart pounding. Her whole body is energized. She orders herself to calm down. She needs to be less eager. She waits for him to continue.

"See, no sweat." He stands up, leans across the table and kisses her cheek.

"We are prepared to offer you a salary of eighty-five thousand dollars…"

On impulse, she interrupts and, much to her own surprise, says, "I'm available for a hundred thousand."

Jesse takes his time responding. He sips again from his glass, then says, "Your salary is fifty-two thousand now. You want a 100 percent raise?"

Teresa inhales, then exhales discreetly and watches Jesse's face, especially his eyes.

"That's what Mary Ann was making. It's the same job and same responsibilities. And it's my opinion that I have been underpaid for quite some time. I am not inclined to continue that trend."

He smiles and raises his hands in a defensive gesture. "That was between you and Mary Ann."

Teresa relaxes. She smiles. Jesse is open for negotiations. "And this is between you and me. Equal pay for equal work, right? You know that applies to race as well as gender."

"She earned that after proving herself a capable executive."

"I don't see the relevance of that line of reasoning." Teresa feels she's on solid ground on this one. "The job is worth what it's worth and more now than when Mary Ann started. She was compensated accordingly."

Jesse rubs his smooth chin as if stroking a beard. His chubby face contrasts sharply with his trim physique while those hazel-colored eyes focus somewhere beneath her eyes. He pushes on his forehead as if to lift his to look at her.

"Can we start out with the eighty-five thousand and revisit, say, in six months?"

Teresa's eyes are focused, unwavering, and reveal the confidence she's feeling. She says, "How is it possible to do eighty-five percent of the job?"

Jesse chuckles. "How about ninety-thousand initially and revisit it in six months?"

"How about a hundred thousand and revisit in three months?"

"Not enough give there," he says and laughs.

"Okay. The hundred thousand and review in a year."

"And you want the same fringe benefits as Mary Ann?" he asks.

"No less," she says.

Jesse summarizes. "You're asking for a hundred thousand dollars beginning salary, an increase of forty-eight thousand over your current salary. And you want to revisit that salary, presumably for an increase, in twelve months. In addition, you want Mary Ann's benefits package, which is an additional twenty-five thousand. I think I have that right."

Teresa feels giddy. So close. She inhales softly, covers her mouth and fakes a light cough. She picks up her glass of water and sips. Teresa has been contemplating two more terms she wants as part of the deal. They came to her while she wandered around the Loop, waiting for this meeting. A perk Mary Ann never had.

"I want a title change to President and CEO," she tells him, "and a seat on the board as a voting member."

"The board, that's my lane," he says.

"I want leverage. Mary Ann got it by picking the board. I need to be on the board," she says.

"Again, that's my lane. And it may be a hard sell for the other members," he says. "To be frank, most of the members wanted a full-blown executive search to be conducted."

"They wanted a white replacement for the white woman?" Teresa says.

Feeling her temperature rise because of that assumption, she closes her eyes for an instant and breathes deeply but discreetly. Now is not the time to attack Jesse's board. But it feels like he's sacrificing her interests for his own purposes. It's like a déjà vu moment for her. A moment long ago when her mother made a similar move.

"Maybe, but the official reason is that they want a major change going forward. And I agree with that. I convinced them that you deserved the opportunity to take us where the board wants the organization to go."

Jesse's explanation doesn't quell her roiled emotions. "That's why Mary Ann made you the chairman. To move this tired board forward, you'll need some help," Teresa says.

"It is a hard sell that I do not want to spend any chips on right now." Jesse's tone is firm, indicating no give on this one.

"Mary Ann knew it would take your salesman skills to lead the board after she was gone. You've been working the members and selling them on you since day one. You received unanimous support after your nomination. It's your board now." Teresa's intuitive flattery surprises her yet also impresses her. She forces herself to suppress the smirk that is threatening to make an appearance.

"Our deal cannot be contingent on your board membership," he says. "That's a big ask on top of everything else. Can we table that for now? Revisit in a few months?" Teresa looks at him, then looks past him as she ponders her response.

After a few seconds, she says, "The title change?"

"I can make a case for that. A new day, right! We have a deal?" he asks. The board membership was more a tactical move than a desired outcome for Teresa, and she sees that the request ruffles his feathers.

"We can table the board membership for now, and yes, we have a deal." Teresa reaches across the table, and Jesse meets her halfway. They shake, and their deal is done. Teresa's heart is racing. She's ready to leave. Ready to retire to the privacy of her own space, where, with unrestrained exuberance, she can rejoice over this major career achievement. Jesse signals their waiter, who comes to the table with two bottles of champagne.

"The lady needs her meal packaged," Jesse says, then points at the champagne, "and she will be taking them with her, too." Then he tells Teresa, "I ordered the second one for your celebration with friends."

* * *

On the sidewalk in front of the restaurant, they say goodbye. Teresa stands on the semi-crowded street and watches Jesse head east. She punches the air with a balled fist and whispers, "Yes." She's intoxicated by her change in status: she's head bitch in charge now. She begins to feel woozy, almost drunk, as if she had downed both bottles of Jesse's champagne.

She can't think but only feel. Teresa giggles, then shakes her head in wonderment and remains frozen in place, staring in the direction Jesse has gone. He's no longer in sight. She crosses to the other side of Michigan Avenue, hails a taxi and slides into the rear seat. She gives the driver her address, closes her eyes and gives in to the overwhelming joy.

The taxi ride is a calming influence as her body gently sways with every red light and every change in direction. She feels the gentle vibrations of the tires kissing the textured pavement and smiles every time the squeaky brakes are applied. Fifteen minutes later, the taxi rolls to a stop in front of her high-rise. She pays the fare and adds a ten-dollar tip, an act of generosity she wouldn't have performed three hours ago.

The magnitude of what has happened in the past twelve hours crystallizes. She's now making $100,000 a year and can get a new car, save more and pay off the condo note sooner. Then her mind begins to meander away from the euphoria of the day as she makes her way past the security desk. She greets Rob, the attendant, as she passes and makes her way to the bank of elevators that take her up to the twenty-ninth floor and curses when she recognizes the direction her thoughts are going. A darker mood begins settling over her like an old, torn, musty blanket.

Back in Hannibal is a family that can use her help. A family that hasn't received money from her in two years. An underwater family she has tired of trying to rescue: siblings who have no desire to be rescued and a mother who only wants to be subsidized. Teresa believes they have been made too small to want more than what Hannibal has to offer. Increased requests for money had taken their toll when she decided that enough was enough. So, without giving them any advance notice or an explanation, Teresa stopped the flow of cash from Chicago to Hannibal.

She's also avoided going back to Hannibal for the past six years. Her one regret is that she hasn't seen her nieces and nephews during these intervening years and probably wouldn't recognize them if they approached her on the street. And they'd be lucky if she didn't point a can of pepper spray at them if they did. Teresa sighs, punches the code pad, pushes open the door and steps inside her dimly lit and silent apartment.

The blinds are open in her living room, and lights from the surrounding high-rises, along with a full moon, illuminate its interior. She drops her bag and briefcase and flops on the sofa. The silence and solitude she cherishes whenever she comes home aren't serving her well now. She doesn't want to be held hostage to these unwarranted feelings of guilt. What she needs is someone with whom she can share this moment. Someone who doesn't have skin in the game. That means Toni is out.

She can call her college friend Lela who lives in Texas, and now seems to be following the same program as Teresa: no kids, a full-time job and no husband. But Lela's too competitive to offer an enthusiastic pat on the back. The most Teresa will get from her friend is *sounds good,* and then an hour-long bragging session by Lela about her own life achievements despite the two broken marriage engagements and the three different career changes in the past five years. They haven't spoken in the last year since they fell out over Lela's comments that Teresa was a fool to let Terrance get away.

She can call Valerie, her other college friend, now Mrs. Charles Johnson, who lives in Charlotte, North Carolina. Teresa is always amazed at how content Valerie sounds. She loves her job as an accountant and is proud of her two kids, eleven and seven, a son and a daughter. Charlie, her guy since freshman year, is a tech engineer who got her pregnant with their son in their senior year and married her immediately.

Teresa is convinced that Valerie has moments of wishful thinking. Her original plan was to stay single until she was at least thirty and to live abroad for five years after graduation. Valerie will playfully chastise Teresa for not communicating for the past several months but will be expressively overjoyed with Teresa's good news. She makes the call, and Valerie answers her cell on the second ring.

"Teresa! So, you're still alive and not dead or in a coma?"

"I see the same holds for you, too."

"Touché. How are you? Everything okay?" Valerie says, her voice reflecting concern.

"I'm okay. No, better than okay, and that's why I called."

"Let me go out on the veranda," Valerie says.

"In a few months, we'll be able to FaceTime on our cell phones," Teresa says. "That'll be fun."

"Hope that new technology has the capability to remind you to call every once in a while."

"That goes both ways," Teresa says.

The veranda, Teresa knows, is a large open porch at the front of Valerie's 2,500-square-foot house with three bedrooms, three full baths, and an attached garage. Once Valerie and her family moved into their new home two years ago, she called Teresa to share the good news. The two talked and celebrated over the phone. Valerie drank champagne, and Teresa drank a diet cola, the only beverage other than the water she had in her fridge at the time. The last time they talked was three months ago.

"We can talk now," Valerie says. "I need the privacy just in case your news is wild. Like you're married."

"I've been promoted. I'm now a CEO." Teresa grins while she waits for Valerie's scream to run its course.

"When? The same place? Where's Mary Ann?"

"Today. Yes. She's moved on. Take a breath, girl," Teresa tells her friend.

"You have a bottle of champagne, I hope," Valerie says.

"I do. You?"

"You know I do."

They both laugh. After they have opened the bottle and filled their glasses, they toast, then sip their drinks. Valerie demands a minute-by-minute description of Teresa's day. Despite the hundreds of miles and the intervening years separating them since college, Teresa feels the same closeness she had more than a decade ago. She's glad she made the call.

After Teresa recaps her day up to this very moment, Valerie sighs, then says, "You know, a good man would come in handy right now. That attorney you met sounds interesting."

"He might be."

"You going to use that number?"

"I'm not sure," Teresa says.

"Call him. Give the man a chance."

"A chance to do what? Disappoint?" Teresa groans.

"What's the worst that can happen? You go on a couple of dates and let the chips fall where they may."

"So says the girl who's been out of the dating game practically all her life."

"This wasn't the plan. You know I didn't like Charles at first." Valerie's voice lowers to a whisper. "Give it a chance, and who knows, he may be the one."

"He is fine. Seemed charming. And very determined." Teresa pauses, then adds, "I am getting a little tired of my own company."

"What will you say if you make the call?"

"He's a smooth talker. All I have to say is hello, it's me." Teresa laughs.

"I'm so happy about your promotion. And if you can snag a good man to boot, well, go for it, honey."

"Stop talking like you're all old and wise." Teresa laughs again.

"And you stop acting like you're afraid of men. Terrance was good until he wasn't."

"Please, let's not go there. Again. He's water under the bridge. Gone and forgotten." Teresa snaps her fingers.

"I've got to go, girl. Domestic duties call."

"Well, good luck," Teresa says.

"You, too. Kisses." Valerie smacks her lips and is gone.

Teresa feels good about the call. It brings back memories of the good old days when she felt liberated from her mother's world. Could reinvent herself and did reinvent herself. So far, college has been the most fun she's ever had in life. She met Valerie in a freshman geology class, where both struggled to eke out a 'C' but got to be best friends. Lela, on the other hand, became a transactional friend only. Both were members on the volleyball team. The only two Black girls. Both were juniors, but Lela was a starter, while Teresa came off the bench. Teresa always felt she was the better player, but Lela was the better teammate to the other girls.

After a few more minutes of reflecting on her college days, Teresa fills her glass with some more bubbly beverage and sits on the floor with her back against the sofa. She doesn't sip now but takes a big swig. And thinks about Valerie's advice. *Should I? It's something to do to keep my mind off Hannibal.* Recalling his smooth though somewhat corny rap brings a smile to Teresa's somber face.

She reaches for her bag, searches through the contents, and pulls it out. His business card. Turning it over, she stares at the scribbled number to his cell phone. She takes another swig of the champagne. The buzz feels good. Allows her to abandon her reservations and dial his number. While it rings, she sips more bubbly. Damn. His voicemail. "Why not?" she says and leaves a brief message telling him it's her.

Then she stands, hikes up her skirt, eases down on the sofa and scoots backward. She lifts her feet off the floor, tucks her knees under her chin, and presses her heels deep into the softness of the sofa. Remembering is an act of courage for her. Courage is now fortified by Jesse's first bottle of champagne.

A journey into a past along a path shrouded in anger, rutted in pain, and littered with regrets. It's a journey she seldom permits herself to take. Memories from her childhood are tawdry and sad. They are reminders of how her life could have turned out differently. Reminders of how narrow her escape has been. She sighs again and closes her eyes, letting the guilt, something she's come to accept as the price every survivor pays, settle over her.

Three

It's 9:00 p.m. when Marcus turns down his street and, seconds later, is easing up the driveway of the box-shaped two-story brick mini-mansion inherited from his grandfather. He pushes a button, waits while the garage door recoils into its steel shell, and then pulls into the space twice the width of his car and yawns. A quick dinner—the sub sandwich he's picked up in Hyde Park—a cool shower, and into bed.

He steps through the back door into his kitchen and flicks on the light. Edna's handiwork is evident. The hardwood floors gleam like spit-polished army boots. The dirty dishes from this morning are now washed, dried and put in their proper places. The stainless-steel surfaces of the stove, dishwasher, and refrigerator are now smudge-free. An immigrant from Poland, she's been the housekeeper for the past eighteen years, since 1992, the year of his grandmother's departure.

When, after Edna's interview, Marcus told his grandfather he felt uncomfortable with her cleaning the house, his grandfather informed Marcus that if not Edna, then the grandson would get the job. And like a poker player staring at a bad hand with no inclination to bluff, Marcus quickly folded.

It's 10:30 when he's finished eating and has taken his shower. He drips water across the cool hardwood floor as he makes his way to his bed. He has a towel wrapped around his waist but has never liked using a towel to dry off. He leaves it to Earth's natural forces to do their work. He drops down on the edge of his bed and pulls his cell phone from his gym bag. He has two voicemail messages. The first is from Ana. He deletes it.

He hasn't talked to Ana in weeks despite her calls from New York, Miami, and Rio. He's been avoiding her since their breakup.

Ten months ago, they met at one of Fraser Letcher's parties featuring attractive women along with Fraser's exotic paintings. Marcus had been drifting from one room to another, taking in the sights, sipping on a beer, when he noticed Ana's eyes, a strange but magnetic shade of green. She was facing the doorway when he entered.

Ana's eyes met his for an instant as he made his way into the room. Set up like an art gallery, the circular room showcased thirty black-and-white framed prints of nude women in various poses hanging on the wall. He made his way over to the print with the lady on a divan, where Ana was standing. She turned to face him and smiled, then greeted him as if they were old friends. She worked for Fraser's firm and remembered Marcus from his visits to their offices. They huddled the entire evening in the corner of Fraser's expansive living room, engaged in light conversation.

That night when they left Fraser's place, they'd ended up in a nearby north-side restaurant on Halsted. After eating, they went to her apartment. A nice two-bedroom townhouse with a balcony. Without saying a word, she nudged him down onto a small sofa designed for two and disappeared somewhere behind him. A soft jazzy singer's voice began to fill the small space, and Ana returned to the sofa. She lay her head against his shoulder. *Bewitching* was the only word he could conjure up to describe her.

She sat up and took his face between her hands. Then slowly pulled his lips to hers. He hesitated. Even now, he can't explain his hesitation. She stopped, disappeared into another room, and came back with a marijuana cigarette. He told her he didn't indulge, but she lit it and tutored him on the proper form for inhaling and exhaling. It worked, and he entered the beginning stages of mellowness. He closed his eyes and asked her to tell him about herself.

So, she did: about being Brazilian, about being born and raised in Belo Horizonte, about her name, *Ana* meaning "grace" and her last name, *Teodoro,* meaning "God's gift." Her voice had a soothing effect on him. Whenever he opened his eyes and tried to focus, her lips seemed to dance around words like they were part of an animated video, opening and closing slowly; her tongue at intervals caressed both her bottom and top lips in alternating patterns.

Then she stopped talking and kissed him again. She pushed gently against his chest to stop him from rising. Ana unbuckled his belt, unhooked and unzipped his pants, and reached inside. He watched as she lowered her head into his lap. The swiftness of his orgasm stunned him. Ana continued after his eruption, keeping the tremors shaking his body longer than any woman ever had. When she released him, his right arm sagged, and his hand dropped to the floor. His body went limp. He felt powerless to move. He felt drained. He mumbled an apology for being unable to reciprocate, but she cupped his face between her hot hands and said his pleasure was her pleasure.

For five months, she dominated his life. They were inseparable until Ana left Fraser's firm to start a hair trading business of her own. It required her to be on the road a lot. New York. Miami. Rio. But there were trust issues on his part. He had gone to Rio with her once. Men from all over the world, hordes of them, made their way to the city. Most of her friends were or had been working girls, but Ana said she had never lived that life.

But he had his doubts. About her history. About her sincerity. Girls like Ana were hustlers, Fraser told him. Smart. Clever. Survivors. Manipulators. There were days he couldn't reach Ana. She always had an explanation. Reasonable and believable. But he would challenge her story, and she would cry. Would tell him he's being unfair. That she has to make a living. Has to support her family in Brazil. He felt he had gotten in a little too deep and had to pull back. Had to protect himself.

Ana's second month on the road was when Marcus decided to end it, and told her as much during one of their long-distance phone calls. It was a tense and tearful conversation. Between her dramatic outbursts, Ana kept saying she loved him. But he had never said those words to her. He felt bad about how he ended the relationship and still does, but it's history. No reason to be friends after being lovers. At least, that's always been his rule of thumb.

* * *

Marcus listens to the second voicemail message and is caught off guard. It's Teresa. She's left her number. Despite the late hour and without reservations, he returns her call. She answers the phone on the second ring.

"Yes?" the voice says.

"Teresa?"

"Yes."

"How are you? It's me."

"I know," she says. Her voice is low and sounds sad.

"Did I catch you at a bad time?"

"No, not at all," she says.

"Glad you called."

"Are you?" she says.

"The tenth time is a charm."

"Meaning?" she says.

"The number of times I've prayed for this call since we met."

Her laughter is soft, almost demure. "I bet you did."

"If not God, why have I been blessed with your call?"

"I've been drinking champagne," she says.

"You don't need an excuse to call. I *begged* you." Marcus laughs, and so does Teresa.

"My girlfriend told me to call."

"She did?"

"She did. She said any man as determined as you deserves a chance."

"What exactly did you tell her?"

"Exactly what you said about our fate." Teresa giggles.

"Sounds like you really are drinking champagne."

"Something really good happened to me right after we parted ways. Made me think you might be a genie and granted my secret wish." She giggles again. "You want to hear what you did for me?"

"Please. But let me ask a question that's been dogging me since I approached you today," Marcus tells her.

"Really? Well, go right ahead and ask away."

"Why were you carrying pepper spray?"

"Don't you keep up with the news? There's a downtown snatching spree. Guys are out here grabbing purses and cell phones left and right. I'm not giving mine up without a fight."

Teresa's laugh is the same one that infected him earlier that day. He laughs too. "I had a close call then," Marcus says.

"Your shoes and briefcase saved you."

"Not my charm?" he says.

"That charm got you *this* call. Now for my good news. When I left you on Franklin, I was second in charge at my job. An hour later, I was the boss. Totally unexpected."

"The boss?" Marcus says.

"*The* boss."

"That *is* good news." Marcus claps.

"Thank you. I'm still in shock, I think."

"What happened to your boss?"

"She resigned. Immediately. No warning at all."

"No reason either?"

"Not one she shared with staff. But she's strategic. She's had this planned for a while. My chairman of the board knew for a month."

"What did you do to celebrate?"

"Called my friend, and we toasted with champagne. She's my best friend from college, and we hadn't talked in a few months, so we got caught up."

"I'd love to celebrate with you," Marcus says. "You need a night on the town to really celebrate. No offense to your friend."

"You may be right about that." Teresa pauses and then asks,

"So, what are you doing tomorrow night?"

"Spending time with you, I hope."

"How about a movie? My treat."

"Right. A *big* raise comes with a *big* promotion. I accept. Wait. Is your real name Teresa?"

She laughs loudly for several seconds. *The champagne at work,* Marcus thinks.

"Yep. Teresa Casteel."

"Teresa Casteel. I like it. Classy sound."

"Why thank you, sir."

"Would it be rude to ask what you're wearing at this time of night, Teresa Casteel? I'm only wearing a towel. Just got out of the shower."

"Well, I'm naked, with one foot on my dresser. I can send you a photo if you like."

"You're kidding, right?" he says.

"Men! You want way too much way too soon."

"I won't deny the charges. But are you or are you not going to send that picture?" They both laugh.

"It really is late."

"I'm glad you didn't lose my card."

"I stashed it inside my bra," she says. "Who am I to ignore the winds of fate?"

"Really?"

"No, not really, Mr. Greene."

"Well, I'm looking forward to some sweet dreams tonight," he says.

"Good night."

"Bye, Teresa."

Four

They reach his car and lean against it. They stand pressed, shoulder to shoulder and knee to knee, while they finish their discussion.

"It didn't work for me."

"Why?" she says.

"She's too unathletic. Her character wasn't believable."

"But she's selling sexiness, not athleticism."

"I'm not sold on that either, although she's got a nice pair," Marcus says.

"She bought those breasts, you know."

"Get your mind out of the gutter. I'm talking about her lips." He presses a bit more against her.

"I bet she bought those, too."

Their first outing feels to Teresa less so. Picking the right movie hadn't been a chore. He let her choose, and she likes the tall, skinny actress. Sharing a big bag of popcorn and a bag of bite-size Snickers was an intimate experience. All is going well so far. When they leave the theater, he takes her hand, and his is warm and soft but firm. She keeps finding things to like about him: this easy familiarity between them, this effortless light chatter. And he smells good too. She inhales quietly. The scent isn't too heavy or sweet, with hints of lime and cinnamon. She thinks it's his soap. Teresa leans in and smells his arm. *Yup, it's his soap.*

"Did you like the plot?" Teresa says.

"Russian assassin gets caught up in her cover story as housewife working for the CIA and goes rogue?" he says. "And you buy that?"

"It's as plausible as Bond," she says.

"He's 007, woman. No comparison."

"Her being a woman has nothing to do with your skepticism?" she says.

"She wasn't believable. There were better choices for the role."

"Sean Connery is athletic?"

"Hmm. Good point." He squeezes her hand.

"Did you like the love story? She went rogue, as you say, to save then avenge her husband."

"Love is a powerful message? Skeptical."

Teresa gives him a hard stare, then says, "Don't tell me you don't believe."

"Miracle cures give me cause for concern," he says.

"*What* about the myths of love make you skeptical?" she says. "That it's magical? Can heal the sick and save the sinners?"

"And turn water into wine." Marcus moves a hand through the air like a magician waving a wand. "Even raise the dead after it's killed them."

"Who broke your heart?" she says.

"Michelle Turner."

"Where is she now?"

"According to her Facebook page in Texas."

"What happened with you two?"

"I went to third grade, she didn't."

Teresa gives him the side-eye. The punch line is that good, and Teresa can't contain her laughter. Soon they're both doubled over, holding their stomachs. Several seconds pass before they regain their composure. She hugs him and says, "I'm hungry." Once inside the car, they head to the Fiesta del Sol.

* * *

They reach the popular restaurant in less than ten minutes, enter its airy interior and discover, as he predicted and she declared as no problem, there's a thirty-minute wait for a table. To navigate through the congestion in the waiting area, they slide by and between patrons both standing in their carved-out spaces and those sitting at tall round bar tables. They find a tight nook to stand in next to a window and claim it, then turn to people-watch in silence while his hand alternates between caressing and squeezing hers.

Names are called. Patrons rise and follow a hostess out of the waiting area, while new arrivals take their place. Now and then, Marcus leans over and whispers a comment about an individual or a couple who catches his attention. She nods in agreement or laughs softly in response. Then she turns to look at him, their faces just inches apart. She can feel his breath when it ricochets off her lips each time he exhales.

"See any behinds here that look unique?" she asks.

"I only have eyes for one." Marcus rubs her arm.

"Good answer."

"The truth always is."

Marcus tilts forward and kisses her forehead. For a brief moment, she closes her eyes. Finally, the hostess dressed in faded jeans and a pink T-shirt, calls out for the Greene party of two and leads them to a seat at a small square table in a cozy corner in the rear of the restaurant.

When the waitress arrives, Marcus orders the combo platter for them. Teresa adds two margaritas to the order. Teresa stands and removes her black thigh-length silk jacket for the first time that night. She's wearing a cropped tank top that showcases her midsection and grapefruit-sized breasts. Her blue-jean skirt curves with her curves and then falls short of her knees by three inches. And those shapely calves he's been privy to the whole evening are still her crowning glory. When she turns to place the jacket on the back of her chair, he lets out a low whistle.

"Have I told you how good you look?" he says.

"No. Do I?"

"Yes."

"Thank you." She tugs at the hem of her skirt.

"Thank you."

"For?" she says.

"For giving me this chance."

"It was our destiny. Remember?" She remains standing, hands on hips and smiling. "Excuse me while I go freshen up."

"I'll be right here waiting." He's grinning.

Teresa winks as she turns to leave. Her self-assured stride catches the attention of more than a few diners sitting along her route as she breezes past their tables. Marcus feels a little cocky. Teresa, as fine as Halle in his opinion, is with him at her request. His eyes stay on her until she makes a left and disappears. The waitress arrives with the customary appetizer of chips and salsa, along with their drinks. Marcus makes a quick trip to the men's room to wash his hands and returns before Teresa. He dips, nibbles, and sips while surveying the room.

Marcus discreetly shakes his fist when he sees her coming back. It's a congratulatory gesture; it's an acknowledgment that he took his shot and bull's-eye. When Teresa takes her seat across from him, he pushes the chips and salsa closer to her. They sit content in their tranquility while she devours the appetizer and chases it with her margarita. Impressed by her lack of self-consciousness, he watches her every bite and sip. She pauses to smile at him but doesn't stop eating until the bowl of chips is gone.

"Mmmm. These chips and salsa are delish," she says. "And this place is marvelous."

"Marvelous? Why thank you, madam."

"Madam? Mocking me, are you?"

"Enjoying you," he responds.

"Since this date is on me, I have and will exercise my prerogative to interrogate you." She moves the emptied dishes aside and places her elbows on the small table and leans toward him until their faces are within kissing distance.

"An interrogation? Is that how it works when the woman foots the bill?"

"Exactly," she says.

"Well, let's do this." He leans in and slides his forearms across the table until his fingertips stop in the spaces under her elbows.

"This is fun, don't you think?"

"The most fun ever," he tells her. He slides his fingers up and down her arms.

She tilts her head away from him, lays the back of her hand against her forehead, takes a deep breath, then says, "You flatter me so."

"I see it's working." He tickles her elbow. She snatches her arm out of his wiggling fingers and laughs. "Ticklish, are we?" Marcus says.

"Yes," Teresa says as she looks around the room. She puts her arms back on the table, and he slides his hands back in place.

"How old are you?"

"I'm thirty-three," he says. "You?"

"I'm thirty-two."

"Never married?" he asks her.

"Right."

"And no children?" he says.

"No. This is my interrogation, remember? Why are you still alone in the world?" she says.

"You think I'm alone?"

"Answer my question, please." Teresa points a finger for emphasis.

"Too many people in the world for me to be alone," he says. "Now, why is a fine woman like you still available?"

"Says who?" Teresa arches an eyebrow.

Marcus tries to arch his own. "Where is he? Incarcerated? The military? Out on the town with the boys?"

"I'll ask you the same question."

"So, you think I'm fine and available?" Marcus says.

"That qualifies as evasive, but I'll give you some leeway since you probably can't help it. You *are* an attorney."

Her breath carries the aroma of salsa that reaches his nose when she laughs. They lift their margaritas in a silent toast, then gaze easily at each other and sip their drinks. His intolerance to alcohol is becoming apparent; its intoxicating powers are making their way along his arteries, crossing the blood-brain barrier and invading his brain cells. He closes his eyes and rubs them with the back of his hands.

"You okay?" She sounds more amused than concerned.

"I'm fine." He opens his eyes.

"These margaritas are potent," she says. He has to smile. The woman is sharp.

"I'm trying to impress. My usual is a light beer and preferably no more than one on any given occasion." Teresa nods. Their eyes don't separate until the waitress arrives with their food. Marcus looks on while Teresa cuts one of her enchiladas into smaller portions and slides the end of her fork under two pieces and lifts them to her mouth. He's charmed by the dimples that keep reappearing when she chews.

"Your food's getting cold," she says. "Don't waste my money, mister, or you'll be in big trouble."

"It's only money," he replies, picking up his own fork and pushing it through the enchiladas assembled on his plate.

"It's only *my* money. So, clean your plate." She signals the waitress, who comes right over. "Another margarita, please." The waitress nods, then looks at Marcus. "No more for him," Teresa says.

When the waitress returns with her margarita, Teresa raises it in the air and says, "To my new friend who can't hold his liquor and is not afraid to show it."

He lifts his half-empty glass and says, "Hear, hear."

She sets her glass down and shakes her head. "I'll let you slide on that drink."

"Ah, but that will be wasting your money."

She reaches over and takes the glass from his upraised hand and moves it to her side of the table. "There are two things you should know about me. One, if I like you, it's easy to be yourself around me. And two, I like you." She takes his now empty hand in hers. He knows all thirty-two of his teeth are showing, and he's fine with letting her see how she's affecting him.

"Do I really have to finish this?" he says, pointing at his half-empty plate. "Too much of that big popcorn at the movies."

"You're a big baby," she replies and sighs.

* * *

They head north on Lakeshore Drive with the car windows down and the sunroof open. A cool breeze off the lake bounces around the car's interior. Teresa sits sideways in her seat, facing Marcus. He seems to have recovered. His eyes are clear, and he seems alert. She studies his profile. His smooth caramel-brown skin shows very little need for a razor. His nose is a bit broad, in her opinion, but it works with his full lips. Handcrafted lips made to perfection. *Wesley Snipes lips.* The recognition makes her smile.

"What?" he asks, shifting his eyes toward her.

"Just thinking about the date," she says. "Really had a good time."

"A free movie and a free meal. Me too."

"Free? That's not how you guys see things, right?"

"You expect to get lucky tonight?" Marcus says, then laughs.

"You think a lot of yourself, don't you? *I* would be lucky, huh?" Teresa reaches over and pinches his cheek, then settles back in her seat. The fresh night air strokes their faces as the Jag deftly slides into and then exits the many curves that mold the Drive.

The moon glides along above them, letting its reflected sunlight shimmer across the lake's undulating waves. *So romantic,* Teresa thinks and stretches her arms up and through the open sunroof. She tilts her head back against the seat and closes her eyes. The serenity of the moment engulfs her. She imagines herself floating above the car, lying on her back, legs crossed with her hands behind her head and watching the stars.

She's so close to one, she can reach out and touch it. Teresa thinks about the woman she read about who had a near-death experience that was so peaceful and so tranquil, she didn't want to reenter the world of the living. Right now, she's feeling the same way: at one with the universe. She no longer hears the hum of the motor or Marcus breathing. Teresa knows those margaritas have a little something to do with this fantastic mood. Then she feels the car slow and turn, then stop. They have come to the end of the Drive and the end of her out-of-body experience. She pulls her arms down and opens her eyes. They are at a red light in the middle of bumper-to-bumper traffic, polluting the summer air with a mixture of noise and fumes. She sits forward and surveys the scene. "This sucks," she says. While they wait for the green light, Teresa decides to probe some more. "You grow up here?"

"Yup, on the South Side."

"Your parents still live here?"

"Raised by my grandparents, but they're both gone."

"I'm so sorry."

The red light turns green; he eases out into the intersection then turns south back toward downtown and her place. "What's your law practice?"

"It's a small firm, so I take on a variety of cases. It was my granddad's firm before I took over."

"Impressive. Is there anything you don't mind sharing about your childhood?" she says.

He glances sideways. "Yes," he says. "There is the summer of hell, 1987. I was ten." He tells her how his grandfather enrolled him into a YMCA summer day camp. "It was only a few blocks from my house but on the other side of the tracks, literally and figuratively speaking. I grew up very middle class, and the kids at the summer camp lived far less privileged lives. I didn't know a single person there. Not one. My friends were sympathetic. Their parents were shocked. But my grandfather was determined to acquaint me with a world similar to the one that shaped him."

"Your grandfather thought you were a little soft?"

"Probably. He said I was living the good life and needed to see what it was like on the other side. And that summer, I did."

"What did your grandmother think?"

"She didn't say anything in front of me, so I'm not sure. On day one, I was a target and got bullied twice the first day. The second day a roughneck slapped me around. A supervisor barely out of his teens advised me to fight back or get my little ass kicked every day.

I didn't fight back, and by the end of that first week, I averaged a smack or push or punch a day."

"Didn't you tell your grandfather?"

"I didn't, but apparently somebody did because when my granddad took me back that Monday, we had what he called a man-to-man talk. He said, 'Son, you're probably the smartest kid there, and you have a brighter future than any of those kids kicking your butt. However,' he said and paused for emphasis 'that don't mean shit to those little brothers from the hood.' He poked my chest lightly with his finger. 'And if you don't defend yourself, it is guaranteed that by the end of the summer, your little egg will be scrambled.' He then took my head between his big hands and looked me dead in the eye and whispered, 'Having brains isn't near enough if you don't have the balls to back them up.'"

"I wish I could have met him," Teresa says.

"Really? Why?"

"He sounds like the dad I never had." Marcus glances at her but says nothing. "Did you get your egg scrambled by the end of the summer?" she asks.

"No way, not after that pep talk. My granddad drove off, leaving me with no plan, just a mission." Marcus pulls the car over into a parking space along the curb and shuts off the motor. "I strolled into that gym where all the kids gathered in the morning and saw Weasel Face, the name I gave to my number one tormentor. The last thing Weasel Face told me on Friday was that he'd better not see me on Monday. I watched him shooting hoops without a care in the world while I hadn't spent a second of summer camp without looking over my shoulder. Something came over me at that moment. At an emotional level, I think I came to understand that there was no point in being a victim. To my right, against the wall, was the canvas bag with the Wiffle balls and bats…"

"No, you didn't."

"…I grabbed one..."

"Oh, no."

"...And headed toward that short, skinny kid with a front tooth missing..."

"Oh no," she says again and squeezes his upper arm.

"I was sweating bullets, scared to death. I started jogging through that crowded gym..." He glances sideways. "...fighting the urge to turn and hightail it the other way. I think the embarrassment and humiliation of being a victim energized me."

"Nobody stopped you?"

"A wild-eyed boy sweating bullets with fire in his eyes? And about to be the source of entertainment? They parted like the Red Sea. Weasel Face was in midair taking a jump shot, a pretty nice jump shot, as I recall, when the bat caught him smack-dab in the middle of that little knot at the top of the back of his head. Needless to say, I didn't finish up the day there, let alone the summer."

"Marcus! How bad was he hurt?"

"I'm not sure. Probably not very. A lot of commotion followed, but no ambulance ever came while I was there. Somebody called my grandmother, who arrived in five minutes. My teenaged supervisor slapped me on the back and told me 'Way to go' and then told us Weasel Face's family was on the way and we needed to make tracks. And we did."

"Wow!"

"Yeah."

"You never saw that boy again?" Teresa is staring deeply into his eyes.

"Nope." Marcus tilts his head to the side when he answers.

"What do you think happened to him?"

"Who knows? I don't remember his name, and hopefully, he doesn't remember mine."

"Unbelievable." She squeezes his arm again.

"Unforgettable," he says and flexes his bicep.

"Now I'm starting to get impressed."

"Just getting started?" He displays a mock frown.

"What did your grandmother do?"

"She was a housewife."

"Really? So, she raised you."

"Only so far," he says.

* * *

Two hours later, they are sitting in the circular driveway in front of her building.

"When did your grandparents pass?" she says.

"My grandfather died six years ago. My grandmother is still alive." His tone tells her he's finished with the subject. She drops her head on his shoulder, and they sit in silence. She wraps both her arms around his right one and waits for him to speak.

"What about your family?" he says.

"I have one."

"Are you close to them?"

"That's why I'm here, and they're there."

"Sibling rivalries?" he says.

"If it were that simple."

"Kind of bad, huh?" Marcus says.

"It was pretty bad. I'm lucky I got out. My brother and sister didn't. No, that's not true. I wasn't lucky, I was determined."

"I know," he says, "becoming CEO is proof of that."

Teresa hugs his arm tighter. "If anyone had bothered to ask me, I would have chosen a protected childhood like yours."

"Grass always looks greener," he says.

"Doesn't always mean it's not," she counters.

"Okay, how about something you don't mind telling me about your childhood," he says.

"Hmm," she says. Then she tells him about an incident when she was in fifth grade. One of a handful of Black students in an otherwise all-white school, she tried out for the school's chorus. She had sung briefly in a church choir but missed so many weekday practices and so many church performances on Sundays, she was kicked out.

"My attendance at school was just as bad, but I had this passion for singing. I wanted badly to be a member of that chorus. I was required to sing a solo, the national anthem." Teresa sings a few bars. Marcus grimaces. "That was the chorus director's response, too," she says, then sticks out her tongue. "He didn't even let me get halfway through the first verse before he unceremoniously yelled at me to shut up and sit down. That old dried-up cracker. Can you believe that? I was only ten, and I was nervous."

"Uh-huh."

"Then he announced to the whole room, about thirty of us, as he directed me to the scarlet letter section, where the other musically challenged kids had been exiled, that I was the first person of my race that he had ever heard who couldn't sing. That bastard. He was such a racist..."

"Well, now..."

Teresa slaps at his shoulder before Marcus can finish. "After he made his stunning announcement about me disappointing my ancestors, the only sound in that auditorium was the rustling of clothes as every kid turned to look at me. Ever since then, I've had a clue that I can't carry a tune, but I'll be damned if I'll stop singing." Teresa begins singing the national anthem again. Marcus applauds before she finishes the first stanza, but she closes her eyes and increases the volume of her solo.

There is something about him that tugs at her in unfamiliar ways as she watches him watching her. It had tugged at her on the street and on the phone. It had tugged at her this whole date. He's charming. And smart. And sexy. But those redeeming characteristics are not what draws her to him. Though more rare than common, she's met men who possessed them. She feels Marcus has something else going for him. Then it hits her. *He has this boyish innocence. Can't hold his liquor. Uncomfortable with his emotions. He's vulnerable.*

Teresa trusts her instincts with men. It's her ability to overlook her intuition that worries her. That's how she ended up in Chicago with

Terrance Boyd. Kappa man. Journalism major. Kansas City boy. For two years they dated, and despite the fights and the breakups, Teresa still felt she had to give it a chance even though Terrance was a poseur: life of the party but boring when sitting across from her at a restaurant, flirtatious with every girl who gave him the eye but a very weak lover, and he had ambitious dreams, but, she found out later, Terrance had no stamina.

When he got a job offer with a large news organization in Chicago, and because she had no other plans upon graduating, she came too. But once she got a job and got comfortable in Chicago, she was overjoyed she had come. But his was a different story. He lost his job a few months after they arrived and went into a funk. Maybe even got depressed. Kept calling home and whining to his mother, who urged him to come back to KC and restart. He tried to convince Teresa to move to Kansas City for that fresh start. She remembers the whole scene, word for word. Teresa also remembers her sense of relief when she accepted the truth; their relationship wasn't going to work.

"Move to your momma's house?" she said when he told her they needed to discuss their next move.

"Yes. I can get back on my feet there."

"*You* can get back on your feet here," she countered.

"I don't like Chicago."

"I love Chicago."

"You love me more," he said, staring her directly in the eyes. She hesitated. Stared back at him while registering her feelings. Terrance didn't look the same. Wasn't cocky anymore. Wasn't charming. He was no longer attractive. Had the same features, of course. Full lips, flat nose, curly reddish hair and perfect orthodontist-maintained teeth. Those square shoulders, however, were sagging now, and those strong hands were entangled in his hair, obviously expressing his frustration. His masculinity was less so. He looked defeated. No, she didn't love him more. She didn't love him at all.

"I'm not going to Kansas City," she told him.

"What am I supposed to do?" he asked.

"What's best for you," she said. He had cried, but she hadn't. She was ready to move on from him and had, at that moment, realized she'd been ready for a while.

Then there were the other brief flings with other men to pass the time and were destined to die on their vines. Teresa's career has kept her too busy to be out looking for love or trying to grow a long-term relationship. Teresa also knows she needs passion as a fundamental requirement for her to even fantasize about a serious entanglement. She had it once, long ago when she was too young, but the feelings she had for that boy were almost overwhelming. But it hasn't happened again. Yet. Teresa opens her eyes and sneaks a glance at the vulnerable man sitting next to her. *Maybe,* she thinks.

Teresa lowers her eyelids and begins singing again. But it's not the national anthem. This time it's a Prince song. Marcus joins in. She opens her eyes and stares at him.

"You can carry a tune," she says.

"A little."

"You're full of surprises." Teresa nods her head in approval.

"You like diamonds and pearls?" he asks. "Are you a high maintenance woman?"

"I like Prince. Are you a fan too?"

"He gave me some of my best lines." Marcus grins at her, then begins to sing again. "Just want your extra …" Teresa disrupts his Prince imitation when she leans over and pecks him on the lips.

"You gonna be my little red Corvette?" he asks.

Teresa laughs and says, "Time will tell. But right now, it's after two o'clock. No Corvette tonight."

"It's still early," he says, then tries to stifle a yawn.

"Past my bedtime," she says, pointing at the car's clock.

"If you want, I can tuck you in."

"You really are spoiled," she says.

"Not spoiled, just don't want to be left here alone in a cold world."

"You are good, counselor, but it's only the first date, so turn on your heater. You'll be fine," Teresa says.

"Is that an invitation for a second?"

"It's an invitation for an invitation." Teresa bats her eyes at him.

"May I have the pleasure?" he says.

"I'd be delighted."

He gets out and goes to open her door. She waits.

"Thanks," she says. "And I really had a great time. I really got my money's worth."

She slides out, leans into him and plants a kiss on his right cheek, then brushes past him and heads into her building. When she reaches the entrance, she turns and waves, then strolls past the security desk and disappears into a hidden space behind it. *Sex appeal.* Teresa shakes her head in recognition. *The man has sex appeal.* She steps onto the elevator and pushes the button to her floor. "The man moves me," she says, shivering with the memories of their bodies pressing and brushing against one another all night.

After her breasts grazed his chest that first day they became acquainted, her nipples had gotten rock hard. She attributed it to her hormones at the time because she was on her period. But it's Marcus. The man arouses her just by his presence. She shivers again, then smiles. He's the first, she realizes, to affect her like this. For Terrance, it was about his popularity on campus. Others because they were convenient. Or persistent. Or interesting. But not exciting. Marcus excites her. By the time the elevator shudders to a halt and Teresa steps into the quietness of the carpeted corridor, her smile has morphed into a grin.

Five

It's early Monday afternoon, and the restaurant is half full. They sit by a window, eyeing two well-shaped legs dangling a pair of yellow flip-flops before sliding out of a black compact SUV onto the cracked pavement.

"A nine, easy," Bird says, then breaks off a piece of coco bread and stuffs it in his mouth.

"I give her a six." Marcus lets his eyes follow the woman as she sashays toward their window, then turns right. She's working a yellow plaid mini-skirt and walks with short quick steps. A bit chunky for his taste.

"No way. Look at those legs." Bird points in her direction.

"Yeah, but she's hauling an oversized butt. Throws off her symmetry."

"Yep, my type," Bird says.

"Absolutely. She looks nineteen."

Bird shifts in his seat and keeps his eyes on the young woman until she disappears. He shakes his head and whistles softly. The waitress arrives, a plate of jerk chicken for Marcus in one hand and a bowl of oxtail stew for Bird in the other. She'll bring the rum cake and bread pudding shortly, she tells them. This is Bird's favorite eatery, nestled in a northwest corner of Restaurant Row in trendy Hyde Park, where Bird makes his home in a high-rise building overlooking the lake. Further discussion waits until the last of their desserts disappears.

"She called," Marcus says. "Her name *is* Teresa. And she asked me out. She's from your neck of the woods."

"From St. Louis?"

"A hundred miles up the river," he says.

"Not my neck of the woods."

"It's close enough," Marcus says.

"What's her story? Kids? Divorced?"

"No and no. And she can't sing." Marcus makes a slashing gesture across his throat. "And she paid for the date. Movie and a meal."

"An independent woman who can't find a man to meet her expectations," Bird says.

"Until now."

"I imagine the right man would have to want a relationship that lasts longer than a sitcom season." Bird chuckles.

"If she's the right woman, I'm capable of a long run like *The Jeffersons*," Marcus responds.

"Not my favorite show," Bird says. "George was too short to be the lead."

"That's a reflection of your self-hate, brother. You've only got him by a couple of inches." Marcus leaves little room between his thumb and forefinger to make the point.

They both laugh. Bird Man's real name is Walden Byrd Mann, III, and they've been friends since their freshman year at Howard. It is an alliance formed over time and is now void of surprises. With him, Marcus knows what to expect. And that's the most you should expect from a friend, according to his grandfather. The waitress, reed-thin but full of personality, smiles as she returns and places the bill on the edge of the table.

"That smile for him or me?" Bird says. Her long fingers press the side of her face as she looks back and forth between the two men. A concentrated frown wrinkles the space between her eyes as she considers the question.

"I'm not sure," she says, pursing her lips.

"I'm the big tipper." Marcus slides his credit card to her.

"But your friend's so cute," she says, then winks and takes his card. She swings her hips when she strolls away.

"Add a few pounds and I would take her out," Bird says.

"Like fifty pounds," Marcus tells his friend.

"I could live with twenty-five," Bird replies. He makes a large circle with his arms simulating a big bear hug. "I need a body to fit snugly in here." When they leave the restaurant, the woman in the yellow minidress strolls toward them. Bird clears his throat as she approaches. "Good afternoon, Ms. Lady."

She waves but passes without breaking stride. They watch her descend the concrete stairs, cross the narrow driveway, and glide over the cracked pavement of the parking lot and climb, not too ladylike, into her car. They turn at the corner and head west on Fifty-third Street, the heart of Hyde Park.

"How's George's case going?"

"I'm working on George," Marcus says. "You should have told me the brother would be a project."

"I told you his wife is white. Guess that's backfiring on his ego." Bird shakes his head. "Don't know why a brother with that kind of bank doesn't keep it in the diaspora."

"He didn't discover love in the diaspora."

"He's about to discover the price of colonialism," Bird says and laughs.

"The diaspora screwed you," Marcus says.

"Maybe. But all I lost was the woman. Not my fortune."

"How's Malik?" Marcus asks.

"Thinks he wants to play football," Bird says.

"Think he's ready?"

"You know he's thin as a rail." Bird holds up his baby finger.

"Didn't get that from you."

Marcus pokes the chubby midsection of his friend. "He could be a wide receiver."

"Tonya won't let that happen."

"You talk to her?"

"Just long enough to put Malik on the phone."

"So, she's still Tonya the shrew," Marcus says.

"She thinks as much of you."

Tonya's a touchy subject between the two friends. She was Bird's high school sweetheart who came to live with Bird in his senior year at Howard. She persuaded him to apply to law school instead of going for that master's in education he wanted. Got him to marry her in his third year of law school, then she moved back to St. Louis after one of her many tantrums. The estranged couple reunited after Bird finished his law degree and followed her back to St. Louis. A year later, Tonya was pregnant. Or, as Marcus describes it, she had tightened the noose.

She thought Bird was going to make big bucks as an attorney, but Bird never got around to practicing law. Says he never wanted to be a lawyer but just did it to please Tonya. That was Bird's M.O., his mindset. It had been in college even before Tonya came on campus. He strove hard to be the good guy that he imagined women preferred: agreeable, chivalrous, and solicitous. He could reel them in, but keeping them was a different story. Bird lacks an edge when it comes to women. He lacks an edge, Marcus believes, because he lacks confidence. He doesn't give off a manly enough vibe, and women don't find that acceptable over time.

Marcus tells his friend this every time one of Bird's relationships fizzles. When things do go south, Bird gets confused and full of self-pity before finally accepting that the woman doesn't want to stay in the relationship and has simply lost interest in him. It's only at this point that Bird gets assertive. So, when he moved back to St. Louis and Tonya began making it clear he wasn't enough, Bird abandoned all his plans to practice law. Instead he taught at a high school and worked as a youth worker at the YMCA in the evenings. Tonya wasn't a happy camper.

By the time Malik was born, their fragile union had fully and finally disintegrated after Tonya said she was tired of living as broke-ass man and wife. Talk about irrational, Marcus had said, a part-time church secretary complaining about being broke. But there was nothing Bird could do to save his family, so they separated, and six months later, the divorce was final. Six months after that, Tonya married the minister, her boss and the couple's former counselor. Six months after Tonya remarried, Bird arrived in Chicago to save his sanity.

"Tonya was the biggest mistake you ever made."

"Takes two to tango. I could've done better. She could've been more patient. No villains in this story," Bird says.

"Not even Reverend Backstabber?"

"He's doing right by Malik," Bird says.

"You've got two peas for balls."

"Told me that already and got your ass kicked for it. Remember?" Bird purses his lips and points his finger.

"Better than you do, it seems," Marcus says.

"Pops double-teamed me."

"I remember he pulled me off your non-fighting ass." Marcus stops and looks down at Bird, whose height falls shorter by five inches.

"Your old man knew whose ass he was saving." That night had tested their friendship. Although battered and bruised, it had managed to survive.

"Tonya was a wannabe gold digger."

"She's still my boy's mother."

"Quit defending her."

His friend is weak in ways Marcus cannot respect. Falling in love with her, okay. Abandoning his self-respect and pride for her, unacceptable.

"When are you going to see Malik?"

"Not sure." Bird does not look at his friend.

"He needs you." Marcus pats Bird's back.

"He's okay. Likes his life just fine. He's in a groove and got a rhythm to his life. I mess up his rhythm when I drop in."

"That's ass backwards." Marcus shakes his head when he says this.

"This is my life, my son, and my business. I got this."

Marcus pulls Bird by the shoulder and says, "You ain't got shit."

Bird shrugs and starts walking. Marcus follows. His disappointment covers him like a third layer of skin: heavy, stuffy, and confining. And he's tired of being a witness to Bird's failure as a parent, but he can't stop.

"I want to see my godson. Can you arrange that?"

Bird stops. He turns to face Marcus. "What?"

"Bring him up here."

"So he can tell me how much he misses them? Talk to me like I'm just an uncle. I hate that. I let him feel free to talk about his life to me, but I hate it. Sometimes I'm not up for dealing with it."

"You can't disconnect. He won't have a nine-year-old's mind a few years from now. Then what? How will you convince an eighteen-year-old that you abandoned him for his benefit?" Marcus says. His sense of disappointment deepens. For a man ambitious to save the race, Bird's nothing but a fraud if he can't commit to his own son.

"Let me think on it," Bird says. "It's my life and my kid. I'll do what I feel is best."

"Tonya wants a fairy tale with no Bird in the picture."

"Says a man who can't commit to anyone."

"Whatever," Marcus says.

"Yeah, whatever."

Six

Her first staff meeting as the boss is about to begin but Teresa's calm. These are the same people she's been working and meeting with for the past several years. Twenty of them, all seated and waiting for her to move them into the future. Her agenda is a short one. She'll tell them to keep doing what they've been doing and that she will, over the next two weeks, meet with each one of them to get new ideas about how to move CEC forward.

"Good morning," she says. "This meeting will be brief, as you can see by the agenda. Any pressing items that we need to add?"

"No offense meant to you, Toni," Michael Brown says, giving her a quick glance. "But why only consider Toni for the VP job?"

"That's a discussion we can have later if you want," Teresa says.

"I'm not the only one interested in the position," Michael Brown replies.

"Who else is interested?" Teresa surveys the group sitting around the large black oval-shaped conference table. They're more young than old, bright and capable for the most part. Silence greets her question as they look at her, then at Michael Brown and then back at her, every face alert with anticipation. Except one.

"Teresa chose Toni like Mary Ann, and the board chose her without using a more inclusive process because that's how it's done here. This position was probably created just for Toni." That's Maybelline Watts. At forty-five years old, she's the oldest and most senior staff member. "The bosses do it however they feel like it now."

Teresa ignores her. Good old Maybelline, with all her limitations and backward thinking on how things used to be. She's not a fan of the changes in the organization over the past twelve years since Mary Ann took over. She's a relic of the past, but she mostly camouflages her resistance and maneuvers through other people. Maybelline leans forward with her forearms on the table. Neat and stylish in appearance, clever and provocative in her speech, Maybelline possesses the least amount of formal education among the staff and is the least productive.

For reasons indecipherable to Teresa, Mary Ann has tolerated Maybelline. Protected her by finding nice little niches to hide her in while the organization's evolving needs continue to confirm Maybelline's expendability. Indifferent to her insignificant status, Maybelline will nudge any staff discontentment into a conflict and then hide in the eye of the storm. Teresa sees Maybelline's fingerprints all over Michael's challenge, but Teresa knows he will be on his own when, as her mother would say, the shit hits the fan. Maybelline's comments are as close as she will come to outright supporting Michael.

"So, you're interested in the vice president position?" Teresa knows the smell of money can make a person do foolish things, and Michael Brown is definitely sniffing that additional $30,000 if he were to get the job.

"Well, hell yes, I want an opportunity to interview before you anoint Toni," he says.

"I'll give you five minutes. Tell me why you're more qualified than Toni."

All eyes turn to Michael, whose own pupils grow wider, registering both his surprise and uncertainty. A blush appears beneath his pasta-colored skin, and a faint twitch pulls at his thin lips. "I would prefer meeting privately if at all possible. I think it would be the more appropriate way to handle an interview."

"Or to request one. You chose to raise the issue here, so make your case. You've got four minutes left," she says.

Michael looks embarrassed, then perturbed. "I think this is blatantly unfair. I would like the same courtesy you extended Toni. No offense, Toni."

"Time's running out, Michael."

"Fine, we can *debate* it right here. I think you are starting your administration off on the wrong foot. I am sure most of us do not want a repeat of Mary Ann's style of management."

"You've got three minutes left to make your case. It's your time; waste it if you want," Teresa says.

"I refuse to submit to your bullying tactics." Michael's voice rises as his eyes narrow.

"The only one trying to be a bully is you."

Teresa wants to take him on. He and Maybelline are always holed up in someone's office bitching and complaining. Mary Ann overlooked their shenanigans. Had always stepped in to save them from drowning in a river of miscalculations when Teresa had been prepared to make them pay. He won't be so lucky today. She looks at Maybelline, who shows no inclination to rally to Michael's aid. This is good. One at a time *is* better.

Michael sits back in a huff, his defiance captured in the set of his jaw and the glare in his eyes. Teresa is relaxed, chair pushed back from the table, legs crossed ladylike at the knees, and waits while silence fills the room. No one clears a throat or scratches an itch. She knows, and they know, Michael Brown's not finished.

Maybelline stares at the unreflecting blackness of the table's surface, a somber expression shrouding her thoughts. Toni has leaned back in her chair with arms crossed, resting on her chest. A microscopic smile thins her full lips, and her keen eyes focus on Teresa as if to record every arch of her eyebrow, tap of her finger, and curl of her lip, all intended to emphasize who is in charge.

"Time's up," Teresa announces without so much as a glance in Michael's direction. "So, to continue, Toni will be…"

"This is bullshit." Michael pushes away from the table and stands.

"Beg your pardon." Teresa also stands.

"This anti-male shit that Mary Ann perpetuated," he says.

"Yet you never got up in her face." Teresa's hand aims a finger in his direction.

"I had hoped you wouldn't be a Black-faced version of her," he says.

"Sit down or get out." Her hands-on-hips stance signals she's had enough of his disruption.

Michael's lower lip curls inward and catches beneath his bared teeth. He sits down on the table, his eyes never leaving hers. "I am not intimidated," he says.

"Good for you." She puts her hands on the table and leans forward. "This is why you're not qualified to be *anybody's* vice president."

"You are acting like a damn dictator."

"Get your ass off my table," she says.

Michael's forehead glistens with a light layer of perspiration. His pale face turns crimson as he appears to take a quick survey of the others sitting around the table as if seeking a coded message of moral support. There are none. But all are paying rapt attention. All are engrossed in the drama. Teresa knows this is entertainment at its best. Live and unrehearsed. And like her, they're waiting to see the next move from a man whose bluff has just been called. Michael gets off the table, falls back into his chair and puts his clasped hands on top of his head.

"Fuck you."

"In your dreams," she says.

"Try me," he says.

"I don't believe you are man enough. It takes more balls than you've shown."

Michael springs from his chair, sending it screeching on its rollers into the wall behind him. "Bitch!"

"I don't see your momma in here." Teresa knows as soon as the words leave her mouth, she's gone too low. She's the CEO. *Damn.*

"You are supposed to be the motherfucking boss. You need to check yourself. Or I will."

"Michael," Teresa says, her voice just above a whisper, "I *am* the motherfucking boss."

"You think I'm impressed?" His voice is a low growl.

She shivers as streams of warm sweat turn cool against her skin. Her stomach is heaving and her feet are numb from standing in one place.

Her knees start to give way, and her whole body starts to sag, but she grips the edge of the table and keeps herself upright. It takes an act of extraordinary will to maintain eye contact with him. What if he attacks? Knock her around like they're in some goddamn tavern, some fucking hole in the wall? Would he hit her with his fists or open hands? There is a difference. A child caught in places no child should've been, she heard women bragging about the men who didn't hit them with closed hands, who didn't beat them down but only slapped them around.

Is she going to get lucky today? Will Michael Brown turn out to be one of those men who only slaps women? Only leaves her with black eyes and small knots across her forehead? No broken bones, no missing teeth. Teresa can see herself like old Lucy Brown, knocked over on her back, legs flailing in the air, skirt and underwear ripped from her body, leaving her bare ass exposed. *Oh, hell no*, she tells herself, *that's not going to happen. If he crosses that floor and makes it to me, I swear one of us will fucking die in here today. This ain't fucking Hannibal, and I ain't fucking Lucy Brown.*

"You need to check yourself, Michael." Toni rises from her seat, walks to the side of the table where he stands and steps into a space where only inches separate her from him. "Are you out of your freaking mind? Calm down before you do something you'll regret for the rest of your life."

He looks at Toni but says nothing. Furrows crease the middle of his forehead, signaling his emotional stew is bubbling. Toni moves to his right side and positions herself between him and the quickest route he would take to reach their boss. The male staff begins to stir, to abandon their spectator roles as they, too, seem prepared to help stem this dangerous turn of events. Three of the men hurry around the table and stand next to Teresa, who's still staring down Michael with a cultivated fearlessness. The other four men move to Michael's side of the table; two stand between him and Toni and the other two behind him.

"Michael, you're completely out of line. Completely." Maybelline is firm in her tone. "You've shown us why you weren't considered for the position."

Toni leans in and whispers in his ear for several seconds. His head drops, and the tautness in his body begins to slacken. Teresa observes the change and relaxes a little. Michael says he needs to go to no one in particular and turns toward the door, but the four men have him hemmed in and do not step aside.

"Let him go," Toni says, and the men move away.

Michael keeps his eyes cast downward as he hurries past them. Toni follows, escorting him through the door and into the empty corridor. A collective sigh of relief echoes throughout the otherwise quiet conference room. The men return to their seats. Toni comes back into the room, stands next to Teresa and whispers in her ear.

"I'll go handle Michael, okay?"

Teresa nods, and Toni leaves. The staff wait for Teresa to speak. She takes her seat and feels the tingling sensation in her feet as the blood begins to circulate again. She stretches each foot and then taps it against the floor. Her hands ache from gripping the table so hard. She winces as she realizes how bad things could have gotten. Like her mother, she always needs to have the last word.

"Thanks," she says. "Anybody else want to interview?" Their laughter reverberates with both the nervousness and the awkwardness the moment deserves. Teresa laughs too.

* * *

The staff have gone for the day. The suite is quiet and filled with shadows. Teresa and Toni sit in the conference room, shoes off and relaxed. A lamp sitting on the credenza near the door is the only light in the room; its subdued glow leaves most of the room in the dark. They talk while they eat sandwiches bought at a Subway nearby.

"He won't resign," Toni says as she sips cola from a paper cup.

"He thinks I'll forgive and forget?"

"Michael has issues. He grew up in North Lawndale. He's a Westside boy who's had it pretty rough. His head's a little screwed up, but he cares about the clients, and they respond to him. And you know he's an effective project manager."

"You're saying I should keep him after his performance today?" Teresa says.

"Of course not. Michael was way out of line, completely out of control."

"Do you think there's a general feeling among the men here that they're discriminated against?"

"There were always rumblings that Mary Ann was a crusher," Toni says. "Know what I mean?"

"That's a trope for women in charge who aren't shy about being in charge."

Toni bites into a chocolate chip cookie and closes her eyes. Then after sipping from her cup again, she says, "I don't lose a lot of sleep worrying about men in the world getting a bum deal."

"It's always been about power with them," Teresa says. "It's the reason Michael lost it today. Power's a natural instinct for them, but for us, it's an acquired taste."

"I'm liking it," Toni says and laughs. She finishes her cookie and stretches, her blouse rising above her pudgy midsection.

"Girl, you should've gone for the veggie sandwich and left that steak and cheese alone."

Toni pulls her blouse down and sucks in her stomach. "It's not that bad. I do sit-ups every day."

"Teresa." The voice coming from the shadows of the corridor startles them. It's Michael. His slender silhouette hovering just outside the doorway sends nervous shivers down Teresa's spine.

Toni rushes to the door. "Michael, what are you doing back here?"

"I need to talk with Teresa," he says, his tone neutral.

"Tomorrow," Toni says.

"What do you want, Michael?" Teresa moves toward them, wanting to see his eyes. Wanting him to see hers, to see there is no fear.

"Excuse me." Michael tries to slide past Toni into the room.

Toni pushes against him, pinning his spare body between hers and the doorway's frame. "No," she says.

"Let him pass," Teresa tells her. "Have a seat, Michael." She points to a chair. Toni steps back, and Michael walks past Toni and takes his designated seat. He sits down with the heaviness of a deflated man.

"I want to apologize. There's no excuse for my behavior." *He's grown smaller since this morning,* Teresa thinks as she analyzes his every twitch. He's discarded his earlier bluster and now sits, head bowed as a sign of repentance, his clasped hands a request for mercy.

"What do you want me to say? That all is forgiven? You were way over the line. Disrespectful not only to me but to the whole staff. Making us all afraid you had lost your mind. Not good, Michael, not good at all."

The remorse he displays misses its mark. Teresa's more rather than less determined to get rid of him. She has never truly mastered the art of forgiveness, the act of absolution.

"I told you earlier you had forced her hand and needed to resign," Toni says.

"I want to keep my job. I need my job. Toni, you know that." He doesn't look up while he speaks.

"How can I let you stay? Then everybody gets a free 'fuck you boss' moment?" Teresa studies Michael's profile. In some ways, he reminds her of her own brother, too young for his years and full to overflowing with self-destruction.

"I've been here for six years, and I've done very good work. Suspend me and put me on probation for a lifetime, but don't fire me over this, my first mistake on your watch."

"The first day of my watch. It can't get worse than that." Teresa feels her lip start to curl in disgust. Michael is begging. "I need to review this whole situation. Give me a couple of days. But now you need to leave. Give me your office keys, please."

Without another word, Michael stands and sets the two keys on the conference table. Teresa and Toni escort him to the door. He reaches out to shake Teresa's hand, which she declines, then leaves the room. The two women exchange looks of astonishment before Toni follows him out into the corridor.

Teresa leaves too but goes to her office, plops down in her chair and begins checking her voicemail messages. There's one from Marcus. She dials his number. Toni strolls through the door just as Teresa is leaving her own voicemail message. Her voice is soft and sweet when she says goodbye.

"Sorry. I should have taken his keys earlier," Toni says, a curious look on her face.

"Both of us slipped up on that," Teresa tells her.

"Why are you smiling?"

"Am I?" Teresa says.

"You sure are. Who is he?"

"Who?" Teresa says.

"The man on the other end of that message." Toni lowers her voice to a whisper and says, "Goodbye."

Teresa gives Toni a "don't worry about it" look that goes unacknowledged.

"Well?" Toni raises her eyebrows.

"Well, what?"

"Who is he?" Toni moves away from the door and takes a seat. Teresa and Toni are close but not friends. Teresa has been in Chicago for more than nine years and has no real friends. Her two college friendships are mostly based on their college days, and it often feels like her connections to both of them weaken every year they don't see each other. Growing up, she never kept girlfriends. Engaging in petty jealousies, meaningless competition for the same boys, and other banalities weren't her style.

But with a distant family, both physically and emotionally, and no close friends, Teresa has moments where the loneliness is too much. Her life is more complicated than it was in college, and her friendships there added more than they took away. She accepts now, especially after getting this position, that she can use a good friend.

She eyes Toni and thinks, *maybe*. Toni is poised on the edge of the chair, her eagerness to share in Teresa's life is evident. Teresa likes her, always has, but never saw her or Mary Ann or anyone else at CEC as a prospective friend. *Toni, maybe.* Teresa decides to share.

"He's Marcus G. Greene," Teresa tells her.

"What does he do?"

"An attorney."

"How'd you meet?"

"That's a story for another time," Teresa says.

"Is he tall, dark, and handsome?" Toni leans in far enough across the expansive desktop to be within arm's reach.

"Taller than me. Darker than me. Wesley Snipes kind of looks."

"Oh my." Toni fans her face southern damsel style. "Can I have your life, please?"

"Parts of it, but I get to choose." Teresa admits to herself that she's enjoying the moment.

"What's he like?"

"Charming. Intelligent. Sexy."

"A dream man?" Toni asks.

"He's fun. So far. What's a dream man?"

"Tall, dark, handsome, gallant, generous, a gentleman." Toni gives Teresa an inquisitive look. "And a great lover."

"The first six I can speak on."

"It'll be awful if he's lacking in the lover department." Toni groans.

Teresa grimaces. "Really awful," she says. "Clark Kent with no superpowers."

"Bruce Wayne with no bat mobile," Toni adds.

Teresa laughs. "Marvin Gaye with no talent."

"Michael Jackson with no rhythm." Toni closes her eyes and prays. "Please, Lord, let her man have rhythm."

"Amen," Teresa says. She then beckons to Toni with both hands to move closer, then whispers, "Tell me, now that we're sharing, what's the deal with you and Michael?"

"Michael?"

"Yes, Michael. Were you two a couple like the rumor mill alleges?"

"A couple, nope. We went on *two* dates. No big deal. I discovered he has serious issues. Too angry about too many things: growing up poor, growing up on public aid, growing up without his father and on and on."

"He's a train wreck waiting to happen."

"Michael's a train wreck that's already happened," Toni says.

"What are we going to do with him?"

Toni frowns but says, "Maybe give him another chance. He knows he's all out of chips. He might be able to control himself under short-leash conditions."

"You don't think it looks like he won?" Teresa says.

"Not if we drag him into a staff meeting and make him apologize to everybody with the same humility he did with us."

"That's cold."

"He's gotta wave the white flag. Right?" Toni purses her lips and pushes a balled fist into her other open hand.

"I'll let this be your call, but you've got to handle him," Teresa says.

Toni nods and with that simple gesture they form a new bond. Teresa feels closer to Toni than she had just yesterday. Maybe, just maybe, she has also found herself that friend. But only time will tell.

Seven

It's **late Saturday** afternoon, and Marcus is on the Drive headed north to Teresa's place. To his right is the lake, still reflecting the dimming light from a westbound sun. After a week of them both having chaotic workloads, one shared but short lunch, several missed calls, and one late-night phone conversation on Thursday, this is their official second date, and it's her treat again. He thinks about the first date and smiles. At Fifty-seventh Street, two young women in colorful bikinis stroll along the walkway next to the Drive. Marcus honks. They glance over and wave animatedly. He knows it's the Jag getting their attention.

A warm breeze drifts through the open windows and provides a slight reprieve from the lingering heat. This is one of the hottest days of the summer so far, but still, the air's filled with the sounds and smells of summer fun. Kinetic energy covers the beach like a low-lying cloud. An old white Dodge idles next to him at a red light. When the light turns green, the Dodge emits a cloud of smoke as it darts forward. Marcus chuckles as he floors the accelerator. The Jag hunkers down, then shoots past the Dodge and its young driver, who keeps his eyes pointed straight ahead.

Inside Teresa's building, he stops at the security desk where an alert young man, with glistening dark skin and wearing a green uniform with gold seams, greets him with a smile. The young man dips his head when Marcus gives his and Teresa's names, pushes several silver buttons on a console built into the desk's top, then speaks into a phone. "You're welcome, and have a good evening, Ms. Casteel. Sir, go straight back to the elevators." The young man points to the area behind him. "The twenty-ninth floor. Unit 2924."

The lobby's décor showcases a Victorian motif: arches over the two entry ways on each side of the front desk leading further into the interior of the building, large houseplants stationed three in a row along one side wall, multicolored tiles cover the floor, and patterns displaying garland and wreaths adorn the walls. Two black loveseats face one another along an opposite wall. The lobby is a small, cozy foyer near the front entrance. Beyond the security desk, a bank of elevators waits to take riders to the various floors. On each floor is where a select number of condo owners reside. Marcus leaves the security desk and enters a space where a gray-and-white-marbled floor feels like concrete beneath his sandals.

His sweaty feet squish as he walks. The noise from the soles of his sandals slapping against the hardness of the building's somber floor rises into the hollowness of the circular space. The amplified sounds reach the high vaulted ceiling and reverberate all around him. It feels like the inside of a cathedral. "Teresa's probably the only owner living here who's younger than sixty," he says, somewhat loudly, and waits for the echo he knows must come. The elevator is small, slow, and dated. A cracked mirror covers the ceiling. He stares up at his distorted reflection and rubs his index finger against the front side of his teeth, then cups his hands together over his nose and mouth and blows gently. All seems well, but he still pops in a breath mint.

The elevator jolts to a stop. The door opens, and he hurries out into the dim, narrow corridor before the elevator can do him harm. The hallway floor is in stark contrast to the lobby's downstairs. Its dark plush carpet absorbs the weightiness of each footfall and reduces its movement to a series of soundless footprints. In the quietness of the hallway, only his breathing can be heard. No noises escape from behind the four doors interrupting the long mauve-colored walls.

When he reaches her door, it opens to Teresa's smiling face. She pulls him inside and hugs him. It's brief but firm and reveals that beneath the clingy tan tank top she's wearing, there's no bra. As she leads Marcus farther inside, he notices that beneath her sheer beige shorts, there are no panty lines and that her nicely curved butt jiggles when she walks. The living room's not large, but its sparse furnishings create a spacious feel.

"Nice," he says.

"Thank you. It's not huge, one bedroom, one and half baths. But it's mine. And the bank's, of course." She laughs. "Follow me for the grand tour. But stay close so you don't get lost."

In the living room, floor-to-ceiling mirrors cover one whole wall. Four long, narrow windows stretching from the floor to the ceiling offer a sliced view of Chicago's downtown skyline. "Great view," he says, leaning against the window. The right side of his face presses the smooth glass.

"Moving along," she says, then grabs his hand and pulls him past a closed door. "That's my bedroom," she says. "But there's no need to peek inside."

"Why?"

"It's only available for the VIP tour."

"I thought this was the VIP tour," he says.

"Nope."

"Who gets the VIP tour?" he asks.

"Not a man who's practically a stranger."

"Define *stranger*, please," he says.

"A man who doesn't know my mother's name."

"Mother Casteel."

"Aren't we proper? I call mine *Momma*."

"But they mean the same thing. I'm right," Marcus says.

She walks him back to the bedroom door, opens it and lets him take a quick peek inside, then closes it. The lights are off, but he sees a full-size bed and maybe a dresser. "This isn't a full tour stop. No lights, no history?" he says.

"That's extra." She laughs and pulls him close. Face to face, her eyes lock into his as if daring him to cross that threshold. Marcus takes a step forward and kisses her forehead, a soft and quick touching of bodies. He feels no awkwardness, and when he steps back, he sees her eyes are closed. He smiles.

"Shall we continue on?" he says.

"Yes, of course. Now over here is my laundry room." She opens what appears to be a storage closet but, instead, houses a small washer crowned with a compact front-loading dryer.

"Cute and clever," he says.

"Yes, it is. Now to your immediate right is the half bath." Teresa takes his hand and leads him back to the living room. She points and says, "As you saw when we came in here, there is my petite kitchen." It's on the other side of a dining counter that separates the two rooms. She guides him to the sofa. It's so soft that he sinks deep into its cushions. At the end of his long frame, his heels come off the floor. It's like being pulled into a sinkhole.

"Whoa," he says, falling backward.

She releases the hand she's been holding. "This is a take-off- your-shoes, put-up-your-feet kind of couch. Make yourself at home."

He slips his feet out of his sandals, struggles to turn horizontally, and stretches out on the long sofa that runs the full length of the wall. He crosses his arms behind his head and his legs at the ankles, and peers at her from beneath half-closed eyes admiring her backside as she goes into the kitchen.

"What's on the agenda for the evening?" he asks.

"Agenda? Please, there are no agendas. Just a nice evening of dinner for two."

"Sounds good," he says. "I can help if you need me."

"You're fine right where you are." She reaches into the kitchen cabinets above the sink and takes down several dinner plates, and places them on the counter. "You like Chinese, I hope." The phone rings, and she picks up a glittery red portable phone. "Our fare is here, piping hot and ready to be served," she says after setting the phone back on the counter. Soon there's a soft knocking at the door. On the other side is a polite young man holding three large bags. Teresa takes the bags; they exchange words of gratitude, then she returns to the kitchen.

"That looks like a lot of food for just two people," Marcus says. "Are you expecting *more* guests?"

"I have assumed you're a man who likes options," Teresa says as she makes her way to the closet near the front door and pulls out a picnic basket. She comes back into the living room, kneels next to the sofa, and begins exploring the contents of the basket. She takes out a folded burgundy tablecloth and spreads it on the carpeted floor.

"An indoor picnic?"

"That okay with you?" she asks.

"I like your style."

She stands and turns, brushing against him as she heads back to the kitchen. He follows her with his eyes, and in the mirror wall, as she passes, he sees the smile she meant to conceal. A warm feeling presses the inside of his chest, making his hand tap a light rhythm against his leg. His own smile isn't as discreet. The meal is delicious. By the time they finish, the sun has disappeared over the horizon. The bright lights of the surrounding high- rise apartments begin dotting the view from the living room's windows. After their team's effort in clearing the picnic setup, they head to the sofa.

Marcus is on his back. Teresa's on his arm against the side of his chest, her right leg wedged between his two. His left arm forms a pillow beneath the back of his head. His eyes stare, without seeing, up at the ceiling. He can feel hers trained on his face; her right hand lies motionless under his shirt and atop his stomach. The shrimp fried rice, pepper steak, chicken and broccoli, and egg rolls have left him full and satisfied. The weight of her leg on his and the heat of her hand against his skin feel good. There's magic in the moment.

There's a time-defying quality to it, too. It feels like he's known her far longer than he has. Miss Teresa you-don't- get-my-last-name, lying next to him on *her* sofa in *her* condo. Unbelievable. He had wanted to meet her; had hoped he would get her attention when he pursued her in the Loop. Took his shot. Bull's-eye. He relishes the warmth of her body as it presses against him. Her touch ignites every nerve ending attached to his skin. She's gently stroking his arm and chill bumps rise like small moths attracted to a flame. She's enjoying his company. This formerly mysterious lady couldn't resist his charm.

Teresa raises an eyebrow. "Why are you grinning?" she asks.

Marcus turns to look at her and is mesmerized by the boldness of her intelligent eyes and the lushness of her lips. Her face is one he wants to touch and kiss. "Just thinking," he says, "how lucky I am to have a friend that points me in the right direction and assures me I am a marksman."

"Meaning?"

"When I spotted you that day, I pointed you out to my friend and told him I was smitten..."

"You were smitten?" Teresa laughs.

"...and wished you would stop, turn around, and come running to me because you were smitten too."

"And he said?"

"Go, my friend. Don't let that beauty get away without even trying."

"And you said?"

"But it's too improbable. What if I stop her, and she sprays me with a chemical that blinds me?"

"And he said?"

"Be brave. Take a chance. Shoot your shot."

"Oh. I get it." Teresa chuckles. "Good shot," she adds, then lowers her head and kisses his stomach.

* * *

His unblinking eyes gaze into hers as if searching for an answer to an unasked question. This is different for Teresa. It lacks awkwardness and uncertainty. His warm breath blows against her face. Their sexual chemistry is real. She leans even closer and kisses him. A soft, tender kiss with a lightness that says she likes him. Marcus closes his eyes. Teresa keeps her lips close to his, but they don't touch. She's teasing herself. She's not sure how far she wants to go, but he raises his head. This time the kiss is deeper and longer. Her tongue presses past his lips. She can feel her own body heat rising as her breasts dig into his side. She shivers when his erection strains against her.

Teresa pulls away, not abruptly but with uncertainty. She places her hands against his chest and disentangles their bodies. He yields, lies back and groans. She sits upright and scoots backward against the sofa's arm for support, then pulls at her blouse and then her shorts. His eyes are shut. She closes her eyes and waits for the turmoil within her body to subside. Neither of them gives voice to their thoughts. His erection is still evident. She studies it. Her own body is still poised too. Her nipples are still sensitive as they press against the warm cotton. The heat and wetness between her legs are still sending pleasure signals to her brain.

Marcus opens his eyes and reaches for her. He squeezes one of her nipples then rubs it gently. Teresa shivers. Her body stiffens. She caresses his thigh, then slides her hand slowly upward until it finds his erection. She rubs and strokes it. By now, his eyes are closed, and he's stroking and massaging both her breasts. Then she stops, releases a long breath, and moves away from his overpowering hands. *Damn, it's too soon. We can't do it before he knows my momma's name.* She laughs at the thought. Marcus opens his eyes and peers sideways at her.

Teresa slides her legs off the sofa and stands up. Her shorts are now scrunched between her cheeks, and the rounded bottoms of her butt are exposed. Marcus closes his eyes and groans. She bends over and strokes the front of his pants one more time, then straightens her back and then straightens her shorts. She goes to the refrigerator and takes out two cans of light beer, his preferred alcoholic beverage because he can handle it, he's told her. Teresa returns to the sofa and places the cold cans against his groin.

"Thanks, I needed that."

"I know," she says.

Marcus sits up, takes one of the cans and pulls open the tab and takes two long gulps. Teresa does the same. They sit in silence, drinking and looking at each other. Ten days ago, she was seconds away from blinding this man with pepper spray. Now she's been two moves away from fucking him. Two moves. She shakes her head and shifts her body to break their eye contact. "Wow. I guess we're past the stranger-danger phase," she tells him.

He holds up his can and proposes a toast. "To the next phase."

"Hear, hear," Teresa says.

"And the next phase will be?"

"To becoming friends before lovers," she says and raises her can.

"How about this? To lovers becoming friends."

"How about this? Let nature take its course. Just not tonight," she says.

"How about this? You come over to my place, and we let nature take its course in the wee hours of the morning."

"I repeat my last offer," Teresa says. She reaches down and rubs his ebbing erection. "I'm convinced it'll be worth our wait." Marcus moans, then grins and raises his drink. They clink their cans to seal the deal. She pulls him to his feet and helps him fix his clothes. Then pulls him toward the door.

"Are we sure I should leave?" he says.

"No, but that's why you should."

"Right now?"

"Right now," she says.

Eight

The buildings along Michigan Avenue cast cool shadows across the sidewalks as Marcus heads to his office. He's late for a meeting with Fraser Letcher regarding George Womack's case. His lunch with Teresa lasted longer than planned. She talked, and time flew. Her mother's name is Taylor Lee Casteel, who also gave birth to an older brother and younger sister. Teresa's 34-27-34, five feet eight inches tall, and likes her face but thinks her forehead is a bit big. She describes her butt as a bit too round but not too big, her calves less shapely than she would prefer, and her hair too stubborn to tame. Marcus listened to all her alleged insecurities with a healthy skepticism, and now, they're friends. He smiles in anticipation of what comes next.

Missy greets him with a luminous smile when he enters the suite. It's 2:15 p.m, and his meeting's scheduled for 2 p.m. Being a little late is a bad habit he needs to break. He hears laughter booming from behind the blue half-wall separating the reception area from the long corridor connecting the other offices and rooms in the suite. Fraser rarely visits, so Marcus knows he's catching up with Seleste.

"How was your *lunch*?" Missy asks, raising her eyebrows.

"Great," he says.

Melissa "Missy" Mills is twenty-five and single and Seleste's goddaughter. She's also flirtatious as of late, and he's not sure what's up with her. She's started to stand too close when they're leaving the small conference room after a staff meeting, and she looks him in the eyes for a little too long. He needs to tell Seleste to put Missy in check.

He continues past Missy and toward the laughter coming from Seleste's office. She and Fraser are old friends from the days when Fraser worked as an associate for his grandfather, Walker

Mitchell Greene. Fraser attributes his renowned business savvy and aggressive—Marcus prefers the word *cutthroat*—lawyering to lessons learned from his time as an associate. Marcus pops his head through the doorway of Seleste's office. She's leaning back in her chair at her workstation holding her stomach. Her curly ponytail swings wildly as she shakes her head from side to side. Fraser sits perched on the edge of her workstation, hunched over and laughing, too.

"What's so funny?" Marcus says.

"Just revisiting old times." Fraser stands, steps over to the door and puts his arm around Marcus, pulling him close. "Why do you still have this beautiful woman stuck behind this antiquated, outdated piece of junk?" Seleste starts laughing again. She always acts silly around Fraser.

"I won't let him waste good money. Besides, this workstation and I have a history. We're old spiritual friends who know each other's secrets," Seleste says.

"There's nothing like loyalty," Fraser says, "even to a piece of furniture." He winks at Seleste and walks back over to her.

"Sorry I'm running a little late, counselor. Can I get another five minutes to get settled?" Marcus holds up five fingers for emphasis.

Fraser looks at his watch and frowns. "As long as I'm on George's dime. My time is my money."

Seleste has placed the Womack files on his desk. As soon as Marcus unstacks them, Missy calls on the intercom. "There's a Teresa Casteel calling."

"Put her through. Thanks."

"I can tell her you're busy."

"I'll take the call."

"Hey," Teresa greets him.

"Hey, yourself."

"I wanted to say again how much I enjoyed lunch," she tells him.

"I enjoyed you," he responds.

"I'm blushing."

"I'm grinning."

"Such a silver-tongued flatterer. I didn't mean to disrupt your meeting. Your receptionist said I was. So, am I disrupting your meeting?" she says.

"You always get the VIP treatment with me."

"I don't think your little receptionist agrees with you," Teresa says.

"I'll get her up to speed," he tells Teresa and laughs. "Besides my guest is being hosted by my business partner at the moment. I'll get him away from Seleste in a minute." Marcus sits down and plops his feet up on the desk. "How's it going over your way?"

"Nothing's routine for me right now. I'm not complaining, though. To paraphrase my mentor, 'Ain't nothing bad about being the boss.' I'd just add that it ain't no cakewalk either."

"True it has its ups and downs," he says.

"Do you like it?"

"Being the boss? Compared to being bossed? Without a doubt," he says.

"Great perspective."

"You having regrets?" he asks.

"The adjustments from my previous role are huge," she says, then groans. "You know, a lot of people can't handle a woman being in charge."

"That's not your problem. It's theirs," he tells her.

"If it were only that easy, counselor."

"Maybe it is," he says. "Just avoid making other people's issues your issues."

"I'll try. Thanks for listening."

"That's what friends are for. We are friends now, right?" he says.

"I think so."

"So, it's on to the VIP tour at your place," he says and growls.

"Phone sex, huh?"

Fraser's voice is like a sonic boom in the dead of night.

Marcus flinches, then he puts a finger to his mouth to shush Fraser and whispers in the phone, "My guest just walked in."

"Your guest is a little rowdy," Teresa says.

"More than a little." Marcus frowns at Fraser.

"Well, I believe that's my cue to sign off," she says.

"About tonight?"

"Oh, darn. That's why I called too. Have to reschedule. Work stuff. Sorry."

"Okay, tomorrow then?" Marcus knows Fraser is watching him, knows there's a smirk plastered across that broad face. Fraser sits in one of the three leather chairs he's probably sat in a hundred times during his tenure with Walker Greene.

"We'll talk later. Bye," Teresa says and disconnects.

"You should close and lock your door when you plan to get your rocks off during office hours," Fraser says.

"Get my rocks off? Man, you really sound old."

Fraser takes out a cigar, unwraps and sniffs it, then encircles it with his thumb and index finger and leaves it resting lightly on his middle one. Fraser won't smoke it because he doesn't smoke. It's just a prop, an affectation, a part of his act. Fraser's the consummate showman and a self-styled enigma. He wasn't born into money but comes from the streets. Marcus has seen that side of Fraser. Most people who experience Fraser for the first time are often shocked at his casual slide into vulgarity. But most also come to accept it as a part of who he is, and Marcus is no different. Fraser is Fraser.

"That expression is a classic, and it is timeless, or a young man like you wouldn't have understood it. But that is not the real issue. The real issue is that you weren't making any money while you were getting mind-fucked over the phone. Pussy's a poor substitute for currency and can be a damned liability if you have to pay for it." Fraser's baritone voice is so rich and full it makes his crassness sound poetic.

"That's why I feel blessed to have you as my guru. But, for the record, I don't pay for what I can get for free." Marcus wags his finger at Fraser.

"For the record, you'll pay for pussy sooner or later. It's never free. Ask George," Fraser says and laughs.

Fraser takes several folders out of his briefcase and sets them in a horizontal row on the desk. He rolls the cigar between his fingers, then points it at Marcus. "This, my young friend, represents what George's little lady is salivating over. He's done pretty well for himself, and that's why Miss Rhonda is on a mission to show him just how expensive a piece of white pussy can be for a Black man. Let me give you the numbers."

Marcus knows the numbers are huge. George is the spouse that made the money and claims total credit for the accumulation of his immense wealth. George is also a man whose stubbornness and anger short circuit his intelligence, which makes him a difficult client. And his wife feels entitled to a lot of it, which adds fuel to his raging fire.

"These are the coveted spoils of this authentic war of the sexes, my young friend," Fraser says. He opens each folder one at a time and slides them across the desk for Marcus to review. "In addition to the '51 Rolls Silver Wraith, there are three other classic cars. All four are valued at $200,000. There are several pieces of real estate, including the residence, valued at $5,000,000. Bank accounts, stocks and bonds, jewelry and other personal property, are valued at $2,000,000. And then there is the medical practice." Fraser pauses while Marcus scans the contents of the folders. "I think we can make a good case for the practice being nonmarital property. And we can also make an effective argument that the goodwill value of the practice is zero," Fraser says.

Most of the valuation issues are foreign to Marcus, except those regarding real estate. In the majority of his divorce cases, a home or condo is the only real appreciating asset his clients have to fight over. These gigantic valuation issues are routine for Fraser's well-to-do clients. He's a specialist in divorce cases where there's enough at stake to lob hand grenades.

When Fraser takes on a case, he is willing to bomb the opponent, women and children be damned. In an online magazine article, Fraser was quoted as saying, "I know my business, and I know the law. I win cases because I understand divorce is war and defeat is dishonorable.

If a person wants a quick, negotiated peace to avoid bloodshed, then don't bother me. A negotiated peace means all parties lose."

Fraser wants all his cases to go to trial if the opponent doesn't surrender. But George is not Fraser's client, and Marcus is determined to negotiate an acceptable settlement. This goes against Fraser's instincts for a big fight in the limelight. He wants the win, period. Marcus has been challenged by Fraser at every turn while the relationship between George and his wife is becoming more volatile.

She's changed all the locks and codes. His classic cars are being held hostage. George is furious and threatening to break into the garage. Even more unsettling are George's declarations that the children would be better off with him. He's contemplating a custody fight. Marcus knows he's losing control of George and knows that his more notorious co-counsel, Mr. Fraser Letcher, Esquire, is poised and ready like a feline predator to lead the bloody attack.

Fraser concludes his presentation, leans back in his seat, and makes a pronouncement. "This case is not going to be settled. I can feel it in my bones. That white woman is going to make that Black man pay and won't settle for anything less than his balls. How's George holding up?"

"He's pissed, and he's itching for a custody fight. He's raising questions about her fitness."

"That could be an effective tactic. Something to shake her up, make her understand there's a price for being greedy. Right now, she's only focused on how much she can snatch. George has to show her she has a little something to lose," Fraser says.

"That little something being her kids."

"Sometimes I think you're too sensitive. *George* is your client. George is paying your bill. Let Rhonda's little cute-ass lawyer make her case." Fraser stands and walks to one of the two windows facing east and Lake Michigan. The window's view of the lake is blocked, except for a paltry sliver of the blue water, by tall corner high-rise office buildings. He raises the unlit cigar to his lips.

"I don't believe a knock-down, drag-out fight is in our client's interest," Marcus says.

"You know George dreamed big and worked hard to become successful. Miss Rhonda, on the other hand, wasted her talents and time on petty ambitions and mediocre men. It seems to me she caught a break when she suckered George into marrying her. It seems to me like little Miss Rhonda hit the lottery. She'll be sitting pretty after *this* failed marriage because she married a rich Black man and not another hillbilly who took off with the truck and trailer." Fraser turns to face Marcus. "Don't waste your tears on her. Save them for George. Your job, our job, is to make sure he doesn't get his ass handed to him on a silver platter he bought. That's what I lose sleep worrying about at night. And you should too. Miss Rhonda is going to be just fine. She's about to get paid, and I think right now that's *all* she cares about."

Marcus isn't going to argue because he knows he can't compete with Fraser in or out of the courtroom. George was referred to Marcus by Bird, who was serving as an adviser on two real estate deals. During the real estate transactions, George's marriage, already a heavy wounded bear on thin ice, crashed through and was sinking fast. Marcus took George on as a client in the divorce case, and once he understood how many assets were at stake, called in Fraser for his expertise in handling complicated and volatile cases like this but also as insurance just in case the other side craves blood. If that happened, Marcus didn't want to be outgunned. Marcus needed a grenade launcher.

Still, Marcus isn't ready to give up on his strategy to negotiate a settlement. "We've got to get George down off that cliff. He's teetering on the edge. And I think we can get Rhonda's lawyer to lower her weapon. They're just reacting to George's threats. I think if you and I try hard enough, we can avoid a scorched-earth outcome." Marcus doesn't expect Fraser to encourage this stubborn effort to protect people from themselves, but he knows Fraser won't fight it. Fraser will let him tilt at windmills until it becomes an obvious waste of time and energy.

"Feel free to give it your best shot, and in the meantime, I'll draw up plan B," Fraser says.

Nine

Bird speeds up the driveway in his yellow bug and slams to a stop just inches from the bumper of the Jag. Marcus glances in his rear-view mirror, shakes his head, and then drains the last of a protein shake. They exit their cars and walk to the back of the house. Bird looks around while Marcus unlocks and opens the metal storm door.

"Think he's home?" Bird says.

"Go see." Bird shakes his head.

"I don't know the man. You do."

"I don't know the man any more today than the last time you were here."

"You live here all these years and don't know the man?" Bird says.

"Nope."

"I've got some ideas, and he's got the clout."

Bird's an entrepreneur. After coming to Chicago, he got into real estate and other enterprises. He owns several condo units and has a few angel investments. He's been bugging Marcus forever to introduce him to the neighborhood celebrity businessman as a contact.

"Send him an e-mail," Marcus says.

They enter the kitchen, and Bird takes a seat at the kitchen table while Marcus takes a seat across from his friend. The sun flares through the arched windows, its rays full of swirling dust particles suspended in midair. The house is clean and smells fresh through the efforts of his housekeeper. Since he became its owner, Marcus has kept the spacious house uncluttered, unlike his grandmother, who kept a disorganized and junk-filled mess in every room.

Now because of the hard work he and the housekeeper have put in since Marcus took over, the house is comfortable and impressive. At least he thinks it is, and he figures Teresa will think so too. He's come to understand, as a result of his divorce practice and social life, that women find a man's expensive cars and big houses as key indicators of whether he's deserving of their time and attention.

"I'm serious," Bird says.

"You always are."

Bird gets up and walks to the refrigerator and peeks inside. "You need to get some food in this place." Closing the fridge, he says, "Glad I finally get to meet Miss Teresa."

Marcus stands and stretches his stiff lower back. The two of them ran and walked five miles along the lakefront on the north side. It's Bird's plan to reduce his burgeoning midsection. Marcus does it as an act of support for his friend.

"You'll be long gone by the time she gets here," Marcus says.

"I'm a reference for you. All women want to meet somebody connected to a new prospect."

"I need a good reference."

"I'm the only friend you got," Bird says.

"There's no way you're going to be here when she comes."

Bird reopens the refrigerator door and grabs a handful of grapes from a plastic bowl. "I'm offended," he says.

"The first time you'll meet her is at the wedding."

"Doubt there will be a wedding."

"You can take the bowl," Marcus says, "and hit the road. She'll be here in an hour, and I need to shower."

"You? Settling down and giving up the chase? Don't think so." Bird reopens the fridge and grabs up the bowl of grapes.

"I don't chase, my friend. I explore options. You're proof of what happens when you don't."

"Maybe she has a friend I can explore," Bird says.

Before Marcus can respond, his cell phone rings. It's Teresa.

"I'm in your driveway sitting behind a cute little VW. You've got company?" She sounds energetic and upbeat.

"A friend of mine who's on his way out as we speak." Marcus motions to Bird to follow him and heads for the door.

"Early. Get to meet her after all," Bird says when they head down the driveway. "Might as well invite me to stay for supper too."

The door of the small silver Benz opens, and Teresa emerges with a dazzling smile on her face.

"Not bad," Bird whispers barely moving his lips.

"I know," Marcus whispers back. "Just say hello and goodbye. Got it?"

"Hello, Ms. Casteel. I'm Walden Byrd Mann III, the one and only friend that Marcus Greene can claim. I guess now you make two." Bird extends his hand as he walks past his car to greet her. Teresa ignores his hand and hugs him.

"I'm glad to meet you," she says. "You'll be joining us for dinner?" Teresa winks at Bird.

"I asked, he said no." Bird grimaces and points a thumb.

"Nope, he's not invited." Marcus pulls at Bird's arm.

"Maybe soon," Teresa says and hugs Bird again. She walks past Bird to Marcus and slips her hand behind his head and pulls his face to hers; she reaches briefly inside him with her tongue, then lets her lips linger. "Hey, you" she says.

"Hey, yourself," he says. "We need to let him out." Marcus takes her hand and guides her back to her car. "I'll see you later, Walden."

"So, you're from my home state," Bird says, trailing behind them.

"So, I'm told. We'll have to get together and see if we know any of the same people. I met a lot of folks from St. Louis at Mizzou." She opens the rear passenger door and stands back so Marcus can retrieve the groceries.

"Can I get your number?" Bird says.

Marcus steps back from the Benz holding three plastic grocery bags. "You think it's that easy to get her number?" He shakes his head, then tells Teresa, "Let him get his little sunshine buggy out of here, then pull your car all the way to the back after he leaves. Goodbye, Walden."

"Want some insights after he goes inside?" Bird says.

Teresa laughs and says, "I'm all ears."

Marcus leaves them standing in the driveway.

* * *

"The steak and baked potato were delicious." Marcus smacks his lips.

"Your friend says you have very unrealistic standards about everything."

"You've exceeded my wildest expectations."

"Really?" she says, unable to stifle the smile that parts her lips.

"Really. You two had a nice chat, I see."

"Just got a heads-up," she says.

"He's not credible. Too biased."

"How long have you been friends?" she says.

"Since college."

"I'd say he's a very credible witness."

"He's a gossip."

"Well, he's good at it. Kept my attention." Her voice is soft when she giggles.

"That he is," Marcus says, standing up and moving behind Teresa. "But gossip is fabrication, you know."

He grasps her shoulders, turns her away from him and begins to massage her back. His thumbs slide along her muscles in an up-and-down motion, then in a circular fashion. She catches her breath, then sighs in approval. Using the palms and fingers of both hands, he eases up the center of her back, pressing and rubbing in rhythmic movements. Teresa closes her eyes and feels her whole body relaxing. Then she's being spun around, and the warm moistness on her forehead opens her eyes.

"Your friend says you're what's called a charmer. That seems more factual than gossip."

He kisses the tip of her nose and then her lips. Her eyes close again, and her lips part. He pulls Teresa to her feet, and minutes pass as they cling to, claw at and mash against each other. No words are spoken. His frenetic kisses touch every square inch of her face. His hands are hot pads heating up her skin. She trembles when he raises her tank top over her head and moves his mouth across her eyes, her chin, and her neck. He inhales her nipples between his lips and paints them with his tongue.

The friction he creates when his teeth pinch her hardened nipples makes her gasp. His tongue eases past her breasts and slides down her stomach and circles her navel. He pulls at the waistband of her jeans. Teresa unfastens the snap, lowers the zipper and squirms out of them. She slides to the floor until she's in a sitting position, then lifts her butt, and he slides off her lacey green thong. He pushes her sandals that lie under one of his arms to the side and pulls at her ankles until she's flat on her back.

Teresa closes her eyes and lets him have his way. Her arms lie limp beside her on the floor. Her body stiffens when his lips pull at her toes. Her breath comes in short, heavy bursts as his mouth and hands move in tandem from her feet to her legs and upward along her thighs. Her soft moans echo off the sunlit walls of the kitchen. Her movements in response to his every touch urge him onward. Everything he's doing speeds up. She bolts upright when his tongue penetrates her wet center. He puts his hands against her stomach and eases her back down.

"Oh, God." She's upright again but this time pushing at his head.

"Relax, baby," he whispers.

She wants to comply, but she's not in control. She twists away from the island, her hands scraping the hardwood floor as they try to grab on to the unyielding surface. Her body twists and jerks, then scoots away from him. He scrambles after her, his nose buried deep between her legs. She stops when her head bangs against the refrigerator. He presses forward and slips his hands under her butt and lifts her. Her body stretches, then grows rigid. She sucks in air in big gulps. Then an uncensored scream. He clutches her legs and keeps his face buried deep between her moving thighs while the thunderbolt tearing through her body threatens to blow it apart.

Seconds later she is still. She opens her eyes but only the top of his head is visible. His face lies below her pelvis. Her hands stroke his head as she struggles to catch her breath. She thinks she heard him grunt. His breath is as labored as hers. She wants to move but he feels like dead weight. She wants to wiggle her toes, but it seems a monumental effort is required. She closes her eyes and relaxes. Minutes pass in stillness. Then he moves his face from between her legs and lays a cheek on her thigh. His breathing is now soft and metered. So is hers. She struggles up on her elbows and says, "Did you have an orgasm?"

"Yeah," Marcus says, "I did."

* * *

The water feels good, and Teresa's body against his feels even better. The spray drenches them as they stand, his front to her back, leaning against the shower wall opposite the shower faucet. Her eyes are closed, and her arms are wrapped around his neck. The back of her head rests on his shoulder, and he holds it there, gently moving his fingers in and out of her tangled curly hair, holding on to the moment, not wanting it to pass. His eyes are open but unfocused. The misty spray bounces off her onto his face and clouds his vision. He thinks about the day he followed her and feels a sense of astonishment. He rubs each eye with the back of his finger and looks at her, thinking, *I beat them long odds.*

"A penny for your thoughts," she says, turning her head slightly toward his face and smiling.

"Just thinking about what I could have missed."

"Meaning?" she says.

"If I had passed up the chance to meet you."

"You mean if you hadn't stalked me?" she says and laughs.

"It's not stalking the first time."

"Is that a legal definition?"

"It's in the stalker's handbook. The first pursuit is *not* a stalking incident. It's classified as *Fatum tuum persequi*. If the followee is amenable to your invitation to get together, it is *Fatum tuum occurrit*."

Teresa turns fully around to face him and puts her hands against his chest. "Gibberish," she says.

"Absolutely not. It's Latin, the stalker's handbook's official language. Fatum tuum persequi means 'pursue your destiny,' and Fatum tuum occurrit means 'met your destiny.'"

"You're good," she says.

"Thanks for recognizing."

"And I'm glad you pursued and met your destiny," she says. "But at some point, I wanna know why you have that handbook." She traces the word "good" in the streams of water flowing down his chest. He shivers beneath the feathery touch of her fingers. He tilts her head upward and kisses her lightly. She presses her lips firmly back, and the kiss takes on a weightiness that causes his manhood to harden between them and brings a soft moan from somewhere inside of her. The huskiness of her voice makes him smile. Her hands grabbing his butt make him press his body against her. Her lips slip from his and, as if melting; she slides down his body, leaving a heated trail of kisses. Kneeling in front of him, she takes his erection in her hands. She caresses it with a knowing gentleness. He moans without inhibition when she takes him into her mouth.

* * *

They're back in the kitchen cleaning up. Teresa's wearing one of his sweatshirts and nothing else. His only attire is a pair of jockey shorts. She's putting the dishes in the dishwasher. Between singing a medley of Smokey's songs and using the sink's faucet sprayer to rinse each plate, pan, glass, and utensil thoroughly before passing it on to Teresa, his work is proceeding at a leisurely pace. Teresa waits patiently for each handover.

"What's your favorite song?" she asks.

"Old-school stuff but variety," he says. "Some Marvin Gaye. Temptations. Smokey. Louis Armstrong. Miles Davis, etc."

"How old are you, really?" Teresa asks as she takes a fork from him.

"When it comes to musical taste, my late sixties. Raised by an old man who liked soul music and an old woman who liked blues and jazz. What can I say?"

"I'm hip-hop," she says.

"Talk about a generation gap. Come here, girlie." He goes over to her, puts an arm around her waist, takes her hand, and moves her around the floor while he hums the melody to *My Girl*. "We old folks call this slow dancing."

"I remember this," she says, "Barack and Michelle, inauguration night."

"They did the clean version," he says, then bends her backward, stops moving his feet and does some deep grinds. "Now this is what my grandfather did." For the next several minutes they glide around the floor, then stop and do deep grinds and then move some more.

When he stops, Teresa says, "My turn."

"What you got for me?"

She slides away and faces him. "Do what I do," she tells him. Then she stretches her arms in front of her, leans side to side, starts bobbing her head, and sings. She watches his face and knows he's clueless. She laughs and keeps singing and dancing. The lyrics are edgy, and the beat in her head is controlling. She closes her eyes and lets the imagined beats move her body.

Her feet and knees and arms and head keep time to the rhythms pulsing through her brain. She keeps going until she completes the whole song. When she stops and opens her eyes, Marcus has taken a seat, palms cupping his face, a big grin flattening his nose, and he's bobbing his head like he can hear the music too. "Sorry," she says, "got a little carried away." She slides over to him and wraps her arms around his neck.

"What was that?" he asks.

"It's *The Dougie*."

"I couldn't do those moves if you offered me a million bucks," he tells her. "But that was so hot."

"Why thank you."

"No. Thank you. I got me a hip-hop girl."

"Yes, you do," she says and squeezes tighter.

Ten

Teresa listens to his shallow breaths. She studies his face. Marcus is asleep. Less than three weeks ago, this man was a stranger, and now they've made love more than five times in a day. Her orgasms were powerful. She remembers screaming during the last one before blacking out for a couple of seconds. When she opened her eyes, he was staring at her. His eyes were glassy and unfocused. Then she must have fallen asleep. This is the best sex she's ever had. Her body shivers with the recognition. A clock on the small table next to her reads 9:00 p.m.

Teresa lightly caresses the dark flesh of his naked body from head to feet. She enjoys the slickness of his head. She eases her fingertips in and out of the few acne divots bunched on each cheekbone. His arms and chest are muscular but not buff, and he's a little soft around the middle, but it's nowhere near a potbelly. He's a man who takes care of himself. She trails down his stomach but avoids his groin and slides her palm down one leg. His quads are well developed although his calves are less so. All in all, she likes his body. Is drawn to it.

The interior of his bedroom is dark except for the slivers of light coming through partially open blinds. A ceiling fan stirs the warm air. The walls, a pale blue, hold only a single framed piece of art. The painting portrays an exaggerated version of Black life. She recognizes it as the same scene on the cover of a Marvin Gaye album: images of dark dancing women with spaghetti waists and pumpkin butts all draped in fabrics of blood red, lemon yellow, and money green. They are in the company of long, thin Black men with leering smiles, sweaty brows, with philandering eyes trained on those bouncing big asses full of promise.

Teresa studies the painting a few moments longer, then eases off the side of the bed. Marcus has changed his position, but he's still asleep. He won't be offering her the VIP tour anytime soon. She puts on his robe and with the stealth of a burglar tiptoes out of the bedroom into the short hallway and closes the door behind her. The hallway is dimly lit, but she can see three doors: two off the same hallway as his bedroom, and the third door is on the other side of the stairs that lead to the first floor. Teresa starts with the door across from his bedroom. When she peeks inside, she's met with the same smell of jasmine that hangs in the air in his bedroom. The light is better in here, and she can see two large bookcases full of hardcover and paperback books, a twin-sized bed and an oversize oak dresser.

She steps into its sterile stillness and walks through to the back into a concrete, enclosed solarium with four wide windows, two facing east and two facing south. Both views overlook the houses and yards of neighbors. She's surprised there are no alleys separating backyards. The solarium's furnished with a treadmill and a weight bench. A few dumbbells of various weights lie on a windowsill and on the floor along one wall.

In the room across the stairway she finds a smaller space, but it has a separate full bath with a marble floor and an enclosed glass shower. It appears to be undisturbed. It has no bed linen or towels, and the wooden dresser's drawers and the bathroom cabinet are empty. The third room, next to his bedroom, is neat and ordered but has a more lived-in feel to it. The room has contemporary furniture and a half bath with a marble floor. It has a second connecting door that leads to the smallest room on the floor, his home office from the looks of it.

She steps back into the hallway and gives the second floor a summary inspection. The varnished sheen of the wooden doors with their transparent glass doorknobs are classy. The spacious rooms are, to her surprise, uncluttered. It's a big house. All five of those little houses her family lived in when she was growing up could fit in this place.

He said the housekeeper is from Poland. Now, *that*'s interesting. Her grandmother cleaned the houses of white people when Teresa was growing up. She remembers the time she went with Momma Neva on a cleaning assignment and hated it. She goes down the stairs and lets her hand glide along the wooden banister. She kneels down and slides her hands across the bare hardwood floors. She admires the Polish lady's work.

To her right is the living room, as long as the house is wide. At one end of the room is a brown sofa fronted by a short, square, glass-topped table. At the other end is a fireplace encased on each side with built-in shelves with mirrored walls. The shelves are empty except for three framed photos of the outside of the house from three different angles.

No family photos here nor anywhere else in the house. Interesting but also sad, she thinks. The remaining two-thirds of the room are empty except for the two brown wing chairs forced into corners away from everything else. Two chandeliers hang from the high ceiling, an equal distance from the middle of the room. "Hello," she says, expecting to hear an echo. She steps back into the hallway and looks into the dining room where a large antique dinner table swallows up the space.

Six high-backed chairs stationed around it are covered in green cloth and feature soft plump cushions on the seat and back. Behind the dining room at the back of the house is a small sunroom furnished with a loveseat. She passes through the dining room into this sunroom. It offers a view of the backyard through a large picture window. There is a short narrow hallway between the sunroom and the kitchen that leads back to the front hallway. At the end nearest the sunroom is a half bath. She starts to head back to Marcus but stops to open a door to her right. *Ah, yes, the basement.*

Marcus is still asleep. Lying there with that half smile painted on his face, he looks like the most satisfied man on the planet. She blows him a kiss, takes off the robe, and walks over to the dresser and explores the drawers. She selects a black T-shirt with a picture of Muhammad Ali outlined in yellow on the front. After putting on the shirt, she goes into the master bath and searches his medicine cabinet for some toothpaste. The cabinet, like his bedroom, isn't quite as neat as the rest of his house.

A tube of toothpaste lies half hidden behind a pile of shaving paraphernalia: an electric shaver, a manual razor, two large bottles of shaving cream, and a bottle of shaving lotion. It's not her preferred toothpaste, but she puts a dab on her index finger and rubs her teeth in circular motions. Back in the bed, she moves close to him, and his body turns toward her like a flower to the sun. Teresa sighs. There hasn't been a night spent with a man for quite some time. She rolls over, then scoots backward until she's flush against his warm body. Teresa pulls the top sheet up to her chin. Soon she's fast asleep.

* * *

Teresa pulls on the front of the T-shirt as she sits down. Marcus, wearing a tank top, a pair of tennis shorts and no shoes, stands at the counter next to the sink. He looks fresh. She opened her eyes a few minutes ago to discover it was 11:00 a.m. and his side of the bed was empty.

"Ali never looked that good on me."

"You're looking bright-eyed and bushy-tailed," she replies. "And don't sell yourself short."

"Well, I've seen us both in it and, believe me, it's no contest."

"I'm happy to concede the point," she says. "By the way, I gave myself a tour this morning since you weren't available."

"I enjoyed my nap."

"More like a coma," she says. "This place is huge. So much house for one person."

"I thought about selling." His expression changes for a brief moment. "But it's the only house I've ever lived in, and I can't see myself living anywhere else. Gave yourself the tour, huh? What's the verdict?"

"I love it. Can I ask you a personal question, though?"

"Sure," he says.

"Why no family photos?"

"They're packed away in a trunk in the basement. My grandfather put them away, and I've never gotten around to doing anything else with them."

"Oh," she says and decides to let the subject drop for now.

"Why didn't you wake me?" he asks.

"You looked so content with that smile on your face."

"I was smiling, huh?"

"More like grinning," Teresa says. She goes over, stands behind him and leans her chin on his shoulder. "Are you any good at this?"

"I can cook a few things. My specialty is scrambled eggs. You'll love them."

"I grew up eating some of the best scrambled eggs in the world," she says. "My brother would fix me and our sister a big skillet of scrambled eggs, sometimes with onions, cheese, and peppers. Maybe, when we had them, he'd add some ham and bacon. Sometimes apples and honey. You name it, he'd give it a try. Those are some of my better memories." Teresa moves from behind him and walks over to the open door.

Two squirrels dart in and out of the garbage cans that are lined up next to the side of the garage. A trio of huge black birds sit perched in the limbs of two long trees standing guard along the wrought-iron fence at the back of the yard. The lawn is cut but brown in a few spots. *What a nice place to grow up in,* she thinks.

Marcus collects a mixture of ingredients and begins cracking eggs, dicing an onion and apple, adding bacon bits, shredded cheese, and multiple spices. Then he removes the link sausages he's been browning in the cast-iron skillet, sharply inhales the aroma of the fried meat, nods his head in approval, drops in two butter chunks, and pours in the yellowish contents of the bowl.

"Breakfast is about to be served, Madame," he says five minutes later. He sets a platter full of eggs and eight link sausages on the table.

"Wow. If it tastes as good as it looks and smells, I'm a fan." Then the clanking of forks against plates fills the room.

"Um, these eggs *are* delicious," she says.

For the next few minutes they eat in silence while exchanging flirtatious glances. When Teresa scoops up the last of the eggs and dumps it onto her plate, she says, "I know I'm being a pig, but when I'm hungry, I don't pretend I'm not."

"I know. I've seen you at work. Remember?" he says.

"Your eggs may be as good as my brother's." She winks. He winces.

"Competing with memories is hard," he says.

Teresa puts another forkful of eggs in her mouth, doesn't chew, casts her eyes upward and taps her forehead. Then begins chewing and swallows. "It's so close," she says, "but it's not fair to compare just yet. I'll need a few more samples of your work."

"Deal."

"This is such a big house for one man."

"But perfect for a family of three or four." He laughs.

"Don't you prefer being a single, childless man?"

"Do you prefer being a single, childless woman?" he says.

"I never decided to be. Just how things have gone. So far." Teresa is putting the last of the eggs in her mouth but glances up from beneath her bowed head and leans it sideways to look at him.

"The forks in the road you took, as opposed to the ones you didn't take, brought you to me. That's fate," Marcus says and sits back in his chair.

"Has fate kept you frisky and single? Or was this your plan?"

"My only plan was to have a law career. I guess like you, this is where I landed." He smiles, rubs her hand, then adds, "So far." Teresa stands, hovers over the empty dishes, pulls his face toward her, and brushes her lips across the shiny baldness of his head. He tilts it backward until their lips meet. His mouth opens and lets her eager tongue inside. The kiss, though deep, is brief. Although their sexual chemistry is evident, Teresa doesn't believe it's just sex with them. This isn't pure horniness on her part. She's been *there*, and this isn't it. "Well, where do you go from here?" Teresa asks.

"A better question is where do *we* go from here?" he counters. Teresa would love to express how she's feeling about him. Them. Right now. How her heart races when she remembers and when she anticipates being in his arms. Being his lover. But her caution is like the worried parent she never had, holding on to her hand, urging her to go slow because life isn't a fairy tale.

"You think you would like living here?" he says.

"And where would you live?" Teresa laughs, but her eyes try to intuit his intent.

"In sin. With you," he says.

"That's the good sex talking."

"Good sex, huh?" He grins, then thumps his chest.

"Yes, Romeo. You're the man."

* * *

They're on the sofa in his living room facing a dark fireplace. The room's covered in shadows. It's late afternoon. Marcus sits upright at one end, while she lies with her head in his lap. She's asked him about his family again.

He sighs. "It's not a heartwarming story. My mother, Desiree Greene, died on October 25, 1977, in a twelve-car pileup on the Dan Ryan. Six months after I was born. She was nineteen. She was alone driving home from a friend's party when it happened."

"That's tragic." Teresa rubs his leg.

"She came home from college newly pregnant during Christmas break her freshman year. But would never tell my grandparents who the father was."

Teresa adjusts her position and sits upright next to him, her hand on his arm. "Never? She never told them?"

"My understanding is that she just shut down and refused to talk about it. Kathryn suspected that Desiree might have been raped. She pushed for an abortion, but my granddad refused and so did Desiree. Then she pushed for putting the baby up for adoption and got overruled by my granddad and Desiree. So here I am."

"Raped? Oh, Marcus," Teresa says, then caresses his face. "Who told you this?"

"Seleste. After Kathryn took off. And bit by bit over a significant period of time. In secret. And to not let anybody know who told me."

"When did your grandmother leave?"

"Left my senior year in high school."

"What happened?" Teresa's eyes don't leave his face.

"Seleste says she doesn't know those details."

"Your grandfather never said?"

"He died of a heart attack six years ago. He took that secret with him." His voice carries a sad undertone. "They were old school. Kids had a place, and it wasn't in grown folks' business." He laughs.

"What else did Seleste tell you?" She slides her finger up and down his cheek.

"That Kathryn got her divorce, went back to her maiden name of Thornton. When she left, she went back to Arkansas. Little Rock."

"And you two haven't seen each other since you were eighteen?"

"No."

"No? She didn't attend your grandfather's funeral?" Teresa turns to face him.

"No. I left her a voicemail message about his death and service arrangements, but she never responded and never came."

"You haven't talked to her in fifteen years?"

"Twice," he says.

"She didn't explain why she left?"

"We talked about how I was doing in school. How she was enjoying being back home. But would never address my questions about why she left. Just said, 'Maybe the same reason you hit that boy in the back of the head.' The second time I called her, I got so frustrated that I hung up on her. And that's been that." He caresses her cheek with his finger and says, "Water under the bridge."

"Fifteen years is a long time," Teresa says.

Marcus hears a hint of accusation in her tone. "She left me. Left me and never blinked as far as I know."

"Did you two fight a lot?"

"I didn't fight with my grandparents. They raised me. I owed them," he says.

"Any theories on why she left?"

"No clue. And the way Granddad fell apart, I don't think he had any either," Marcus says.

"Don't you want some answers? Some closure?"

"The details don't really matter in the end. She left me and never looked back. No indication. No explanation."

"Maybe you missed the signs. Did you ever see them kiss? Or hug? Or argue? You ever see them laughing together?"

Her questions are like small slaps across the face. They get his attention, but he's not happy about it. Does he have any memories of his grandparents doing anything together? None. He was either with one or the other. They never ate meals together, but Marcus credited that to his grandfather's long work hours. Out by eight o'clock in the morning and back in at eleven o'clock at night. Never ate breakfast. Ate leftovers at night when he got home.

Sometimes on weekends Marcus would go to the office with him, but it was Kathryn who parented him on a daily basis. But, Marcus acknowledges, he always felt a distance between him and his grandmother. She never hugged or kissed or complimented him. Teresa shakes her head in sympathy. They let the shadows and the silence in the room reign. Teresa closes her eyes and lays her head against his chest. Marcus stares into the dimness and stillness of the room and ponders the significance of what his memories mean.

* * *

Teresa's setting the small cartons of food on the table. Marcus has put the libations in the fridge and is gathering plates and eating utensils. They haven't eaten since breakfast. It's 7:00 in the evening and during the eight hours between breakfast and now, they've put in a full day: they've had sex twice; taken two baths, one together and one separately; engaged in long discussions mostly about movies, sports, and work; called into their offices for updates; shared tidbits of information about themselves and their families, and took two brief naps. Teresa finishes unpacking the food and turns to watch him. They've been together for more than twenty-four hours. She juxtaposes the man she kind of knows now against the stranger who chased after her through the Loop. Unreal. Crazy. Wild. *Life is something else,* she thinks.

"I'm famished," she says.

"You should be. Let's go for two in a row."

"I think we need a break."

"Mind in the gutter again," he says. "I'm talking about hanging out again tonight and tomorrow. But, of course, sex is a given."

"Oh, bae," she says and is surprised she's called him this.

"*Bae?*" Marcus asks.

Teresa laughs and tells him, "My hip-hop slang. A term of endearment."

"Like *baby?*"

"Like before anyone else. *B-A-E.*"

"I'm that special," he says.

"You are, but back to going MIA tomorrow. I can't go MIA two days in a row. I just got the job."

"You're entitled to a brief break. To acclimate to your new role." He moves behind her and slides his hand inside her shorts and beneath her panties and rubs.

Her lids flutter to a close. She sighs softly.

"Please," he says in her ear.

"You ain't right." She gently removes his hand and turns to him and brushes her lips softly against his. "One more day. Okay?"

Marcus grins and pulls her tightly to him. "Okay."

* * *

They've moved into the sunroom, but it's the moonlight coming through the picture window that illuminates their faces. They snuggle on the small loveseat behind the small coffee table that holds his two empty beer cans and her third glass of wine. The television was turned off after they watched two episodes of *Bosses Undercover.* They had fun with those. Now Teresa has asked him, and she suspects it's the wine that's sent her careening out of bounds, about other women who've sat in this loveseat.

"Hmmm," he says, lifting his leg and stretching it across her lap. "There have been a lot of them. Kathryn's friends. Neighbors. Family members."

"Lovers." She smacks his leg. "Just in the past two years, let's say."

"Lovers? Not girlfriends?" he says.

Teresa smacks his leg again and reaches for her glass. "Lovers and girlfriends," she says, even as a small knotty pressure grows in the center of her chest just below her breasts. Even with Terrance, she hadn't cared about his past romances. Maybe because they were both young and she'd had her own history. Maybe because on a college campus it's expected that various life experiences come with the program. But with Marcus she feels differently. And she's not sure why. Imagining him enjoying a moment like this with another woman raises her blood pressure. Then it hits her like a fist in the gut. Takes her breath away. *I want to be special. Be that unique ass he was drawn to.*

"Well," he says, dragging the word out like it has three syllables. *I need to stop him. I don't need to know.* Teresa's mind stumbles around in a wine-induced haze, limiting her ability to produce clear-eyed thinking.

"I'm waiting," she says, her slightly slurred words evident to both of them.

Marcus studies her face. "Let's save this discussion for when we're both free of the influence of the joy juice," he says.

"I'm waiting," Teresa repeats, working hard to eliminate the slurred speech this time.

"If you insist," he says, taking in a deep breath. His words are spoken at a slow, halting pace. "I'll tell you the last four. Valerie. JoAnn. Melanie. And," he hesitates, then says, "Ana."

Teresa frowns. The name rings a bell. She eases upright and moves an imperceptible few inches away. She's heard something in the way he said Ana's name. Teresa's now on full alert.

"Ana? My ass twin?" she says.

He tries a laugh that dies in its infancy.

"Lover or girlfriend?" she asks.

"A relationship."

"How long?" Teresa feels her body temperature rising. It's like she's caught him cheating. Like she's caught him in a big lie. But that other voice still free from the alcohol-induced dementia she's experiencing says *no, don't answer Marcus. Like you said, it's not the time to engage in confessions.*

"A few months." His eyes close briefly.

That other voice is losing any semblance of influence. Teresa aims her eyes at his mouth. A lie or a bent fact won't get past her. "When did it end?"

He shrugs. "Five or six months ago."

That other voice has shrugged and walked away. "Who ended it?" Teresa asks.

"Me."

"Does she hate you?"

"I doubt it. She still calls."

"Oh, Lord," Teresa says and scoots a few inches farther away. She stretches her arms, Christ-like, across the back of the love seat and closes her eyes. "I don't want any stupid ex-lover drama. That's not my thing."

"There's no drama." Marcus waves a hand dismissively.

"Why did you quit her?"

"It wasn't working. Too big a difference in age. Very incompatible lifestyles." He eases over into the space between them.

"She Black?"

"Yes, from Brazil."

"Is she pretty? Brazilian women are supposed to be very pretty, very sexy." She crosses her legs in the direction away from him. She's having some serious reactions and fighting hard to corral them.

"She's attractive." His eyes close briefly then pop back open.

"So, Ana still calls you?" She studies his eyes, his forehead and the movement of his lips.

"Every now and then she leaves a phone message just to say hello."

"No, Marcus, she's calling to talk to you."

"Too bad," he says, "but there's nothing there." He slips her arm off the back of the love seat and drapes it around his shoulder. He leans over and pecks her on the cheek.

She inhales and slowly exhales. Then turns to face him. "I'm sorry. It must be the wine. Ana's none of my business." Her agitation doesn't subside despite her assertions.

Marcus squeezes her hand. "You were getting pretty wound up. Are you jealous?"

She wants them to get back to that earlier mood. She really does. But he's mocking her and ignoring his own ass-twin deception. She moves out from under his arm and reaches for her glass of wine. While she sips, Teresa tries to calm a new second wave of volatile emotions. And it's not working. Teresa wonders if she resembles Ana and that's why Marcus was drawn to her. Maybe Ana dropped him, and now he wants her as Ana's replacement. She drains her glass, sets it gently back on the table and turns to face him.

"Not jealous as much as suspicious," she tells him.

"I told you there is nothing there."

"You also told me that Ana was a *friend.* Not your lover. And I'm sure you would have recognized your lover's ass. You started off with a lie." Teresa narrows her eyes, more to focus than intimidate.

"It was a pickup line. Not a great one, I admit."

"I need you to tell me about Ana," she says and takes in a long deep breath.

He shakes his head. "I don't think we're ready to go down this road given the condition we're in."

"I am."

"I'm not." His voice has an edge to it.

"Tell me about her."

"Tell me about your lovers. I haven't heard a peep about any of them."

For some indecipherable reason, Teresa's caught off guard. She closes her eyes and leans back. She folds her arms across the top of her head.

"How many?" he says. "How recent?"

"Let's not flip the script."

"Let's."

"Worried I might have my own Ana hiding in the woodpile?" Teresa remembers the time her mother and her mother's man friend were arguing. She may have been six. The man friend kept telling her mother to shut her mouth, but she kept taunting him. Wouldn't shut up until he made her. "Think that would make us even?"

"This isn't a competition."

"This is about trust." Teresa opens her eyes. She winces when she sees the hurt look in his eyes.

"Why keep going down this road?" he says.

"Just tell me about Ana." Teresa's voice is filled with resignation.

"You're intoxicated. We both are. I'm done talking about it."

Marcus grabs the armrest to his left and abruptly pulls himself in the opposite direction, away from Teresa.

"What does that mean?" she asks.

"You're a smart girl. Figure it out."

"Well, that settles that," she says, rising from the sofa and heading out of the room.

"Nothing's settled." Marcus rises too and begins snatching the empty glass, bottle, and cans off the table.

Even as she strolls past him, Teresa wants Marcus to stop her. But there's no mistaking it; he's angry. She keeps walking because she doesn't know what else to do. She *is* flaking. Faking. Manipulating. This is on her, she knows, but knowing doesn't make her change course. She's stepped in it. She holds her breath. In the newly arrived quiet that surrounds her as she leaves the sunroom and heads for the stairs, Teresa expects to hear his footsteps hustling across the hardwood floors in hot pursuit. She wants him to call her back. She knows she's being silly. Her rational thoughts try to get back in the game.

Fucking wine. Still she continues up the stairs.

Teresa thinks she hears him mumble, "Silly bitch." She's not sure he said it, but she's finding herself getting thoroughly pissed. This is madness. She's too damn volatile for her own good. She storms into his bedroom and snatches her clothes from the chair near his bed, hurriedly puts them on, all the while telling herself that if Marcus gives a damn, he'll be up here persuading her to stay and not let the great time they'd been having end like this. The sober brain responds. *He must think I'm crazy. I am crazy.*

Teresa slips on her shoes, pats her hair in place, and goes back downstairs. Marcus is back in the sunroom stretched out on the love seat. She stands in the doorway and watches him a few seconds, but he doesn't look her way or acknowledge she's there.

"Thanks for the hospitality," she says and turns to leave.

"Don't mention it."

It's all she can do to hold her tongue. She storms through the kitchen and out the back door. When she's in her car with the seat belt snug across her breasts, she presses her head against the steering wheel. She feels like crying. She likes that man. She's had a great time with that man. He hasn't done a damn thing to her. Taylor Lee would say she's as wrong as two left shoes. She needs to go back in and apologize.

But the wine's hold still grips her fuzzy thoughts. *He should be feeling the same way. He should get his ass up and come out here and stop me. He shouldn't let me leave like this.* Teresa glances over her shoulder toward the back of the house. Her eyes strain hoping to see him pop out the door and rush to her side of the car. But she knows he won't. *He's right. We're intoxicated. I shouldn't be trying to drive. What to do? Call him.* It's her rational voice again. Teresa pulls her cell phone out of her purse and dials his number.

"Yeah."

"Get out here and stop me." She hangs up and peers over her shoulder just in time to see him shove the back door wide open.

Eleven

Marcus can't believe Teresa continued her workout for another hour after he hit the wall. Now she's sitting here looking refreshed and sexy as hell. He never took her for the athletic type, although when he gives it a little more thought she *is* something of a bedroom athlete.

"Why the smile?" she says.

"Just thinking how athletic you are."

"You didn't think I was?" She flexes her biceps.

I didn't know it transferred from the bed to the gym," he says.

She smacks his hand. "I played volleyball in college. And I ran track in high school, dude. One hundred, two hundred and four-x-four relay."

"State champ?"

"That would've been the lead in my story. Did you do sports?" she says.

"Nope."

"Didn't think so," she says.

"Another cocky athlete."

They're waiting for their lunch to be served. Josh's Café is on the corner of Sheffield and Webster in an upscale north side neighborhood called Lincoln Park. Its sparse setup is made to order for beginning couples who need only each other's company and little else by way of entertainment. There are six tables situated around a narrow sidewalk and another ten tables inside. The café's menu offers a variety of heart-healthy meals. Neither of them has ever eaten here, but it caught Teresa's eye that morning on the way to the gym. They sit at a table near the curb on the grass between the sidewalk and the street. They are the only Black people here. Same as they were at the gym.

"All these white folks beginning to grow on you?" She squeezes his hands and chuckles.

"Definitely not that dude at the gym. It's more like he's sticking to the bottom of my shoe."

She taps his hand with the tips of her fingers. "Are we jealous of Mr. O'Brien?"

"No, not really. I just had my share of certain kinds of white boys back in high school. He looks like one of them."

"You didn't like your high school?" She rubs her thumbs across the back of his hands.

"It was a private high school on the north side, not far from here. Not too many of us going there, so it was their school and I was in *their* world. Know what I mean?" Marcus says, then laughs. "I got along with most of them in general, but not so much with the white boys. Some of them had issues with my arrogance. That's the role I played with them. The girls found it compelling, though."

Teresa laughs when he makes that last comment. "I bet they did. Probably another reason the white boys weren't fans of yours."

"That and the fact that I was smarter than all of them."

"You know, I felt the same way in high school *and* college. I never had any conflicts with white girls; I just resented the hell out of them."

"Really?"

"Yup. But the white boys found my smarts and athleticism appealing." Teresa winks, then smiles at him.

"That's exactly why I kept my eye on your Mr. O'Brien. So, you knew he wasn't just being a nice guy?" Marcus points a finger at Teresa.

"I did, but once I saw how cute you are when you're jealous, I gave him a pass." Teresa squeezes his hand. "Next time, though, I'll grab you in the crotch and let him know I've got a man, that you're a handful, and you are all I need." Teresa grabs a fistful of air to demonstrate her point.

"That's exactly what a man wants his woman to do." Marcus nods vigorously.

The prissy waiter, ponytail swinging, returns to their table and says, "Voilà," as he sets down the food.

"Merci," she says.

"That's all I've got," the waiter tells her and laughs.

"Me too." They high-five, then ponytail prances back inside.

"Now, him, I'm fine with his flirting," Marcus says.

"Of course you are," Teresa smacks his hand. "Doesn't look like he's ever been to a gym."

"So, Mr. O'Brien's your type?"

"Maybe he'd had a shot at a date," she says.

"I'm surprised."

"Why? Because he's white?"

"Yes."

"You never dated any of those white girls in high school?" Teresa puckers her lips so he'll know it's a question that needs no response.

"Let's eat," he says, then laughs.

Both have post-workout appetites, so they eat without uttering a word between bites. The chatter of other patrons and passersby buzz around them. It's a beautiful sunny Saturday afternoon, and it's one of the better days of the summer so far. They're sitting beneath a slender tree, where a gentle breeze tickles the leaves until they flutter. The shaded sunlight slides intermittent rays between the tree's branches, moving in light and dark patterns that play across their table. The ice cubes clink against his glass when Marcus sips some of the best lemonade he's ever tasted and watches Teresa.

She's not wearing makeup or even lip gloss, and she looks twenty years old. He eyes the crumb lingering in the corner of her mouth and wipes it away with a gentle dab of his finger. She smiles at him, then gets back to eating. His mind wanders between thoughts of other relationships and how they started and how they ended, to some of the divorce cases he's handling and to the fact that he needs to pay some bills when he gets home. This is the third day in a row he's spent with Teresa, and their time together has been unbelievable except for that little incident Thursday night.

"A penny for your thoughts," she says when the last bit of food has disappeared from her plate.

"My thoughts are worth a lot more than that, at least a dollar."

She raises an eyebrow. "A dollar?"

"Easily. They're all about you."

"Clever boy."

"I was thinking about how you polished off that burger without taking a breath." Marcus imitates shoving food into his mouth.

"I was hungry. But you, on the other hand, eat like a picky little kid." She picks up his half-eaten tuna sandwich and takes a bite. "Yuck. This is awful. Where's the mayo? The eggs? The pickles? You should send it back and order something else. My turkey burger was fantastic."

"I'm good. Don't know what I'll get back if I hurt the cook's feelings." He hunches his shoulders and adds, "I figure why bother. But this lemonade is great."

"It's to die for." Teresa drains the last of hers.

They continue to sit, touching hands. They stare into each other's eyes, refusing to say what they each are feeling, while cars cruise past, people move in and out of the restaurant, and unintimidated birds swoop down and snatch bits of the remaining crumbs off the plates of amused patrons. Despite the background buzz of people and things, the air surrounding them is quiet and still. Marcus likes this place. "Our new spot?"

"Done. Is it okay if I do a little work today?" she says.

"You ask so little of me, it's embarrassing," he replies.

"I'm capable of asking for so much more. Be patient." Teresa laughs, pushes her chair back from the table and stands. "I need to go to the little girl's room. Lunch is on me." She lays a credit card next to his plate and pecks him on the top of his head. "Be back in a sec."

Marcus gives a low whistle while he watches Teresa as she leaves their table. Her derriere seesaws under the burgundy leggings, and her bare shoulders sway as she struts through the café's door and disappears inside. He closes his eyes and enjoys the feel of the cool breeze brushing across his face and the unnatural sounds of urban life that envelops him.

Even with his eyes closed, Marcus feels when Teresa's headed back his way. He turns toward the café's entrance to confirm his intuition just when she sashays back through the door with the waiter following close behind. She picks up the check and the card and hands them over. She doesn't sit down but stands next to Marcus and caresses his head until the waiter returns with the receipt.

"Ready to go, Romeo?" she asks.

"Always." He rolls his tongue around his lips, then blows a kiss.

"Let's go," she says. Then adds, "I do like how your mind works."

* * *

Teresa pulls into an outside lot near her office and parks beside a red Camry. "I see Toni's still here," she says.

"Your assistant, right?"

"She's the vice-president."

"You make your folks work on Saturdays?"

"She's in an MBA program and comes into the office to study."

They get out of the car and walk south to a five-story red brick structure. The building's lobby is a narrow corridor with a marble floor and fancy chandeliers hanging from a high ceiling. A winding staircase stands opposite the bank of three elevators. The brass railings put the finishing touches on a classy act. Their mild metallic odor from a recent polish waft through the confined hallway. Marcus takes in a deep breath, sighs audibly, then crowds close behind Teresa as she steps into the elevator's car. He pushes against her when the door closes. He strokes her thighs and nuzzles the nape of her neck.

"What exactly do you do?" he asks as she pushes the elevator button.

"Whatever you like," she says, reaching behind her to fondle his rising excitement.

"Even with your assistant here?"

"Vice-president, and if you're game, I'm game." Teresa laughs.

"Are there any hidden cameras in here?"

"It's a little late to be worrying." She pulls away and turns to face him. She presses her hands against each side of his face and draws him to her. Their kisses quickly lead to heavy breathing, frantic groping and total distraction. They don't notice they've reached the fifth floor and the doors have opened.

"Get a room, people."

His eyes spring open. He jerks his head around and sees a light-skinned Black woman with straight hair tied in a ponytail. He turns back to Teresa to find her eyes still shut, but the look on her face is not one of passion but embarrassment.

"Ms. Toni, I presume," Marcus says, keeping his voice light and controlled.

"Mr. Marcus, so pleased to meet you." Toni steps part way into the elevator to keep the doors open and then extends a hand. Toni's eyes reveal her amusement but also her friendliness. Marcus likes her.

"Boss, I know that's you, so don't try to go incognito on me." Toni looks at him and adds, "I know she started this, so don't worry about your first impression."

Marcus takes Teresa by her shoulders, moves behind her and pushes her toward Toni and off the elevator. Teresa keeps her eyes closed and holds her hands over her mouth.

"See you Monday. Or will I?" Toni says.

Marcus turns back to Toni and winks. She waves goodbye as the elevator doors begin to close.

"See you Monday, Toni," Teresa shouts just as the doors bang shut. She opens her eyes, turns to face Marcus and drops her head on his shoulder. "Oh my God," she mumbles into his shirt. "I feel like a teenager caught necking in the church basement. Damn."

She lifts her head and offers her lips again. They kiss. "Welcome to my world," she says and turns to open the doors to her office suite. She fumbles with her keys until she gets the door open, then stumbles inside and plops down on one of the soft cushioned chairs in the reception area. She closes her eyes again and groans. Marcus sits down beside her and takes her in his arms.

"Kissing me can't be the worst thing she's ever seen you do," he says.

She opens her eyes and gives him an exasperated look. "I can't imagine what she's thinking. Probably thinks we're in here now, like a couple of hot-blooded rabbits, getting it on in every office in the suite."

Tentative at first, but it's soon imitating the rising waters of her hometown river as it gathers steam, and much like the Mississippi River's clay banks, which, during a spring flood, can't contain its surging waves, neither can Teresa's insides hold back the laughter caused by her embarrassment. It's loud. It's boisterous. It's infectious. Once Teresa has lost it, Marcus tries to hold back but can't avoid being caught up in her uncontrolled reaction. Soon he's lost it too.

Like a couple of juveniles, they surrender completely to the hilarious moment. To the impetuous absurdity of it all. They don't stop until the laughter becomes a means of catharsis for them. Minutes pass before Teresa gets it back together. She stands, one hand over her mouth and the other grasping her stomach, and makes her way down a long corridor toward the back of the suite.

Marcus gathers himself together long enough to watch her as she stumbles away from him. He sees her turn right off the corridor and go into an office. He gets up and follows her. Along the way he notes how spacious, modern, and neatly laid out the suite is. There are cubicles with tall, clear, cylinder-shaped partitions lining the corridor on his left, and several glass doors to small offices are equally spaced along the wall to his right. He ducks in and out of each one.

Several short corridors branch off the main one, and he briefly explores each of them too. Meeting rooms, additional offices, a kitchen area, and several storage spaces and file rooms are located off these shorter hallways. Ten minutes later, he heads back to the main corridor, then turns down the short corridor where Teresa has gone. He finds her seated behind a large desk with her shoeless feet folded under her. She has some paperwork in her hands.

"You've pulled yourself together, I see," she says, glancing up, then covering her mouth.

"Please," he says, "don't get us started again."

Teresa takes in a noisy big breath, then exhales slowly. "Okay. I'm good."

"Can we do it in here? Right there against the wall?" he asks.

"Don't you start up again," she warns. "I need to get this done. Then we can go to your place and do whatever you want."

He walks over to a small bookcase that stands against the wall behind him and across from her desk, and begins skimming the titles of several books. One novel has a naked woman on the cover, so he picks it up, sits on the carpeted floor next to the bookcase, and begins thumbing through it. He's never heard of the author. He stops on a page near the back of the book and asks, "Who's this Miller, and why is he talking about somebody dancing like a nigger?" He glances at her for an explanation.

"He wrote it in the 1930s. It's an interesting novel and has nothing to do with race."

He turns back to the page and reads some more. He skims a few more pages, then sets the novel back on the shelf and picks a small thin volume. "You've read these books?"

"Every last one of them." She looks over her shoulder at him. "You haven't read any of those?"

He hesitates. To answer 'no' seems like confessing to one of the seven deadly sins. "I haven't read nearly as much as I should."

"That's a good novel you're holding. Take it. You'll like it. It's one of my favorites."

He looks back down at the cover and reads a glowing quote about the novel. "I think I will. Thanks. I take it you like to read?"

"Love it, but I don't get to read as much as I used to. Most of those books I read in college."

Marcus stares at the book, then looks up but Teresa has turned her attention back to the paperwork. He sits and watches her. She's focused. She's cerebral. She's athletic. She's emotional. She's eclectic. She's different. She's hot. He sets the book next to him on the floor and explores several others; for those with book covers he reads the front jacket, then the back part of the jacket giving bio on the author. He scans the first paragraph of each book he pulls off the shelf and then the last paragraph to determine if it convinces him to read the whole book.

An hour and a half have passed when Teresa says, "I'm about finished." Her head is still bent forward over some paperwork. "Thanks for being so patient and so well behaved." She chuckles.

"Take your time, I'm in no hurry. Take all the time you need," he says, then picks up and opens the book he set on the floor and starts reading her favorite novel.

Twelve

The sun is still on the rise, but the early August heat is already working its sweat-popping talents at 8:30 on a Monday morning. The windows are up and the air-chilled interior is cool. "Voilà," Toni says when she slides into the passenger's seat and places a placard on the dashboard. "The brothers were glad to help," she tells Teresa. The placard authorizes them to park in this reserved lot.

Inside the department offices, they're led to a small conference room. Minutes later, several low-level bureaucrats enter the room. The two men, one Black and one white, are wearing expressions seemingly intended to give an air of authority and the two women, one white and the other Black, look as if they don't want to be bothered with the whole affair.

"Thank you for coming." It's the short Black man speaking. "I suppose we should start off with introductions. I'm Judson Williams, Program Liaison."

The teenaged-looking white woman to his left says, "I'm Melissa Reilly, Assistant Program Liaison..."

Teresa scrutinizes each bureaucrat's face. There's too much tension in the room. It feels like a fight's about to break out.

"I'm Boris Frain, Assistant Director of the Fiscal Unit." He's a tall redhead with a freckled face. A man whose eyes never blink as they pass across Teresa's and then Toni's face.

"I'm Mary Jo Allison, Program Coordinator." She's about Toni's age.

Teresa tunes out Judson when he begins saying that the history of the department is long and illustrious. She doesn't like him. He's too short, too chunky and has a misguided sense of his status in that room. When she tunes back in, the speaker has changed.

"Again, thank you for coming," the Paul Bunyanesque Boris says. "I know the e-mail we sent was a little nonspecific, but that's because we are not totally sure ourselves what's going on. This is..."

Teresa stops listening again. Her heart's pounding. Her mind becomes occupied with the unlimited number of bad possibilities. Several of them zip through her brain at the speed of light. She has been summoned here to be warned that the shit will soon start rolling downhill. Headed her way. She forces herself to tune back in.

Melissa, the teenager, speaks more properly than Teresa had thought the girl would. "Of course, we are all partners and, in this endeavor..." Teresa tunes out again and wonders if this will cost the organization money. *Clawbacks* they call it. Grant money earned and spent and now may be demanded to be paid back to the government. A drain on CEC's much-hoarded reserve funds. And on her watch. She taps her foot in response to the anxiety spreading from her chest to her lower limbs.

It's Mary Jo's turn to talk now, and the sister is fidgety. She shifts in her seat and clasps her hands as if in prayer. "Let us remember this is a program audit and not a fiscal audit. For the past two years, we haven't conducted full-scale program audits. Most of the program data submitted to us by you service providers, we trusted and still trust its accuracy..."

So, there it is. Teresa looks over at Toni and grimaces. Toni's frown says that she, too, recognizes the deception.

"...the city and its service providers are a team," Mary Jo continues, "it's not about finger-pointing. That's not why we are here."

Teresa pushes back in her seat and says, "Of course." She studies the room's decor. It's borderline plush. Like the whole building, it's done in an impressive and lavish style. It seems such a contradiction. It seems like such an inappropriate office complex for public servants. They use taxpayer dollars like corporate profits. And now they're going to force her little organization to pony up big bucks if the city has messed up.

"We obviously do not know the outcomes of the audits yet, but believe me, we wouldn't be holding these meetings if insignificant amounts were involved," Judson says, keeping his eyes away from the faces of his guests, who are both glaring with obvious dislike for what he's saying.

"I'm sorry," Toni says, "but what are we supposed to do as the result of this meeting?"

Teresa doesn't wait for any of them to engage in more half-assed double-talk. "We pray, Toni, and get the shovels ready." With that, she stands to leave.

* * *

It's later that Monday afternoon, and Teresa has at last finished replaying every word, every facial expression, and every nuanced interpretation of every declaration made by the four minions in her meeting with the city. Prepping for this city audit will be a major challenge that will suck up significant amounts of time and resources.

The hum of office activities echoes off the walls and floats through the corridors and past her door. Not too loud and not too quiet. She likes the air of professionalism permeating the suite. The atmosphere's so unlike the loose culture she was thrown into when she came on board five years ago. Three promotions later, Teresa became the organization's associate executive director and imposed more order on the organization.

It took a mulish effort on Teresa's part to make the changes. Mary Ann had never been one for operational details, according to her own confessions, which is why she created the associate executive director's position. However, Teresa found out, implementing changes was easier said than done. Staffing changes that were begging to be made and long overdue systemic reorganizations would be uncomfortably disruptive and messy. Mary Ann balked, then stuck her head in the proverbial sand.

It took weeks of pulling Mary Ann around by the arm daily and forcing her to "look at this and check that out" until Teresa got the support she needed and was able to transform an unsophisticated nonprofit organization with an undisciplined staff into a professional business enterprise. "Yep," Teresa says. "I was key to this transformation." But this audit represents a threat that was not anticipated. A test that has come way too soon. She's barely gotten used to sitting in this office and not being here to request Mary Ann's permission, approval, or opinion on some issue. She sighs, leans back in *her* executive chair, and closes her eyes.

The disruption comes in the form of loud voices. Angry voices. Voices that are escalating by the second. Then Teresa hears the screams. She bolts upright, banging her knee against the desk in the process. The clicking keyboards stop. Hurried footsteps speed through the corridors. The commotion is coming from the direction of the training rooms. Toni's head pops through the door. "I'll handle it," she says, then she's gone.

Teresa scrambles out of her chair, rushes into the corridor, and races toward her staff, who are gathered outside Training Room A. The adrenaline rush, like a cold arctic blast, makes her catch her breath. She pushes through the clump of clients and staff forming a gaper's block in the narrow corridor.

"Michael, do something." Toni is standing just in the doorway of the training room. Teresa squeezes next to her. Two young women in their early twenties are fighting in the middle of the floor. A blouse, torn and bunched, hangs off the top of one table. A silver earring lays a few feet away, near the leg of another table. Small knots of women stand and watch from the far corners of the room, a safe distance from the combatants. Michael Brown stands off to the side, also at a safe distance and watches.

"Get off me, bitch." The smaller of the two women, her voice strained but fierce as she speaks, lies trapped under her much larger adversary.

Her hands, in contrast to the rest of her body, look strong as they tug and pull at the bigger woman's long weave. She wraps the weave around one of her hands like a bandage and uses the other hand to pull at it as if in a tug of war. The heftier woman sits astride the smaller woman, her arms rotating like windmills, her fists raining down blows against the smaller woman's face and her arms.

Some of the blows slam into the bigger woman's own legs. The penned opponent, in a state of frenzy, bangs her legs against the floor like a child having a tantrum. Teresa is stunned. Toni screams at Michael to break it up. He doesn't move. From her position near the door, Teresa's frozen in place too. Unable to act. Unable to fully digest what she's seeing.

Clients fighting in her training room? One with only a bra covering her upper body and the other's lime-green thong on display. And nobody is moving to stop the madness. Teresa realizes that no one, including herself, wants to intervene. The possibilities for pain are too great. She ponders what to do. She hears somebody tell somebody to call the police. "No, don't call the cops," she shouts over her shoulder as she rushes to the center of the room and orders the two women to stop.

Teresa looks over at Michael and questions him with her eyes. He doesn't move. He shouts at them to get up.

"Shut...the...fuck...up...Michael," the smaller woman shouts back.

Teresa reaches down and grabs an arm of the woman on top, but she's too big and strong and snatches her arm away. Next, Teresa tries to pry the hands of the smaller one off the other woman's hair but pulls back when she's almost hit by a wild swing.

"You get her left arm and I'll get her right one." It's Toni at her side. Using all four hands, they grab the smaller woman's arms and pull. The big woman screams. Clumps of weave dangle from slim fingers with brightly colored nails. Up close, Teresa can see that blood, like smeared lipstick, covers the full lips of the skinny one and a big ugly knot looms above her right eye.

"Anthony, get over here and help us," Toni hollers.

Anthony, with his thin arms and undernourished body, hustles over. The two combatants seem exhausted and ready for someone to intervene and with little resistance allow themselves to be separated and dragged off to opposite sides of the room. Teresa picks up the torn blouse and hands it to the larger woman. There's a patch of her real hair missing near the front of her head. The smaller woman yanks down on her skirt until her panties are hidden again. Her face is badly marked with scratches and bruises. Teresa's hands are shaking.

"Toni," she whispers, "get them the hell out of here. I can't believe this shit." She looks straight ahead as she leaves the room. "None of us are trained to handle shit like this," she declares as she passes through her staff who part like the Red Sea. After she makes her way to her office, Teresa plops down on one of the two guest chairs facing her desk. She closes her eyes. This violence has unnerved her.

She's known the work they do carries risks. Their clients, for the most part, come out of neighborhoods where violence is commonplace and unrelenting stress a component of the air they inhale on a daily basis. She's all too familiar with the kinds of toxic air they're forced to take in but the odds of someone on her staff becoming a victim of a client's knee-jerk violence, she now realizes, is greater than the possibility of any of them becoming a client's savior. But still, Teresa doesn't understand how Michael let the situation get so out of hand. She regrets listening to Toni and letting Michael keep his job. She should have gone with her gut instinct and fired his ass.

But, to be honest, none of her staff were impressive in the situation, which is why she had to put her ass on the line to stop that craziness. Still, how the hell did Michael manage to let a fight break out between two clients? Was he out of the room when the argument started, or was his stupid ass parked right there when it escalated? Teresa can only shake her head in disbelief and sighs when she realizes her whole body is shaking.

Thirty minutes later, Toni breezes into Teresa's office and closes the door. She takes the chair next to Teresa and says, "Girl." Toni looks and sounds like a woman about to choke on a juicy bit of gossip. "I don't know what to think about all of this. I don't know what to believe. One of the girls, Lola Willis, the petite one, told me they were fighting over Michael." Toni scoots forward to the edge of her seat, her knee bumping against Teresa's knee.

Teresa eyes widen in disbelief. "Fighting over Michael? Why would they be fighting over Michael? They call themselves having a crush on him? That's some really silly shit."

"Lola claims it's more than a crush. She says Michael has been playing them both." Toni pauses, then whispers, "This stuff is off the chain."

Teresa blinks when Toni's words begin to penetrate. "Michael's been sleeping with the clients?" She grips her head in her hands. She falls back in her chair. "I don't believe it. Not even Michael's that stupid."

"He's denying it. Says Lola's a pathological liar."

"What's the other woman saying?" The air in the room has gone stale. Teresa closes her eyes, then reopens them, stares at Toni and tries hard not to blame the messenger.

"Her name's Mamie Dixon, and she told me Lola needed 'her little ass kicked and she got it.' She claims Lola said the wrong thing to the wrong person on the wrong day."

"Do you think Michael's that dumb?" Teresa says. The absurdity of it makes her laugh. Here's a man with a college degree, living in trendy Lincoln Park, driving a late model SUV and earning $40,000 a year. He isn't a bad-looking brother, and even Toni has gone out with him. As much as she dislikes Michael, Teresa isn't prepared to believe this about him. At least not just yet.

"Believe it or not, it gets worse," Toni says. She lowers her voice and leans so far into Teresa's space that Teresa feels Toni's warm breath against her cheek. "Lola says she's pregnant. By Michael. And Mamie jumped her to cause a miscarriage."

Teresa's shoulders sag. "Pregnant? What the fuck? This is not happening. This ridiculous shit is not happening." She closes her eyes again for an instant, then aims them at Toni. "Is this for real?"

Toni shrugs her shoulder. "Maybe. Michael says bull crap."

"Give his ass a lie detector test," Teresa says, inhaling a large dose of the heavy air that hangs stagnant in the room and then sighs as she blows it out again past her puckered lips.

"Maybelline," Toni says. "She'd know what's what. Michael confides in her."

Teresa's hands, usually animated and expressive, lie hapless in her lap. Her eyes no longer focus but look off somewhere over Toni's head trying to imagine the immediate future if this bizarre shit turns out to be true.

"I don't think she'll back Michael on something like this. Let me go talk with her." Toni rises.

"Let's both meet with her. In here. No, let's meet in the conference room in ten minutes. And tell Michael I want to talk with him after we finish with Maybelline. And close the door behind you. Please."

Teresa stares at the phone. She needs to call Marcus. They're supposed to meet at six for dinner, but this mess will probably take her well into the evening. She'll call after she calms down. Teresa turns her chair away from her desk to face the wall and closes her eyes. Her thoughts are debris caught up in a hurricane of emotions. Can she fire Michael? Can she dismiss him because he fucked two grown-ass women who consented? What if she fires him and he refuses to leave? She laughs at the question.

Call the police? She can't expect her other male employees to haul his ass out the door. The image of Michael being dragged out by his feet, his head bumping along the floor into the elevator and in the lobby, tossed out the door, landing hard on the sidewalk, then bouncing into the street where he's hit by a passing truck. Problem solved. She laughs again.

Mary Ann fired two people during the past five years, but Teresa had never witnessed the act. Mary Ann did it behind a closed door, one-on-one. "Kept it short and sweet and made them an offer they couldn't refuse," Mary Ann declared when Teresa asked what happened. No police were ever called. Teresa decides to let Maybelline and Toni wait a few minutes before making her appearance. She needs time to prepare her thoughts.

After a call to Marcus can't get past his little receptionist, Teresa feels a growing dislike for the girl. She's too curt and too quick to tell Teresa he's not available. Very unprofessional. But that problem belongs to Marcus. She's knee-deep in her own mess, and it'll probably get a lot messier by the end of the day.

Thirteen

When Missy stands to leave after their meeting has ended, she uses a high arc to uncross her legs, and her short skirt rises. His eyes linger long enough for both women to notice.

"You like this dress?" Missy says. Marcus smiles but doesn't answer.

"Marcus, you do remember that today is Missy's first-year anniversary?" Seleste says.

"Of course, I do," he says. A lie all three of them seem willing to accept.

"Good. Then you have plans to take her to dinner?"

"Yes, all three of us. Lunch." Another lie.

"What time?" Missy asks.

Seleste shakes her head. "I can't close down my office to go with you two."

"What time?" Missy repeats.

"How's one o'clock?" he says. "All three of us. The office will be just fine."

"I think you two can do without me," Seleste says. "I always bring my lunch. You know that. Restaurant food, no thank you."

"One o'clock is great," Missy says and steps between the two chairs to stand next to where he's still sitting. Marcus looks up past the curved hips and modest breasts and sees that Missy's eyes are filled with shameless joy. "I'll be in your office to remind you fifteen minutes before," she assures him. Missy brushes against his shoulder as she slides past. The two women with their brazen manipulations leave him shaking his head and fighting the urge to watch Missy's departing backside. He waits a few seconds before he follows.

Seleste's small office is decorated with paintings of Jamaican scenes. Several green plants hang from the ceiling in front of her bare window. She clings to her Jamaican ancestry like a drowning woman to a raft.

"What do you expect to happen?" he asks.

"I don't expect anything." Seleste shuffles the papers on her desk. "Listen," she says, "you think too hard and worry too much. Just go to lunch and enjoy yourself. You'll find that Missy is good company."

"I'm sure she is."

"A pretty and clever young woman too."

"*Young* is the operative word, and fraternizing with office staff is not my cup of tea," he says, eyeing Seleste as if she were a stranger.

Seleste laughs. "That's because I am the only office staff you've ever had an opportunity to fraternize with. Besides, Missy's not the messy type, so just go to lunch. Get to know her better. It has been a year, and she feels like you have ignored her all this time."

"The truth is," Marcus says, "anybody can get messy." He stands to leave and shoots Seleste an annoyed look, but she's back to typing and singing to the reggae beats pumping out of her computer.

* * *

The restaurant is packed as usual. It's the lunch crowd. People sit at the bar or stand shoulder to shoulder in the waiting area just inside the front entrance. The tight space gives Missy an excuse to press against him. A large round earring dangles from each ear, and her dark hair, pulled back in a shoulder-length ponytail with streaks of blonde, may be Missy's or it may be purchased.

"I'm glad Seleste didn't come." Her mouth is near his ear, and her heated breath tingles.

"This is not a date."

"I know." She keeps her lips near his ear while she speaks. He tries to step back, but there isn't room. People keep entering the restaurant, closing down the space around them. "Oops," she says, "that man just bumped me." Missy wraps her two arms around one of his and holds on tight. "I almost fell." He feels her small, spongy spheres yield against his arm. "You have a new girlfriend?" He glances at her but says nothing. "It's just a question."

"Do you have a boyfriend?"

"Not really." She wraps her arms tighter.

"*Not really* means what exactly?"

"I date this guy, but I don't like him like that. I can date other people."

"Well you're young, so it makes sense to keep your options open," he tells her.

"I'm not that young and the guys I date are your age."

"I've been told never to keep my honey where I make my money." Marcus glances sideways at her and winks.

"By who?"

"It's conventional wisdom, and it makes a lot of sense." He's going to make her understand that a personal relationship isn't in the cards.

"You never dated any clients?" The question catches him off guard. "What about other lawyers you work with?"

Seleste's been talking. He rubs his forehead. Over the years he's confided in Seleste about a lot of things, including his love life. "I take it you and your godmother talk a lot."

She leans her head against his shoulder. "Did she tell me something she wasn't supposed to?"

"It doesn't matter." After his grandmother disappeared on him, Seleste took on the roles of big sister and confidante. She's been the one he talked to about girls. Even in college. Even now. Maybe too much, he realizes.

"I'm not like you," she says.

"What?"

"I know what I want." Missy squeezes his arm tighter.

"I don't even know what that means."

"That *you* don't know what you want," Missy says.

"More insight from Seleste?"

"Yep."

"I thought the purpose of this lunch was for me to get to know you better," he says.

Missy raises her head from his shoulder and then raises her eyebrows. She smiles, then leans in again and blows into his ear. He tries to move away without bumping into the people surrounding them. There isn't enough room. Although embarrassed and flustered, Marcus finds himself becoming aroused. Seleste once told him a man's nature is tailor-made for a seductive woman. Missy shifts her position to face him. He bumps into the couple behind him when he tries to step back.

"Sorry," he says.

"Greene. Party of two."

Missy turns and waves to the hostess, grabs his hand, and pulls Marcus along through the crowd, following the pert young lady wearing a short skirt that pretends to offer more intimate glimpses but, in fact, only intermittently reveals a pair of matching shorts underneath. He and Missy are led to the rear of the restaurant and seated at a table for two beside a window that frames a section of Michigan Avenue. Missy doesn't look at him but stares out the window while her foot, which has discarded its sandal, rubs against his ankle. He frowns and moves his leg.

"What's wrong?" she asks, a touch of petulance evident in her tone.

"Beg your pardon?"

"Why'd you move your leg?"

"To give you room."

She looks at him and sighs. A waiter arrives with the obligatory water and menus and announces the day's lunch specials. Missy orders a big salad, and Marcus orders a Monte Cristo sandwich. He asks to hold on to his menu to study desserts. Missy returns hers, tells the waiter she watches her weight, and then turns her attention, after the waiter leaves, back to Marcus. He tells himself he has to put Missy in check and not allow this to get messy.

"That wasn't the smartest thing to do back there," he says.

"It's what I felt like doing."

"You need to *think* a little more; it's never a bad idea," he tells her.

"You liked it."

"Maybe, maybe not. But this isn't the place nor the time to behave like that."

She rolls her eyes and sticks out her tongue. Then she turns to watch the scene outside on Michigan Avenue. He's amused by her reaction. "How old are you really?" he says.

Missy laughs. "I'm playful. I like to have fun."

"Try telling a joke or a humorous anecdote."

"Anecdote? What's that?" she says.

"A nice little story that's funny."

"I've got one." She giggles. "That time my mom and Seleste gave me a surprise party when I was sixteen."

"And?"

"I didn't show up."

"Because?"

"I was a little wild back then. So, I was supposed to come straight home from school, and I didn't. I met up with my so-called boyfriend, and we hung out until way past midnight. He cheated a lot. Anyway, by the time I got home, all the food was gone. The birthday cake and ice cream too. Mom and Seleste were the only two left." She's rubbing her foot against his leg again. "They just stared at me, then rolled their eyes and kept on drinking their wine. Didn't even say *happy birthday*. But I knew I was wrong. Funny, right?"

Marcus chuckles even though there's a whole lot of stuff out of place with that story. But he can imagine their faces when Missy strolled in eight hours past her curfew. "All your guests had gone?"

"Fifteen people." She runs her bare foot up under his pant leg until her surprisingly soft foot presses against his shin.

"Seems to me you're still a little wild," he says, maneuvering his leg away from her cool foot.

"Whatever." She bites her bottom lip. "I've seen you watching me, and I know when a guy's interested in what he's watching."

"More like curious," he says. "I've been wondering why you've taken this sudden interest in me."

"I've liked you since the first time I met you. I just never thought you'd be interested in me because I wasn't in your league."

"And what changed your mind?"

"Seleste told me there's no league when it comes to men. She said it's all about timing, and men won't know when the time is right until they're shown." Missy's pupils are the large dark marbles he associates with aliens.

"And therefore?"

"And, *therefore,* I decided to let you know I was interested and see if the timing is right."

"I see."

"And since you don't know your own mind when it comes to women, I think I'm a good fit for you." A smile lights up her face. A frown darkens his.

"I know a little something about my own mind despite what Seleste says."

"Maybe she knows you better than you know yourself. She knows me better than I do. She says I have damaged self-esteem because my father never claimed me and I never got to be daddy's little girl. She says the worst thing that can happen to a young girl is to grow up out of the protective shadow of her father's love. Seleste understands people."

The air stirs around them as people hustle to and from tables. Waiters bringing food, tables being bused after patrons finish their meals and move on, opening the way for others to take their places. The appetizing aromas of fresh-baked bread, pasta, and even garlic wafting from the plates of food zipping past his head pull on his attention. The food looks delicious. His eyes scan the small, packed area around him. A Monday lunch crowd. His stomach growls.

"Earth to Marcus," Missy says.

"Well, help me understand Seleste. What does she expect to happen?" he asks.

"I think Seleste wants you to be my mentor."

"And not your boyfriend?"

"If it happens."

"Which it won't."

"You never know. Seleste says you're a lot like your grandfather in some ways."

"Your point?" He's growing irritable. He should've eaten breakfast this morning but he had overslept. His almost weeklong sabbatical with Teresa came at a price. Marcus can't help but smile with that thought. He looks around for their waiter.

The little lunch timer the waiter set on their table is at fourteen minutes and counting. A few seconds longer and they'll get a free lunch. He turns back to Missy. Has she forgotten the point she was making? Or did she even have one?

"Here we go." It's their waiter and he beats the timer by mere seconds.

After the waiter leaves, they both turn their attention to the food and begin to eat. Marcus looks out the window, while Missy's eyes alternate between her plate and him. On the other side of the glass are crowded sidewalks and bumper-to-bumper traffic. A menagerie of lunchtime strollers, fast-moving corporate types, and sightseers move into, then back outside, his real-life picture frame. Vagrants and street vendors are hard at work. The noise, though muted, still reaches him inside the restaurant. He turns away from the window and continues eating. After Marcus finishes off the last of his food, he looks at Missy and asks, "How's your salad?"

"Fine," Missy says. Her extraterrestrial-looking pupils can be disconcerting, and he concedes to their power and lowers his eyes and picks up the water pitcher. He pours a glassful, then turns back to his window view.

Marcus enjoys summers in Chicago but sighs when unappreciated thoughts of winter flit across his mind. Yet even with its dreary winters, he loves this city. His grandfather sold him on it when he was a kid. "If a Black man can't make it here, he can't make it anywhere." Marcus remembers the first time he saw the city on a map. He was about five. It was a simple dot placed alongside Lake Michigan. It was so small. But his grandfather assured him Chicago was a big place, and every weekend for the next thirteen years, they explored every square inch of the city.

"You want to know my point, right?" Missy's voice disrupts his thoughts. She's finished her salad.

He turns to face her. "Absolutely," he says, picking up his glass of water and sipping.

"That your grandfather didn't think about Seleste in that way at first either." Her eyes hold his in a steady gaze. The waiter reappears. Marcus sends him away.

"What way at first?" he says.

"A girlfriend. But then he did."

"Did what?" Marcus stares at her in disbelief.

"Became her boyfriend."

"Seleste told you that?" he says.

"No." He begins to breathe easier.

"My mom told me. I just now figured it out that nobody told you."

Marcus checks his watch, sees it is three o'clock and tells Missy it's time to get back. He avoids those alien eyes again. He's annoyed. Why? He isn't sure. His grandfather and Seleste? Missy stands but he doesn't move. She sits back down. He glances out the window.

"My mom said Seleste worshipped the ground he walked on. My mom and Seleste were best friends back then but not now." He turns to look at her. "It doesn't change my mind about you." She continues as if he hasn't spoken. "Like I said, in the beginning, he didn't think it was a good idea either. Seleste used to tell my mom how she always caught him looking at her. He was interested but never acted like he was, until one night and it happened. They ..."

"Let's go." He stands up.

"You're mad at me?"

"No. It's just time to get back to the office."

"Seleste *said* you don't deal with things you don't like dealing with."

"For a woman who likes telling everyone else's business, she does a pretty good job of keeping her own skeletons buried deep in the closet."

Despite the anxiety gnawing away at his insides, he manages to smile at Missy. Despite the smile, he doesn't like her right now. It's some absurd shit. It's out the box. His grandfather and Seleste? It's too stereotypical. Too cliché. Too trite. Too ordinary for a man like his grandfather. But he feels it's the truth. An intuitive understanding of how it all makes sense now. And if what Missy has just dropped on him *is* true, Marcus wonders if the affair was before or after Kathryn left.

He sees their waiter watching from across the room and signals him to bring the check. The waiter comes, takes his credit card, and hurries away while he and Missy stare out the window. Missy moves around the table and steps next to him, then brushes against him, but he doesn't lean away. He tries to ignore her. The waiter returns; Marcus signs the slip and heads toward the exit. Missy hustles to keep up. He stops at the door to let some other patrons enter. She catches up to him and wraps her arms around one of his.

"I didn't mean to make you mad," she says.

Marcus doesn't respond. He doesn't bother to try to pull his arm free. He's gone numb on the inside. His mind is full of frozen thoughts that lay lifeless like corpses encased in ice. Useless and without purpose. Who approached who? Were they in love? He walks south on Michigan Avenue with Missy clinging to his arm. They stumble several times as Missy hangs on and tries to lean her head against his shoulder.

"I'm sorry," she says. "I shouldn't have told you."

"Didn't we come to lunch to share?"

"But you're mad."

"I'm not," he tells her. "Just disappointed."

"With me?"

"Seleste. And my grandfather."

"You shouldn't be disappointed," she says.

"We both should be." He peers over at her. She turns his arm loose but says nothing as they cross the intersection a half block from the office. He doesn't say anything else. They enter the building and make their way to the elevator. After Missy steps into the empty car ahead of Marcus, she turns to face him.

"Don't be mad at Seleste, please," she says.

"Not mad. Just disappointed."

I don't know Seleste, he thinks. Nor did he know his grandfather as well as he thought. When Kathryn packed up and disappeared, and he had felt lost and abandoned, Seleste filled in the empty space. Now he's learned it wasn't only *his* empty space Seleste moved to fill-in, and most likely, his wasn't even first on her to-do list.

Fourteen

"**This kind of** nonsense happened before, back in '88 when Charles Harris, dog that he was, started fooling around with a teenage client. He was a real lowlife." Maybelline purses her lips as she speaks. Her fake eyelashes sweep upward as she looks beneath them at Teresa. "Mr. Haynes, he was the executive director then, fired him with few questions asked."

"So, what do you know about Michael and these two clients? Was he messing around with either or both?" Toni asks.

"I cannot say with one hundred percent certainty one way or the other, but several of the guys have hinted as much. I'm surprised neither of you were privy to these rumors. Especially you, Toni. A few clients have hinted that Michael was 'kicking it' with those two girls, but who knows what's really going on around here? I would hope that Michael would not be that stupid. But who really knows anybody for sure?" Maybelline's hands are intertwined. Her head's bent forward as she speaks, and it looks like she's about to pray.

Teresa squints as she stares and imagines the three sixes she knows are lodged beneath Maybelline's long wavy weave. Even as she listens to Maybelline cleverly avoid direct confirmation of Michael Brown's indiscretions, Teresa is convinced he's an unsalvageable lowlife and has to go. Fifteen days since Mary Ann's last day, but it seems a lot longer than that. Teresa strokes her cheek hard. "Do you believe Michael's been acting inappropriately with those two women?" Teresa says.

"Like I said, I can't say. But if he did, I would hope his itch came wrapped in packages small enough to fit in his wallet. You know what I mean?" She chuckles but maintains her pious pose.

"Anything else you can tell us?" Teresa asks, working hard to avoid sounding exasperated. Maybelline has a way of getting under Teresa's skin.

"Just that this may be as good as it gets. I do not believe anybody else will have too much to tell. People here respect you, Teresa, but they also want to stay off your radar. Always have."

"Will they talk to you, Toni?" Teresa asks.

Maybelline chuckles again. "Not about Michael, I am willing to bet. I know you are young, Toni, but dating Michael was not a good idea. No disrespect, but I am just saying."

Toni glances at Teresa, then directs her comment at Maybelline. "I don't think that's true."

"Then why have you not heard the rumors?" Maybelline says.

"I think we've finished here. Thanks for your help in this matter, Maybelline. I think it's time I talk to Mr. Brown." Teresa stands and guides Maybelline out of the room.

"You want me to bring Michael in here?" Toni asks.

"In a minute. You let her put you on the defensive."

"I know, but Maybelline is so treacherous."

"Of course she is. But the truth of the matter is she's right. And since you didn't know, neither did I. Now go send Michael to me."

* * *

Michael avoids looking at Teresa when he enters the conference room and takes a seat. He keeps his mouth stretched thin, his shoulders slumped, evoking a thin veneer of humility that she's not buying. He's a small-minded, deceitful man. She pays close attention to the pulsing vein near his temple like she would a dark sky full of whirling clouds. Teresa knows Michael hasn't arrived unaware of what he's facing, and she's on guard for any sign of the volatility that lurks inside the man sitting across from her.

"I assume you know why we're here," she says.

"Because I didn't break up the fight?"

"Because it's rumored you're the cause of the fight." Teresa's arched eyebrows reveal her concern about the possibility.

"I can't be responsible for rumors."

"Are they just rumors?" she says.

"They are."

"Then why are they saying the fight was over you?" Teresa keeps her eyes on that pulsing vein. The door to the conference room has been left open, and she hears soft sounds in the corridor beyond her view. That means Toni's not taking any chances either. Teresa almost lets a smile slip past her tightly sealed lips.

"I can't be held responsible for their fantasies. I do take responsibility for letting the situation get out of hand. I should have stepped in as soon as I saw the tension between them escalate. But the fight broke out after I left to get some handouts. They were going at it by the time I got back. To be honest, I panicked and didn't know what to do. Just like everybody else. Nobody knew what to do, not even you."

"Why were they fighting?"

"I guess they don't like each other."

"But they *do* like you?"

"Apparently, according to the rumor."

"The rumor also says *you* like them. So much so that you're about to be a new dad." Teresa shakes her head when she makes this comment.

"News to me."

"Is that a denial?"

"You know it won't make any difference what I say. Your mind is already made up."

"But the fact of the matter is you haven't answered the question. I only need a yes or no." Teresa rolls her chair back from the table and crosses her legs.

"What difference does it make? What, if any, rule would've been broken even if the rumors are true?"

Teresa pauses before she answers. There are no rules that forbid him from becoming a father. Or sleeping around with grown-ass women who happen to be clients. At least none in writing, but it is a well-accepted understanding. There are potential liabilities associated with men fucking female clients. "How about sexual harassment?"

Michael blinks but doesn't respond. Teresa realizes she's put him in a bind. He can't admit he did anything but then say it wasn't sexual harassment.

Finally, Michael leans forward in his seat and says, "Let me ask you a question. Do you want me out of here? That's the rumor I've been hearing. And I only need a yes or no."

Teresa stares at him, unblinking, and says, "Yes."

He sits back in his chair and, for the first time since he arrived, gives her a tight smile. "Since that episode we had in the meeting? You're still carrying a grudge?"

"No, it's not a grudge. But I don't forget," Teresa says, tapping her forehead.

"Because of your man-sized ego I have to go?"

"It's *your* outsized ego that bothers me," she tells him, "and your lack of professionalism and now your ethics. Or lack thereof."

"What do you have against men?" He sits up straight again.

"Have you been screwing those two women? A simple yes or no will do."

"What? You think I'm going to confess to you?"

"Not confess, Michael. Just tell me you didn't do it. Tell me you're an upstanding professional who wouldn't slink around at night, stealing in and out of the projects, to sleep with women you wouldn't take to a public restaurant."

His laugh is harsh. Closer to a grunt. He crosses his arms in front of his chest. He stares at her. "Ass is ass. If you're gonna be a man, that's the first lesson you have to learn."

"So, our clients' asses aren't off limits?"

He uncrosses his arms and continues to stare. "What do you want from me? To resign? To cave in and walk away from a job I need? It's not going to happen."

"What do you want? To stay here and work for me? To get reassigned to clerical duties because I don't trust you with clients anymore? To report to Maybelline? Is that what you want, Michael? There are worse things than getting fired," Teresa assures him.

"What do you prefer?" he says.

"What do you prefer?"

"That you make me an offer." Michael's eyes narrow, but his face is relaxed.

"Three months' severance, three months of insurance or until you find another job, whichever comes first, and I'll give you a layoff letter for unemployment."

"Six months of severance pay," Michael counters.

"I can live with four. Today's your last day."

"I can live with that. Nothing goes into my personnel file except that I was laid off because my position was phased out."

"Fine. Goodbye, Michael. And good luck." Teresa stands and walks to the door. She hears the muffled footsteps hurrying away. She doesn't bother to hold back the smile now.

"Mary Ann would shake my hand and pat me on the back," Michael says.

Teresa ignores his remark, holds the door open for him, and pushes it closed as soon as his back clears the doorway. She walks over to the big window overlooking the boulevard below, closes her eyes, and takes a deep breath. She has done something Mary Ann wouldn't or couldn't do. Had Mary Ann been intimidated by Michael? Or was there another possible reason she let him slide for so long? "Ass is ass," he had said. That would qualify Mary Ann's pancake-flat backside. Teresa laughs. It's such a loud laugh that she's sure the whole staff hears it. Mary Ann doing Michael. It takes a minute for Teresa to regain her self-control. Toni taps on the door, pushes it open, steps into the room and eases the door closed behind her.

"Michael's telling everybody that he's out of here. You did it?"

"Like you don't know," Teresa says.

"You knew I was there?"

"I knew you had my back." Teresa puts a hand on Toni's shoulder and squeezes.

"You think I screwed up big time with him, don't you?" Toni says.

"You could've used more discretion."

"I know. Like you say, I need to see around corners. I hope I'm not *too* big a disappointment."

"It's a lesson learned, for both of us. Don't beat yourself up over this one. Besides, Mary Ann's the one who hired this fool and kept him here far too long. We need him gone today. You know what to do. Also transfer those two clients back to their case workers at Human Services. They don't step foot back in here, and get this all done today. I want a fresh start tomorrow."

"Yes ma'am, boss," Toni says.

* * *

Teresa looks tired to him. She sits slumped in the seat beside him, her eyes closed. It's 9:30 p.m., and he's just swung by her office. She hasn't spoken more than four words since getting in the car. He pulls out into traffic, turns on the radio, keeps the volume low, and finds a jazz station.

"Hmm, nice," she says, head tilted back against the seat. A saxophone croons through the speakers.

"It's all Kathryn ever listened to."

"Again, I'm sorry about messing up our dinner plans. Things got really hectic."

"Things went a little sideways at my place today too. Feel like telling me about your day, or do you just want to chill?" Marcus takes a quick peek at her. She turns her head in his direction and opens her eyes.

"Are you really interested?"

"Why wouldn't I be?"

"For a lot of reasons, not the least of which is that my day ruined our evening." By the time they reach Michigan Avenue, she's summarized her day's unexpected twists and turns. Marcus thinks *hectic* is an understatement. It sounded wild.

"Want me to take care of Michael boy? I know people."

"I think it's handled. But you know people, huh? Walden Byrd Mann III? I thought there was more to him than he lets on." Teresa's laugh lacks its usual gusto.

"Do you think it's over?"

"He's a reckless man, but he's not dumb. He figured out his best move and took it," Teresa says.

"What happens to the objects of his affection?"

"They're gone. No longer my problem," she says.

"That seems a little unfair. They *could* be viewed as victims."

"They were anything but. To be honest, Michael was probably played. For heaven's sake, the man had unprotected sex with at least one of them and maybe got her pregnant. She knew what she was doing, I'm not sure about him."

"Still a case could be made he took advantage of them."

"I can't let them stay. I have to clean up every bit of sordidness associated with this. Come tomorrow I want the whole affair to be in the past. I have to keep the bigger picture in mind." She rubs the lids of her closed eyes. "Let's talk about your day." Marcus tells Teresa he's learned that his grandfather may have had an affair with Seleste.

"*She* told you that?" Teresa sits up and lowers the radio's volume.

"Not hardly. Missy told me."

"How would Missy know?" She turns sideways, rests her head against the seat, and pays rapt attention.

"Her mother told her. Seleste is her godmother."

"Wait a minute," Teresa says. "Why would your little receptionist's momma tell her about that?"

"I don't know and didn't ask. Mothers and daughters gossip. Right?"

"Mothers don't usually gossip about their best friend's love affairs to their immature daughters," she says.

"I think Missy said her mother and Seleste aren't best friends anymore."

"And why would Missy tell you about *her* godmother's affair with *your* grandfather?" Teresa's face has lost its tired look, and the weariness in her voice has dissipated.

"She's immature. Remember?"

"How did that become a topic of conversation?" Teresa asks. She sounds suspicious of Missy.

Marcus changes the facts as he continues the story. He's convinced himself it's to protect Missy from getting on Teresa's radar any more than she already is. "Over lunch. It's her one- year anniversary with us."

"And?"

"I really don't know her that well, and I wanted to celebrate her anniversary by taking her to lunch and getting to know more about her. All I knew was her name and that she's Seleste's goddaughter."

"And?" Teresa says.

"She talked about her mother, her boyfriend, and Seleste. Nothing about her father. So, I asked about him, and she said he left when she was a baby. Then she said it was like my grandmother did me except I was older. I was surprised Seleste had told her about that."

Marcus shrugs, then pauses and studies Teresa's face. She's intrigued by this bit of juicy gossip. "She went on to tell me, which I already knew, that Seleste's father had abandoned the family when she was about seven. That revelation led Missy to say that her mother told her that Seleste needed a father figure, and that's why she fell for my grandfather."

"How do you feel about that?" Teresa says.

"Disappointed."

"Do you believe it?"

"I don't know what to believe. I'm not sure if it should even matter."

"Do you think that's why your grandmother left?"

"I don't know."

"What if it was? Would that make a difference in how you look at things?" She moves closer to him and puts her hand on his leg. Her hair smells like citrus fruit. He likes it.

"That might explain why she left him, but she also left me." He's irritated and he knows it's not Teresa's fault. But she is annoying him with her subtle defense of Kathryn. "And your father?" he says, not sure when he hears his words why he asked that question.

"He was never in my life. No comparison to your grandmother." Teresa moves away from him and looks out the front window.

Her reaction triggers yet another impulsive remark from Marcus.

"Despite all the negative things you say about your mother, she never left you. She stayed. From where I sit, she deserves at least one call a year," he says.

"I was with her until I was eighteen, then left. You were with your grandmother for the same eighteen years, then she left. The difference is I've seen my momma a lot since I was eighteen, despite our differences." Teresa gives him a quick stare before turning her eyes back on the darkening scene outside the car's windows. They're headed east on Randolph Street toward her place. They haven't discussed where she will stay tonight but he's made the decision on his own. It's late and he's fatigued. "I need to go to my place tonight. I think we're both too tired to be good company."

Teresa reaches in the back of the car to retrieve her briefcase and handbag. "I agree," she says. Five minutes later, Teresa's walking through her building's front entrance, and Marcus is driving in the opposite direction.

* * *

Marcus punches in the number on his cell phone. While it's ringing, he considers disconnecting. "Curiosity killed the cat," Kathryn always said when he asked questions she didn't want to answer.

"Hello, counselor." Fraser's booming voice vibrates against his ear.

"Hey, Fraser, you got a couple of minutes? I need to ask you something. About my grandfather."

"Shoot," Fraser says.

"And Seleste?"

"What about her?"

"Was she more than *just* an employee?"

Fraser's laughter tumbles through the phone and spills over into the car. "You asking if she fucked the old man?"

"Were they involved?"

"What makes you think I know something like that?" Fraser says.

"You know everything else."

"Even if I knew, what makes you think I want to get in some shit between you and Seleste?"

"There's no shit between me and Seleste."

"Then ask her. She's better suited to know who she's fucked." Fraser chuckles.

"She hasn't bothered to tell me in all these years."

"That should tell you she thinks it's none of your business," Fraser says.

"It's like that?"

"It's the right way to go," Fraser says. "But if you're all hyped to uncover her dark secrets, talk to Seleste."

Three minutes after talking with Fraser, the cell vibrates in his hand. It's Seleste. "I understand you want to know something about me but are too afraid to ask."

"Says Fraser?"

"He said you needed to ask me something. I'm wondering why you called him instead of me. So? And what?"

"I called him to avoid a confrontation with you," Marcus says.

"We confront all the time. So, what's your issue now?"

"It's very personal."

"What exactly do you want to know?"

"It's about you and my grandfather."

"What exactly do you want to know?" she repeats. Her tone challenges him to ask a direct question.

"I want to know if you had an affair with my grandfather."

The silence hangs in the space above his head like the calm before a storm. He can't hear her breathing. He waits.

"Marcus," she says, her voice just above a whisper, "your grandfather's dead—may his soul rest in peace—and may those things he didn't see fit to tell you when he was alive, stay buried with him as he rests in peace."

"I'll take that as a yes."

"Be my guest."

"So that made you the other woman," he says. Click. She's gone. His anger, driven by a nervous anxiety, is like a caffeine rush. A million thoughts and emotions tumble against one another after he's parked. He eases out of the car and makes his way through the city's still bustling downtown streets to his office. It's 10:30 p.m. when Marcus enters the suite, goes to Seleste's office, and opens one of the locked file cabinets. He finds Missy's personnel file, sits down at the desk, and dials her number.

"Hello?"

"Missy, this is Marcus."

"I'm really popular tonight. I've got Seleste on hold; she just called. I'll call you right back."

"Okay," he says. He shakes his head. He doesn't know how he, Seleste, and Missy will get past this.

* * *

Marcus is pulling into his driveway when the cell rings. It's Teresa. He doesn't answer. By the time he parks in the garage, the phone rings again. It's Missy.

"Thanks for calling back." He turns off the ignition and sits back in his seat. "I just want to apologize for the way I reacted today. You did nothing wrong. And for the record, I didn't tell Seleste you told me anything."

"She asked me and I said yes, and she said I was out of line and that my mom was out of line. And that neither one of us knows what we're talking about."

"You still believe your mother?"

"My mom does a lot of things that I don't like, but she doesn't lie. Never has and never will. Not about her own personal business and not about anybody else's. Seleste just doesn't want to admit the truth."

"What else did your mother say?"

"That's all about Seleste and your grandfather. Can I lose my job behind this?" she says.

"You won't lose your job. Good night, Missy."

"You sound sad."

"I'll see you tomorrow."

He ends the call and goes into the house. His family's home. He's the only one left. He refuses to try to make the puzzle pieces fit. His grandfather and Seleste. Kathryn's sudden departure from his life. He drops onto the chair nearest the backdoor and stares unseeing in the lightless room and listens to the refrigerator's motor change gears. Other than that, the house is silent.

Fifteen

It's **11:00 a.m.** when Marcus arrives at his office the next day. He had a restless night and overslept. Missy looks subdued when he enters the suite, and the absence of cheerful energy feels like stepping into a sealed chamber. She raises her eyebrows and offers up a strained "Good morning." He moves through the short corridor, and when he comes to Seleste's door, it's ajar but not wide open like she usually keeps it. He can only see the corner of her desk.

He pauses and glares at the door, then continues on to his office. Piled on top of his daily newspaper lay several pink message slips. Fraser called at nine, ten minutes after George Womack's message says he called. Rhonda Womack's attorney, Bridget Nathanson, called. What the hell has happened?

He calls George, but he's out. He calls Fraser. While Marcus waits for his call to go through, he feels the anxiety flutter like a trapped fly in the pit of his stomach. Fraser comes on the line as upbeat and boisterous as ever without a hint of self-consciousness in his voice when he says hello.

"What's all the excitement about?" Marcus says, his irritation with Fraser over the Seleste thing muted beneath his somber tone.

"Rhonda pulled a gun on George, threatened to shoot him in his head if he comes to the house again. He's blown a fuse, says he's going to fuck her up. Your negotiations are unraveling at the speed of light. He's on his way over here right now. Says he couldn't get in touch with you, and Seleste couldn't tell him when he could. George just walked in. You need to come on over because we've got some work to do." Fraser hangs up.

"Damn," Marcus says. His case is careening out of control, and people's lives are at stake. The floor seems to shift beneath his feet when he stands. Marcus reaches out to grab the edge of the table to steady himself. He straightens up and eases around the table over to the window where he visualizes the boats sitting on the lake. He can almost feel the coolness. The breeze. He envies those unseen people out there sunning and drinking without a care in the world at the moment and feeling free.

He rubs the full length of his face. *What the hell is Rhonda thinking? What the hell is George thinking? What the hell are they doing to their kids?* He takes a deep breath. Fraser sounds like a man in charge. Marcus rubs his face again. Why hadn't Seleste called him? The biggest client they have needs to talk to him, and she doesn't call to let him know. He wonders if she called Fraser instead. How else would George and Fraser have hooked up? The idea changes the signals from his nervous system, replacing anxiety with a smoldering fury.

Before turning away from the window, Marcus looks over at the taller buildings that hide the lake from him. Then he lowers his eyes and takes in the scene of the crowded street below where the magic of the city comes together. Its energy and its crowds, its big buildings and its big ambitions all crammed together in every available space in the air and on the ground. It inspires him. Like his grandfather, he claims this city. And like his grandfather, he claims this firm, and if he and Seleste can't work together, then she has to get the hell out. He focuses on that coveted angle between the two buildings that frame his puny view of the lake. It isn't much, but it's his view.

He slings the strap of his briefcase across a shoulder and strolls out of his office. Seleste's door is still half closed but in the confines of the quiet corridor, Marcus can hear the soft rhythms of Jamaica coming through the narrow opening as he approaches. He pushes through the door and steps into the sun-filled space. Seleste is seated at her desk, her heavy fingers thumping away on her keyboard. She doesn't turn her head when he enters, only her eyes.

Her fingers move even slower as she corrects the numerous mistakes underlined in red on the monitor's screen. This feature of word processing convinced her to retire the typewriter she'd used the previous two decades. He closes the door and takes a seat. She stops pecking and turns to face him but says nothing. The ball's in his court. The crow's feet wrinkling the corners of her eyes seem more pronounced as he sits scrutinizing her scrutinizing him. The skin beneath her chin sags a bit.

"We need to talk."

"Aren't you needed at Fraser's?" Seleste removes her hands from the keyboard, places one on her knee, tucks the other under her chin, and poses like Rodin's Thinker.

The question catches him off guard. He looks at a woman he's known most of his life but is seeing someone else. A person he does not really know. A person whom he may not like. Marcus realizes Seleste is losing her youthfulness. He can see her harder edges. Her dismissive attitude is tantamount to pouring emotional gasoline on a simmering anger.

His slow burn is fast becoming deep resentment; roiling emotions color his perceptions of her, and now Seleste is looking like the proverbial bitch. "So, you knew George was going to meet with Fraser? You called Fraser?" he says, more as an accusation than a question.

She smiles but not a cheerful smile. It's more like the smirk of an adversary. And she does not answer his questions.

"Why didn't you call me?" he says.

"You should have checked in with me this morning."

"You're confused. I'm the boss here." Marcus keeps his eyes unwaveringly on hers.

"Then act like it." Seleste doesn't bat an eye either.

"You're out of line," he tells her. There's a part of him that is bewildered by his feelings and what he senses are hers.

"You were out of line when you went behind my back," she tells him.

"This is not about that. This is about the firm's biggest client."

"I think it isn't about the firm's biggest client. If it were, you'd be on your way to the meeting."

"If you were doing your job, the client would be meeting me here," he says.

"If you were doing your job, the client wouldn't be asking Fraser to take the lead on his case."

Her retort catches him off guard, once again. "Enough, Seleste."

"What makes you think you can talk to me like that? Leave my office. Please."

Marcus stands to leave. "This is not over." He turns his back to Seleste and steps out into the corridor. The furious clacking of the computer's keys is her only response. Missy offers a weak smile when he comes into the reception area.

"Leaving?"

"I'll be at Fraser's," he says, not slowing to acknowledge her smile.

"It must be important. He's been on the phone a couple of times with Seleste."

He stops at the door and glances back at her. "You okay?" he says.

"Things are getting a little out of hand, huh? Seleste is really tripping."

"Her guilty conscience, maybe."

"She called me disloyal and said I don't appreciate what she's done for me. Says I'm just like my mom and I talk too much about what I don't know. She said some things about my mom that I didn't like. She's mad but I'm mad, too."

"You two will kiss and make up, I'm sure."

"You will too," Missy says.

Marcus steps into the outer corridor but turns back to look at her. She waves. He knows she caught hell from Seleste this morning. The elevator opens and he steps in, and when he turns around, Missy's on the phone. She frowns and points toward the back of the suite. Marcus knows it's a pissed-off Seleste giving Missy more grief.

"This shit's not going to work itself out," he says as the elevator doors close.

* * *

Teresa's day has been filled with stressful demands. The city's sent a compliance order for submission of six hundred client files from the past two years. Their preferred time frame is within thirty days. The number of staff and staff hours needed to comply is daunting. She has to put together a plan for getting it done. The board is demanding a detailed report on the issues with Michael Brown's resignation and severance package. Their stated time frame is within the month, which gives her two weeks from today. This is a new move for a board that has never required personnel reports from Mary Ann.

Teresa's not sure what the move means, but she's not optimistic. The memo came from Jesse and raised several questions for her. First, how does the board know about Michael's resignation? She hasn't informed them yet. And why did she get a memo rather than a call from Jesse? She opens her laptop and begins to outline her plans for responding to both demands when the receptionist calls.

"Mr. Greene's calling."

"Put him through, please."

"I'm sorry about last night." His voice is strong and reassuring, giving Teresa a bit of a lift.

"Me too," she says. "I need to see you." She's tired of being alone in her office, tired of dealing with the stresses of the job. She needs to get away. Needs to get some distance from the work, relax her mind and clear her brain. Maybe even get a little loving in the afternoon. The thought makes her smile. "Can you get away now?"

"I'm sorry, but I can't right now. I'm on my way to meet with a client who's sinking fast and is in shark-infested waters. Can we get together later? Tonight, all night? I need some loving, bad."

"Me too. Call me when you're free," she says.

"Will do." He pauses as if he wants to say something else, then just says, "See you tonight."

"Bye," Teresa says and blows him a kiss.

* * *

With an hour left before Marcus arrives, Teresa wants to relax and get her head straight. He's going to spend the night for the first time. Marcus sounded like his day has been a shitty one too. Teresa yawns because she didn't sleep well last night, and she's a woman who needs her seven hours in dream world. An evening with Marcus and she'll sleep like a baby fully fed and comfy dry. She smiles in anticipation. Thirty minutes later, the soft knock on the door means the doorman has let Marcus up without calling her first. Marcus can be a charmer, and the tips he's thrown the doorman's way haven't hurt. She puts on her robe, pulls the belt tight around her waist, and heads for the door.

"Who's there?" she asks, her voice a teasing soft whisper.

"It's me." His voice is low, drained of all its energy.

She hears his weariness, feels his frustration even as he stands unseen on the other side of the door. She wants to console him, to relieve his stress. Be his rock.

"You look tired," she says when he enters.

"Not angry?"

"That bad?"

She leads him over to the sofa, where they both drop down into its receptive softness. But before he can answer, she leans over and kisses him. He knocks his briefcase to the floor and turns his body into hers. They stay this way, their bodies not moving as if posing for a picture while their tongues dance a slow tango. And those crashing waves of frustration inside her, brought on by the day's events, subside. And when their lips part, the calm remains.

"You want to talk about it?" she asks. Her hands massage the nape of his neck.

"You sure you want to hear about the snake pit? Or wouldn't you rather take this action into the bedroom?"

His smile's not convincing. He wants to talk, and Teresa's willing to listen. "Tell me what happened." She continues to massage the nape of his neck with the tips of her fingers. He moves his head from side to side, leans it forward, and rolls it around in response to her touch.

"Basically, my co-counsel has stolen my biggest client."

She moves her hands up to his head and massages his dome. She searches for the subtleties hidden in his voice. At a level far below her radar of consciousness, his enemies can easily become her enemies. "That's so foul," Teresa says.

"I've known Fraser Letcher since I was a kid. I brought him in on this case because I respected and trusted him. Now he's convinced my client to go right when the plan was to go left."

His voice strains to stay strong and even. She can hear the anger and the disappointment.

"I know Fraser's aggressive," Marcus continues, "and prefers to attack rather than negotiate, but he knows that's not my style."

Teresa cups his face and presses gently. "Relax, bae."

"I get to his office, and my client—his name is George—starts yelling at me. He's holding me responsible for a confrontation that happened with him and his wife. She pulled a gun on him. Now he wants Fraser to be in charge."

Teresa starts massaging one of his shoulders. His tensed muscles are like stone under her hand. "That is crazy."

"And then George starts in on my weaknesses as an attorney. Too willing to compromise, he tells me, too willing to give away all the gold in his treasury."

She loosens his tie and unbuttons his shirt collar. "He's rich?"

"He has a large portfolio. I calmly try to explain the law and the odds of not winning a bloody divorce fight by a man with a lot of gold and no prenup. And Fraser just sits there like a spectator, doesn't say a word."

She disengages three more buttons and strokes his chest. "He sounds treacherous."

"Not so much treacherous as self-righteous. He obviously knew what George was going to say and let it play out. Then he speaks up supporting George's point of view. More hours, more fees. He's exploiting the situation. He doesn't care about George. I do." His voice sounds defeated.

She leans in and kisses his nipples. Then she sits upright, plants a peck on his lips and then says, "George will get what he deserves. He sounds too self-righteous."

"He is an arrogant fool for sure. But my job is to protect him from himself."

"Is that even possible?"

"If Fraser was on the same page. But I knew what I was getting into with Fraser."

"So, what now?" Teresa begins unbuckling his belt.

"I don't know. And the same goes for Seleste. I have to figure out my next moves."

She leans her head against his shoulder and rubs both of her hands along his thighs. "You'll figure it out."

"Fraser's a big part of my biggest case, and Seleste just about runs my practice." He sighs and closes his eyes.

She slides a hand up between his legs and massages there until she feels his response. She puts her lips next to his ear and blows. They need each other right now. Her mind is no longer filled with troubling thoughts. Teresa maneuvers her body over his and sits on his lap facing him. She kisses him. First on the forehead, his nose, and then she takes control of his mouth. His hunger is instant and fierce.

"Thanks for the sympathetic ear," he says, his voice hoarse, his breath hot against her face.

"My sympathy hasn't run its course, bae," she says, then pushes her tongue deep inside his mouth.

Sixteen

The sound of breaking glass startles her awake. Teresa bolts upright in the bed, her heart pounding, her mind struggling to find its bearings. A head pokes through the open door of her bedroom.

"Sorry. I dropped a glass."

"How long have you been up?"

"About fifteen minutes. I'm hungry."

"Me too." Then Teresa summons Marcus with a beckoning finger and says, "You can eat later."

Marcus angles his body against the frame of the doorway. "I came to you last night for sustenance. I was deep in a funk."

"And?"

"I'm on cloud nine now." Marcus strolls over to the bed and crawls in between her bare legs. His baldness rises like a dark boulder above her mound of hair. "You're about to see what it's like on cloud ten."

"Oh, my," Teresa says.

When Marcus flicks his tongue over what he calls her pearl button, her eyes flutter closed. She drapes her legs over his shoulders and begins to move her hips, slow and steady, up and down, in rhythm with the beat of his bobbing head. Then he changes the beat. His hands, now cupping each butt cheek, pulls and pushes. Fast then slow then fast again.

Teresa opens her eyes and watches in fascination. His lusty movements between her legs turn the tingling sensations into electrified pulses. She gasps when the pulses turn into rhythmic tremors. Her eyes snap shut. Her mouth forms a circle, sucking in oxygen with each heartbeat. He takes control of her body.

Her knees tighten around his neck, as he begins to extract the last remnants of her free will. Soon waves of intense passion sweep the entire length of her body.

Teresa grabs his shoulders and rotates her hips. He slides his tongue inside her and slowly pulls it out, then in again. He moves it rapidly in circles pausing to inhale, then exhale in sharp cool bursts. She snaps upright then backward. Her head bounces off the headboard. Somewhere, somebody screams. Every muscle in her body has grown taut. Then he stops abruptly. She hears a grunt, then feels herself being yanked across the bed.

She becomes airborne as her legs unwrap. Her eyes won't open, and her mind can't function. She only senses it all as she tumbles through space. Her eyes come unglued. The two of them are on the floor. Marcus is on his back, one foot still on the bed. She's lying face down, her stomach covering his face. Her elbows are embedded into the fabric of the carpet beneath them. Her sexual excitement masks what she knows should be painful.

"You were choking me," he says, his voice a warm and moist vibration against her flesh.

"What?"

"You were choking me. I couldn't breathe."

"What?" She isn't comprehending. She feels his body shaking. She rolls over and off him.

When she scoots down and turns to face him, he says, "Didn't you hear me choking?" She hadn't. "I couldn't pry your legs loose," he tells her. "I jumped backward to escape. It was my only option." Teresa covers her mouth and closes her eyes. She's not sure if it's because she's embarrassed or if it's to stop herself from laughing.

This temporary confusion dissolves when a cartoonish rerun of Marcus flashes across the movie screen that is her imagination, him in the death grip of her killer thighs, eyes wide with fear, desperately pulling at her legs in an unsuccessful attempt to free himself and finally taking the only way out that he could see. So he leaps backward off the bed in order to save himself. Her hand is stuffed tightly inside her mouth to contain the laughter. Her closed eyes strain to keep the tears damned up.

"I got greedy," he says, "and made the mistake of throwing in my s-curve swirl. The next thing I knew, I was fighting for my life."

She, on the other hand, had been rendered breathless and nearly unconscious. Teresa slowly removes her hand and says, "I'm sorry."

"If anyone needs to apologize, it's me," he says. "That was all Marcus G. Greene. You couldn't help yourself."

Now that the intensity has subsided, Teresa feels a sense of vulnerability. It's not overwhelming or even anxiety producing. But it's there. The depth and intensity of the passion she experiences with him is way beyond anything she's fantasized. She likes him far more than she's been willing to admit. She plasters his chest with several soft kisses. "I guess I have to take you in doses. You had me screaming like a madwoman."

"Nope, that was me. You stabbed me with your fingernails." He leans his right shoulder forward to show the proof. She winces at the deep imprints in his flesh. Marcus laughs. A sweet laugh that sends a soft breeze blowing through her hair. Yes, she likes this man a lot.

"I'm hungry now. I need food," she says, then slides her lips across his chin and up to his lips. Their kiss lasts several minutes until she rolls away and stands on wobbly legs. The digital clock on her nightstand reads 9:10 a.m. He reaches up and pulls her back down. She lies perpendicular to him, the back of her head on his stomach. He strokes her hair.

"How's your day looking?" he asks.

"I'm not sure."

She glances at the clock again and stands back up. "We need to start moving."

"Not really." He rolls over on his stomach and does thirty pushups, then jumps to his feet. He pulls their bare bodies together and slides his hands up her backside.

"No sir," she says taking a small step backward. "I'm still reeling from your s-curve swirl."

"Good," Marcus tells her. "It was my first test run."

"I highly recommend you add it to your repertoire. But—" Teresa pauses for emphasis "—be very careful with it. I need you to stay alive and healthy. Now, we have got to eat."

His eyes scan her body, and the way he looks at her makes Teresa grin. Makes her feel like she's the hottest woman on earth. She realizes she has a hunger for him too. A closeness. A bond. *This is not love but lust,* she thinks, *the best sex I've ever had.*

"Let's shower first," he says, running his fingers down the center of her back. She shivers in response.

"Shower only, please." She giggles and steps beyond his touch. Her hips sway as she walks to the bathroom. She hears him groan behind her and smiles.

It's 11:00 a.m. by the time they finish showering and eating. Outside, the weather's sunny and hot, but a cool breeze keeps it tolerable. He kisses her, the hunger still evident when he presses his body into hers. She isn't one for public displays but discovers this is yet another one of her idiosyncrasies she can get past for him. She presses back and they stand like that for several seconds.

"This is nice," he says. "We're good together."

"Yes, we are," she responds, then adds, "mostly."

* * *

Marcus makes his way down Michigan Avenue and thinks long and hard about what his next move should be. He checks his cell phone, and there are three voicemail messages.

"Marcus, you need to call Seleste." It's Missy's voice. She left the message at 10:30 a.m.

Another is from Seleste at 10:15 a.m. "Marcus, Mr. Womack called this morning and demanded I send his files to Fraser. Since you can't be reached, I've made arrangements to accommodate his requests." The third one is also from Seleste calling at 9:45 a.m.

"Marcus, I need to talk with you. Call the office."

"Damn it." He trots across the intersection against the red light and shoves through the revolving door of his building. It's 11:30 a.m. He chastises himself for not checking his phone sooner and not calling the office to check up on things. That damn Fraser. That damn Seleste. If only he were double-jointed, he'd kick his own butt up and down Jackson Boulevard. Beads of perspiration dampen the back of his neck as he enters the elevator. He takes a deep breath. He needs to slow down, get his thoughts together.

George wanted Fraser to take the lead on his case, so Fraser had a right to the files. But Marcus believes that Seleste should have waited until he gave her the go-ahead. And before yesterday, she would never have sent those files without his consent. It's a serious breach of protocol. When Marcus steps off the elevator, Missy is peering through the glass doors. The look of concern on her face becomes a frown after he flings open one of the doors and covers the space between it and her desk in three long strides.

"Seleste sent those files over to Fraser?"

"Yes."

"When did the files go over?"

"Bout half hour ago. Seleste took them." Missy keeps her eyes trained on his face.

"She lost her mind?" He pushes past her desk and heads toward the back offices.

"She's not back."

He returns to the reception area. "She took copies of all the Womack files?"

"Originals. She left the copies here."

His anger erupts into a volatile mix of words and emotions. "Get her ass on the phone. Now. I can't believe she pulled some crap like this."

The look of panic on Missy's face makes him stop. He's ranting. Something he never does. Seleste has gotten to him.

"Call Fraser's place and get her on the phone. Please."

"Right away, boss."

He goes back to his office and plops into his chair. Missy buzzes him on the intercom. She's talked with Fraser who says Seleste is on her way back.

"Is there anything you need done? You want me to get Mr. Womack on the phone?"

"No."

"You sure? You don't want to know why he wants his files sent to Mr. Letcher?"

"I already know."

"I don't."

He starts to blow her off, but she's part of the team. And right now, he needs her on his side. "His case has turned ugly. His wife pulled a gun on him. He doesn't think I have the right stuff to lead the charge and wants Fraser to be new lead counsel."

"It's our case. Can he do that?" she says.

"It's his life, his divorce, so yes, he can."

"Are you still his lawyer too?"

Marcus hasn't thought about getting off the case, but maybe he should.

"I may not stay on, but you're right, I need to talk to George."

"You want me to get him on the line?"

"I'll call him."

"Can I please do my job?" Missy says.

"Okay. And thanks."

"No problem, boss. I work for you."

Until the other day, he's never thought of himself as the boss. He was the lawyer and Seleste the manager of everything else that needed managing. And it's obvious Seleste never thought of him as the boss either. Or her peer. The level of her indignation is evidence of that. He feels the anger rising again. Things have changed in the last forty-eight hours, and Seleste is about to find out who runs this goddamn place.

"Boss, Mr. Womack's on hold, and he says you've got three seconds to pick up."

"Thanks. Put him through. George?"

"You had your girl call me." George's heavy breathing means he's ready for a fight.

"You know my position. Turning this into a fight to the death isn't the answer. You won't win, can't win. There'll be no winners in the end."

"That skinny little washed-out bitch pulls a gun on me and I just negotiate how much money I give her?"

"What you should have done before she pulled the gun on you was leave her alone, not threaten to take the kids and not try to break out all the windows in the garage."

"We settled this the other night. I need Fraser to take the lead. I want a win, not a tie. Are you in or out?"

"I'm out," Marcus says and disconnects. A few minutes later, Missy calls and tells him Seleste is back and Fraser's on the phone. Marcus tells Missy that he'll take the call and wants to see Seleste in five minutes.

"Don't be so damn petulant." Fraser laughs but his voice doesn't reverberate across the lines as usual. "You can't get off this case. He just wants a change in strategy. This case won't go to trial. That little cute-ass lawyer of Rhonda's doesn't want to go up against me, but we do need to give her a taste of what she'll face if she does. And George needs the inspiration."

"I'm off the case, Fraser. That's it. He's your client now. Look, I have something pressing I need to handle."

Marcus disconnects. Seconds later, Seleste struts into his office and sits on the edge of the chair, the one not directly in front of him. Marcus has to shift to an angle to face her. She hasn't brought a tablet or pen. He can tell from the set of her eyes and the stiffness in her posture that she's come to fight. And he's not going to disappoint her.

"It wasn't your place to turn those files over to Fraser."

"The client requested that it be done immediately. When you were unreachable, I made the decision to respect his wishes. I don't see the problem."

"The problem is that you're not the attorney." His tone is stern.

"Why is that suddenly a problem?" Her tone is nonchalant.

"Why are you suddenly taking orders from the client? Or Fraser?"

"I made a judgment call," she says.

"Don't do it again. Ever." He's lowered his voice and paused between each word. He points at her to dramatize his intense feelings.

"Or what?" she says, a smirk pulls at the corners of her mouth.

"I don't expect us to have to find out."

"Is that a threat?" she says, the smirk disappearing, replaced by what looks to Marcus like a snarl.

"No," he says. "I don't resort to threats."

"It sounds like a threat to me. I don't like them, and I don't think much of people who resort to making them."

"It's a directive. This is my law firm, and you work for me. Not for Womack. Not for Fraser."

"Is that all?" She stands up.

"I'm not finished."

"I am. I've got work to do. You may be the boss, as you say, but I'm here day in and day out, while you come and go at your leisure. I run this office. I did when your grandfather was alive. I did when you were only a child. So now you want to play boss? Well, enjoy yourself but I've got work to do." She heads for the door.

"Don't test me." The calm in his voice is an act of will, but inside, his gut is bubbling.

She glances back at him over her shoulder. "Don't test *me*. You've gotten in my face several times already. One more time may be one too many."

"Is that a threat?" He's borderline shouting.

"It's a warning. I've given so much for so long to this firm that I won't let you disrespect my place in it."

Through sheer willpower he stops himself from going over the edge. He senses this is a pivotal moment for him, for her, and for the firm. What he's learned during the past forty-eight hours has left a bitter taste in his mouth. He frowns. "You need to sit down," Marcus tells her.

Seleste opens the door and, without a glance back at him, leaves his office and slams the door behind her. He sits there, unable to move, unable to respond to her act of defiance. His mind races in a haphazard fashion through the limited options available to him. Ignore what she's just done or fire her. But he doesn't know how to fire her. He doesn't know how to tell Seleste Brown, who's been with the firm before he even knew what a lawyer does, to get out. And what will he do without her? She runs the office; he doesn't. He closes his eyes in order to focus. "Goddamn you, Seleste," he says.

Seventeen

Shattering voices and frenetic energy greet Teresa when she steps through the front door of the office suite. The conference room is the epicenter for all the activity. Inside, Toni and several staff are pouring over stacks of files. Others cart more piles in and organizes them on chairs, the floor, and the conference table. The madness has begun. The room smells of disturbed paper. Dust particles float invisibly through the air. Teresa sneezes.

"God bless you," Toni says.

"Thank you. How's it going?"

"You want to know how I feel? Or what I think?" Toni says.

"Both."

"I feel overwhelmed, but we *can* get these files ready and sent over by the deadline."

"Do we need to bring in some temporary help?" Teresa says.

"Could we? Please?"

"Get what you need. And don't forget to let these folks get some lunch."

Teresa lingers outside the epicenter and observes her staff's intense faces and anxious eyes. The next several weeks are going to be hell on everybody. Later, sitting at her desk trying to figure out just what it is she needs to do next, Teresa checks the phone calls she's ignored earlier. There are three. All from her sister.

"Momma's in the hospital. Call me right away." Tisha sounds hysterical. Teresa doesn't know how to feel. She's expected this call ever since she left home.

Taylor Lee's in the hospital and Tisha's falling apart, but that means nothing. Her sister lives her life afraid of everything. It has to be something like diabetes or high blood pressure. Taylor Lee has no self-discipline. Eats what and how much she wants whenever she wants, and her bulging body attests to that. She also drinks beer in lieu of water and smokes a pack of filtered cigarettes daily. She believes that the filters make them a healthier choice. Despite her bad health habits, when challenged, Taylor Lee has always declared that people have to die from something. Teresa, disconcerted by her uncertainty, lays her head on her desk. Her mother is in the hospital and that means she is sick. How sick? Teresa won't know unless she calls Tisha back. Teresa stares at her sister's number. She doesn't want to call. She doesn't want to know. But the reality is that she has to make the call. She has to because she's obligated. Teresa takes in a deep breath, then exhales. Acquiescing to what she considers her unavoidable burden, Teresa inhales again while Terri's cell phone rings somewhere in Hannibal, then lets the stale air seep back out into an office whose walls seem to be closing in on her.

Tisha's voice is close to a whisper. "Where the heck have you been, Resie? Momma's been asking about you. Hold on."

"Don't give..."

"Hey, girl, I've been waiting to hear from you." Taylor Lee's voice is weak and hoarse. So much so that it startles Teresa.

"Hey, yourself. I just got Tish's message. You sound a little tired, so I don't know why she stuck the phone in your face. Let me speak back to Tish. That girl doesn't think sometimes."

"I've got lung cancer," Taylor Lee says. Teresa's speechless. The silence lasts for seconds. "Did you hear me?"

"Yes," Teresa says.

"Here's Tisha Lee."

"When are you coming?" Tish is crying.

"Coming?" Teresa's mind can't focus. Her thoughts are fragmented. They fall apart before she can finish forming them.

"Tonight? Tomorrow?" Tisha sounds like she's talking with a mouth full of water.

"I'm not sure. My job..."

"Resie, Momma's dying. Forget your job." The fear in her sister's voice rattles Teresa.

"I'll be there tomorrow." Teresa runs her hand through her hair.

"You promise?"

"I'll be there," Teresa tells her sister. She fidgets in her chair. Then sits up straight with one hand holding her forehead while the other presses her cell phone against the side of her face. Rocking back and forth, Teresa closes her eyes and lets the helplessness she feels have its way.

"What time?"

"I'm not sure. I'll call you later tonight after I've made the arrangements. Tell Momma I said bye and I'll be there soon."

Teresa ends the call before her sister can utter another word. *Tomorrow. I have my staff meetings on Fridays. Damn.* She punches the do-not-disturb button on her desk phone, gets up, and locks her office door. She sits back down and lays her head on her desk. *What the fuck am I supposed to do?* She's feeling overwhelmed. Put-upon really. Guilty too. Emotionally confused. How should she feel? Sad? Sorry?

She begins to sniff, then she blinks. Droplets pool in the crevice beneath each eye. Then the crevices fill to overflowing, then wet streams trickle down her cheeks. Minutes pass while her eyes shed what have become full-blown tears and her mind meanders in thoughtless anxiety. When Teresa finally lifts her head and wipes at the slowing stream, she urges herself to get it together: stop the self-pity and figure shit out.

"Jesse can cancel the board meeting," Teresa says out loud. A good move. It will give her more time to work on some of the other board members. Try to get her ducks lined up like Mary Ann said. That'll work. Stay in Hannibal for a couple of days. She won't be able to take Hannibal and her family longer than that. If she has to make a return trip later, so be it. She'll take a flight to St. Louis tomorrow night, rent a car, and drive up to Hannibal the next morning. She'll figure out the next step once she gets there. This will work. The knock on the door is light. Teresa swipes at her eyes. "Yes?"

"It's me," Toni says. Teresa starts to tell her to come back later but instead gets up and opens the door. Toni looks concerned once she has stepped inside and sees Teresa's face. She closes the door behind her and locks it again. Teresa walks back to her desk and sits down.

"What's going on?" Toni says.

"I'm sorry, Toni. I look like hell on wheels, to quote my momma. I just learned she's sick with cancer."

"Oh no." Toni puts her hands to her mouth.

Teresa looks at her own hands, trying to focus, trying to keep her emotions in check. No need for her and Toni to throw a pity party. Another one of Taylor Lee's memorable quotes. Teresa shakes her head and smiles.

"That's terrible news," Toni says, her eyes narrow with concern.

"Totally caught me off guard."

"What do you need me to do?" Toni asks.

"Here's the plan. I'm leaving tomorrow night. I'll ask Jesse to change the date of the board meeting for two weeks down the road. I'll be back by Tuesday, but you'll have to make sure the audit moves along."

"Don't you think you might need to stay longer than three days?" Toni says.

"Not in the plan."

Toni frowns. Teresa suspects, that to Toni's eyes, she doesn't look as confident as she's trying to sound. After crying, her face usually loses its color and little lumps dark as coals materialize under her eyes. Teresa's certain her face looks haggard and weary. It's also how she feels. She needs to go home, make her travel arrangements, and get some rest. An hour later Teresa slips on her sunglasses and leaves the office.

As she makes her way along Jackson Boulevard, headed toward the Loop, thoughts of her family and Hannibal buzz around her brain like bumblebees, irritating and intimidating. Six years have passed since Teresa's last visit. She hasn't spoken to anyone except Tisha, only four times and the last time a year ago, after Teresa cut off the flow of money from Chicago to Hannibal. The first time Tisha pleaded with Teresa for help to pay for school clothes for her kids and the second time for rent after Tisha had lost her job. The third time was after Tisha had been evicted from her apartment and had to move in with Taylor Lee, who was demanding some help with the bills. The last time Tisha called was to say she was working again, that everything was going well, to thank Teresa for the money and to promise that she wouldn't be bothering Teresa for money *ever* again.

Teresa feels a sense of shame when she remembers her sister's last call. She feels selfish. She shakes her head vigorously as if trying to dislodge that memory. When she reaches the first intersection, Teresa stops next to a bus shelter and calls the travel agency she's used in the past for trips home. She finishes making her travel arrangements and continues toward the Loop with no real destination in mind.

Teresa calls Toni to update her on the travel plans, and when the call ends, she's only a block away from Marcus. She needs to let him know about her new plans. She starts to call him but decides to pop in.

* * *

Teresa pushes through the revolving door and enters a lobby that's small and clean but unimpressive. A faint smell of fried rice lingers in the air from the adjacent Chinese restaurant. A chubby security guard, popping his fingers to hip-hop music from an unseen radio, grins and tells her to sign in. She catches the elevator to the ninth floor and steps out into the dim light of a short corridor. Inside a set of glass doors, a young woman, her hair laced with blonde streaks, looks up but doesn't smile when Teresa walks into the suite.

"Yes?"

"Is Attorney Greene in?"

"Does he know you're coming?" the young woman says while her eyes travel the length of Teresa's height.

"No, but I'm a friend. Is he in?" Teresa flashes a big smile but imagines her red eyes and washed-out complexion say something different.

"Your name?"

"Teresa."

"Teresa what?"

"Casteel."

"Okay, I'll check."

Teresa watches the young woman when she gets up from her desk and, rather than use the phone, walks behind the single wall partition, then turns left. She's shapely and attractive; her light blue blouse is cute, but her white pants seem a bit too snug.

Teresa turns her attention to the suite's decor. She likes the ambience of the space with its soothing muted light. The colors are soft and warm, the paintings lush with scenes of Black life in Chicago.

She sniffs the air and recognizes the smell of cinnamon. Being in his office adds a new dimension to her perceptions of Marcus. Offers her some additional insight into the man. She ponders the differences in the activities that animate his office and the activities that animate hers. She imagines that here there's a slower pace and less energy but a mellow atmosphere. She likes that vibe for Marcus. It fits him.

The young woman returns and beckons for Teresa to follow. They make their way through a narrow corridor where two offices occupy the wall on her right. One door is closed. And the other office door is open, but it's obvious to Teresa that it is not being used. Straight ahead Teresa can see Marcus sitting with his back to her, talking on the telephone.

"You can see he's busy," the woman tells her. They stop at the entrance to his office, and Teresa's young guide steps to the side.

"Thank you. And your name?" Teresa asks.

"Melissa."

The young woman turns and strolls back down the corridor letting her hips sway and her rump bounce. Teresa's gaze follows until Melissa turns the corner and disappears. Teresa closes the door and walks over to Marcus. When she kisses him on the nape of his neck, he looks up and smiles, then puts his hand over the phone and tells her he'll be finished in a minute. She nods and goes over to a window that has a partial view of the lake. She's impressed. The uninspiring view from her own office keeps her away from windows.

She looks down at Wabash Avenue just in time to see an el train rumble down the track. It's loud. She looks over at Marcus, who seems undisturbed by the noise. Teresa takes one of the leather guest chairs and lets her eyes roam. It's sparse but neat. Two pictures of colorful African scenes hang on one wall. There's a tall burgundy-colored bookshelf with several thick volumes on another wall and next to it a four-drawer matching file cabinet. She likes the oval-shaped table that he's using for a desk. She likes how he looks sitting there in his dark suit and red tie. *He's a handsome man*, she thinks. He turns to face her and winks.

"Don't sweat that, Mr. Bailey. You're just days away from being able to move on with your life," he says to whoever's on the other side of the call, then is quiet while he listens. He wrinkles his forehead. "You're right of course, but the kids shouldn't be made to feel as if they have to choose sides."

Marcus takes in a shallow breath and appears to hold it for seconds before releasing it into the room. "Mr. Bailey, I'm going to need you to bring in the balance of your fees ASAP," he says, his voice sterner than it had just been. He's silent for several seconds. "I know you will. See you in the morning, bright and early. Okay? Uh-huh." He is listening again.

Teresa focuses on his lips when he talks and wonders if they've ever touched Melissa's. She studies his face, now deep in concentration, and wonders if it has ever been between Melissa's legs. She rolls her eyes at the prospect. She tries not to visualize the two of them on his floor, her legs up and wrapped around his waist.

Why is her imagination playing these games? She doesn't as a general rule consider all men dogs. She hasn't as a general rule been the jealous type. Since her junior year in college when her body crossed over into full womanhood, Teresa has felt confident she can hold her own against any woman. Especially if the guy is already into her.

So why was she even giving a second thought to this cute but clearly immature receptionist? Maybe it's the intimacy of the office itself. But mostly, Teresa realizes, little saucy Melissa has a crush on Marcus, and flaunting her sexuality around this cozy little enclave could be distracting. Teresa forces herself to refocus on something else and sends her eyes roaming again. She zooms in on one of the paintings and imagines herself being in Africa and seeing the scene live that's being depicted.

"Hey, bae," Marcus says and chuckles.

"Hey, bae."

"You're a sight for sore eyes," he says and gets up and walks around the desk. She stands to meet him and sighs as her hands press against his body, its firmness evident under his suit, as they embrace. Then he kisses her. Lightly at first. Then he pulls her tightly into him, pushes his tongue past her parting lips, and probes deeply.

His hunger excites her. "So are you," she says when they finally separate and take a breath. "Glad I caught you in. Surprise."

"A beautiful sight for sore eyes," he says again, keeping her firmly pressed to him.

Does that mean your petulant little receptionist doesn't qualify? The thought bumps against her mind like an uncontrolled heartbeat, a thought she doesn't need to entertain. She's feeling way too insecure.

"As are you," Teresa says.

"My day's been hectic," he tells her.

"Am I going to meet Seleste?"

He wraps his arms tighter and squeezes. "I may have to fire her."

She takes a step back to look at him. "Really?"

"Yes."

"Because of that thing with your grandfather?" she asks.

"She's confused about who runs this place. Stormed out of a meeting this morning. She also transferred files to Fraser without my permission." He releases her and sits down in one of the guest chairs. She sits down in the one next to him.

"Stormed out? Why?" Teresa says.

"Because she felt like it."

"After all these years?"

"She obviously doesn't need this job." He releases a long hard breath.

"Do you think *she* believes her job's in jeopardy?" Teresa leans across the distance between their chairs and rubs his shoulder. She can see the stress that's settled in the space between his eyes.

"Probably doesn't. And probably doesn't think I have the cojones to fire her." He offers a sheepish grin.

"First you have to decide if you really want to."

"I can't go back to the way things were last week. We don't have the same relationship." He stands up and walks to the window. Teresa follows.

"Just don't make a rushed decision."

"I won't. Your place or mine tonight?" He takes her back into his arms and kisses her again but with less hunger and fire.

It's a tender kiss that touches her in a different place. She closes her eyes, lays her head against his shoulder and sighs. Her arms circle his waist. He wraps an arm around her back. He doesn't say anything, and she's grateful because she doesn't want to think or talk. Just feel. Resting tall and snug within his embrace and in this moment and in this place, his small corner of the world, Teresa feels like she felt that first night she lay in her own bed in her own newly purchased condo: safe, satisfied, and secure. His office phone buzzes. He doesn't move.

"You going to get that?"

"No," he says but loosens his arm.

A few seconds later, there's a brisk knock on the door. They pull apart, and Teresa sits down. By the time Missy enters the office, Marcus is standing at the desk facing the door.

"What do you need, Missy?" he says, irritation coloring his tone.

"I'm leaving. Seleste is gone too."

"Okay. See you tomorrow," he says. Teresa says good night.

Missy spins back around and is out the door. "Have fun," she says over her shoulder and closes the door behind her.

"Running your own place wouldn't be half bad if you didn't need employees," Marcus says. He moves away from the desk and sits back down in the guest chair.

"Or money," Teresa says.

He nods. "Or clients."

"Or records especially," Teresa says and laughs.

"Why are we even bothering? We're not likely to get rich, and it's a lot easier just to be an employee." Marcus looks at her and hunches his shoulders.

"And go home at the end of the day and not give it a second thought. Sounds like heaven," she says.

"So why do we bother?"

"It's our burden to bear," Teresa says and pats her chest near her heart, "and somebody's got to do it." She reaches over and strokes his leg.

"And we're among the chosen few," he says. They look at each other and grimace.

"I know," Teresa says, "but we should've run in the opposite direction."

The rumblings of another el train drift up from below and cause the windows to rattle. The sound of sirens can be heard after the train passes.

"How do you put up with that?"

"What?" he says.

She laughs and wonders how long it's taken him to get used to it all. "The noise."

"Oh," he says and shrugs.

But still, she likes his office. She likes her office. She likes the fact that he's his own man and she's her own woman. They are a good fit. And now as she sits here watching him, a handsome, successful, and educated man who's probably in love with her, Teresa wonders if they will ever get married. She doesn't know what to think about marriage, not really. Although it's never been an incessant itch driving her to distraction, there have been times in her life when she did think it might be something she wanted to do. She squeezes his leg and looks into his eyes. He leans in and gazes into her eyes.

"You okay?" he asks. "You look drained." Teresa smiles. It took him a minute but he's discovered her red eyes and pallid complexion.

"I've received some not so good news. It's why I came to see you. I just learned that my mother has cancer..."

"I'm so sorry."

"...and I need to leave out of here tomorrow."

"Is there anything I can do?" he says. She shakes her head no.

"I need to go home, pack and get some sleep."

"I'll stay with you tonight."

"Thanks. I'd like that," she says.

Eighteen

Teresa sits in the bathtub scooping up bubbles and blowing them apart. Three raspberry-scented candles light up the otherwise dark interior. She's left Marcus on the floor in front of the sofa reading her favorite novel while he waits for his turn to take a bath. Their lovemaking earlier had been more low-key than what has become their norm. More whispers than grunts and screams. For the past three hours Teresa's thoughts seldom strayed to her upcoming trip back to Hannibal. Talk of work didn't make its way into their conversation either.

She mostly talked about her books, and he asked a ton of questions. He made a list of her favorites and committed to reading all ten of them by this time next year, the anniversary date of what he called the best decision of his life, the day they met in the Loop. Teresa spreads the suds across her breasts and feels her nipples rise in response.She can't remember the exact number of days, months really, of her dry spell before Marcus. She never felt deprived even though she's always had a healthy sex drive. But Marcus is a new kind of experience.

"Hallelujah," she says softly. "But sex is sex, so this is beyond the sex. It's too strong to just be the sex. It's also a little scary." Teresa covers her eyes with the wet sponge, leans her head against the back of the tub, and takes in a long slow breath.

Marcus, Marcus, Marcus. You've definitely gotten my attention. This thought makes her laugh. *What is going on with me? Am I in love with this man?*

The question makes her shiver, and she doesn't try to answer it. She closes her eyes and lets her upper body slide down into the warm water until it's fully submerged. She inhales and savors the scent of raspberry sorbet body wash. Then she holds her breath and lowers her face until it's completely under water. *You know,* she tells herself, *it's okay to wait to exhale.* The water rushes in and chokes her when she laughs.

* * *

"I'll miss you," he says. They cuddle in her bed, unable to sleep. It's past midnight.

"I miss you already," she tells him. She rubs his bare chest and licks his nipples. He groans.

"Hope all goes well with your mother."

"My sister's a drama queen, and my mother's an attention addict, so I'm not convinced it's as bad as they make it sound."

"Whatever way it goes, I'm here for you. You know that," he says.

"While I was taking my bath, I was thinking about us. Can you see us married?"

"Huh? What?" Marcus pushes her away from him and sits up straight. "Married?" he asks, a mock frown accompanying his question.

Teresa laughs and slaps his arm. "I'm not asking you to marry me, so chill. But seriously, have you wondered about where we're headed?"

Marcus pulls her back to him. "To be honest, not really. Being a divorce lawyer and with my family history, I don't entertain fantasies about marriage. Can *you* see us married?"

"We have a lot going for us."

"Like?" he says.

"We make each other laugh. A lot. The sex, we're intense. We're both too old to keep having a ball as single, childless, well-paid success stories."

"Hmm, you may have a point. We should be racing toward lives like, uh, who exactly?" he says.

"I like *The Simpsons*," she responds.

Marcus shakes his head in disagreement. "Not *The Simpsons*. I was looking at the *Family Guy*'s marriage as our model."

"Hmm, maybe," she says.

"Or maybe *Modern Family*. They all seem sexy and happy."

"According to *their* scripts," she reminds him.

"We can write our own scripts. What would be the theme?"

"Well," Teresa says, "the Huxtables come to mind, but without four of the five kids."

"We keep Rudy, right?"

"Yes, yes, yes. She was my favorite," Teresa says and claps.

"So, is this the first time you've ever considered marriage?" he asks.

Teresa hesitates. Then leans back, cradles his chin between her thumb and forefinger. "Once. I never told you, but I came to Chicago with a guy. A college romance."

"You wanted to marry him?" He sits upright and turns to face her.

"I did before I got to Chicago. But once we got here, I knew he wasn't *the one*."

"Why?" he asks.

"As many reasons as you have for not marrying any of your gazillion women."

"Now *you* sound like a lawyer." He leans over and kisses her forehead. "For the record, gazillion is three too many. And I've never married because I, too, never found *the one*."

"So, you *have* thought about taking a relationship to the next level?" she says. "Ana?" The question surprises her. She hadn't known it was coming. They haven't spoken of Ana Teodoro since that first time at his house. But the story of Ana has never been free of her curiosity.

He reaches his arm around her head and pulls it against him. "Not Ana again. Please."

"Well, it was you who brought *Ana* to my attention. Remember? You threw *her* name at me. Not *Linda* or *Mary* or *Sharon*." Teresa turns her head and kisses his shoulder. "I think we need to clear the air of her. So, did you think about marrying her?"

Marcus drops his head, puts up his hands in surrender, and says, "I wouldn't say I wanted to marry her."

"Okay. Then tell me why she wasn't *the one*."

"Ana could be overwhelming."

"Overwhelming? In what way?"

"Uh, just overwhelming."

"Emotionally?" she says. Even as Teresa feels her pulse kick-start, her unwavering stare tells him she wants an answer.

"You could say something like that."

"Not me. What do *you* say?" Teresa softens her voice.

"Just overwhelming sometimes." Marcus throws his hands up again. "She was sexually aggressive and..."

Teresa interrupts, her voice rising a little higher. "Sex. She overwhelmed you with sex?"

"The whole thing got overwhelming," he says.

Teresa's amused by his inability to express himself. He's really uncomfortable. But this plane is already in the air. "Sex overwhelmed the relationship? How?"

"Her style was intense. I figured she must have learned that on the streets of Rio and..."

"Slow down, Marcus. I need a minute here. Her style was intense? Meaning what exactly?"

"Ana, she worked like a pro. I got caught up."

Teresa's feeling too many things at once. She feels fearful and jealous of Ana, but she also feels an urge to defend her. He had judged Ana on what he supposed was her past and found her what? Immoral? Unworthy?

"Got caught up?" she says.

"She wanted to be engaged and asked me for a ring. I got her one, but I should have realized it wasn't love; it was just sex. It was just an addiction..."

An addiction? Goddamn! What the hell did she do to you? Please shut up, Marcus, please.

Teresa knows her emotions are being hijacked by the green-eyed monster, but she feels helpless to stop it. Ana's sexual prowess, although it's beginning to effect Teresa's confidence, it is, at the same time, mesmerizing.

"...And I knew, once I had looked back on everything, that it was never going to work. I couldn't see a future with her, and so I ended it."

Teresa stares at the ceiling. Then his face. Then back at the ceiling. She's working hard to digest what he's said. But he needs to stop. To shut up.

"And I made the right decision. She wasn't *the one*," he says.

"Ana's not a thing, bae."

Teresa can feel the blood pounding the walls of the veins in her head. The sweet feminine smell of her bath oils on his skin drifts across the short distance between them, and she wonders how many baths he took with Ana, the goddess of sex. Her mind is short-circuiting. Her eyes remain staring at the ceiling with its shiny speckled swirls and circular fixture casting its dim light. Then the room becomes a blur. She blinks to clear her vision before she realizes there are tears trickling down her cheeks. *What the fuck?* is the only thought that emerges from the internal turmoil she's feeling.

Teresa closes her eyes and presses them hard trying to hold back the flood she dreads is imminent. Marcus lifts her off the bed. When she's standing, he pulls her to him, tilts her head back, and kisses her. She sags against him from the weight of her petty jealousy, the frustration caused by her unhinged behavior, and the anxiety her impending homecoming has triggered. He wraps her in his arms and holds her tight.

"You okay?" he asks.

"No, I'm not okay. I'm a mess," she tells him.

"I'm sorry," he says.

"Me too," she says. "Me too."

Teresa inhales deeply and silently counts to twenty-five. She pleads with herself to not lose control; to not let her floodgates open and release the rising tide of emotional insecurities she's now acknowledging are real. She covers her face. Add to her already chaotic emotions: embarrassment and disappointment. She can't begin to imagine what's going through this man's mind. For the next few minutes, Marcus rubs Teresa's back, then her shoulders. He strokes her hair, navigating through her damp, tangled curls.

Finally, feeling she's held on to her self-control, Teresa says, "I think it's time for me to go to bed."

"You and me both," he says.

Teresa keeps her head down and tells him, "I don't think I'd be good company right now. Do you mind?"

"You want me to go home?"

"If you don't mind," she says. "I'm feeling overwhelmed by the job, my momma's situation and my flakiness with you. I'm weary, I'm embarrassed, and I know I don't want to put all that weight on you."

"I can handle it. I understand what you must be going through."

"Maybe," Teresa says, "if you didn't have your own challenges to work through."

"Isn't this when we're supposed to show up?" he says, the irritation in his voice a cracking whip in an enclosed space.

Teresa flinches when he says this. She looks at him and says, "Let's not do this tonight." She feels like every cell in her body is ready just to go to sleep and rest.

"Let's not," he says, stepping away from her. "What time do you leave tomorrow? I'll take you to the airport."

"I've already made arrangements. I'm sorry."

"I'll come by before you leave."

"I wouldn't be much fun," she says.

"I don't expect you to entertain me."

"I'm sorry." Teresa takes a deep breath. "I'll call you in the morning. Okay?" She looks apologetic.

"I can stay the night."

"I'll call you in the morning," she says again.

* * *

It's now 9:30 a.m. the next day, and Teresa knows she needs to get up. She tossed and turned all night. Her mind couldn't rest. When her sister's call came around six o'clock, Teresa was already wide awake. Tisha wanted reassurance, so Teresa assured her sister she was leaving out today. Teresa pushes the thin cotton blanket off of her and sits upright. *What to do first?* "Oh shit," she says. "I forgot to call Jesse yesterday." She retrieves her cell and dials his office's direct line rather than his mobile phone. She's in no mood to talk to Jesse and hopes he's in a meeting as usual and won't pick up. She calls and leaves a brief message. Although she told Marcus she'd call him this morning, she's not feeling him right now, either. Maybe she'll call after she takes a shower. Teresa eases out of bed and stumbles to the bathroom. She wants to feel sorry for herself but her thoughts turn against her.

There's nothing wrong with your life, so it's got to be you. Jesse should've been a breeze. Momma's cancer. Well, you knew you'd get a call like this one day. You should've been prepared. And the way you didn't handle Marcus was pitiful. What's wrong with you?

She turns on the shower, then walks over and stands in front of the mirror. Her eyes look terrible. She lets her robe slide to the floor and steps into the shower. The warm water drenches her from head to toe as she tries to think about nothing. And after a few moments, it works.

* * *

Marcus sits with his back against the headboard. Twice during the night he found his eyes being pulled open by strange sounds in his room, but it was only his own heavy breathing and thumping heart. He eases out of bed, goes into the bathroom, turns on the shower, and brushes his teeth. The man in the mirror doesn't look as uptight as he feels. There are no wrinkles etched into his forehead despite the tension balled up inside his gut.

The whir of the exhaust fan overhead, the steady downbeat of the shower spray against the glass cage, and the muffled voices hidden inside the clock radio beside his bed make it hard to tell, but he thinks he hears his cell phone ringing. He rinses out his mouth and steps into the shower. The hot water stings his skin. He leans against the wall and lets his mind, so well-trained to break down confusion and get to the heart of the matter, go to work.

Lust, Love & Family Legacies

His thoughts wander through the debris that litters his relationship with Seleste. Her assertion that prying into her personal life was out of bounds is laughable. Making herself out to be a victim is equally disingenuous. She's clearly in counterattack mode. She can't be trusted. And Fraser, he can't be trusted either. There will be no more partnerships in their future.

And Teresa, he's not so sure about her either. She'd suckered him into running his mouth. True, he knew better but he'd taken the bait, and then she couldn't handle it. She should've known her limitations. Right? Her topsy-turvy emotions are keeping him guessing what to say and when to say it, and he's not built for that drama.

But she is dealing with the bad news about her mother, and he has to make allowances for that. Still, the way she let the situation play out bothers him, makes him feel like she can dismiss him anytime her life hits a bump in the road. Like she acknowledged, he's dealing with stuff too.

Marcus begins to feel a familiar discomfort in his chest. It first made its presence known when Kathryn disappeared. It feels like a hard knot encased in flames. Heartache is what Seleste said he was feeling then. *Heartache*. Marcus hates the sound of the word. He slips into his robe, and once back in the bedroom, he plops down on his bed and inhales. He remembers the phone might have rung and checks it. He has missed Teresa's call. When he calls back, the phone goes to voicemail. He doesn't leave a message.

* * *

Teresa's sitting on her bed with her phone in her lap when it rings. It's Jesse. He's calling from his office. She hesitates, then decides to answer.

"Hello."

"Hey, Jesse."

"I got your message. Hope the news is not too bad."

He sounds concerned. She feels a slight sense of relief.

"Well, it's my mother. She's seriously ill." Another call shows up on her phone. It's Marcus. Her stomach tightens. The anxiety is like a leech gripping her insides. She lets it go to voicemail.

"Sorry to hear that," he says.

"We need to reschedule next week's board meeting."

"Go take care of your mother. Your family is your priority right now."

"Thanks. I appreciate your concern."

After they hang up, Teresa takes in a deep breath. She hates how uptight she feels. She steps into the kitchen and pours herself a glass of wine. "This," she says, "is proof I've lost it." She manages another weak laugh. Teresa sips the wine as she surveys her closet and drawers. "I'll call Marcus after I pack," she tells the glass of wine. Then she sets the glass down and gets to work.

Thirty minutes later, she has two suitcases and a carry-on bag packed and ready to go. She takes a seat on the bed and tries to figure out what to say to Marcus. She wants to keep it simple and drama free. She wants to avoid any discussion about the night before. She doesn't need the added stress. Going home's stressful enough. *Home.* The word snuck into her thoughts yesterday from some place deep within her psyche. She hadn't thought of Hannibal as home since the day before she left. She picks up her half-empty wine glass and sips once. Then twice. Then takes a third sip that slowly seeps down her throat while she returns her lover's call.

* * *

Marcus sees it's Teresa calling.

"Hello," he says.

"Hey, yourself."

"Feeling better?" he says.

"So far so good."

"All packed?" he says.

"Two suitcases and a carry-on."

"When are you coming back?"

"A week," she says.

"I'd like to see you before you leave."

Her voice is low, almost inaudible when she says, "I know, but I wouldn't be good company." He waits for something more, but she's silent. Her place is only a fifteen-minute ride from where he stands, yet she seems much farther away.

"I'll call you later tonight."

"Okay." He sighs when she disconnects.

* * *

The limousine arrives at 4:30 p.m. The sweet smell of oranges greets Teresa as she settles into the back seat. She takes in a deep breath and exhales. The soft sounds of jazz float down from above her head. She slips off her sandals as the driver eases the car away from the curb and gets her started on the first leg of her journey. She's on her way. Teresa stares through the tinted windows and watches the frenzy of the late afternoon rush hour engulf them as they drive down Michigan Avenue.

The outside noise is muted by the limousine's thick glass windows. She broods over the friction between her and Marcus. She's made him unsure, and now she's unsure. She ponders the move that Jesse's made. He's flexing with those written demands for information, and she's not sure how to take him on. Back him off.

Both situations are like simmering embers that she's leaving behind unattended. Those simmering embers, she fears, can die out in one case and become more than just flickering flames in the other. Teresa shakes her head and wills herself to put those concerns on hold somewhere in the back of her mind. It works. She sighs again, takes another deep breath, then closes her eyes. When the car makes its way onto the expressway, the increased speed helps her relax. Being sealed inside the limo helps her embrace the illusion of being safe and insulated.

Hannibal here I come, she thinks. No matter how many bad memories the place holds for her, it's where she grew up and spent more than half her life. She wonders how she'll feel when she sees Taylor Lee. Or Tisha and Tommie and their kids. She's an aunt who doesn't know her nieces and nephews. She knew all her aunts and uncles when she was growing up. A knot finds its way inside her stomach. What does this say about her? She refuses to let that train of thought take her on an unwanted excursion. A childhood memory crosses her mind.

It's in the form of scenes from the carnival that came through Hannibal every year with its raggedy rides and cheap prizes. The whole town got up for it. Hundreds of people each day for seven days filled a narrow pathway down the center of Broadway. She remembers the fun she had trying to win dingy teddy bears or plastic knickknacks and eating cotton candy. She conjures up images of her and her friends, standing in long lines, filled with excitement, and anticipating the thrill of getting on one of those rides that took you off the ground and spun you through the air away from your routine life. The carnival had been the highlight of her summers.

The memory makes her smile. Soon her night of loving, fighting, and a restless sleep catches up with her. Her thoughts begin drifting between the sounds of jazz and the disjointed memories of her hometown. Those soon fade as her mind becomes weighed down in darkness. Then there's no more thinking when she slides into deep sleep.

* * *

Sitting in the same restaurant where he'd first seen Teresa stroll past, Marcus peers through the window at the half-empty sidewalk. Small groups of people pass by, seemingly intent on enjoying a quiet Friday evening. When Teresa strolled into that small space where his eyes had been gazing, she was there for only a split second and then was gone. He smiles at the memory. He glances back across the table at Bird, who's still talking on his cell phone. His friend's face looks strained. The weather's beautiful, and the westbound sun spills its rays on the opposite side of the avenue, leaving the restaurant window in the shadows. At a table next to him are two young women, so he shifts his body partially sideways to put the women in his peripheral line of vision. Both are blonde, attractive, and animated. They wear deep tans and short skirts that leave three quarters of their legs on display. He takes in a few furtive glances until one woman catches his eye and offers a subtle smile to let him know she's on to him. He isn't embarrassed. She turns back to her friend, and he turns back to Bird, who has finished his call.

"The boy says hi." Bird's voice lacks enthusiasm.

"How's he doing?"

"He's fine."

"And you?" Marcus says.

His friend shrugs and sits back in his seat, his eyes well-hidden behind dark sunglasses. He turns toward the window. Marcus turns and stares out too. Neither speaks again until the waiter brings their orders.

"Looks like you're really missing him."

"I'm failing as a father," Bird says.

"What?"

"I live here and he's in St. Louis. Can't parent long distance."

"You stay in his life any way you can."

"Can't bond with a kid in absentia," Bird says.

"Kids are more resilient than you think. Is he asking to see you?"

"No."

"Don't you want see him?" Marcus asks.

"He's my son."

"You need to get down there," Marcus tells him.

Bird takes off his sunglasses and begins eating. Marcus shakes his head, lets the subject drop, and thinks some more about last night. He should have been more assertive with Teresa and stayed the night. Teresa's more vulnerable than she lets on, and he needs to stop reacting to her irrational moments. She was emotionally distraught and bone weary when she lost control. Teresa needed his support even though she wasn't receptive to his offer. He promised her he would be there for her, and he needs to keep that promise.

Marcus begins to plan the logistics of a trip to Missouri. Teresa said Hannibal was about a hundred miles north of St. Louis, two hours or so by car. He can drop Bird off in St. Louis and make that short drive to Hannibal and surprise Teresa. It's something that both he and Bird need to do. They can't sit around here doing nothing and feeling impotent.

"We're going to Missouri."

"What?" Bird says.

"You need to handle your business. And so do I."

"You're going to Hannibal?" Bird says.

"That's the plan."

"Where's your invitation?" Bird says. "And for the record, I didn't get one either."

"I do what I gotta do, and so should you. Are we going or not?"

"Could both be going where we're likely to get disappointed," Bird says.

"There's only one way to find out."

* * *

Teresa is sitting in bed watching a comedy on television. It's late Saturday night, and the anxiety that clung to her like a second skin throughout the flight to St. Louis and the drive up to Hannibal has somehow fallen away. She arrived late the night before and has been in the motel all day resting and getting her head together. Tisha said that Taylor Lee's been released from the hospital and is scheduled to begin chemotherapy on Wednesday. Although they've spoken three times this morning, Tisha doesn't know Teresa's in town. Each time they spoke, Tisha chastised Teresa for reneging on her promise to come today.

The television screen begins to blur, which is a sign it's time for bed. She turns it off and tunes into a radio station playing a Beatles song. She sings along in her head until the music fades into the background and ten minutes later, she's deep into a dreamless sleep. It's 8:30 Sunday morning when Teresa opens her eyes again. She forgot to close the curtains last night and now she's blinded by the penetrating rays streaming in from a bright sun.

Her window overlooks a backside parking lot filled with mostly older vans, sedans, and pickup trucks sporting license plates from all over the Midwest. Her rental, a new black Jeep Sahara, stands out. *Good,* she thinks. It's summer and for Hannibal that means it's the tourist season. Mark Twain put Hannibal on the map, so this morning she's going sightseeing.

She is, after all, an out-of-towner now, and Teresa's more than ready to see how much has changed since she's been gone. Teresa can't wait to sink her teeth into one of those delicious maid-rites. It's the *one* thing she's missed. The thought of being this close makes her giggle. A maid-rite and a mug of root beer. The anticipation makes her stomach growl.

Teresa runs her hands through her curly locks and inhales. The musty smell of the room doesn't bother her now. She bends over her suitcases and starts separating the layers of clothes to put together her outfit for the tour. She selects a pair of cutoff blue jeans, a yellow tank top and her yellow sandals. Being back in small-town America feels surprisingly good, and it reminds her of a quote she's read somewhere that said *seeing an old world with new eyes is the same as discovering a new world.* She snaps her fingers and shakes her head in affirmation, then dances her way across the room and into the shower.

Nineteen

It is 10:00 a.m. by the time Teresa rolls out of the motel's parking lot. The temperature is heating up fast. The forecast is for a hot muggy day. The Mississippi River flows past Hannibal on the east, and the humidity at this time of the year can be stifling. A slight breeze, warm but not yet hot, blows through the open window against her face as she makes a right turn and heads toward the river.

She drives along the narrow, uneven street past familiar small one-story houses, which have been there for as long as she can remember. They look old and forlorn as they sit tilted on the ever-present hilly terrain. They could all use a little paint and some repairs. The traffic is heavy by Hannibal's standards. A host of pasty faces gawk and wave as she passes them, riding high in the Jeep, and she waves back.

Within minutes Teresa has entered the heart of downtown and makes a left off Broadway and heads up one of the innumerable hills that take you high above the river. She's walked this particular hill a million times in her life. Just over the hill, down in the valley, is her old neighborhood. It's a stone's throw away, but big bucks removed from the hilltop homes she's now passing. Homes that only white folks had been able to afford back in the day, and Teresa figures this hasn't changed much. But now, she's pleased to realize, this doesn't bother her anymore. With her salary Teresa knows she can easily afford any of these houses.

At the top of the rise, Teresa makes a right turn and passes the huge haunted mansion that stands tall beyond a concrete wall. Throughout her childhood the abandoned and scary mansion had been home to a variety of ghosts and the walking dead.

Now renovated and turned into one of the town's biggest tourist attractions, it still triggers a foreboding as she drives through its broad shadow at the crest of Hill Street. Her breath catches in her throat when the framed image of the steep drop pops into view. The decline is nearly a ninety-degree angle to the flattened bottom of the street, which is at least a city block away.

As a kid she'd run up and down this paved hill a million times without a second thought. Driving down it now makes her anxious. What if the brakes give out? Or a front tire blows? The trepidation makes her stomach churn and her breath cower inside her chest as the SUV picks up speed. The cracked pavement rushes at her, then quickly disappears under the Jeep. *This must be what it's like going down in a plane fully aware of your fate,* she thinks. It isn't until she reaches the bottom of the hill that she exhales.

Then she laughs. Teresa's missed her turn and does a full circle in the middle of the block. She notices that most of the small, dilapidated houses that used to be on each side of the street are gone. In their place stand newer, more modern structures. A white family sits on lawn chairs in front of one. "Wow," she says as she cruises past them. "Gentrification in Hannibal?" The family, all four of them, wave, and Teresa honks in response.

The area is called The Douglass Village, but she can't remember why. The neighborhood had been mostly all black, a little depressing, and the air always seemed filled with the smell of defeat. As she takes in the scene, Teresa realizes this sense of dreariness had more to do with her memories than the actual neighborhood she is driving through now. All the houses are new construction and sit on the sides of steep banks covered in dried-out grass. The place has changed. The Jeep plods up her old street, still steep, narrow and badly in need of patchwork.

All three of the old shacks she'd lived in at different times while growing up are gone. The three row houses that had been home for her family and her relatives for the first ten years of her life are also gone. They've been replaced with three single-family brick homes with a well-equipped playground nearby, where the chicken coop used to be. She sees few kids outside playing. Things have changed a lot.

Teresa spends the next half hour driving past all of her old stomping grounds. She sees several people when she passes through familiar streets but recognizes none of their faces. Several wave and wonder, she's sure, who the hell she is. Teresa smiles and waves back at every one of them. Then it's noon and she is back on Hill Street headed east toward the Mississippi. Lunch at The Dinette where a maid-rite with her name on it is waiting.

* * *

It's 12:15 Sunday afternoon, and Marcus is headed north on a rural interstate to Hannibal. He's been on the road for more than an hour and is stopped again at another light in yet another desolate-looking tiny town. He yawns. The place is so quiet. The only discernible sounds coming through the open windows are birds chirping and the barking of a dog somewhere unseen in somebody's yard. He accelerates through the intersection when the light turns green. A warm breeze stirs up when his car gains speed. It brushes against his face in soft, sweeping motions.

The smells here are different: a nauseating mixture of manure, grass and trees. Marcus is in and out of the place in less than a minute. Since he's left the St. Louis area, people seem to have disappeared. This is a different experience for him, traveling through these long, empty expanses of highway with nothing to interrupt the monotony but crop fields, farmhouses, animals, and machinery. These endless acres of fields leave him feeling alone and vulnerable. At the same time, being surrounded by such isolation, he also feels an abiding sense of tranquility.

Marcus speeds along at sixty miles an hour accompanied only by the solitude of the gray narrow strip of highway. He's gotten comfortable with the two-lane road because the traffic coming his way has been light. He hasn't turned on the radio or the CD player. The sign shooting past on his right says the next town is twenty miles ahead. He doesn't know what he'll do once he gets to Hannibal.

He hasn't talked with Teresa since Friday. She hasn't called him, and he's avoided calling her. But Marcus knows he should talk with Teresa before he gets there. He pulls to the side of the highway and parks on a patch of grass and gravel. Then makes the call. His cell rings twice, and then her voice comes through the phone speaker and fills the car.

"Hello."

"Hey," he says.

"I miss you."

"I miss you too." His smile is instant; his heart celebrates without reservation.

"How are you?" she asks.

"Fine now. And you?"

"Fine now too," she says.

He enjoys hearing her voice coming through the phone like music on the radio and imagining the grin lighting up her face because he's called. He longs for the feel of her heat. Several seconds pass in silence, but there is no awkwardness.

"I haven't seen my family yet," she says.

"No?"

"I wasn't ready. I needed some time to rest. I was a basket case. But you know that." Her laugh is soft. It's her apology.

"We both were a little edgy," he tells her.

"I was the worst."

"You're staying at a hotel?" he says.

She laughs. "No hotels here," she says, "The Hannibal Mark Twain Motel on the outskirts of town on the other side of town from where they live. Didn't want to run into any of my family before I'm ready."

"What would you do if I showed up?"

"I'd make you glad you did."

"Then maybe I will."

"Then maybe you'd regret it once you got here. This is not your cup of tea, city boy," she says.

"You're my cup of tea, no matter where you are."

"You and your pretty talk."

"What are you doing?" he says.

"I'm in heaven. I just ordered my maid-rites and root beer."

"At last?"

"Yep."

"And after you finish?"

"Back to the motel until later in the evening about six, then go see the family."

"I'd love to meet your family."

"It's a deal. Let's say in ten years." She laughs.

"They'll love me," he says.

"That's not my concern. I'm sure you'd charm the heck out of them. It's about what they might do to your opinion of me."

"It can't be that bad."

"Well, we'll see in 2020," she says.

"I can't wait that long. You know me when I want to meet people." They both laugh. He sits back in the low-slung seat and starts the engine.

"Where are you going? You're driving?" Teresa says.

"I'm about to head into the parking garage. I have a meeting scheduled, but I'll call you later this afternoon before you hook up with your family."

"Okay," she says. "I'll be waiting."

* * *

Teresa had just taken the maid-rite off the tray, unwrapped it, and is about to take a big bite when the cell rings and startles her. She snatches the phone off the car seat thinking its Marcus calling back. It's not. It's Tisha.

"Where are you at?" her sister asks.

"In St. Louis. Getting on the road about two-thirty this afternoon. I had to see someone."

"Who?" Tisha asks.

"A college friend."

"When are you getting *here*?" Tisha's voice doesn't sound as frantic.

Teresa looks at the phone clock. It's 12:45. "I'll be in by five o'clock or so, and after I check in, I'll be over. Say about seven tonight. How's Momma?"

"Raising heck like she ain't sick and mostly complaining about your behind taking your sweet time getting here. Saying she could a died and gone to the devil by the time your slow self gets here. I got to save my minutes, so call me when you get in." Tisha hangs up.

Teresa knows Taylor Lee was ranting more than complaining, with most of it laced with more spice than Tisha's rendition. She glances at the time on her phone, sets the phone back on the passenger's seat, and stretches. *He made the call I should have made*, she thinks. Still, Teresa's glad he did. In fact, she's excited by it. Teresa finishes her maid-rite combo and heads back to the motel. She wants to take a shower, catch a quick nap, and be ready for the big family reunion.

The motel has digital cable with a bunch of stations, and it's been a luxurious indulgence Teresa's denied herself back in Chicago. A rerun of a sitcom is airing, and she uses it as background noise while she lies back and thinks. Her thoughts drift back and forth between Marcus and her family. Now that she's here and given herself time to get reacquainted with her hometown, she feels more at ease. She will be gracious with her family and sensitive to Taylor Lee's situation. Teresa's brought $1,500 in cash to give away but only on her terms.

After the show ends, Teresa makes her way to the shower. Ten minutes later, she sets the alarm on her phone for two hours, turns on her side with a pillow between her legs, and waits to drift off into a needed slumber. When the alarm goes off, Teresa sits upright, yawns, and then stretches. She is still groggy and blames it on an unrestful sleep. That is until her stomach starts growling. That one maid-rite, small order of onion rings, and root beer haven't been enough. Teresa puts on the new pantsuit she recently bought and decides to eat again before hooking up with her family.

The only restaurant in the motel had some pretty tasty food, so that's where she'll go. She leaves the room with her cell phone snug in her hand. As Teresa makes her way through the narrow corridor toward the elevator, there's a small group already there waiting. When her phone begins to vibrate and Teresa sees that it's Marcus, she walks past the elevator to take the stairs. The phone continues to vibrate in her hand, but Teresa doesn't answer until she reaches the landing on the next floor, where she can be alone. She sits on the ledge of a window overlooking an open field covered in dry grass and takes the call.

"Hello, handsome."

"Still missing me?"

"You know I am," she says.

"Tell me anyway."

"I miss you Marcus G. Greene. More than you realize and more than I imagined," she tells him in a soft, whispery tone.

"What are you doing this very moment?"

She smiles. "I'm in a stairwell headed down to the lobby to the restaurant."

"Picture me waiting down in the lobby for you and looking like the happiest man in the world."

She closes her eyes. "I see your cute self. That too-tight blue tank top, those tacky khaki shorts, and those ugly sandals. Still, I wish you *were* here."

"What are you wearing?"

"A white pantsuit, no bra, and white sandals."

"Ah, I can see you," he says.

The call disconnects. "Damn," she says. Teresa gazes out the window and waits for Marcus to call back. Several minutes pass but no call. Frowning, she turns from the window and continues down the stairs.

* * *

Marcus is perched on a small couch next to the motel's front desk near the entrance. He's been sitting here, legs crossed, and ignoring the stream of white faces staring at him as they pass by heading for the exit while he talked with Teresa. The restaurant is across from his position but not directly. From this vantage point, he should see Teresa when she enters the establishment. She'll stand out like a red dress in a black-and-white photo. He hasn't seen another Black person yet.

He looks among and between the guests milling about. His eyes dart from left to right with anticipation. What will she do when she sees him? Run to him, arms spread wide, shock and surprise written all over her face? Or will she stand there amid the crowd, unable to move and shout out his name? Maybe she'll walk over to him, cool and unaffected, and ask what he's doing here.

He couldn't handle that. Maybe he should move over to the side and approach her as she walks pass. Ease up to her and whisper *it's me* in her ear. When she turns, he'll pull her to him and kiss her before she can react, before she has a chance to hurt his feelings. Marcus gets up, walks past the front desk toward the pool area. Just past the front desk is a doorway with a small enclave. It offers a concealed position nearly directly across from the restaurant. It's the entrance to the men's restroom. Depending on how she responds, it might be the appropriate place for him to run and hide. He leans against the wall and waits.

* * *

Teresa strolls through the damp and noisy pool area like she owns the place. To her continued surprise, many of the white faces, when she breezes past, offer smiles or nods. Several are quick to speak. But, of course, none of these folks live in Hannibal, so that may explain their civility. Or things have changed more than she imagined they had. Or her memory is flawed and things were never as bad as she led herself to believe.

Instead of turning right and heading through the lobby to the front entrance of the restaurant, she keeps straight and enters it from the back door. Despite the crowd in the pool area, the restaurant has plenty of open tables available. It doesn't possess an extraordinary ambience, but it's clean. She spots a small table near the wall of glass that borders the lobby across from the motel's front desk.

She lays down her phone and picks up a menu. Her curious eyes leave the menu to take in the scene on the other side of the transparent wall. There's a steady stream of people making their way toward the motel's front entrance. Teresa studies their animated faces as they float past, headed for a day of muggy heat and unhurried sightseeing. She continues to scan the crowd, now almost looking without seeing.

Then she discovers it, another Black face, a man, off to the side, out of the way of the human traffic heading for the exit. Her line of vision is disrupted by a large group of adults struggling with several small children as they drift past. She finds herself leaning and straining against the glass. From where she sits, he looks a lot like Marcus. She scoots her chair a little to the right, where she can get a better view.

* * *

He strains his neck to see over the heads of the people streaming by or just standing around blocking his view. She should be coming through by now. Maybe she went back to the room for something. She must have gone back to her room. He pulls out his cell phone and calls her. Then disconnects. *Patience,* he thinks. *Don't spoil the surprise.* He decides to move. He steps away from the enclave's entrance and back into the lobby. His phone rings.

"Hey," he says.

"Marcus?" It doesn't sound like a question as much as a revelation.

"What are you doing?" he asks.

Teresa's behind him now and touches his arm. "I'm dreaming," she says.

He turns. She grabs him by the front of his shirt and pulls him to her. Her lips press against his lips. He looks at her with wide eyes. She's appeared out of nowhere. He's startled at first, then bewildered. His heart's racing. His mind goes blank, and his body stiffens as if paralyzed. Teresa steps back. She caresses his face. Her eyes are misty. And then she melts back into him. Her mouth is hungry and insistent. It encircles his lips, then pries them apart.

He holds back, inhibited by the gawking people surrounding them. He stares at her intense face with its furrowed brow. She doesn't care about anybody else, doesn't see anybody else. Only him. In that moment, the full force of the love he feels for this woman takes over. He closes his eyes, and the crowd disappears. The inhibitions slip away. They cling to each other and kiss without regard to time or place.

He hears nothing but their breathing. His hands begin to roam: her head, her shoulders, and down her back. Then she pulls away. She looks at him. She surveys the colorless faces with their bold eyes trained on them. Then she laughs and buries her own face in his neck, her laughter vibrating against his skin. Soon he feels the wetness of her tears, then he feels his own rolling down his cheeks and into her hair.

* * *

We need to stop being a tourist attraction, Teresa thinks and pulls away again, shocked to see tears trailing down his cheeks. Grabbing his hand and pulling him along behind her, she edges past the dozens of pale faces, unrepentant and unashamed, who meet her stare with clumsy smiles. They take the stairs and stop on the second-floor landing. Teresa pulls him to her. His eyes are red. His lip curls up on one side. Marcus looks over her shoulder out the window behind her. She understands this is a moment of vulnerability for him.

But for her it is a moment of truth. She places her fingers against his cheeks and guides his lips to hers. She keeps her eyes open and stares deep into his. It's a light kiss, but it's heavy with promises being made. She wipes the corner of his eyes. He attempts to smile. She pulls him to her, and they hug. Minutes pass in silence. She feels his arms tighten around her waist. The concerns of a few days ago have faded. She loves him. He loves her. They are a couple. She eases his arms from around her waist and steps back.

"I love you," she whispers.

"I love you too."

"I missed you," Teresa says. Her eyes glisten, still wet from the tears of joy she's shed at seeing him here in Hannibal, in the motel and within arm's reach of her touch.

"Me too," he says.

"I'm sorry about everything."

"It doesn't matter now." He kisses her forehead.

"No, it doesn't," she says, taking his hand.

"You look so good," he says.

"You too."

"I had to come," he tells her.

"I couldn't believe it was you."

"I wasn't sure how you'd react," he says.

"I still think I'm dreaming." She strokes his face. "You are really here?"

"I am. In the flesh. And that's a good thing, right?"

"That's a great thing," she says, the tears welling up again and then sliding down her cheeks.

* * *

It's early evening and they're on their way to see Teresa's family. He's feeling relaxed and feeling like all is right with the world. Sitting beside Teresa watching the Hannibal landscape unfold around them.

"Am I ready for your family?" he says.

"More specifically, are you ready for Taylor Lee?"

"How can I get ready?"

"By understanding she carries the mark of the beast."

"What's that?" he asks. Teresa laughs.

"No Sunday school for you?"

"Oh, a religious thing. Nope. I grew up in a house of nonbelievers."

"I don't know about God, but I know there's a devil, and her name is Taylor Lee Casteel."

"That's pretty harsh," Marcus says.

"Oh really? My momma didn't like her middle name. Loathed it. Despised it. Cursed her momma out for putting it on her birth certificate. So, can you guess what she did?"

"Legally had it changed?" he says.

"Oh, you little innocent. Nope. Her revenge was to saddle every one of her kids with the name. That tell you anything?" Teresa shakes her head.

"Your middle name is Lee?"

"Thomas Lee. Teresa Lee. Tisha Lee. See what you're up against?" she says.

"I think it's cute," he says.

"Oh, you poor little dove."

"What's the worst that can happen?" he says.

"That my whole family's been converted."

"I see you're really looking forward to this," he says. "It'll be fine."

"When I say run, don't jog."

"You can't scare me," he says and laughs.

Twenty

Her family lives in a recently built subsidized housing complex on the outskirts of the town, near the high school. Tisha, her four kids, and Thomas, all live with Taylor Lee in the three-bedroom duplex. After making a left turn onto a winding street, the dark faces start appearing as if by magic. They continue along the curving street until the buildings come into view. "Here we are," Teresa says. "If you don't look too closely, it reminds you of a middle-class subdivision."

But only from a distance. Teresa remembers the first time she saw this complex, the last time she'd been back home, was right after they were built and her family moved in. Green grass, freshly painted exteriors, and few tenants. But based on the updates Tisha has shared with her over the intervening years, things had changed. She can see what Tisha meant. There's little grass to keep the dust down as hordes of small children tramp through the front yards of the brightly colored duplexes.

"There's my family estate just ahead and to the right." Teresa pulls onto a side street and enters a parking lot filled with older cars and trucks. Most are damaged and rusted. "Well, it's showtime, Mr. Greene." She leans over and kisses him. The anxiety she's managed to tamp down for the past three days is reemerging and fast. It's been six years since she's seen or talked with Taylor Lee. Now she'll be facing a woman suffering from cancer and may be dying. Teresa isn't sure how to feel about her mother's condition. Taylor Lee's a woman whose own sympathy and compassion for others couldn't fill a thimble, let alone a human heart. Teresa lays her head against Marcus for a brief second, then sits upright and sighs.

"Let's go," she says.

"I'm ready."

"You think?" she says. "Ah, you poor sacrificial lamb. When they interrogate you, expect handcuffs, a blindfold, and sharp instruments with electrical cords to make you spill the beans on us."

"Now I'm scared."

They both laugh as they climb down out of the Jeep and make their way to the sidewalk. It curves in a semicircle in front of rows of duplexes. The one Teresa points at is colored a dingy blue, and its brick façade pockmarked and badly in need of tuck pointing. Teresa doesn't realize she's grasping his hand in a death grip until Marcus pries it loose and assures her he isn't about to turn tail and run.

"Sorry," she whispers. Turning on to the short cement path leading up to Taylor Lee's duplex, Teresa clears her throat as she prepares to greet two young girls sitting in chairs near the front door.

"Hello," she says.

"Are you Auntie Resie?" It's the smaller girl in a short green sundress who asks.

"Yes, I believe I am. And which of my nieces are you?"

The girl jumps up, runs over, and hugs her. "I'm Willa."

The taller girl joins them and says, "My name's Samantha." She's wearing a short yellow sundress. Both girls have their hair done in long braids, and Teresa wonders if it's all their hair or extensions. Neither Taylor Lee nor Tisha nor she have ever had hair that long. Both girls' teeth are a bit crooked but white, and their smiles make Teresa smile.

A shout comes from inside the apartment. "It's Resie. Momma, Resie's here." The door swings open; Tisha runs out and barges between her daughters and gives Teresa a big bear hug. "You finally made it," she says. Tisha's the same height as Teresa but heavier than Teresa remembers. She's put on at least fifteen pounds. She's wearing a burgundy sundress similar to her daughters' but not as short.

"You've grown some hips," Teresa says as they separate.

"Hey, girl." The voice is weak and comes from behind the screen door. "Glad you made it." Taylor Lee pushes open the door and shuffles outside.

"Hey, yourself." *Wow,* Teresa thinks, looking Taylor Lee up and down. *She's lost weight. A lot of weight.*

Taylor Lee's head is wrapped tightly in a red and white scarf. It covers her like new skin. Tisha had already warned Teresa that Taylor Lee had shaved her head because she didn't want to wait for it to fall out. Her blue jeans are wrinkled and a bit too short. Her white T-shirt is also wrinkled, and her breasts, without a bra underneath to stop them from sagging, are almost kissing her navel. Her brown sandals are new and cute, but her feet could use some lotion.

When Teresa, arms outstretched, takes a step toward her, Taylor Lee takes a step back and doesn't extend her own arms. Teresa stops short. Neither one says anything else. Then with all the awkwardness Teresa had hoped to avoid, she and her mother stand there in silence, just a foot apart, and look at each other.

"My name's Marcus." In their excitement to see Teresa, they haven't focused on him, but now he's a magnet that draws everyone's full attention.

"Resie didn't tell us she was bringing no man. I'm Tish, her baby sister. This is Samantha, my oldest daughter. She's twelve, and this is my younger daughter, Willa, and she's ten. And this is our mother, Miss Casteel."

Each of the girls makes direct eye contact, offers up a sheepish smile, and says hello. Marcus gives Tisha and her daughters brief embraces and then turns to Taylor Lee and says, "I hope you're feeling better." He avoids attempting to put an arm around her, given that he's just witnessed Teresa's failed attempt.

"I could be better, but I ain't complaining. Come on in out of this hot sun." The forlorn look Taylor Lee sported, when she first stepped outside, vanishes behind a broad smile. Teresa reaches for Marcus, but each of her nieces grabs each of her arms and holds on tight as they all follow Taylor Lee inside.

The apartment's neat and clean. There's even a vase of yellow flowers on the small rectangular coffee table in front of the couch, and the small air conditioner in the window keeps the interior much cooler than outside. Teresa is pleasantly surprised because she's expected the same disheveled and cluttered mess that characterized all the places she remembers from her childhood and adolescent years living under Taylor Lee's roofs.

"Tommie and the boys went to get some pizza and fried chicken," Tisha says, and she takes his hand and leads Marcus to the couch. Teresa slides down next to him before Tisha can plop her burgeoning butt there. Taylor Lee takes the chair across from the couch, while the girls sit on the floor at opposite ends of the coffee table and stare at their aunt and her boyfriend.

"Teresa Lee doesn't tell us nothing, Marcus. How long you two been seeing each other?" Taylor Lee asks.

"Not real long, Momma."

"See what I mean? That wasn't answering my question." Taylor Lee rolls her eyes.

"We met a few weeks ago," Marcus says.

Taylor Lee eases forward in her seat. Marcus unconsciously leans backward, then looks at Teresa who turns her eyes away and begins to chuckle. He should've left well enough alone. Teresa crosses her legs, slowly folds her arms across her chest and winks at Tisha.

"We ran into each other downtown in the Loop. You've never been to Chicago, right?"

Taylor Lee coughs before she says, "I've never been invited, but I hope to see it someday before I die."

"Momma starts," Tisha's voice trembles and she pauses. "Momma starts chemotherapy Wednesday."

"How are you feeling?" Teresa asks.

"I got out the bed just to see you all," Taylor Lee says. "I've been in bed for the last two weeks. You know, I'm *really* sick. Tisha Lee thinks I'm dying."

"What's your doctor saying?" Teresa asks.

"There's a spot on Momma's lung, but they won't operate," Tisha says.

"They claim the chemo will work, but I don't know. Miss Ruth—that was our neighbor, Marcus—she died of lung cancer last year. Chemo didn't work so well for her," Taylor Lee says, then rolls her eyes.

"I told Momma we need to get a fourth opinion."

"You've gotten three opinions?" Teresa says, looking at Taylor Lee.

Tisha answers before Taylor Lee can. "It's cancer and they won't take it out."

"What did the doctors say?" Teresa tries to feel some sympathy for Taylor Lee but feels no emotion at all. Not fear or sympathy or sadness. Not even pity.

"Not much that I could understand," Taylor Lee says. "They looked inside, said it was bad, and now they're going to try to kill it by filling me full of chemicals. But they'll probably kill me before they kill the goddamn cancer." Taylor Lee moves her bloodshot eyes over the five faces in the room before she leans back and closes them.

"Momma, stop. You're scaring the girls," Tisha says. "Go on outside, you two. Aunt Resie's not leaving anytime soon." The two girls stand, step over Tisha and Marcus to give Teresa another big hug, and then they scurry out the door.

"They've done a bunch of tests," Tisha says, "but I don't trust them. White doctors don't care about us. They have Black doctors in St. Louis. We need to get Momma down there."

Teresa shakes her head. "Tests are tests, sis."

"I'm feeling a little better now that my long-lost child has come home to see me before it's too late." Taylor Lee coughs again.

Teresa stands and crosses the few steps to Taylor Lee. She leans toward her mother, who leans back but can't go far enough to avoid her daughter's kiss on the forehead. "You'll be fine, Momma. Just do what the doctors tell you. They're the professionals." Teresa straightens and turns to Marcus. "Want something to drink?"

"Pop, beer, and Kool-Aid," Tisha says, jumping up and heading to the kitchen. "What will you all be having?"

"Kool-Aid for me," Marcus says. "Haven't had that since I was a kid."

"Make that two, little sis. In fact, let me help you." Teresa pecks her mother on the cheek before Taylor Lee can react, then follows Tisha into the kitchen.

"Marcus, I could use some help with the stairs. I need to get back in bed. I've been up for three hours waiting on you all."

Marcus stands and makes his way over to Taylor Lee, lifts her out of the chair and into his arms. Teresa steps back into the room after hearing how fast Taylor Lee's become weak and helpless, and marvels at how easily she includes Marcus on the list of people who owe her something. Tisha steps back into the room too and says, "Don't spoil her 'cause nobody else here is strong enough to carry her around like that."

"Where to?" Marcus asks.

"This way," Tisha says. Marcus pulls Taylor Lee tight against his chest. Tisha giggles as she leads the trio upstairs to the second floor where three small bedrooms and one full bath fills the space. Teresa brings up the rear, shaking her head and thinking, *He's good. I see why I made that call that night.* The upstairs is as neat and clean as the downstairs. Tisha leads them to a bedroom door at the end of the hallway. Once inside the room, Marcus lowers Taylor Lee onto her bed.

She lets a soft moan escape from between her full lips and says, "There was no need for you to do all this." Marcus smiles and pulls the light sheet over her legs. Taylor Lee grins. Teresa's appreciation for him takes on an added dimension after witnessing this taming of the shrew. Taylor Lee curls up in a fetal position and tucks a pillow between her knees and yawns. "Wake me up in an hour, Tisha Lee," she says.

"Okay, Momma."

The three of them leave the room, and Tisha gives a tour of the other second-level rooms. In a second bedroom are one twin bed and a bunk bed that Tisha explains is her and the two girls' room. The third bedroom has two twin beds and is where the boys claim their share of the duplex. Tisha explains that Thomas has a bedroom on the first floor that was meant to be a dining room.

After the brief tour of both the upstairs and the rest of the first floor, the three of them settle back down in the living room. The sisters sit on the couch, while Marcus lowers himself to the floor between them and slides his long legs under the coffee table. The sisters spend the next half hour talking about the duplex, the subdivision, and Hannibal in general.

"Whose new black Jeep sitting pretty in the lot?" It's Thomas with his two nephews blowing through the front door. "Come here and give big brother a big hug." He's thinner than Teresa remembers but looks dapper in his khaki pants, tan long-sleeved V-neck shirt, and a red Cardinals baseball hat. He strolls across the room, steps between the small table and couch, forcing Marcus to stand up to avoid the combat boots being slung through the small space.

"Hey, Tommie," Teresa says, her voice strained from the pressure of his embrace. He yanks her away from the couch and twirls her around until her feet come off the floor. He puts her down and yells to his nephews, who have taken the food to the kitchen, to come and meet their auntie. They shuffle over to Teresa, each one encircles her waist gingerly, then they stumble away.

The taller one is about Teresa's height and darker than any of the other family members. His hair's cut in a stylish fade. The other nephew is reed thin, has hair that's bushy and unkempt but a smile that beams. Teresa loves him already. Thomas reminds her that the tall one is fourteen-year-old Eddie, and her shorter, thinner nephew is Damon, who's thirteen. They're both handsome but don't resemble Tisha or each other. Before Teresa can introduce Marcus, Thomas is all over him.

"I'm Tommie, Resie's big bro. And you?"

"Marcus Greene." They shake hands.

"Glad to make your acquaintance. These are my nephews Eddie and Damon." Both boys extend their hands, and Eddie executes a two-hand-up-and-down shake while Damon does a quick squeeze. Thomas pats Marcus on the back, then says, "Hey, let's eat before all this delicious food gets cold. Where's Momma?"

"She's sleeping," Tisha says.

"Good," he says and heads into the kitchen. Teresa hears the door open again and turns to see her nieces bumping into each other as they try to get through the doorway at the same time.

"We saw the food," Samantha says.

They all pile into the small kitchen. The adults let the youngsters go first, after Tisha prepares a plate for Taylor Lee and wraps it in aluminum foil. Teresa studies her nephews and nieces while they go about the business of filling their plates. She's thankful the four of them are nothing like the kids who lived in her imagination: the truant ones destined for bleak futures. And she's flattered by their attention. While the younger family members prepare their plates, Eddie asks Teresa about Chicago. All four hang on to her every word. Teresa describes the skyscrapers, the el trains, and the lake. She exaggerates the hugeness of the city as being two hundred times bigger than Hannibal and compares the diversity of the city to the United Nations, with all its different ethnic groups, and to her delight, Eddie knows about the United Nations.

Teresa tells them that Chicago has a lot of Black people who own businesses, are lawyers and doctors, and live in wealthy neighborhoods. She tries to be modest when they ask about her job, her house, and her car, but she also feels compelled to brag in subtle ways. When she's finished, only Thomas seems indifferent to what she's said. After the kids have filled their plates and gone into the living room to eat, the adults take their turns and take a seat at the small kitchen table.

"Hey, bro, you wanna see Hannibal's popping nightlife?" Thomas says.

"Sure. Why not?" Marcus glances in Teresa's direction, and she's shaking her head, telling him to decline the invite.

Tisha snorts at the invitation. "Marcus, we've got one joint for Black folks, and it's not really legal."

"It's the only gathering place open on Sundays," Thomas tells Marcus, "and it's an open secret as long as hard liquor isn't sold."

"It's raggedy and everybody and their mommas pack the place. Hoodlums and dope peddlers included. You all don't need to be hanging out there," Tisha says.

"Marcus, you sure?" Teresa says.

"Womenfolk," Thomas says. "It's safe, bro."

"I'll check it out," Marcus tells Teresa.

"Everybody knows everybody, and the authorities don't hassle. Our only Black policeman drops by all the time." Thomas winks at Marcus, then laughs, picks up a slice of pizza, and takes a big bite. "Good to see you're your own man." Teresa glances at Marcus and raises her eyebrows but says nothing.

After everyone has eaten, Thomas and Marcus stay in the kitchen discussing sports, the boys go back outside, and Teresa follows Tisha and the girls into the living room. Teresa takes a seat on the couch next to her sister, and her two nieces sit on the floor, arms on the coffee table, facing the two women. For the next fifteen minutes, Tisha shares the latest family news and gossip. Two updates make Teresa gasp.

Taylor Lee's sister, Willa Mae, who lives in Bowling Green down the highway, lost a leg to diabetes. Taylor Lee's other sister, Beth Ida, who lives in Quincy across the river, has at the age of fifty-eight taken on a nineteen-year-old boyfriend. The rest of the updates are interesting but not surprising. Most of their cousins are lost and confused and making a mess of their lives as far as Teresa's concerned. Tisha, on the other hand, finds their problems amusing if she likes them or feels they got what they deserved if she doesn't.

"Where's Geraldine?" Teresa asks. "I expected to see her big butt sitting up under the family like always."

"Oh, that's right. I forgot to tell you. She's gone. Got ran out of town 'bout a year ago."

"Ran out of town? By who?" Teresa says.

"Momma."

"Say what?" Teresa frowns at her sister. "Spill the beans, girl."

Tisha glances at the stairs that lead to the second floor, lowers her voice, and says, "Some truck driver from Georgia came through on his way back home from Michigan and somehow hooked up with Geraldine and stayed for about two weeks." Tisha looks disgusted. The girls don't seem bothered.

Teresa's flabbergasted. She puts her hand over her mouth to stifle a laugh as she turns to face her sister. "She messed around with a man? You've got to be kidding."

Tisha glances again in the direction of the stairs, then says, "I know, right? But Momma didn't know, and she and Geraldine were still together. Then Gracie busybody calls Momma up and tells her about Geraldine and the trucker."

Teresa interrupts. "Lord have mercy."

"At first Momma acted like she didn't believe Gracie. Called her a lying two-faced nappy-headed B-I-T-C-H. And then just went on a rant after she slammed the phone down. But then she started calling Geraldine all kinds of nasty-name fools. Said she was tired of being a D-Y-K-E anyway and was gonna get herself a man too."

Teresa sits, unable to react. She isn't sure whether to laugh or cry but says to Tisha, "And then?"

"And then a couple days later, she goes and spies on Geraldine. Has Tommie to borrow Stanley Jackson's car..."

"Stanley Jackson moved back here?" Teresa says.

"Sure did about two years ago. Had a drug problem, and they discharged him from the service."

"Not straight-'A', going places Stanley?" Teresa shakes her head in disbelief.

"He told Tommie the Navy was the problem. Had them out in the ocean for months at a time and somebody always had good dope."

"That's really too bad," Teresa says.

"Anyway, Tommie and Momma trail Geraldine, and she leads them right to the motel where the trucker's staying. Momma tells Tommie to park near the truck and wait. Tommie said they waited for four hours before the trucker and Geraldine came out. Tommie said Momma wanted to tell the trucker about her and Geraldine and see if he'd still be interested. But the two lovebirds came out all hugged up and kissing. Tommie said Momma went ape S-H-I-T."

"Stop, Tish. I need a second," Teresa says. She knows now it's clearly going to be laughter rather than tears. "Okay. I'm ready."

"So, Momma jumps outta Stanley's car, runs to the side Geraldine's on, and pulls her out of the truck and starts pulling her hair and slapping her around. Then starts punching her. Beats her up pretty bad. Tommie says Geraldine's lover just stayed in the truck hollering for Momma to stop and for Geraldine to hop in."

"Whoa, slow down. So, Tommie didn't do anything either?" Teresa says.

"He claims he tried to grab Momma when she opened the car door, but she moved too fast. And once she had Geraldine, he knew it was too late."

"Tommie just like messes," Teresa says, but if her nieces weren't sitting there, she would've said that Tommie probably egged that shit on.

"I asked him why he drove Momma there in the first place, and he didn't say anything that made sense. Anyway, Tommie said Geraldine had two busted lips and a black eye. Her head looked like it was growing an egg, and he's sure there was rib damage the way Geraldine was holding her sides after Momma left her slumped against the truck. He said the trucker never got out."

"He said Momma pulled Geraldine on her feet and helped her get back in the truck. Told her she'd better roll when the trucker did or there'd be more where that A-S-S whooping came from. So, everybody thinks that Geraldine took Momma's advice because she hasn't been seen since a week after that happened." Tisha took a deep breath and kept her eyes on Teresa when she finished.

"So, let me get this straight. Geraldine, Momma's lover since forever, got caught sneaking around on her *woman* with some truck-driving *man*, got her behind whooped for it, and Momma ran her out of town."

"Right," Tisha says, glancing toward the stairs again. "And Momma's been with Bailey King—you remember him, the chubby guy who rode the ice cream truck in the summertime—ever since."

"Big Belly Bailey?" Teresa's self-control can no longer contain the laughter that's built up. She falls back against the couch and wraps her arms around herself. The girls are laughing too. The men come out of the kitchen to see what the commotion's all about.

"You all out here talking about us?" Thomas says.

Tears are streaming down Teresa's cheeks. Her nieces have their heads buried in their arms across the table.

"Nobody's worrying about you, boy," Tisha says. "Resie's just being silly."

"Well, me and Marcus are heading on out. Sure you don't want to join us, sis? Might see a few folks you knew back in the day. They're always asking about you."

Teresa fights hard to regain her composure. "I'm not hanging out at that tavern with you," she says with a hint of laughter still in her voice, "and, Marcus, you might want to *run* about now." Despite her best efforts, Teresa can't contain the laughter. Marcus looks at her, as if uncertain, then at Thomas.

"She's laughing at something I told her, Marcus," Tisha says, then looks at Thomas. "I told her about Geraldine." Thomas snickers. Marcus looks confused.

"Tommie, take care of my man," Teresa says as she swipes at the tears still clinging to her cheeks.

"You heard the woman, Tommie. You better take care of her man," Tisha says, pointing a finger at her brother. "And don't let him get you in no mess, Marcus."

"No, ma'am," Marcus says, then leans over and kisses both Tisha and Teresa on their cheeks. "No messes."

"I've got this, people," Thomas says. "Let's roll, bro. You got the keys to the Jeep?"

Eddie leans through the front doorway and says to Tisha, "Damon and I are going over to Ronnie's."

"Fine, but have your tails back in here by eleven o'clock." Tisha points a finger at him for emphasis.

Teresa looks on in admiration at Tisha whose soft but firm voice holds her son's attention. Teresa silently reprimands herself for not giving her family the benefit of the doubt. They aren't the same people she's held captive in her memories. She likes *this* family. Even Taylor Lee's tolerable. Soon the men are gone. The girls leave a short time later, after Tisha reminds them that their curfew is ten o'clock. Teresa and her sister move down from the couch to the floor.

"When are you leaving?" Tisha asks.

"I'll be here a few days."

"I'm glad. Momma said you'd be in and out so fast you wouldn't have time to take a crap."

"Well, Momma's been wrong about a lot of things."

"Like Geraldine?" Tisha laughs.

"Stop it. My heart can't take it," Teresa says, then bites her lower lip.

"I'm so glad you're home. We all miss you."

"You've done a wonderful job with your kids. They're great."

"Yeah, but it's been rough. Not one of their daddies is helping me."

"You take them to court?"

"No, cause none of them have a job or money, and they have other kids. Sometimes I think I'm as bad as Momma."

Teresa swallows a mouthful of questions. But she knows the answers don't reside in her sister's mind but somewhere deeper in Tisha's psyche beyond her sister's reach. She also needs to stop being so judgmental. Teresa vows to be a better sister today and going forward. Far better than she'd been yesterday and as far back as she can remember.

"These men in Hannibal are real catches," Teresa says. They both laugh. "Are our supposed daddies still around?"

"Yours died three years ago. I thought I told you. Mine came back to Hannibal once last year and took me and the kids to McDonald's and haven't heard from him since. Thomas hangs out with his now and then, but they're too much alike to get along."

"How are the kids doing in school?"

"Honor roll, all of them. They better not bring no *C*'s home. I tell them about you all the time. How you got out of here. How you got your education and never had to come back. They worship you, Resie. Not me or Momma, and certainly not Tommie. They love all of us, but you're the one they look up to. I make sure of that."

Teresa's hands clutch each other. She feels elation. She feels rotten. She won't cry, though. Not in front of Tisha, the drama queen. She reaches over and takes her sister's hands into her own.

"You need any help?"

"Always, but I'll make do. I get public assistance, and I have a little side job cleaning two houses a couple times a month."

"I owe my nieces and nephews for a bunch of birthdays I missed. I'll take care of that before I leave. Okay?"

"Thanks, Resie."

"What about my damn birthdays?" They turn to see Taylor Lee creeping down the stairs, hand clasped firmly to the rail. "I think I deserve a little recognition on my birthdays too." She tries to lighten up her words with a chuckle, but Teresa knows better.

"Momma, please."

"Shut up, Tisha Lee, I'm not talking to you. Teresa Lee, you don't think you owe your momma nothing?" Taylor Lee hobbles over to them and looks down at Teresa, then makes her way to her favorite chair. The brief rest has helped. She sounds stronger.

"I haven't forgotten about you, Momma."

"Good, 'cause I'm the only momma you're ever going to get. You only get one." Teresa knows she hasn't and never will feel about her mother the way Tisha's kids feel about theirs. Taylor Lee drops into the chair opposite her two daughters, a crooked smile distorting her dark lips and ashen face. The light from the lamp next to her chair beams off the gold crowns covering her front teeth.

"You want something to eat?" Teresa says, trying hard to sound like a concerned daughter.

"Did Thomas Lee and the boys get back?"

"Back and gone again," Tisha says.

"They eat all the damn food?"

"I put some aside for you, but you know Tommie. Let me see." Tisha gets up and heads to the kitchen.

Taylor Lee shakes her head and says, "That boy's an asshole. Will take the quarters off a dead woman's eyes even if she's his own flesh and blood."

Tisha stops at the entrance to the kitchen. "You spoiled him rotten, just like you're trying to do the boys."

"Thomas Lee's a grown-ass man, and he ought to know better. You can't put that on me." Taylor Lee goes on a rant about how none of her kids appreciate what it took to raise them by herself. Teresa studies Taylor Lee while she talks. The flying hands, the intense eyes, the deep dimples.

Teresa flinches when the reality, live and in person, is flung back at her and can't be denied or ignored in this moment. She's her momma's daughter. The dated and faded but recognizable reflection of herself in the face and gestures of the volatile woman sitting across the room is overwhelming. Teresa slumps lower on the floor and closes her eyes.

* * *

Marcus regrets his decision the minute he steps inside the dilapidated building. The interior is dark and smoky. He hates cigarettes. When his eyes adjust to the dim light, he sees the place is small and crowded with most of the tables and chairs occupied. There's an empty table in a corner a few feet from the bar that Thomas seems to claim by going over and leaning the chairs forward against it.

They go to the bar, and Thomas orders two bottles of regular beer because they don't have lite, and then they proceed back to the table and take seats across from each other. Thomas takes a long swallow from his bottle, then belches. Even though the atmosphere is cordial,

Marcus has lost all interest in this little excursion. After less than an hour with Thomas, Marcus is ready to leave.

"Hey, Shirley, looking good. And you too, Alice Fay," Thomas hollers at two young women sliding past the table. They ignore Thomas but gawk and smile at Marcus. "Little country bitches trying to profile for you. Not happening, hey, bro?" Thomas chugs down a third of his beer and belches again. "Bet they don't compare to the ones in Chicago, but it's all I got to work with, you know."

While back at the house they had talked sports, and the conversation had come easy, Marcus now realizes he has nothing else in common with Teresa's brother. And creeping across the scarred and unpainted table are things about Thomas that are easy to dislike. His nervous eyes don't stay in one place any longer than it takes his crooked smile to disfigure his face, then disappear. He has a hustler's style. He's slick and quick.

An hour later, while watching Thomas drain the last of his fifth bottle of beer, four of which Thomas asked Marcus to cover, he gets what Teresa tried to tell him when she said, "Run." Thomas is a poser. A moocher. Marcus regrets leaving Teresa for a night out with her sketchy brother. By now he and Teresa might have been back at the motel enjoying their last night together. By noon tomorrow he'll be headed back to St. Louis to retrieve Bird, then on to Chicago. Thomas gets up and makes his way through the dimness of the place and returns with two more beers.

"You're running behind," he says.

"I think I've reached my limit."

"You want a little something else?" Thomas takes a big swig from his bottle but keeps his eyes trained on Marcus.

Marcus chuckles at the offer but doesn't answer.

"My family's full of drinkers. Aunts, uncles, cousins, and sisters... all except Tish. She doesn't drink, do drugs, or cuss. Never has. She's just a fool when it comes to men. Not like most of the women in the family, who're mostly ballbusters. Think twice before you dive in." Thomas laughs, then gulps down more beer.

"You've given me something to think about."

Thomas misses the sarcasm. "I'm just kidding, bro. Resie's changed a lot since she left here. She got out, got an education, and got some class. She inspires us now, especially the kids. But she was more than a handful back in the day." Thomas finishes off his bottle.

"You need me to take care of that for you?"

"Be my guest. You paid for this one."

Thomas tips the bottle away from his lips and belches again. "Like I was saying, Resie has turned out okay, but back in the day, she was a little wild. A whole lot like Momma." Thomas takes another swig.

"Yeah, Resie will swear to high heaven she's nothing like Momma, but that's why they fight all the time. Too much alike."

"You fight with your mother?" Marcus knows it's a weak attempt at distracting Thomas.

"Not nearly like Resie. There were times I thought they hated each other after the situation. They hardly spoke to each other after that."

"The situation?"

"Can't go into that. Personal family stuff, you know."

"Want another beer?" Marcus says.

Thomas finishes off his sixth bottle and nods. Marcus gets up and makes his way to the bar and squeezes in between the knot of patrons standing two deep around it. All of them speak or nod and step to the side. A few continue to stare while he waits to order. Marcus turns his back to the bar and looks out into the dark haze in the direction where Thomas is sitting. Too little illumination and too many people hide Thomas from view. *He can't wait to spill his guts,* Marcus thinks. And despite his own reservations, here he is buying Thomas another round. He takes the beer and pushes through the packed butts and hips back to their table.

"Thanks, bro." Thomas takes the bottle and downs a quarter of it, then emits another loud belch. "You didn't have to beat the women off, did you? They don't always know how to act when a new face shows up. That's the thing about Hannibal women. They give it up way too easy, without a second thought. My sisters included. Maybe it's out of boredom." He laughs. "I know we brothers do the same thing, but it's different. It just makes us players. But for women, it makes them hoes."

Did he just call Teresa a ho? Marcus winces.

"Don't get me wrong, bro. I believe women have the right to fuck who they want when they want. I'm not complaining." The Adam's apple lodged in the center of Teresa's brother's throat bobs up and down when he swallows. "But I'm like most men. As long as it's not my sister. Right? I hated seeing them follow the same crooked path as Momma. I took a lot of shit because of them. I hit a lot of motherfuckers too. I still have to watch Tish's back." He gives Marcus a half smile, half sneer. "Do I need to watch Resie's too?"

"She can take care of herself." Marcus doesn't bother to dull the edge in his voice.

"Now, maybe, but not always." Thomas's eyes narrow. "Look, bro. Sure, Resie's gotten along pretty well in life, but she's been knocked on her ass a few times. We all have."

Marcus doesn't want to hear any more about Teresa and wants Thomas to shut up, to keep his family's skeletons in the closet. But Marcus doesn't say a word. He's mesmerized by the revelation he knows is coming. A revelation that, he knows, should stay in Teresa's family archives away from his prying curiosity. But he sits there in silence and waits for every tacky detail of Teresa's half-drunk brother's big reveal. Thomas finishes off the last of his beer. The stale smell from his belching drifts across the small space that separates them. Marcus doesn't flinch. Thomas leans forward on his elbows.

"You and Resie share secrets? What she tell you about us?" Thomas says.

"Some things but not much."

"Only the good stuff, right?" Thomas looks smug.

"Bits and pieces, that's all."

"You know the three of us had it rough. Momma ain't shit as a mother. Set a bad example for Tish and Resie with all the men she brought through our house. She worked at a bar, you know, and brought home all kinds of strays to fuck and fight. As we got older, all of us used to hang out at the bar, play pool, and listen to the jukebox. It was cool for me but not my sisters. Both of them got the wrong message."

"Were there incidents with any of your mother's male friends?" Marcus says. His pounding heart sends the blood crashing through his brain. He's getting a headache, a bad one.

"They never told me anything happened. I guess they knew I would've killed the son-of-a-bitch who did it. I tried to protect them, but I was too busy taking care of my own shit to always do the brother thing right. First, Resie got knocked up and then later, Tish. Resie finally got her stuff together, but Tish is still working on hers."

Marcus feels like he's suffocating. That his breath is stuck in his lungs. *Teresa has a child?* He tries to listen to the music and realizes there is none. "Where's the music?"

Thomas laughs. "The folks who run this place don't know what the fuck they're doing. If I had the money, I'd open my own place and run their asses out of business."

"Where's Teresa's kid?" Marcus says.

"Never happened. Momma made her get rid of it. I don't think Resie will ever forgive her for the way it went down. But, truth be told, it turned out for the best. She couldn't have made it through college dragging a kid behind her. Look at Tish."

Marcus manages to exhale. His head hurts. The place has gotten smaller, darker, and dingier. It's time to go. "This smoke's getting to me. I need some air." They both stand. Thomas belches as they make their way toward the front entrance.

Twenty-One

Things have gone better than she expected. The trip home isn't a disaster. Her family isn't the wandering group of lost souls she'd made them out to be. She enjoys her nieces and nephews. Tisha is sweeter, Thomas is trying, and the cancer has weakened Taylor Lee's roar. Marcus has hung out with her family, and he's none the worse for wear. Maybe it's time for her to change too. Learn to forgive and forget. Life is good. A light breeze drifts in through the open patio door. She can hear the birds chirping outside. She's lying in the motel bed next to Marcus. This moment feels so right. She loves this man. And she believes he loves her.

Hasn't he found his way to Hannibal after she'd left him in Chicago pissed off and confused? A moan escapes her dry lips as she lets her eyes rest on his face. It's early Monday morning, and he'll be leaving soon. His eyes are closed, but she knows he's not asleep. Teresa leans over and kisses him on each eyelid. He smiles but keeps them closed. His lids quiver as she plays with his nipples. Teresa snuggles up against him, tosses a leg over his stomach and eases on top of him. She slides down his body, planting kisses along the way. His forehead. His eyes. The tip of his nose. Then she finds his lips.

His hands clutch her from behind, but she wiggles out of his grasp and continues her journey down his body until her head comes to rest between his legs. He's soft. She resists when he tugs at her shoulders. Teresa wants him to miss her the moment he gets into his car. She reaches up and shoves his hands to the side, then grips him firmly in her hand, then wraps her lips around him and visualizes the blood cascading away from his heart in waves.

In a matter of seconds, he begins to swell. She lowers her head and takes him all the way in until he fills the narrow wet tunnel inside her mouth. Teresa pushes her hands underneath him and begins to maneuver him up and down in long smooth strokes. She keeps her eyes open and trained on his face. His eyes flicker, then close again. His lower lip hangs limp. His breath comes in short, quick spurts.

Her own excitement begins to surge. She shudders as the heat between her thighs grows hotter. Then her own eyes slam shut. Her passion takes over. Hands, lips, tongue and teeth are frenetic in their manipulations. In a few moments it's over. The power of his orgasm makes him curse. Teresa can feel his tremors rumbling throughout his body and keeps manipulating him until he's drained, then lays her head on his stomach and sighs. His soft moan makes her smile.

* * *

He holds her tight. It's been at least ten minutes, and he's still experiencing the aftershocks of his orgasm. Theresa's breathing is slow and steady. She hasn't spoken. Time passes and in the silence his mind bounces from thought to thought until it lands on her brother's words. He wants to release them, but they continue to flit around inside his head like flies between a screen and a windowpane. Why would Thomas lie about that? And should it matter?

"You still awake?" Teresa says.

"Yeah," he says.

"I'm surprised. That last orgasm should've knocked you out." Teresa chuckles.

"Yeah," he says again. Pregnant and an abortion. The words won't escape or simply die. It shouldn't matter. But it does. His stomach's grown a knot. It's silly, he knows, because he'd been down this same road with Ana.

Teresa raises her head. "What are you thinking so hard about?"

"Us."

"You've got my attention."

"To be honest, it's mostly about you," he says. "Was thinking about how honest you want us to be. Or how honest we can be."

Her smile fades. She looks away, then brings her eyes back to meet his. "I guess I've shown I'm really not ready." She taps her forehead to make the point.

"You think it should matter? Our past relationships and stuff?"

"Sometimes I do and then I don't. You?" she says.

"Same, I guess. It's a timing thing. It's got to be the right time," he says.

"Don't know about that. I think I believe it's wise to let sleeping dogs lie."

"Taylor Lee?" he says.

"The one and only. And I get it. The past can't be changed, so what's the point?" She circles his nipple with her finger, then pinches it.

He shudders, then says, "I'm not sure."

"I don't think you really want to see all my warts." Her voice is soft.

"Would it be better if the warts were revealed by others?"

"If I discover something about your past that bothers me, it's my problem, not yours," she says.

He looks into her eyes and believes she means it. His lips brush across the top of her head. The uncertainty is still there, but he accepts that it's his problem, not hers. He's ready to do it the hard way, the right way. Teresa lowers her head, licks his nipple, and asks if he's ready for some more good loving. He gently pushes her head southward and moans in anticipation.

* * *

Marcus gobbles up his first ever maid-rite in total silence. He hasn't eaten a bite since they left Taylor Lee's last night. Teresa feels a sense of exhilaration. The giddiness of intoxication. Sex all night and all morning. They took an hour-long tour of the town. Now both their tanks are empty. She watches with satisfaction as he quickly unwraps his second sandwich.

"What do you think?" she says.

"Delicious."

Without the least bit of self-consciousness, she says, "I love you."

"Me too," he responds, then takes another big bite.

She sits back, unwraps one of her maid-rites and begins to eat. "Damn," she says, this is so good.

They sit in silence and devour their food. She relishes the familiar smell and taste of this childhood favorite. It's a reminder that her life here wasn't a complete bust. Yes, she has to admit, her return home has touched her in unexpected ways, and it does feels like a different place.

Here she sits in the car with her man, the two of them feasting on her to-die-for maid-rites, gulping down this one-of-a-kind root beer and no drama. Then the thought of not seeing Marcus again for several days produces an intense longing. *He'll be gone in an hour*, she thinks and turns in the seat to face him while they eat. *Damn, I'm going to miss you,* she thinks, then says, "I don't want you to leave."

"Great, then I'll stay."

"What about Bird?" Teresa asks.

"He knows how to get on a plane."

"That's not fair to him." Teresa reaches for his face and wipes a bit of grease from the corners of his mouth.

"If the choice is between you and Bird, it's no contest."

"You've got an office that needs your attention too," she says.

"So, you're telling me to leave? Again?"

"It's not the same." Teresa caresses his cheek. "I'm asking you to leave despite wanting you—badly wanting you—to stay."

"It feels the same to me."

His fake pout makes her smile. She fondles him and kisses him deeply, then says, "But it's not the same."

They finish eating and head back to the motel, where she'll give Marcus a little something for the road.

* * *

"Think he prefers the preacher to me." They are an hour outside St. Louis headed north on I-55. Bird's driving.

"I think you're overstating the case," Marcus says.

"He asked if he could call me Bird."

"What does he call the preacher?" Marcus says.

"Didn't ask. Told him to call me whatever makes him comfortable," Bird says.

"Bad move." The leather seat squeaks when Marcus turns sideways to stare at his friend. Light traffic zips along the interstate. The Jag's on cruise control, and the pavement glides smoothly beneath them.

"Talked to Tonya about it."

"Another bad move," Marcus says.

"He needs family stability. I can't keep popping up in his life like a jack-in-the-box."

"Tonya's a witch, Bird."

"She's his mother."

"Yes. The mother. She can't be his father."

"Maybe I can't be either."

"Sounds like Tonya. What does she want you to do, move back to St. Louis?"

"Wants me to consider giving up my parental rights."

"What?"

"Let the preacher adopt him." Bird keeps his eyes straight ahead.

"Tonya must be on crack."

"Told her I'd think about it," Bird says.

"There's nothing to think about. You can't just give away your son."

"Long-distance parenting isn't working for him or me."

"You don't have a choice," Marcus says, then turns away and looks out the window.

"Do have a choice. Being a father is more than biology," Bird says.

"If you do this, you're going to regret it. Don't kid yourself."

"Whatever I should have done, it's too late now." Bird stares straight ahead.

"You're a hypocrite. All that crap you talk about Black people. Always ranting about saving the race and you won't even fight for your own son," Marcus says.

"I'm talking about *sacrificing* for my own son."

Marcus struggles to maintain his self-control, but his anger is gathering steam. He turns to face his friend and shakes his head.

"You don't understand what I'm feeling," Bird says. "You don't have a kid."

"I've been a kid."

"Oh, so this is about you, not Malik or me."

"This is about experiences that affect a kid's life. Yeah, you know I've been there," Marcus says.

"You're no worse off than anybody else. In fact, you're better off than most."

"You won't be any different than all those other deadbeats missing in action. The truth is you're worse. You know better." Marcus closes his eyes and squeezes his forehead.

"Malik hasn't lived with me since he was three. I don't really know him. If I could change that, I would. At least I took a chance. Gave it a shot. More than I can say for you."

"You didn't take a shot. You made a commitment." Marcus takes in a deep breath and counts to thirty before exhaling. His emotional edginess begins to dull and, in its place, emerges a deep sadness for his friend. It's clear. Bird doesn't want to be a father. He wants to resign. Marcus shuts his eyes again and leans his head back against the leather's coolness. The sunroof is tilted open, and the warm breeze slides across his naked dome. Bird's still talking, but Marcus tunes him out. In this moment he doesn't like his friend. "In effect, you're punking out," he tells Bird.

Bird extends his middle finger and says, "Go to hell."

Fuck you, Marcus thinks, then turns his face toward the passenger window and his back to his friend.

* * *

Teresa watches her brother hustling around the kitchen like he did when they were kids. The sizzling sounds and yummy smells of frying bacon and pork sausage make her feel ten again. She can't wait to eat his scrambled eggs even though it's eight o'clock Monday night. Taylor Lee went out most nights when they were kids, and the three siblings had been left to fend for themselves. Thomas had been the chef. Through the efficient use of a limited food allowance and rigorous experimentation, scrambled eggs became his specialty.

Tisha sits across the kitchen table from Teresa, thumbing through a magazine, appearing to ignore Thomas and his silly monologue about the great business opportunities in Hannibal just waiting for an enterprising Black man like him to come along. Teresa's nieces and nephews are still outside somewhere, and Taylor Lee's upstairs sleeping. Day after tomorrow she begins her chemotherapy. Teresa's eyes shift back and forth between Tisha and Thomas, her flesh and blood.

Thomas is still as handsome as he'd always been. If he hadn't been so fine, maybe the girls would have left him alone and he would've amounted to something. Her sister looks worn around the eyes, the only place where the hard years seem to have left their mark. Otherwise, despite the four kids, her pretty face and curvy shape pay homage to the strength of their gene pool.

Teresa always thought her family was, generally speaking, a bunch of good-looking folks. Aunts, uncles, cousins, as well as siblings could make heads turn. But mental health is another story. Irrationality and explosive temperaments are common characteristics of Taylor Lee's lineage. The genes are a mixed bag. Teresa remembers how the three of them had been top students throughout elementary and junior high. But once in high school, their bad genes took center stage. Her own choices almost destroyed any possibility of her escaping Taylor Lee's life. Almost.

Her siblings haven't been so lucky. They've gotten trapped. But now Teresa considers the possibilities that maybe they haven't given up on themselves completely. Thomas is still as upbeat as ever, and Tisha's become a mother much better than the one who raised them. Something balloons inside Teresa that she hasn't felt in a long, long time as she watches her brother and sister. Hasn't felt it since that time Thomas stood up to Taylor Lee to protect her. Or when Tisha won homecoming queen. It may not be true tomorrow or the next day or probably the day after, but in this moment, she feels linked to them.

"You think I'm just dreaming, huh, sis?" Thomas turns from the stove with the smoking skillet. Like her sister seems to be doing, Teresa has tuned out her brother too.

"About what?" Teresa asks.

"Opening a bar and pool hall establishment. If it's nice enough with security, even white folks would come. All I need is a little faith and cash to make it happen." Thomas cracks several eggs into a bowl as he speaks. "It can be a family business, you know. Pass it on from one generation to the next and change the family's fortunes."

"Resie's not giving you no money to throw away," Tisha says. She flips the magazine onto the small table and catches Teresa's eye and shakes her head.

"I'm not talking about giving, I'm talking about investing. Even Marcus could see the dive we were at last night leaves a lot to be desired, and it's full to the gills every night. Negroes standing on top of each other begging for something better." He pours the mixture of eggs, cheese, onions and green peppers into the skillet, and waits for Teresa to speak.

"You need to put a business plan together," Teresa says.

Tisha snickers and says, "Don't be no fool with your money, Resie."

"You don't get it, do you?" He points a long slender finger at Tisha.

"It's all about family. Each one reach one, right, Resie?" His smug look when he points his finger irks Teresa. It's a reminder of why she hasn't always enjoyed her brother's company.

"I believe it's *each one teach one*," Teresa tells him.

"Okay, so let's do lunch tomorrow, and you can show me how to put that business plan together." He sets the eggs and bacon and sausage on the table.

"To be honest, I don't have the inclination or the guts to be an investor." Teresa feels a need to put to rest his mistaken belief that she might be willing to throw any money into his fantasy.

"All the work's gonna be on me, sis. Put up a little front money and sit back and watch the dough flow. These Negroes and white folks will love the place. It's a no-brainer." His laugh is a short empty sound.

His pulsating temples, a dead giveaway since Thomas was a kid, tells Teresa that he's frustrated. She knows he can't *really* expect to get any money from her, but those bad genes tell him he has a right to be pissed. Tells him she's being selfish. And Teresa knows it's partly her fault because, until two years ago, she had let him regularly extort money from her by manipulating her guilt and pity. But those days are long gone.

"Momma seems to be taking this pretty well," Teresa says. She's done with Thomas and his investment pitch.

"Who knows? She'd never admit anything different." Tisha's voice grows soft. "But I'm worried."

"Momma's going to be fine," Thomas says. "She's too ornery to die anytime soon. But Tisha and I'll need some help in taking care of her while she gets better."

"Hah." They all turn to see Taylor Lee standing in the doorway. Although she's slept for the past several hours, she still looks tired. Her eyes are rimmed in red, and dark puffs have formed beneath the skin under them.

"Sit down, Momma," Tisha tells Taylor Lee.

"You need to eat something," Thomas says, then walks over to Taylor Lee and takes her arm.

"I've been lying down all day. I'm fine. You kids haven't changed, still fussing and fighting like cats and dogs," she says as Thomas leads her to a chair.

"Not fighting, just discussing," Thomas says. He releases her arm, and she drops into the seat.

"I heard you trying to shame Teresa Lee into giving you money. You know I'm not depending on *you* to take care of me." She rolls her eyes at her son. "I'm not really depending on any of you to take care of me. It's in God's hands."

Teresa knows Taylor Lee is scared because she's seldom heard Taylor Lee speak of God except to use His name in vain. Now she's betting on Him to save her. The three siblings stare at their mother. The possibility of Taylor Lee's death has left Teresa emotionless. But she knows that for her brother and sister, Taylor Lee's death will be a disaster. Whenever it happens. Taylor Lee's the sun, and they survive in her solar system. She's the matriarch around whom their family life flows. Without her, there might not be a strong enough connection to keep them a family.

Tisha might very well disappear into herself and Thomas into the shadows, where he would become so much less than he already is. Taylor Lee hasn't been a presence in Teresa's life for the past fourteen years and, as Teresa sees it, is a parent in name only. Taylor Lee's death won't represent a loss of anything of value for her. She casts her eyes in Taylor Lee's direction and feels neither love nor sorrow for her mother.

What Teresa feels is a sort of disdain for the woman who brought children into the world but refused to do right by them. Teresa tries to concentrate and describe to herself what she really wanted from Taylor Lee. Love? No, she tells herself, Taylor Lee is not and has never been capable of loving another person. Teresa's known this her whole life. What she had wanted was for Taylor Lee to provide protection, stability and support for the three of them. The bare minimum a parent should bring to the table.

What her siblings feel for Taylor Lee is something different. It's hard to believe they love her. It's obvious they need her. The prospect of losing Taylor Lee frightens them, and their fear frightens Teresa, who isn't sure she can be there for them in the way they might need when the time comes. Tisha and Thomas begin to move around the kitchen. Teresa knows they are trying to put thoughts of Taylor Lee dying in the back of their minds. It's best, she tells herself, for her to do the same.

Twenty-Two

The chemotherapy has gone well, and now Taylor Lee is back at home in bed asleep. Thomas is at the apartment with her. Tisha and the girls play in the water, while Teresa sits in a lounge chair beside the motel's pool on her cell phone, waiting for Toni to come on the line. Although it's only been six days since Teresa took leave time, it seems a lot longer. While she waits for the receptionist to track Toni down, Teresa thinks again about all the problems she's put in the back of her mind since arriving.

"How are you?" Toni sounds out of breath.

"I'm fine. Everything going okay?"

"I'm holding down the fort. Not to brag but I'm getting it done." Toni laughs.

"No issues with the audit?"

"We're going to need to get creative. The federal checklist requires a career plan for each client and a responsibility and service plan, too."

"What the hell is a responsibility and service plan?" Teresa feels a knot form in the pit of her stomach.

"Something they never told us we needed. I have a fix, though. You don't want the particulars, right?"

"Right."

"So far that's the biggest challenge, but it means we've got hundreds of files to fix. It's going to take time, but I got this." Toni sounds confident. "Oh, yeah, two of your board members dropped by. Jesse and Marsha came through early this morning and wanted to talk to staff, but I didn't let that happen. They met with me and wanted to learn a little more, their words, about the audit and Michael. I think I handled it pretty well."

"Good," Teresa says but thinks, *What the hell is Jesse up to? I knew I couldn't trust his ass.*

"I asked them why they didn't schedule a meeting with you for this information. They both looked silly when I asked that one. And I let Jesse know I knew that he knew you were out of town and that I didn't remember either of them dropping by to talk with staff when they knew Mary Ann was not in the office."

"I guess Jesse's flexing for Marsha and the both of them trying to flex for staff," Teresa says. "Or maybe the two Black board members are sending their first Black exec a message. Maybe the flex is for me." Teresa laughs, but that's for Toni's benefit. Her last comment is what Teresa really believes Jesse is doing.

"When will you be back?"

"I plan on leaving here tomorrow, so I'll be in the office on Monday."

"How's your mom doing?"

"She had her first chemotherapy session. It took a lot out of her. But under the circumstances I think she's doing well." Teresa lowers her voice and adds, "Surprisingly, I'm enjoying my family."

"That's great, but we miss you back here."

"Me too. I'll check in again on Friday. But if anything comes up before then, call me. Bye."

Teresa lies back, closes her eyes, and ponders Jesse's moves. The reports. The unannounced visit. What's his game? She's convinced that he's flexing. That he's sending her a message that the board is his. No seat and no votes for her. Teresa decides to put thoughts of Jesse back in mothballs for now and enjoy what to her has become a vacation.

* * *

Sitting slumped low, one hand gripping the steering wheel of the Jeep, Thomas speeds down highway 61. Teresa stares at the landscape rolling by. This is their first time being alone, and to her surprise, he's quiet. Since leaving the house, he's said little except to comment on how much he likes how the Jeep rides. She keeps sneaking furtive glances at him. They'd been close as kids. He'd been his sisters' protector. He'd had so much on the ball too. She really doesn't know what his life is like now. And she hasn't seen any of his children yet.

"I leave tomorrow. Why haven't your kids been over?" she says.

"Me and their mommas don't get along."

"What's that got to do with your kids?"

He raises his eyebrows. "Makes it hard to have a decent relationship with them is all."

"How often do you see them?"

"Often enough. You know Hannibal's too small to hide kids. I see them when they want something. That's just the way it is."

Teresa nods but says nothing. But she does wonder how things might turn out for his iteration of the next generation. Will they end up trapped in Hannibal living some version of their parents' lives? Thomas is saying how he'd like to get a Jeep one day, and Teresa in turn begins to feel guilty. She thinks about the money she's making and the lifestyle she's living and wonders if it's fair.

Does she owe Thomas or his children financial support? Does she have an obligation to care about what happens to them? She rubs her eyes hard. All her adult life she's been burdened with this question. What are her obligations to save her family? Her momma and siblings? The next generation too? The guilt morphs into frustration, then anger. *Nobody saved me. You can't want more for people than they want for themselves.* As usual it works a little bit, but the sense of guilt returns. All she can do is sigh.

"What's up?" Thomas says.

"Huh?"

"You're sighing like you got a lot on your mind. What's up?"

"Just thinking about all the work waiting for me back in Chicago."

"Tish says you're the boss. True?"

"True. Now all the headaches are mine."

"And the big bucks that go along with them, right?" He smiles and angles his face toward her. She doesn't answer because she isn't about to get into a conversation with him about how much money she's making.

"I've thought about coming to Chicago and giving myself another chance to do something with my life. You got a job there for me?"

"You think you could work for me?"

"*With* you, sis."

"No, *for* me, bro." Teresa laughs. "Can you imagine? You've never ever listened to me."

"You're right about that. I'm the big brother and always will be. By the way, what's the 411 on your friend Marcus?"

"You two hung out and you didn't get the 411?"

"He was selling but I wasn't buying. What's the deal?"

Teresa laughs again. "So, Marcus tried to *impress* you?"

"Not really. I tried to get him drunk, but he wouldn't bite."

"I appreciate your concern, but I think I can handle my love life, big brother."

Thomas makes a U-turn at a break in the highway and heads back into town. Teresa monitors the speedometer's needle as it climbs to seventy-five. She wants to tell him to slow the fuck down but holds her tongue. His machismo has always made him annoyingly obnoxious even as a kid. But it could also be endearing. Teresa remembers the time when Thomas tried, foolishly, to protect their sixteen-year-old love-struck cousin.

Not because her boyfriend was beating on her, but because he was cheating on her. Thomas was twelve. He happened to see the boy in his car hugged up with another girl and confronted him. Two black eyes later, Thomas and Taylor Lee, baseball bat and big stick in hand, made the boy pay for his mistake with a short stint in the hospital. Taylor Lee ended up on probation.

"Can I ask you a personal question?" Teresa says.

"What?" Thomas shoots her a sideways glance.

"How do you feel about Momma? I mean...do you love her?"

"Of course, she's our momma. We wouldn't be here if it wasn't for her."

"You don't think she screwed us up?" Teresa's not sure what she wants him to say.

"True, she won't get any votes for momma of the century, but she did the best she could. She could've done worse. She could've aborted us or dumped our asses on the street. Look, I know you and Momma are like fire and gasoline, but to say you don't love her isn't right."

"I've never said I didn't love her."

"Not out loud." Thomas half sneers when he says this.

"I've never heard your ass say you loved her. In fact, if my memory serves me well, you used to call her a bitch to her face, and you're the only one of us who's ever hit her back," Teresa says, knowing she sounds like the petulant teenager she used to be.

"Now I know you ain't going there."

"No, I'm not. I don't know why I still let you get on my last damn nerve," she says.

"Or why you're still a mean little you-know-what? Remember when you threw that butcher knife and damn near killed Knotty Head?"

Teresa laughs. "You shouldn't have slapped me and ran. And your friend shouldn't have stood there and laughed. He only got nicked on the arm."

"This thing with Momma, you really need to let it go. It's over, it's done."

"It wasn't the abortion. It was the betrayal. Like she sold me out to the white folks. Got rid of her grandchild to accommodate their racist asses."

"That's making a mountain out of a molehill. You didn't want that kid either. You were scared to death, remember? That abortion thing probably turned out for the best. Can you imagine if you'd had that kid? You'd still be here with the rest of us."

"Yeah, I know," she says. "I know."

"It's good having you home. You ought to do this more often."

"Yeah, I know," she says, then punches his arm.

* * *

Marcus arrives at his office suite early on Tuesday morning. He sits down at his desk and rests his eyes. It's 6:15 and the silence is all pervasive, except for the soft humming of the copier's motor and an el train roaring past. The rumbling noise makes him smile. He's more aware of it now because of Teresa. Although his trip to Missouri had been a refreshing break, it's good to be back. He rubs his eyes and yawns, then leans forward to pick up the coffee he bought at the café on the corner.

He isn't much of a coffee drinker, but the caffeine always does its job. He needs his mind sharp because he has a lot of stuff to figure out. He stands and walks over to the window. The sun sits low, touching the eastern edge of Lake Michigan, and its early morning rays shimmer across the water's surface. The hot coffee cup stings his palm, and the steamy liquid burns when he holds it in his mouth before letting it drip down his throat. Marcus returns to his desk and sets the cup down. He circles his desk, then sits back down and takes several deep breaths. He forces his mind to focus on the Seleste situation. It's time.

The ball's in her court, and if Seleste doesn't play by his rules, then game over. She's an adult, not some teenager, and if she wants to keep her job, she needs to understand and accept her place within *his* firm. He tells himself he can't let whatever Seleste's relationship might have been with the old man color his perspective, but it gnaws at him so deeply he can't dismiss it. He takes it as a personal betrayal. A deception he isn't sure he can get past. He closes his eyes and tries not to think about it. But it's a failed attempt. Then he tries to break it down. Tries to get at the real problem that's bugging him.

Somewhere, between all the layered emotions that are his to manage, he's discovered a profound sense of longing. A discovery made in Hannibal: Teresa's epiphany regarding her own distorted memories of her family. He realized he may have similar distorted memories. Specifically, his grandmother, whose importance in his life he seldom thinks about since the day she left. He forces his thoughts to go back to *that* day.

It had been his last week of high school. He came home to find his grandfather sitting slumped over, at the kitchen table, staring at a near empty glass of bourbon stuck between his hands. His tie was loosened, and his light-blue shirt collar unbuttoned. His face was an ashen hue. Its skin sagged. His grandfather managed a weak smile, but his eyes never looked up when Marcus entered.

"Hey, Dad." Marcus kept his voice low, nearly a whisper.

"Your grandmother's gone son. Gone."

Marcus froze in fear. He couldn't believe his grandmother was dead. When he'd left that morning, she hadn't looked sick. She hadn't complained like she sometimes did of a headache or of being tired. In fact, she was more upbeat than usual and had forgone her routine morning pick-me-up. He knew because her breath hadn't smelled of bourbon.

And now she was dead? Just like that with no warning? His grandfather set down the emptied bourbon glass and stuck his hand inside one of his jacket pockets. Marcus remembered staring at the small crumpled white envelope inside his grandfather's big outstretched hand.

"Take it," the old man said and dropped it on the table, then pushed it toward his bewildered grandson.

Marcus picked it up, straightened it out, and saw his own name printed in all caps on the front. He struggled to comprehend the meaning of it. She wrote a note before she died? A suicide note? She had killed herself? No way. Not his grandmother. She wouldn't do that to him. "She died?" Marcus said.

It was more fear and sadness than his heart and mind could contain. The dam burst, the tears flooded, and he collapsed, his head banging off the kitchen floor. His grandfather never moved. The bump that rose quickly on his head came without pain. But his mind was filling with it. He struggled back to his feet and sat down at the table across from the old man.

"She's not dead," his grandfather said. "She's just gone."

When Marcus finally understood that his grandmother had left them, he felt worse than when he had thought she was dead. He tore up her note without ever reading it. In this moment, the tragedy of that decision is like a punch in the gut. She had wanted him to know her side.

Her reasons. Probably her pain. All of which he had angrily dismissed. Had made it only about himself and his grandfather. Pops had to know why his wife left but refused to tell his grandson. Now Marcus wonders about that. Maybe Seleste was the reason. He shakes his head.

"Stop looking for scapegoats," he says. "You tore up her letter. You've refused to take that trip south. Refused to confront her and allow her to tell her side." A sadness engulfs him like a heavy fog. He covers his face with both hands, closes his eyes, and tries to remember his grandmother's voice.

When he hears their voices echo through the narrow corridor, it's 8:45 a.m. Seleste and Missy have arrived. Marcus gets up from his desk, shakes his head and walks over to the office window. He has just re-experienced everything he had felt that day. Stunned, he wipes the tears from his cheeks, then hurries over to his office door and locks it.

Twenty-Three

"Marcus, you here?" It's Missy's voice coming through the intercom disrupting his thoughts. He walks over to the telephone to answer. "I'm in," he says.

"How was your little vacation? Feeling better?"

"I think I needed at least another month." He tries to laugh, but it sounds more like a snort.

"Are we meeting this morning?"

He hesitates. "Ask Seleste, these meetings were her idea."

"She said ask you since you the boss."

"Give me a minute." Marcus takes a deep breath. He knows it's time. But he needs to clarify the issues for himself so that he can make them clear to Seleste. The Womack files have already been dealt with and Seleste's relationship with his grandfather is not a bona fide issue to continue to focus on with her.

No, the real issue is her lack of respect. He's not sure why Seleste is struggling with his authority. She's always pushed him to be more assertive with clients and opposing counsels. It's obvious she didn't intend for him to apply her admonitions to his employees. There's no getting around this fact, but today will be the first day of a new day for Seleste.

Marcus summons Missy to his office and meets with her for over an hour. He drills her on what her assignments are and what she knows about office operations. He's surprised at how much she actually knows but how little she does. It seems Seleste wants to keep a lot of control.

He tells Missy to write down all the additional responsibilities she'd like to take on, and she promises to have it ready in fifteen minutes and sashays out the door. He then calls Seleste and tells her to step into his office. Seleste doesn't speak or acknowledge his presence when she walks in and takes a seat across from but not directly in front of him. He has to adjust his position to face her.

"What are we working on this morning?" Marcus demands.

Seleste raises her eyebrows in amusement. Then she pushes her chair back from the table and crosses her legs.

"Why isn't Missy in here?" she says.

"I've already met with Missy."

"What do you want, Marcus?" She scrunches her forehead, purses her lips into a frown and glares at him.

"To clarify our roles going forward," he says.

"Our roles have been clear for six years."

"As defined by you. I'm redefining them," he tells her.

"Leave me alone and let me do my job. Please." Seleste emits an exaggerated sigh.

"First I need to clarify what your job is. And I will be overseeing yours and Missy's work."

"Is that what you think? You don't know half of what goes on here."

"True, but that's about to change, and it's not up for debate."

"I wouldn't get that far out on the limb," Seleste says. She uncrosses her legs and sits upright. "You might find yourself tumbling with no soft place to land."

"I'm ready to take my chances. Are you?"

"The risks are all yours."

While he scrutinizes Seleste's eyes and then her whole face, it comes as a complete surprise to Marcus when he realizes that he dislikes so much about Seleste: her arrogance about being Jamaican, but she's never uttered a single word about going back; her pettiness he's always overlooked, especially when she fronts and talks like she's the only damn *adult* around here; her hypocrisy when she tells everybody else's business but has a fucking seizure when anybody drops a dime on her.

He studies her puckered lips and wrinkled brow. He listens to the drumming of her unpainted fingernails against the arms of the chair. Her eyes refuse to conceal her disdain for all that he has said. His indignation swells deep in his gut like a pending volcano. Seleste has convinced herself that she's indispensable.

"Like I said, I've got work to do," she says.

The chair squeaks as she adjusts her position and offers him her profile. Her eyes roam the ceiling, the walls and settle on the windows. She grabs the arms of the chair, indicating she's about to rise. Seleste is about to walk out on him again. Their last confrontation is still fresh in his mind. She walked out and he had done nothing but sat and watched her leave. But he will preempt her this time.

"Let's review your plans for today," he says and stands. "We'll meet in the conference room."

"I don't have time for this silliness." She stands, smooths out her dress and points at him. "You need to get over yourself."

"A new day, Seleste. This is a law firm, and I'm the only lawyer here. No lawyer, no law firm. You're support staff. If you're having trouble accepting that, I don't know what to tell you."

"This is also a *business* and one I've managed for a long time. Long before you showed up," she says.

"But when I showed up, I did so as boss."

"You may be the lawyer, but you are not my *boss*. And if you have trouble accepting that, I don't know what to tell *you*."

"You were just an employee long before I showed up, and you're still just an employee."

"I was never just an employee. Walker Greene knew that."

"Sleeping with Walker Greene didn't make you more than what you were. It was what it was."

"And sitting in Walker Greene's chair doesn't make you *the* man either." She heads toward the door, then stops. "Anything else you want me to know?"

"Only that if you walk out that door, I will presume you're resigning."

Seleste responds to his threat with a flick of her wrist, then shakes her head as she opens the door. "I always knew you were a bit of a fool." With that said, she steps out into the corridor and quietly closes the door behind her.

Lust, Love & Family Legacies

* * *

Missy stands in the doorway of his office minutes later, her hands cupped around her mouth and nose, her eyes wide with wonder. Then she asks, "What happened?"

"Seleste just resigned," he says, leaning back in his chair, his feet now propped on top of his desk.

Missy steps inside and takes a seat. "Is she really quitting?"

"As far as I'm concerned. There's not enough room here for two bosses." Marcus chuckles because he feels good. There's a sense of relief that he hasn't expected. He feels no anxiety. There's no guilt nibbling at his conscience. Seleste needs to move on, and so does he. Marcus looks at Missy's curious face and asks, "Where do you stand with all of this? Are you going to follow her out the door?"

"I'm staying."

"Sure?" he asks.

"She told me yesterday that I've gotten on her bad side too."

"She did?" he says.

"She said I didn't have the sense God gave a goose. Then rolled her eyes and went into her office."

"Then it's the two of us. First thing we need to do is get a temp in here to handle your job."

Missy's eyes widen. "Why?"

"Because you can't be the administrative assistant and the new office administrator."

Missy giggles. She puts her hands over her mouth. "For real?" she finally says.

"If you think you can handle it," he says.

"What if Seleste changes her mind?"

"Then she's fired." He pulls his feet off the desk and sits upright.

"Can you handle finding a temp?"

"Yes, boss," she says and hurries over to his desk and hugs his shoulders.

"Then hop to it," he says. "We need to talk about the particulars later."

"The *particulars*?" She pauses at the door and gives him a quizzical look.

"Your raise, etcetera."

"Oh," she says. "Okay, we'll talk about the *particulars* later." She almost bumps into the door as she hustles through it and into her new job.

Marcus walks to the window and looks out at his postage stamp view of the lake. Teresa had once said, tongue-in-cheek, that his place with its *partners* sounded like paradise. She had said her job was to make sure the work got done her way. He'd thought at the time she sounded a bit too controlling. Now he understands. There can only be one true boss in a place of business and until today, in the law firm of Marcus G. Greene and Associates, there is no doubt at all in his mind, it had been Seleste.

* * *

Teresa will be back on the road to St. Louis in less than two hours. She's already said most of her goodbyes. Her sister's children, after a series of big hugs and kisses, have gone back to a life that doesn't include her. Thomas, she hasn't seen since yesterday. Tisha says it's because of his little girlfriend, who's almost young enough to be his daughter. Teresa hopes he will come through by four, but it doesn't look promising.

Noise from outside fills the apartment's living room. It comes through the screen door in waves as neighborhood kids shriek and romp around in the dust-filled yards. But after a week of being in this environment, Teresa can hold a conversation inside the apartment without a second thought. The three of them are in the living room. Teresa and Tisha are on the floor in front of the couch. Taylor Lee's in her usual spot in the chair across from them.

"I'm gonna miss you." Tisha reaches over and touches Teresa's arm. "When are you coming back?"

"Soon. I have to come back and help you keep an eye on Momma." Teresa looks over at Taylor Lee and smiles.

"Sure, now that you think I'm about to die." Taylor Lee has been acting funky ever since the chemo session, but with less than two hours left for this reunion, Teresa's not about to go there with Taylor Lee.

"She's looking a lot better today, don't you think, Tish?"

"Resie's right, Momma. You don't look like someone who's about to die. Don't keep talking like that."

"I wasn't talking about dying. I was talking about your sister thinking I'm about to die. When she gets back to Chicago, it'll *take* my funeral to get her back down here. I know her." Taylor Lee rolls her eyes at her two daughters as she sucks air between her teeth. Teresa sits as Buddha-like as possible refusing to show any reaction to Taylor Lee's provocations. Not this close to leaving. Then Teresa begins to wonder if Taylor Lee's real feelings are that she's sorry to see Teresa go and can't express those feelings.

Maybe I should assure her I am coming back, Teresa thinks. *Let her know I do care about her. Maybe this is her limited way of saying she's scared.* Teresa shakes her head as if to clear her mind. *Nah, girl. This is Taylor Lee. If you put yourself out there like that, then you're the fool. What she says is how her mind works. It's messy with mean thoughts.*

Teresa uncrosses her arms, stretches out her legs, and gives Taylor Lee a big smile and says, "You'll see."

"Momma's just being grouchy. Don't pay her no mind." Tisha leans over and touches Teresa's arm again.

"You know you'll be talking about her more than anybody else when she don't show back up. Whistling a whole different tune," Taylor Lee says, then tries to whistle, but only the muffled sounds of air escape her parched lips.

"I'll be back, Momma, and when I get here I want a big hug." Teresa laughs because Taylor Lee winces. "Deal?"

"If you're back here this year, I'll bend over backward and kiss my own ass."

"A hug will do," Teresa says. She's enjoying her momma's obvious discomfort with the idea of touching one of her children in a display of affection.

"I know you, girl. Martians will land in Hannibal before you get back here." Taylor Lee laughs.

Pointing a finger at Taylor Lee, Tisha says, "Maybe if you hug her, she'll come back like she says."

"I hugged both of you when you needed it most."

Teresa laughs at Taylor Lee's declaration. What world does this woman live in to say what she just said with a straight face? She's never hugged or kissed them a day in their lives as far as Teresa can remember. Never. Teresa can't let that lie stand.

"I'm sorry, Momma, but I can't remember a single time you ever hugged or kissed me."

"I can't remember either," Tisha says. She sounds sad.

"You all can't remember every little damn thing that happened when you were kids. You all act like I wasn't a good mother. I raised you, didn't I?" Taylor Lee tries to sound indignant but only manages to sound whiny.

Teresa uncrosses her legs and moves forward on the couch. She puts her arms on her knees and rests her face in the cupped palms of her hands. "You wouldn't do anything different if you could do it all over again, Momma?"

"Yes, I would," Taylor Lee says. "If I'd done with Tish what I did with you, we wouldn't be piled like rats in a cage up in here."

She sucks some more air through her teeth and casts her eyes upward before bringing them back to her daughters' faces. Tisha looks crestfallen. Her eyes fill with tears before she jumps up and runs out of the room. Teresa stands to face Taylor Lee. Tears form in the corners of her eyes but not from hurt feelings. She's livid.

"If you'd done to yourself what you did to me, you'd done all of us a favor. What's wrong with you? How can you be so nasty? Even now, as sick as you are, with all of us here for you, you can say something like *that* to me and Tish? You're too much. I can't take it.

How can you sit here and brag about what you made me do? You're proud of that?"

"Are you proud of what you did? Getting pregnant by that boy, then trying to trick him into marrying you? I did what I thought was right."

Teresa's remaining sense of self-control has disappeared like a single tree leaf caught up in a tsunami. "You forced me to get an abortion because they offered you money. You're such a selfish..."

"Watch your mouth, goddamn it. Don't you even think about calling me out of my name."

"...greedy bitch." Teresa's shocked by her own language. She's never cursed Taylor Lee to her face, ever. She takes in big gulps of air as her mind registers the fury in Taylor Lee's eyes.

"Get the fuck out of my house."

"I'm sorry, Momma. I shouldn't..."

"I...said...get...the...fuck...out...of...my...house, now. Who the fuck are *you* to call me a bitch? I brought you into this world, and I'll take you out." Taylor Lee struggles to get out of her chair. Teresa panics. She doesn't know what she'll do if Taylor Lee tries to hit her.

"Tish, I'm leaving," she yells out to her sister.

"What?"

Taylor Lee manages to stand and get her balance. "You little stuck-up heifer, I told you to get out!" She's screaming now and tries to hobble across the short space between them but falls down.

"Momma, stop it," Tisha yells as she runs down the stairs. "Have you gone crazy?"

Teresa is flabbergasted. Taylor Lee, now on her hands and knees, still trying to close the distance that separates her from her intended victim, is breathing hard. She manages to maneuver under the coffee table and gets within arm's reach of her daughter. Teresa steps backward, almost stumbling onto the couch.

"Get out. Get the fuck out of my goddamn house."

"Stop it, Momma, please!" Tisha shouts.

Teresa's heart is racing full tilt. Taylor Lee's face is contorted with what looks to Teresa like hatred. Taylor Lee grabs onto Teresa's legs and begins to pull herself up.

"You don't think I'll knock you on your ass, huh? You little slut."

Teresa yanks her legs away from Taylor Lee's clutching hands. Taylor Lee tumbles onto her side. "This is crazy," Teresa says. "I'm out of here."

Feeling that familiar anxiety of the intimidated kid, Teresa hustles away from the prone but still raging Taylor Lee and a disconcerted Tisha. With Taylor Lee's shrill threats now coming at her like bullets from a machine gun, Teresa, with one last glance over her shoulder at Tisha, pushes open the screen door and hurries outside into what is now a quiet calm. The horde of neighborhood kids stand staring as she maneuvers between them and makes a beeline for the parking lot.

Moments later, Teresa sits in the Jeep, heart racing, chest heaving and silently cursing her mother. She jumps when Tisha opens the passenger door and climbs inside. Tisha's face is as pallid as that of a vampire's victim. Neither speaks until Teresa says, "I let her get to me after I swore to myself I wouldn't."

"Me too," Tisha says. "I think she just wanted to go off. She's scared, Resie."

"Probably. But our momma's a crazy bitch. Sick or well."

"I know," Tisha says, "but promise that you won't let Momma keep you away again."

"I promise, and here." Teresa reaches into her bag and pulls out a thick white envelope with the $1,500. "This is for you. Not Momma or Tommie. And use it however you want or need to. Buy my nieces and nephews gifts for those birthdays I missed. And I'll send you some help every month."

Teresa leans over and wraps her arms around Tisha's head. A head that's vibrating because Tisha's weeping uncontrollably. They sit like that for several seconds until Teresa says, "I have to get going. Last thing I need is for Momma to come limping out here to finish what she started." They both swipe at their tears and laugh at the same time.

* * *

It's been seven hours since Teresa left Tisha waving goodbye in the parking lot of the housing complex. Now back in Chicago and on her way home, she's listening to the same jazz music in the same limousine that had taken her to the airport a week earlier. Every minute since Teresa hightailed it out of Taylor Lee's place, she's been obsessing over how her trip had ended.

She talked with Tisha for an hour while driving to the St. Louis airport. They shuttled emotionally between laughter and tears during the call. They relived the scene of Taylor Lee struggling to cross the two feet of space separating her from Teresa, intent on giving Teresa a Geraldine beatdown. Each sister recalled several vivid moments when Taylor Lee's awful decisions made each of their lives miserable. The truth, they concluded, was that Taylor Lee never liked parenting.

"They hadn't asked to be born," Tisha said of her kids. "They're here as the result of my choices. I owe *them*, not the other way 'round. Momma has it all wrong." Tisha's life decisions have been far from perfect, but she's trying hard not to mess up the lives of her kids. It's so clear to Teresa that growing up in Hannibal would have been so much better had Tisha been the momma.

Teresa sighs: her sense of equanimity is a warm, fresh, and welcomed mood. It's good to be back in Chicago, her real home. As the limousine rolls along the expressway, the wailing of a saxophone filling its interior, she begins crying again. She accepted somewhere in the air between St. Louis and Chicago that the incident with Taylor Lee has caused more wistfulness than anger for what could have been but never was. Tisha's relationship with her kids has opened Teresa's eyes and her mind. Despite all the problems in their lives growing up, none of it would have mattered, not really, if Taylor Lee had just loved her own kids the way Tisha loves hers. Tisha wants to be a good mother *because* she loves her kids. The limousine veers off the expressway through connecting and winding lanes and then onto the Drive. The saxophone solo ends just as her cell phone rings. She sits up, wipes her eyes, and answers.

"How close are you?" Marcus says.

"Ten minutes."

"I'm in your lobby waiting," he says.

* * *

He's caressing her breasts with one hand and stroking her hair with the other, the short soft semi-curls sliding between his fingers. Her heart still pounds as if it's trying to break out of her chest and join his. She moans when he slides one hand up the inside of her thigh. Darkness descends over the room when her eyelids drift downward. The sweaty sheets streaked with drying body fluids feel cool against her back. A long, dehydrated breath escapes from her dry lips. It took less than a minute after she opened the door for them to leave a trail of clothes behind. Diffused light bounces off her pupils when Teresa's eyes flicker back open.

She turns toward Marcus. He's staring at her, so she closes her eyes again so he can gaze at her nakedness without the need to say anything. She can see him now, in her mind's eye, studying her face, her whole body. She hears him yawn, senses him letting his sex-glazed eyes droop, then close and knows that shortly he'll be asleep.

Teresa thinks about the first time she realized there was this surprising sexual attraction between them. It's when she lowered her pepper spray. That day has turned out be one of the most pivotal in her life. One she could never have imagined: Mary Ann waiting to hand over the reins of leadership, and a cocky stranger waylaying her in the middle of the Loop. Now she's achieved a career goal she's aimed for since joining CEC and maybe has found the love of her life, which she's only fantasized about in her loneliest of moments.

Soon the sounds of his even breaths tell her he's out. Teresa opens her eyes and stares at him. She's worn him out with her unbridled horniness. Her own orgasms totaled five. He had only two, but as

"Then you should hear my heart."

"Tell me anyway," he says. He puts his hands together in prayer.

Teresa laughs and in the lightness of the moment tells him, "I love you."

"You're not nervous?"

"No," she says.

"Come over here." He holds out his arms, and she does.

* * *

Marcus sits at the dining counter talking about his past two days at the office. Teresa shifts about the confines of the kitchen. Between frying the bacon, whipping together the eggs, onions, and cheese in a bowl on the counter next to the stove, she still manages to look his way and nod every now and then. Even as he tells her about the continuing saga with Seleste, his mind's meandering along a different path.

He can see himself living with Teresa. Can see them happy together under the same roof. But there's this other competing glimpse of a future with her that isn't so rosy. An emotional roller coaster ride that would drive him nuts. As his mind darts back and forth between these two visions of a life with her, his eyes, independent of his thoughts, are glued to her bare backside, a moving magnet that holds them captive as she showcases it shamelessly. The perfect behind. Marcus is not aware that he has stopped talking.

"Seleste is really gone?" Teresa says.

"What?"

"You think Seleste is really gone?"

"She's gone. If she didn't resign, then I've fired her."

"Are you sure that's a good move?"

"I think it is what it is," he says.

"That's no answer. What happens tomorrow morning, now that it's just you and that little office clerk left to run things?"

"We'll manage," he says.

"Don't you feel a little sad and maybe a little nervous? You said she was like family and practically ran the office."

He raises his eyebrows but says nothing.

"Well?" Teresa says.

"What do you want me to say?"

"Don't get defensive." Teresa steps over to the counter and leans into his face. "It's just that you don't want to cut off your nose to spite your face."

"Another Taylor Lee noteworthy quote?" he says and rolls his eyes. Teresa raises her eyebrows and leans away from him just a bit.

"You have to be sure that your ego's not getting in the way. I've been there."

Marcus doesn't reply but notes that Teresa's breath's a bit tart and a bit of crust has accumulated in the outer corner of her left eye. He shakes his head in frustration at these petty observations. She's not the problem. She's trying to be helpful. But it's over and Seleste is no longer his concern, and it seems to him that Teresa thinks he might be hapless without Seleste. *Maybe* slowed but not hapless.

"A little ego was in play, but I've dealt with that. The *real* problem is that Seleste can't accept her redefined role as a subordinate." His voice carries more of an edge than he's intended.

Teresa turns away and goes back over to the stove and says, "Maybe it just takes her a little more time after all the years she was in charge."

"She's out of time," he says, "and the fact is that she will never be able to submit to me, no matter how much time passes. And isn't that your expectation for your subordinates?"

"I wouldn't use that word, exactly." Teresa pauses, then adds, "And if you told her she had to submit, I can understand why she reacted."

"She's made her choice. I'm supposed to beg her to stay? Give in to her terms?" He throws up his hands to emphasize his frustration.

"Not give in to her terms, but, maybe, reach out to her and let her know she's too important for you to let her go. She'll appreciate that and step back from that cliff. There's no way she wants to leave you and the firm."

"I've overlooked Seleste's shenanigans since forever. I think I'm tired of doing it. Sometimes you just have to move on," he says.

"Maybe."

"It's happened and now she's out," he says and gestures with his fist like a baseball umpire.

"Even if you can't go back to where you were, I think she deserves a better exit than the one you're showing her now." Teresa's voice is colored with a thin sheet of exasperation.

"Like you showed Michael Brown?"

Teresa turns and gives him a narrowed-eyed look. "You're being immature," she tells him.

"People living in glass houses shouldn't throw stones," he responds.

Marcus is agitated by what he hears as criticisms of him and Teresa's obvious empathy for Seleste, the woman. The same empathy she's exhibited for Kathryn but not for Jesse Waters. Or Michael Brown. Her insistence that he coddle Seleste is familiar too. That's what she's insisted he do for her.

"Living in a glass house might afford a better view of what's happening outside," she says, "and a word to the wise should suffice."

"But it's not the same as a mirror. We all should have mirrors," he tells her with no attempt to keep an aggressive edge from accompanying his words.

Teresa dishes up the eggs, then glances his way but says nothing. She smiles as she goes past him back into the bedroom. When she returns, she's put on some pants. He takes the change as confirmation that's she's pissed. Again. They eat in silence. When Teresa finishes, she takes her empty plate to the sink and moves around in the kitchen, but he doesn't look up.

The sounds of his chewing and swallowing are painfully audible in the silence. He keeps his eyes trained on the last bit of eggs and the small section of bacon remaining on his plate. He scoops up the last of his eggs on the end of the fork and slides it into his mouth. He shakes his head in bewilderment at how fast things have gone downhill.

Teresa pulls his plate to her as soon as Marcus sets down his fork and takes it to the sink without mumbling a single word. He watches as she rinses off the plates and puts them in the dishwasher and wonders how this awkward silence will end. He knows Teresa's capable of letting this little episode get out of hand and automatically expects him to wave the white flag. Teresa looks back at him across the counter as he sips the last of his juice. He offers up a half-assed self-conscious grin again. It seems to irk her. She gives no indication that she's prepared to fix it or help lift them out of this funky place into which they've carelessly stumbled. She picks up the remaining carton of eggs and turns to put them in the fridge but bumps against its door. Several of the eggs tumble out of the carton. "Shit," she says. Marcus doesn't move from the counter.

She starts pulling at the roll of paper towels hanging on the wall behind her. Once she's grabbed a handful of towels, Teresa kneels down and begins cleaning up the sticky mess. He wants to go help but realizes the window of opportunity closed the minute she got down on the floor. He watches her earnestly wipe then fold the soiled towels and wipe some more. She stands and tosses the soiled wads of paper towels into the trash can without raising her eyes. Then she strolls past him and goes into the living room and plops on her sofa.

He rises and goes back to the bedroom. His clothes are no longer strewn haphazardly across the floor but are now stacked in a neat pile on the bed. He sits on the edge of the bed, pulls on his socks and wonders what the hell is wrong with them. With Teresa really. A pattern has developed with them where she'll go through changes, create a dustup, and he ends up working overtime to clean it up. That's how he found his way to Hannibal, right? But let him have a little bit of a reaction to something she says and she reacts to his reaction.

There's no way around it; sometimes it's all about her. Well, she's about to find out that he can play that game too if he needs to. And now, —it's obvious to him—he needs to. He finishes dressing, slips on his shoes and strolls back to the living room. It's apparent that he's leaving. All Teresa has to do is stand up, walk over to him, and pull him to her. It's her turn.

He's been running after her since the first day he saw her. Chasing her through the Loop. Hustling after her when she stormed out of his house. Rushing to Hannibal after she'd put him out of her place and then left town and left him feeling guilty. He walks past the sofa into the kitchen and fills a glass with tap water. He's buying time. Giving her a moment to summon some courage.

Marcus empties the glass and glances her way as he leaves the kitchen. Teresa doesn't look up. Her body doesn't budge.

Her mouth's frozen into a pucker that has drawn her lips into a distorted circle. Even as he walks hurriedly past her, clearly on his way out, he hears the magazine pages turn. Marcus opens the door and pauses.

He hears the pages turn again. He refuses to look back as he steps through the opening out into the empty corridor and lets the door close quietly behind him. As he nears the elevator, he decides to give her one last chance and dials her cell. He'll tell her what she told him when she stormed out of his house. Get the hell out here and stop me.

But the phone rings until it goes to voicemail. When the elevator door opens and he steps inside, he can only shake his head in disbelief. There's something very wrong with this picture. This uncertainty is always there between them, and it's well past the limits of his tolerance for drama.

"This is fucked up," he mutters as he makes his way through the building's lobby and out the front door. Hadn't she just said, again, that she loves him? Now, a nanosecond later, here they are, back on the roller coaster. This ride is becoming too much for him and probably for her too.

Twenty-Five

Her first day back in the office and she can't concentrate. Teresa feels tired and irritated from a night of restlessness. She grimaces at the desktop in front of her. Somewhat organized but covered with a week's worth of overdue paperwork and unopened mail and several sympathy cards from staff. She stares at the time on her computer screen. Fifteen minutes has already passed since the last time she looked. She needs to get back in the game. It's 7:45 a.m., and in another hour her whole staff will arrive.

Her plan had been to get here by seven o'clock, check out whatever work has piled on staff desks in preparation for her briefing session with Toni. She doesn't want to rely solely on Toni to get her up to speed. She's lost forty-five minutes fretting over Marcus. He'll come around. And if he doesn't, well, she has more than enough to keep her occupied. High on that list is keeping Jesse in check.

Another ten minutes pass before Teresa gets up to explore her staff offices. She sifts through the various piles of paperwork in each employee's office and checks on the files in the conference room, then returns to her office. Within minutes the lights flash on throughout the suite and she hears Toni calling her name. Five seconds later Toni swoops through Teresa's door, circles the desk, and pulls Teresa to her feet. After being released from a brief and tender hug, Teresa gives Toni's new pale-blue skirt and matching jacket the once-over and nods.

"Nice outfit."

"I bought five new jackets and five new skirts, and everything matches. It's like twenty-five new outfits," Toni says, then pirouettes.

"Love it," Teresa says and gives a thumbs-up.

"I know you need some time to get settled in, so I'll be back in fifteen," Toni says after eyeing the purse and briefcase in the chair.

"Thanks."

* * *

Ten minutes into her meeting with Toni, the receptionist alerts Teresa that Jesse is on his way to her office. She's barely exchanged glances with Toni when Jesse pushes open the door and, without waiting for an invitation, strolls inside.

"Welcome back, Teresa. And good morning to you, Toni." Teresa is caught off guard. She doesn't speak, but Toni does.

"Good morning, Mr. Waters."

He takes the seat next to Toni and crosses his legs. "I hope I am not being too intrusive, but I was in the neighborhood." He chuckles.

"Of course, you were. Well, Toni's getting me back up to speed, but we can pick this up later." She nods at Toni and tells her, "Give us about ten minutes, please."

Toni pushes up and out of her chair, extends her right hand to Jesse, and says, as he grasps hers in his two, "Good seeing you again." Jesse smiles up at Toni as she steps between the two chairs, the one she's just abandoned and the one Jesse now leans back in, and sashays out of the office.

"Good to see you," Teresa says.

"How is your mother?"

"She's doing fine. Thanks for asking."

Jesse nods and says, "Glad she's recovering. I know it was stressful."

"Things turned out okay."

"Now back to the rat race," he says.

"And I'm playing catch-up."

Jesse nods, then tells her he's glad things are going well for her mother and it's good to see her back. His face looks like he's relaxed, with no hint of any nefarious motives behind his unannounced visit. Teresa offers up her own smile. Maybe he's just come to welcome her back in person, explain his requests for those two reports, tell her it's just a suggested approach, and ask her thoughts on his requests. But she stays on guard just in case his visit means something less gracious.

"So, how's life in corporate America?"

"It is hectic, insensitive, and challenging but pays the bills," he says.

Jesse is the human resources manager for a national energy company and has been for the past five years. According to Mary Ann, he's been frustrated with his stagnant career but refuses to move on to another company for two reasons: he doesn't want to leave the city where his three-year-old twin daughters live with his ex-wife, and he's waiting for his old- ass boss, who's been talking retirement for the past three years, to actually retire. Teresa doesn't know if Jesse knows she knows.

"You don't find it frustrating?" she asks.

"Some days, but so are other aspects of being alive." Jesse chuckles again.

"Since you're here, can we look at dates to schedule that overdue board meeting?" Teresa leans forward and looks over her desk calendar.

"The meeting took place as scheduled."

"What?" Her gaze shifts upward, away from the calendar and directly into Jesse's eyes. He doesn't look away. "I thought we agreed to reschedule," she says.

"I never agreed to that."

"Why would you hold a board meeting without staff?"

"It was my prerogative."

"That is not what I asked you," Teresa says. That feeling she had when Jesse denied her a seat on the board returns. He's undermining her status with the board. It's all about him.

"It was a scheduled meeting, and, amazingly, we managed to get through it without staff." His tone is firm when he says this.

"What suddenly was so urgent for *your* board?" Teresa's tone has a hint of mockery.

"There was no reason to do a last-minute cancellation. I will have the minutes sent over later today."

"I requested a postponement but I guess it was a request you silently denied. Why? Your version of corporate politics?"

"You make that sound like an accusation. There are always politics. Neither the meeting's agenda nor the decisions we reached would have been different even if you were there." Jesse's demeanor borders on nonchalance, as if they are merely discussing the weather.

"We will never know since I wasn't there. No chance for me to represent my ideas on policies. Right?"

"It's the board, Teresa, and I'm the chair. Your attendance would not have changed anything."

"Like I said, we will never know. You're not the only one who has an interest in what the board does, and I think you know this. So, maybe you see me as competition," she says.

"I need you to stay in your lane. Of course, I have plans for the board." Jesse's matter-of-fact tone reminds Teresa of her mother's tone when she had made unilateral decisions for Teresa and her siblings while never failing to let her offspring know that their thoughts and feelings about a situation didn't mean diddly-squat.

"You're worried I want to take over your board? I only asked for one vote." Teresa ends the comment with a snickering laugh. A laugh she honed during her teen years while expressing her distain for Taylor Lee's bullying ways with her kids.

Jesse offers a quiet laugh in response. Then he says, "Not worried. It *is* my board. I just want the line of demarcation between the governance function and the management function to be clearly identified."

"Really?" Teresa says.

"Really."

"The danger of me being one vote on a board of ten members will blur that line?"

"It could for you," he says. "Let's avoid any conflict of interest."

"I would be one vote, Jesse. Conflict of interest or not."

"Then why are you so intent on having that one vote if it doesn't matter?"

"To make sure my voice, the voice of staff, is a factor in the board's decision," Teresa says.

"You are not being excluded from attending our meetings, and feel free to speak your mind when you are in attendance."

"I don't think you're being upfront with me. Why is this such an issue for you?" Teresa stares without any attempt at hiding her frustration with his line of reasoning.

"The better question is why it is an issue for you. I gave you everything you asked for but the board seat. I have been fair and upfront. Why are you fighting me over the board?" Jesse throws up his hands as if expressing his own frustration.

Teresa does not have an answer to his question. She didn't expect to get a seat on the board and had only thrown it out as a negotiating ploy. But now it's more than a ploy to her. But why? It's Jesse's attitude, she tells herself. He's taking the role of board chair too seriously. He's done squat since he's been on the board, and now, all of a sudden, he is the savior of CEC.

"I call BS," she tells him. "I'm not fighting you. It's just the opposite; you're fighting me. And disrespectfully. When I informed you I had to leave town and requested to reschedule the meeting, you could have been upfront with me and told me no. You also waited for me to leave, and then, behind my back, you pay an unannounced visit to the office to quiz staff. Is that your lane?"

Jesse moves his eyes away from her eyes. He looks at some spot above and behind her head while he speaks over the tips of his pressed hands. "The visit happened because many of the board members wanted some insight regarding how the staff is handling the changes, and they insisted on holding the board meeting as scheduled." Teresa laughs, crosses her arms, and leans back in her chair.

Jesse lowers his eyes to look into hers. He offers a half-smile, taps his fingers on the arm of the chair, and then says, "It was a short one with only two agenda items. We revitalized our human resources committee and will require all hiring and involuntary terminations be approved by that committee. In addition, we decided it is better to keep the governance and the management of the organization distinct and separate. That means we don't support your request to be both board member and staff."

"You pulled a Mary Ann on me. Undercut and blindsided your opponent."

"Opponent?" he says, raising an eyebrow.

"Isn't that how you see me?"

"No, no it is not." He points a finger at her, then back at himself. "We are partners in this enterprise."

"Sure, Brutus. Or is it Judas?" Teresa says. Her mind is on fire. Jesse is using *the board* as cover for his own agenda. To what end she doesn't know, but it's not to build a partnership with her. That's for sure.

"Only if you consider yourself Caesar or Jesus. Look, this is not personal, so let us avoid having our discussion devolve into a petty exchange."

"This *isn't* about a partnership with me. If it was, you wouldn't have been so underhanded about it," Teresa says. Now she's certain that Jesse is playing games. Power games where he wants to dominate the organization and reduce her executive role to that of a minion—his male ego out of control. Michael Brown, but with leverage. But like Mr. Brown, Mr. Waters will learn that Teresa Casteel fights back.

"I want to do this job right. Like you, I cannot be bound by the past if we are to move forward," Jesse says.

"Do you have issues with Black women?" His ex-wife is Black, but, according to Mary Ann, she was a unicorn. And his twin daughters are Black, but he's not deeply involved in their lives. So now this juicy Mary Ann tidbit has found its way into the forefront of her attack. Vintage Taylor Lee: personal, aggressive, and disparaging.

His eyes, despite the lingering smile, narrow. "I won't dignify that with a response."

"I may be paranoid, but the only difference I see between me and Mary Ann is color. Every step of the transition from her to me has been a battle with you." Teresa stares at Jesse, whose thin lips are stretched even thinner.

"I am disappointed that you cannot accept a legitimate difference of opinions on how to move forward after a major change in leadership," he says.

Teresa's sense of place, circumstances, and perspective is quickly dissipating. Her mounting frustration and anger are shattering her fragile patience. "These are not legitimate differences. This is a reflection of a power move you're making. This is a reflection of your need to control the organization by controlling me. You're using CEC as a fallback for your lack of power everywhere else in your life. And I'm not having it."

Teresa realizes part of her emotional reaction to Jesse is a carryover from the morning fallout with Marcus. But with Marcus she had willed herself to keep it tightly restrained and not let it turn into angry words to fling at him. There is no love for Jesse to keep her words at bay. They're spewing out, scorching the air as they pass through it. She knows she needs to pull back, needs to keep the discussion about the differences in approaches they want to take. But she needs Jesse's help, his tolerance and patience, to help her reign in Taylor Lee.

Teresa scans Jesse's face trying to gauge his reaction. She's hoping he'll stay calm and help her lower her rising temperature. The silence is heavy. Jesse's smile has vanished. In its place, puckered lips protrude beneath a furrowed brow. His whole head moves, barely noticeably, in slow motion side to side as in disbelief. Teresa feels her chest tighten, feels the blood squeezing through the vessels in her own wrinkled forehead.

Seconds pass before Jesse says, "I do not want to control you. And I do not suspect you want to control me. Mary Ann left the lines blurry. We have to clear them up. That is all we are trying to do."

The rage that erupts and spills out is as startling to her as it is to Jesse, and it's the same conflagration that unleashed her mouth on Taylor Lee. "You're doing a power grab. Pure and simple. You just didn't have the balls to move against Mary Ann. But this little Black girl, no problem."

Jesse looks stunned. He rises slowly to his feet. He shakes his head in bewilderment. "I am not going to continue to subject myself to your discourteous and very unprofessional behavior."

"I don't remember you saying squat to Mary Ann when she cussed out the whole board. *You* have issues that you're projecting on me." Teresa rises too.

"The board has made its decision, and you have to accept it."

"I don't have to accept shit." Teresa's face is now crimson.

"Stop being a bully."

"Stop using your position to feel like a big man," she says.

"I am done with this petty bickering. Decisions have been made. If you cannot live with them, you have options." Jesse's efforts at portraying emotional neutrality have vanished; his voice is now as sharp as a razor's edge. His arms are thrown wide, and the fingers on each hand spread to their limits. The veins in his neck seem ready to pop.

"You're damn straight I do," Teresa says.

Jesse lowers his arms and his voice. "We both need to calm down."

"I don't need to calm down. You and your double standards. I have a right to be pissed."

"Let us agree to disagree for now," he says.

"Let's agree that you need to step back into that little corner where Mary Ann put you and let me lead my organization."

"Do you really want to do battle over this?" he says.

"I do if you do."

"It will not be a contest. You work for the board, not the other way around."

"You want my job?"

"Do you want your job?" Jesse turns toward the door and shoves his hands in his pockets.

"You can't control me. No way. And if your ego can't handle that, then we've got a problem."

"It is not about that, and you know it."

"What I know is you would never have tried this shit with Mary Ann."

"And we both know that you are not Mary Ann."

"Right. I'm the Black woman."

Jesse makes a pretense at laughter. "And I am the Black man."

"Black is more than color," she says.

"That's weak. Playing the race card with me? I'm a professional but don't let this suit fool you," he says, his voice quieter, his shoulders less rigid.

"What's that supposed to mean?"

"It means stop pushing it," he says.

Teresa flings a dismissive hand in his direction and says, "Tokens are for the el train."

Jesse heads toward the door and says over his shoulder, "You need to be careful."

"Or what?"

"The board is mine; management is yours. You report to us. Not the other way around." Jesse tries to lighten his tone.

"You're trying too hard to flex." Teresa is leaning forward over her desk, her neck stretched to its limits.

Jesse shakes his head in a dismissive manner and softly says, "It's not a flex, it's a warning."

"You can't intimidate me, and if you want this job you can have it." As soon as she says the words, Teresa regrets them. She wants her job. She loves her job. She needs her job and the $100,000 that comes with it.

"If you are offering to resign, be careful because the way I feel at this moment I might accept."

"The way I feel right now, I don't give a damn how you feel." That other voice, the sane one, has been lost to the chaos going on inside her.

"*Are* you resigning?" Jesse's tone has hardened. His eyes too. They seem to dare her to take the next step.

"Are you going to get off my back and let me do my job?" Her voice has risen and is borderline shrill. It embarrasses her, which makes her angrier.

"Are you going to let me do mine?"

"Being on the board is just your *hobby*." Teresa manages to work her mouth into a sneer.

Jesse points a finger in her direction and says, "Let us not back ourselves into that proverbial corner."

Teresa senses the threat she poses to herself. Her chest rises, then contracts as she exhales in soft, short spurts. She tries to soften her glare by concentrating on his mouth. She tries to remove the wrinkles that she knows are deforming her brow, by pulling at the creases at the outer edges of her eyes.

She tries to lessen her aggressive posture by sitting down and leaning back in her chair. Despite these efforts she's still in attack mode. She recognizes that boxed-in space Jesse's talking about and the danger it poses. But she needs Jesse to give ground and give her some room to turn around.

"Let's not," she says, attempting to use a softer tone. Attempting to pull back.

"I have heard your concerns, but the board's decisions still stand, and we expect management to comply. Are we clear on that?"

The hardness in his voice is the shove that sends her tumbling into that proverbial corner. Teresa pops up from her chair and shoves it back against the wall.

"You know what you can do with your threats. If you want to run this place, I'll be happy to oblige."

"Your call." Jesse raises his arms with palms up.

"Consider this my notice."

Teresa grabs her bag, pushes past Jesse, and storms out the door into the corridor. A single tear droplet pools in each eye. As she storms through the office, headed for the entrance, not acknowledging the greetings, the smiles, or the inquisitive eyes that follow her silent exit, Teresa knows she's making the dumbest move of her life. But her impulses are far stronger than her thoughts. Her goddamn demons, her mother's legacies, are on full display.

* * *

It's late afternoon when Fraser breezes through the office door. Marcus sighs as he listens to Missy warn him over the intercom that Fraser has just barged past her. The broad-nosed lawyer, his perpetual grin as wide as ever, sweeps into the office, strolls behind Marcus, pounds him on his back, then proceeds to the other side of the desk.

Fraser sports a chocolate three-piece suit, white shirt, and yellow tie. He holds his unlit cigar between the index and middle fingers of his right hand while he poses with his left hand in his jacket pocket. He looks Marcus up and down. Marcus knows he hasn't come to fight about the Womack case since he has arrived sans briefcase. It's about Seleste.

"Missy's there for a reason."

"Because she's a nice piece of ass?" Fraser says.

"To protect me from unscheduled visitors."

"Come on, Counselor, you were expecting me, sooner or later." Fraser eases onto one of the leather chairs and sighs. "Man, Seleste is heartbroken over how you treated her."

"She's a big girl. She'll get over it."

"She's your rock. Can you get over her?" Fraser moves the cigar between his thumb and index finger, puts it between his lips and rolls it around.

"I guess we'll see."

"What's going on with you? That new pussy messing with your head?" Fraser's laugh almost makes Marcus laugh too.

"Sometimes it's best for all involved to part ways," Marcus says.

"How are you going to run this place without her?"

"We'll manage."

"We? You and Missy? You're replacing Seleste with her own goddaughter?" Fraser laughs again as he leans on the desk, moving closer to Marcus. "You know I'll be the beneficiary of Seleste's talents if you two can't work it out. But there's too much history to let it end like this. That shit with your old man is history. It's dead and gone. Work it out with Seleste."

"She's made it plain that she can't work *for* me. That means she wants to work for somebody else and I guess you're it."

Fraser shakes his head and sighs. "I can't turn my back on her."

"I guess that makes you the better man."

"History means something to me." Fraser stands up, his face no longer parading that disarming grin, and sighs again.

Marcus stands too. It's over. Seleste is gone. "This isn't easy for me."

"And worse for her."

"She can have her desk if she wants it," Marcus says.

"She does. Your old man bought that desk for her. She's never forgotten what he did for her. It's that loyalty thing again."

"Yeah."

"Let me tell you something else, and I hope when you get over feeling sorry for yourself, you'll chew on it a bit. Your old man was tough and could be borderline unscrupulous. But he rewarded loyalty, and Seleste was the most loyal of us all," Fraser says, "and if he and Seleste wanted to fuck each other, why should it matter to you or anyone else?"

"Not even my grandmother?"

"If it did, she handled it her way. Kathryn was and probably still is a hellcat. She was nobody's victim."

"I doubt she would have been happy if she knew," Marcus says.

"I know you don't know much about your old man and Kathryn, but he was more than my boss and mentor after I joined the firm. He became more of a big brother. I won't bore you with all the gory details of *my* life, but I needed guidance. And he needed an ear. I know some of what ailed them. You interested?"

"I'm all ears," Marcus says but is not sure, after all these years of ignorance, that he wants to hear anything Fraser has to say about his grandparents.

"I'll say this much and then leave it alone. Kathryn wouldn't run from shit. She was her own woman. She left. She didn't escape. They always had a tense relationship. Your old man pursued his dream, but Kathryn had to defer hers. She wasn't happy."

"What was her dream?"

"New York. Bright lights. Broadway."

Marcus blinks when he hears this. "She wanted to be an actress?"

"She did. But an accidental pregnancy, a hasty marriage, and the old man's selfishness—his word not mine—ended that dream. She resented it and she resented him."

"Accidental pregnancy? Hasty marriage?"

"You can see why they kept you in the dark. But they were just people. Shit happens in life, and you have to hold your breath and move past it." Fraser twirls his cigar prop and keeps his eyes trained on Marcus. "When the daughter got pregnant, they didn't see eye to eye on what to do, so they did what the old man insisted be done. I guess it hit too close to home for Kathryn, and she just tuned out and disconnected. She stayed until you were old enough to handle the shit she was gonna throw your way. Seleste wasn't their problem."

"Thanks for the insight," Marcus says.

"You can step back. I'm sure Seleste would rather be here than my place." Fraser heads toward the door.

"I'd rather she be at your place than here." Marcus shrugs.

Fraser pats Marcus on the back as he moves toward the door. Marcus follows. At the front door, Fraser bows toward Missy, then steps out into the corridor. Marcus stands in the suite holding the office door open while Fraser calls up the elevator. When it arrives, Fraser backs into the car and gives Marcus a half-hearted wave.

"I'll make arrangements for the desk."

"Right."

"See you around, Counselor," Fraser says.

Marcus gives a cursory nod in response, then closes the door and locks it. "The end of a tough day," he tells Missy.

"You okay?" she asks while turning off the main lights in the reception area.

"Yep, couldn't be better."

"Does Seleste want to come back?" she says.

"No."

"Do you want her back?"

"No."

"We can handle things," she says.

"Yep, we can. Just going to take a little time."

"I can do what Seleste did," Missy tells Marcus.

He's headed back to his office with Missy close behind. "To be honest," he says, "I'm not sure exactly what all Seleste did." He takes a seat behind his desk, and Missy sits in one of the guest chairs.

"Are you worried?" she asks.

"No. Looking forward to it. A new day."

"Me too, then," she says, then Missy stands and sits on his desk.

"But let's get something straight about our new day. You and I are colleagues. Professionals. No personal relationship. Not buddies. Not friends. And certainly not lovers," he tells her. Missy looks disappointed and he continues, "So that's part of our deal, or we have no deal."

Missy stands again and returns to the chair. "Deal," she says.

"That means no flirting or touching or anything like that. Got it?"

Even though she pouts, Missy says, "Got it."

Marcus stands, circles past his desk to where Missy sits. He reaches out to her, and they shake hands. "Now it's a done deal," he says.

* * *

Teresa leaves the movie theater and wanders down brightly lit Michigan Avenue headed to no place in particular. Since storming out on Jesse hours ago, she's visited the Art Institute, strolled around Grant Park and wasted an expensive meal at one of the fancier restaurants while being totally preoccupied with the misery she's brought down upon herself. She hadn't really watched the movie either but cried the whole time, sitting in the last row away from the few other patrons.

She's lost control over her life. She's called Marcus several times with no answer but left only one message. He hasn't returned her calls, and she understands why. He has a right to be pissed. He doesn't know why she's so emotionally unpredictable with him and she doesn't know either. What she does know in this moment, as she stares at a young couple hugging and laughing as they pass, is that she feels alone.

The tears begin to pool again, and she knows it's only a matter of seconds before she's making a spectacle of herself in the middle of the crowded sidewalk on North Michigan Avenue. Her phone rings. *Let it be Marcus.* Caller ID tells her it's Toni again. The tears begin trickling out of the corners of her eyes. Toni has left twenty messages over the past eight hours. She's frantic. She's worried. She wants to know what's happened.

Toni's first message says that Jesse met with her and requested that she serve as interim CEO. Despite all the concern that flows from Toni's voicemails, Teresa feels a sense of betrayal because not once has Toni said she told Jesse to go to hell. She doesn't bother listening to this last message.

Teresa squeezes the corners of her eyes to stop the flood of tears rolling down her cheeks. She reaches inside her purse and takes out her sunglasses, hides her teary eyes behind their big dark lenses, then holds her head high and takes extra-long strides to avoid dissolving into a helpless mess. Teresa hopes she looks like a woman on the go and headed somewhere important.

* * *

It's 6:00 p.m., Missy has gone, and Marcus is staring out the office window looking down on the street scene below. Even though he told Missy he wasn't worried about Seleste's departure, there's a knot wound tight in his gut. He's not sure where to begin to fill the hole she's left behind. But that's just how he's feeling now. He knows he can figure out the business and administrative sides of the firm. Eventually. He goes back to his desk and puts his feet up. He's now without any remnant of a family. Marcus knows if he lets himself, he can drown in that river of self-pity. But that's not going to happen. He survived his grandmother's disappearance and his grandfather's death. So, there's no way in hell Seleste's departure from his life will push him off the ledge into those icy waters.

He stands up, looks around his office, and smiles. Walker Mitchell Greene constantly reminded him to appreciate the privileged life he's living. Marcus reflects on his gift-wrapped privileges: the ample trust fund, the cash-generating law firm, the mortgage-free big house, the low-mileage Jaguar, and the debt-free college educations.

Regardless of the bumps in the road his grandparents experienced, they were tough enough to do what needed to be done. Despite the few bumps in the road in his own life, his has mostly been a journey traveled over well-paved boulevards. Marcus moves out of his office and into the corridor. He's been raised to handle shit. He stops in the reception area and looks around. He's feeling a sense of pride.

It's 6:30 p.m. when Marcus packs his briefcase and heads for the door. Tomorrow really will be a new day, and he's ready to move forward, leaving the past to live only in fond memories. *The good times*, he thinks, *will be the only memories to stake out real estate in my head.* He laughs out loud. *I'm a Greene, I can do this.* Marcus begins whistling when he enters the elevator headed home.

* * *

Teresa finds herself a block away from his office. She takes out her phone, dials his number, and feels a little self-consciousness when she says a silent prayer for Marcus to answer. He doesn't. She stops at the entrance to his building and stares through the glass door at an open elevator car. It's seven o'clock. He's probably gone.

She pushes through the entrance and signs in at the unoccupied security desk. The elevator door has closed by the time she decides that if he's in, she'll take full responsibility for their problems. She'll say she really needs him to be there for her now, and she'll promise to be there for him too.

The elevator reaches its destination, and Teresa hesitates before entering the corridor. In four slow steps she's across the small space and is pressing her face against the cool glass door of his office suite. The lights are off. She taps on the door even though it's obvious that no one's in there. Teresa turns away, flops against the nearest wall, and slumps to the floor like a rag doll. Again, the tears start to flow. She shakes her head as she replays the day's worst events.

"Stupid, stupid," she says softly. "You let Jesse run you out of your job. Your hundred-thousand-a-year job. Everything's gone to hell. Gone to hell. Messed up and gone to hell." She goes from crying to sobbing. She slaps herself hard across the cheek. *This is not the place for this shit.*

Teresa pushes herself up on her knees, then stands. She places her sunglasses slowly back on her face and presses for the elevator. It's still there. Inside the car the tears continue to flow as she sends the car back to the lobby. As she passes the now occupied security desk and exits the building, she feels the urge to call Marcus again. But instead she sighs and orders herself to give it a rest. "He'll call when he calls," she says out loud into the evening air. She knows or at least she figures or maybe just hopes that wherever he is, he's as lonely and heartsick as she is.

Twenty-Six

It's the winding down of a long, unimaginable day. Teresa opens the door into her bedroom, says a silent prayer that she knows is useless, and checks her phone. No calls from Marcus. Back in the steamy bathroom, she wipes off the mirror and forces her eyes to look at the face staring back at her. Those eyes, she's sure, are now drained dry. "What," she says to her reflection, "is wrong with you? I'm serious, what in God's name is wrong with you?"

No answers are forthcoming. She stands in silence and continues to scrutinize that face with its puffy eyes staring back at her until, to her dismay, that solemn face becomes Taylor Lee's face, those weary eyes Taylor Lee's eyes, and those drawn tight lips Taylor Lee's lips. Then she realizes she's been wrong. Those sad eyes still have a few tears left to shed. She turns from the mirror and steps into the shower.

Teresa pirouettes beneath the jet stream of water, letting the shower's hot spray cover her tense body. *How fast things can change and how quickly life can turn on you.* She wonders what Tisha and her nieces and nephews will think now. *Will they still think I'm a big fucking deal? Nope, sister auntie, you're just fucking stupid. No not stupid. Mentally ill. They'll say you lost your fucking mind, then your fucking man, and your fucking job all in one day?*

She struggles to relax, to find a lighter thought. Then a glimpse of her sister's shocked expression, when Taylor Lee lost her fucking mind, pops into her head. Teresa almost laughs. One thought leads to another, and like a chain-link fence, images of her trip back home create a heartwarming collage. Her siblings, her nieces, and her nephews, they all love her and look up to her because she's succeeded beyond even her own ambitious expectations. She's been lucky for sure. Her mood begins to lighten when she pats herself on the back.

Yes, she has come a long way by taking advantage of even the slimmest opportunity that made itself known. By being strategic and clever. So how has she let this happen? How has she stumbled into losing a job she's earned and loves? Teresa squirts the lemon-colored shower gel into her palm and begins spreading it across her breasts. Drifting thoughts of how Marcus is feeling make her groan. Teresa knows how vulnerable he feels and how insensitive he probably thinks she is. And he's right to think that because she *has* been immersed in her own feelings.

She's been quick to make Marcus the scapegoat for any discomfort she feels with him. She's been silly and immature and not ready for the vulnerability that comes with the deep passion she's discovered with him. *Marcus is special*, she tells herself. She remembers reading that a good man can provide emotional putty to fill the divots in a woman's life and mend the cracks in her psyche. She knows Marcus is a good man, yet he's where he is, and she's here alone with her thoughts.

She sighs as she gently rubs the sweet-smelling gel between her legs. It feels good. Her body begins to respond. Her thoughts begin to replay images of the last time she made love with Marcus. "Ooh," she says. Before long she's moaning, her solo act taking her mind away from her worries, if only for a brief moment.

* * *

Today has been stressful but busy. Marcus and Missy have put together the beginnings of a plan to move forward. Because the effort has drained them both, Marcus lets Missy leave early. Shuffling back to his office, he pauses in the doorway of Seleste's former office, then steps inside and lets the sadness he feels continue to have its rightful due. He'd been refusing to acknowledge the deep pain he's felt as the result of this split with Seleste, but late last night the sorrow overwhelmed him while he was meandering through his house, a victim of stressed-induced insomnia. Inside his chest a feeling of dejection grew weighty, became heavy enough to cause his legs to buckle.

Marcus moves around Seleste's desk. It's partially covered with papers, files, and office supplies. He drops into the new chair she bought a few weeks ago, props his feet upon the desk and lets the blues have their way. Seleste, the one person who has been there for him for so many years, is now gone, unceremoniously and uncelebrated. Gone without the respect and appreciation she deserves. Guilt eats at his brain with a voraciousness that threatens to destroy any remnants of the self-righteousness he had felt when he was running her away.

It makes him remember. It makes him accept the truth. He covers his face with both hands and massages the skin in short, rough strokes. Seleste's departure has left him with familiar feelings. Familiar echoes from when Kathryn got the hell out of Dodge. He's made her the villain and has held on to his self-righteousness like a life raft. And now he's used that same self-righteousness to terminate his relationship with Seleste. The outlines of his own flawed motives rise up like shadowy spirits from the depths of his repressed thoughts. The ones Bird has seen clearly.

"Go home," he tells himself. "It's been a long day." Marcus isn't quite ready to psychoanalyze himself. Not quite ready to shoulder the unarticulated responsibilities that come with that third eye. He rises and leaves Seleste's former office, softly pulling the door behind him. Standing at the elevator, his thoughts fuzzy with fatigue, he mindlessly pulls his cell phone from his briefcase, and turns it back on. He notes there are several missed calls from Teresa and one from Bird. Teresa has left one voicemail. He sighs as he listens to her tell him she wants to talk, but talking to her is the last thing he wants to do right now. The last thing. He's too weary to climb aboard that rollercoaster tonight.

* * *

Teresa slept well. That blue sleeping pill deserves all the credit. It's Tuesday noon. The clock tells her she's slept for more than twelve hours. She yawns and stretches but has no reason to hop out of bed.

None. So she wraps the thin sheet around her and closes her eyes again. Her dreams are vivid but disjointed. She tosses and turns but doesn't wake up for the next four hours. When she opens her eyes, her head feels like dead weight and her mind empty of thoughts. She blinks to focus and looks at the time.

It's 4:00 p.m. before Teresa wakes up again. She stumbles out of bed, goes into the bathroom, and turns on the shower. After fifteen minutes in the shower, she feels more alert. She goes to the closet, puts on a red robe, and heads to the kitchen. She hasn't eaten in almost twenty-four hours. When she sits down to eat, Teresa decides not to turn her cell back on. After getting no calls from Marcus yesterday and all night, she wanted to stop fretting and being disappointed, so she turned it off. Teresa finishes her meal and goes back into the bedroom. She sighs and closes her eyes. Sleep comes quickly.

When she wakes up again, it's after eight. Teresa turns her cell back on but refuses to check her messages and confirm there are no calls from Marcus. Within minutes the phone rings. It's Toni. Teresa decides to answer.

"Are you okay?"

"I'm fine," Teresa says, her heart touched by the anxiety in Toni's voice.

"Can I visit?"

"Where are you?" Teresa says.

"Out front."

"Out front?"

"Of your building."

Teresa's mood lightens. She needs a friend. "Come on up."

After she calls the security desk, Teresa goes into the bedroom and checks her eyes. They're red but not as bad as they had been. She opens the fridge and takes out the bottle of champagne, the second one Jesse gave her the evening they closed the deal on her becoming CEO. It sits next to the bottle of wine Toni gave her to celebrate her promotion and in front of the three remaining cans of light beer she's kept handy for Marcus.

Teresa feels a sense of dread when she thinks about the possibility that he may never drink another can with her. She will deal with that possibility later. But first, she and Toni will consume the champagne and maybe the wine too. Teresa will give Toni a detailed replay of the clash of wills between Jesse and her that claimed her job as a casualty. She smiles at the thought and has just set the long-stem wide-mouth glasses on the kitchen counter when she hears Toni's soft knock on her door.

Toni scoops Teresa up in a bear hug, lifting her robe in the process well past her naked butt. Teresa's bare feet dangle well above the floor. Several seconds of silence pass between them before Teresa begs to be put back on earth. Toni lowers her to the floor, then takes Teresa's arm, leads her into the living room, and sits her on the sofa. She takes Teresa's face between her hands and turns it side to side, staring into each puffy eye.

"You've really put yourself through the wringer," she says.

"Without a doubt," Teresa replies. "But before we do the postmortems on my career and love life—yes, my love life's in the crapper too—it's time to open what was once a celebratory bottle of champagne. I know, the irony, but it's been calling my name since I got home yesterday."

She unhooks Toni's hands with a tenderness that mirrors the affection she's feeling. For Teresa, in this moment, Toni is the friend she needs to commiserate with on her pitiful career collapse. The role of boss has vanished along with Teresa's optimism about her life. She quickly retrieves the champagne and the glasses and takes a seat on the floor in front of the sofa next to Toni, who has pulled off her shoes. Teresa, her voice a whisper, begins her tale of woe.

She decides to share more than just her career collapse when she sees the concern in Toni's eyes. Teresa tells it all: the slanderous memories of a family of losers that were nowhere near the truth; being chased out of her family's home by a woman who could hardly walk, let alone fight; the frightful treatment of a gallant man who made his way to her as an act of atonement for a wrong he never committed only to get back home and be chastised rather than supported for having made a hard business decision. And her final foolish act, she tells Toni, was the ill-advised confrontation she had with the chairman of her board. "A confrontation," Teresa says, then takes a huge gulp of champagne, "where I foolishly threw my job in his face along with my $100,000 salary plus benefits."

Then Teresa tells Toni that, given her newly acquired status as a member of the unemployed, she had the nerve to waste her now few precious dollars on a good movie she was too upset to watch and an expensive meal she was too depressed to eat. "And well," she says finishing her tale of woe, "the tears I've shed could fill the lake."

The truth of what Teresa says can be witnessed in her dry red puffy eyes and pallid, bloodless complexion. Toni sits in wide-eyed silence and sips her champagne while the tears spill from her own eyes and cascade down her cheeks.

"I don't know what to say," Toni says.

"If you were telling me a story as pitiful as this, I would be speechless too." Teresa laughs.

"You'd tell me to *man* up," Toni says, wiping the tears from her eyes. They both laugh. "You know you haven't really *quit* your job. You just lost your cool and said something you can take back. Just don't give your resignation letter to the board."

"I've thought about that, but I said too much and went too far."

"Too far is handing in your resignation." Toni scrunches up her eyes and puckers her lips. She shakes her head.

"I think Jesse sees that as just a formality," Teresa says.

"Man up. Don't run. Fight." Toni giggles, then sips from her glass. "You can handle Jesse."

"You need to know I've never been as tough as I act. I'm never as sure as I pretend and as far as managing Jesse is concerned, I don't know what I'm doing. I'm mostly reacting to him."

"I think Jesse's doing the same thing with you."

"Maybe."

"And all you did was *threaten* to quit," Toni says.

"No. I gave up my job."

"You're not a quitter."

"But I am my momma's child and crazy stubborn shit is our calling card."

"What will you do?" Toni's crying again.

"I don't know. What are you going to do about Jesse's offer?"

Toni tilts the empty glass to her lips and shakes the last drop onto her tongue. Then she lowers the glass and looks into Teresa's eyes.

"I told him I had to meet with you."

"Take the opportunity when it comes."

"It's your job and not Jesse's to give to me," Toni says.

Teresa tips her empty glass and shakes the remaining drop onto her tongue while she contemplates her response. Sure she wants to keep her job. She loves it. She's earned it. She also needs it and she's good at it. But just as sure as she is sitting here drinking champagne and nurturing a newborn friendship, Teresa's just as sure she'll need to kiss Jesse's ass to keep her job, and she wishes she could. Oh, if only she could, but Teresa knows she's no better than her mother when it comes to humility.

Toni continues to sit, shoulders slumped, eyes reflecting the discomfort she's feeling. Teresa holds on to her own silence. That silence, she knows, is like a strong hand dangling Toni from a noose of uncertainty and apprehension. Despite her genuine affection for Toni, there's still this dark part of her, Taylor Lee's evil gene, which required Toni in the name of loyalty to tell Jesse to shove his job offer up his wimpy little ass. That gene, along with the three glasses of champagne, convince her to leave Toni hanging for a while longer. Teresa closes her eyes and lets the seconds pass. Although lightheaded from the champagne, her mind is still lucid. An emerging honesty like a magnifying glass clarifies some hard truths.

Toni is far from the problem. The truth is you've impulsively and recklessly discarded your job. Your livelihood. And worst of all, you've betrayed the faith Mary Ann had in you. You've never really escaped Hannibal. Never escaped Taylor Lee. You're forever condemned to be influenced by her crazy personality. You've been shaped by it. Those emotional and psychological defects have been embedded in you like hard nails in rubber tires. Teresa inhales imperceptibly and continues her self-flagellation. *It's always only a matter of time and circumstance before the damage gets revealed. Like today. Accept it. It's who you are. It's been a pattern that you've tried to ignore your whole life. You're a real head case. A mishmash of fears, insecurities and volatile emotions over which you have little control.*

Teresa opens her eyes and sets the empty glass on the floor next to her. Toni's still in her trance-like state waiting. "What were you saying?" she asks Toni. "The champagne has me a little tipsy."

Toni giggles and moves over closer and wraps her arms around Teresa. "If I can get Jesse to reconsider, will you?" she says.

"His ego's been bruised."

"He's just a brother with his own issues." Toni sounds so sure of her assessment of Jesse.

"You and your Michael Browns. Always seeing the little boy inside the man," Teresa says.

"They all have little boys stuck somewhere inside. Jesse's little boy works hard trying to be a version of the man he's always admired. You don't think that's cute?" Toni asks.

They both laugh and Teresa knows the alcohol is having its way with Toni. "More bratty than cute to me."

"Bratty is harmless, you know. Michael's little boy is a truant," Toni says.

"Jesse was probably an altar boy."

"That could explain why he's so insecure," Toni says.

"And probably the only Black one in a white church."

"A Black man with a white boy's heart? Now *that* could be a problem," Toni says.

"For a darker sister." Teresa takes Toni's hands, raises them in the air, and says, "I know I won't pass the brown paper bag test but you have a shot."

Their alcohol-induced laughter sends Toni's head into Teresa's lap while Teresa's head falls backward onto the sofa. It takes several seconds before they regain their composure. Teresa has let her guard down with Toni. A sense of well-being settles over her. She's comfortable with it. She feels safe with it.

"We have to figure this whole deal out," she tells Toni, squeezing her shoulder.

"What's there to figure out? You kiss Jesse's little hoity-toity round behind and get back to work."

"Or I tell him to kiss my shapely Black behind and move on, and you move up."

Toni sits up and faces Teresa. "You're really giving up?"

"I've left. Now you need to fight like hell for the job. Okay?"

"There's still a chance you can change your mind, right?" Toni's eyes plead for confirmation.

Teresa closes her eyes before she responds. "There's always a chance," she says, "but I don't see how it can play out."

"We'll sleep on it, get sober, and figure out a way." Toni clasps Teresa's hands in hers.

"I'm not ready for sleep and I've got that bottle of congratulatory wine you gave me. You up for it?" Teresa says.

"Why not? The night's still young. And we still have to figure out what's up with you and Marcus."

Teresa groans, stands and, swaying like a low-hanging branch in a soft breeze, heads to the kitchen. "Yep," she says. "Let's figure out what's up with me and Marcus."

* * *

While he waits for Bird to answer, he thinks about why he didn't call Teresa. With Bird, despite the long silence since their trip, his friend's call means he wants to mend fences. Marcus is clueless as to what Teresa's call means. He's also clueless as to where their relationship is headed. Maybe where all the others have gone: to the end of the road and over the cliff. Is that where they are now? It's her turn to apologize but he doubts that she's calling to do that. And he's determined not to be the one to offer a truce and end this current standoff.

The thought of talking to her increases the tightness in his chest. The weight of his mixed emotions when he thinks about Teresa is familiar and he knows what to call it: a heavy dose of the blues. The same blues that he's experiencing over his failed relationship with Seleste. This bluesy feeling illuminates his imagination like the sun rising on the horizon. It means his relationship with Teresa is over. Another relationship he's too deep in to have it end with no repercussions. He squints his eyes and shakes his head in denial.

"Hey." Bird sounds subdued.

"Just returning your call. What's up?"

"All's well in my world. Yours?" Bird says.

"It's tolerable. We good?"

"Water under a swinging bridge, so let's keep moving. Cautiously."

Marcus laughs and says, "Yeah, right. How's your son?"

"This is moving cautiously to you?" Bird says.

"So, how is he?"

"Talked with him yesterday. Then his stepfather. About an hour."

"How'd that go?"

"The reverend and Tonya aren't on the same page. The reverend says he knows a boy needs his real father in his life."

"Tonya's something else," Marcus says.

"Yeah, sure is. Talked with her this morning and had it out with her. Told her she's out of line and maybe out of her mind for asking me to give up my son. Thanks for the knot on the head."

Marcus is grinning. "Always got your back."

"You and homegirl still good?"

"Well, maybe," Marcus says.

"It's run its course already?"

"Maybe," Marcus says.

"Now are you ready to listen? To visit the analyst's couch?"

"Well, Dr. Freud, you might as well know, I've broken up with Seleste," Marcus says.

"What?"

"Cut her loose. Sent her to Fraser."

"Why?" Bird asks.

"The usual reasons I cut them loose. Too much drama," Marcus says.

"She hurt your feelings and won't apologize? It all starts with Kathryn. She's the black hole that distorts and then swallows up your relationships with women," Bird says.

"I kind of see how that might be."

"An awakening?" Bird says.

"Let's get together. Then you can do your psychoanalysis."

"Finally," Bird says.

"I'll let you know the details tonight."

"Sure you're ready for this?" Bird asks.

"Maybe. I'll holler at you."

Marcus listens to Teresa's voicemail again. "Hope all is well with you," she's saying. "I want to talk. No. What I mean is we should talk. Call me, please." He ponders each word. Each pause. *This rollercoaster of a relationship is getting tiresome,* he thinks, *and it's driving both of us loony. It's too crazy. I'm getting off.*

The second this last thought pops into his head, Marcus feels a sense of dread. Then disbelief. Then a realization, he's not ready to call it quits.

Twenty-Seven

Teresa rolls over on her side to discover she's lying on one of her quilted blankets on the floor of the living room next to Toni. She checks the time, it's 4:00 a.m. Toni's covered by a light green sheet and a light blue sheet is entangled between Teresa's legs. She stands and shimmies free of the sheet. Her robe flies open and she laughs. She spent the whole night communing with Toni with only her robe for cover. No self-consciousness. No awkwardness. She knows the champagne and wine were big factors.

She looks down at Toni, who's sleeping soundly and snoring lightly. Her head's hidden beneath the sheet, and a bare leg, up to her pale, dimpled thigh, protrudes at an angle. The alcohol worked its magic the whole night. When they decided it was time to call it quits and Toni took off her jacket, Teresa began humming the stripper melody. Stumbling while trying to shake her hips, Toni proceeded to perform a striptease that lasted several minutes.

Teresa laughs when she looks at Toni's new outfit neatly laid out with the skirt, blouse, and jacket draped across the back of the sofa. Despite her inebriated state, Toni, with her meticulousness, was not about to leave her new clothes strewn about or left in some heap on the floor. Teresa stares at her former employee and now begins to think of Toni as her friend. Maybe more than a friend. Maybe more like a younger sister.

Teresa's thoughts stray from her growing friendship to the situation that brought Toni to her condo last night. *I don't have my job anymore. I gave up my fucking job.* Teresa gathers the sheet, then goes into and passes through the bedroom and into the bathroom. She turns on the shower, empties her bladder, and goes back into the bedroom where she flops down on the bed.

Teresa drops her head into her cupped hands and starts to cry. The tears flood her cheeks while her screams are held back by the force of her hands pressed tightly over her nose and mouth. Foreboding and grief pervade her whole body. Her sense of awareness disappears under the weight of the sorrow and despair that overtake her. She sits frozen in time and space while the gravity of the enormity of her loss descends over her like a dense fog. Soon her crying comes to an end. The reservoir of tears has been exhausted. The silent screams recede, but the emotional intensity leaves her limp and drained. Teresa lowers her hands and raises her head.

Her awareness begins to return. She recognizes minute details. She's in her bedroom. Toni's asleep in the living room. The shower's on. She can hear it and feels the heated steam that has floated through the open bathroom door and dampened the back of her neck. Teresa eases off the bed, removes her robe, and lets it drop to the floor. She swipes a finger across her face under each eye, then walks slowly into the bathroom and steps into the shower. When Teresa leaves the shower ten minutes later and goes back into her bedroom, Toni's sitting on the bed.

"Your eyes are bloody red. The champagne and wine?" Toni asks.

"The hellhole I've dug."

"It's not too deep," Toni says, "and I've got a plan."

* * *

It's 5:30 a.m. and the two women are sitting on the floor in front of the sofa, drinking coffee. "I guess our night of booze and bluster was a temporary reprieve," Teresa says. "And now that I'm sober and in the light of day, I have to face the facts *again* that I have totally messed up my life."

Toni's voice is soft, below a whisper. "We've got this," she says, "Jesse let this get out of control. I don't think he wants or is ready for this epic failure. Mary Ann ordained you. He can't go against that."

"I backed myself into a corner. And him too."

"You can walk back out." Toni makes a walking gesture with her fingers.

"Meaning?"

"It's still your job. Come into the office and get to work."

"Just like that?" Teresa says.

Toni snaps her fingers. "And Jesse will..." Toni blinks and laughs.

"I *have* to talk with him." Teresa sighs.

"Call him and say, 'I'm back.'"

"Well how about that!" Teresa says. The mocking tone makes her laugh.

"Then it'll be on him. Right?" Toni shakes her head in affirmation.

Teresa squeezes her forehead. "I don't think I have the balls to do that."

"You think Jesse has the guts to fire you? I don't."

"Just get him on the phone and say, 'I'm back'?" Teresa says.

"Yup." Toni grins. "Just say, 'I'm back.'"

"What's he going to say? 'Glad you made it in'?"

"Who cares as long as it's not '*You're fired.*'" Toni winks.

"I don't think I can do it," Teresa says.

"If you quit, I quit. If Jesse fires you, I quit. Period." Teresa smiles. "Don't be silly."

"I won't be if you won't be," Toni says. "That's your job. Not Jesse's and not mine." She raises her fist in a power sign. "To the sisterhood."

Teresa laughs softly, then raises her own fist. "To the sisterhood."

* * *

They agreed to meet in the coffee shop on the corner across the street from CEC offices. Teresa arrives at the coffee shop at 10:00 a.m. Toni's already sitting at a small square table next to a window facing the street. They say nothing as Teresa takes the seat across from Toni, who looks up, smiles, and goes back to fiddling with her phone. Toni has ordered their drinks. Teresa picks up her cup, takes a swig, then leans back and takes in a deep breath. They have rehearsed the phone call Teresa will make to Jesse. Teresa goes through the scenario in her head.

"Good morning, Jesse. I'm heading into the office ready to get back to work. I understand that we may not always agree on board policies or management tactics, but we are on the same team. I would like for us to meet again and finish our discussion and begin this leadership journey on a sounder footing. I also owe you an apology for my erratic behavior, and I do understand that with you and me as the new leaders of the organization, we are not bound by nor should we be committed to the past. So, when can we meet?"

Toni drafted this brief apology and they conducted several dry runs including possible responses by Jesse and possible counter-responses by Teresa. The plan is to call Jesse, at 10:30 a.m., on his cell phone. Toni's assessment is that Jesse understands all the ramifications of Teresa's declared resignation and that he'll be more than willing to negotiate a peace treaty. Jesse's request for Toni to serve as acting CEO, according to Toni, was almost apologetic. "His words," Toni told Teresa, "were really tentative and his voice sounded a little shaken."

Teresa listened to Toni's revelations with more eagerness than she let on and afterward felt a sense of relief and a bit more confident that she could walk out of that corner. Now that she's sitting here minutes from making the call, Teresa's sense of confidence that she can pull this off is growing. Jesse's not a bigger deal than she is.

Or tougher than she is. Not smarter either. Jesse became the board's chair the same way she became the CEO. By anointment. Her misstep was to ignore his ego. To attack his ego really. She knows enough about Jesse to have avoided that mistake. But she hadn't. She'd lost control. She will remedy that mistake. She'll let Jesse have his moment.

"Toni, what are you doing?" Teresa asks.

"Getting my to-do list together for today, boss," Toni says, then looks up briefly and smiles.

Teresa checks the time. It's 10:29. "Showtime," she says, taking her phone out of her bag. She inhales and exhales slowly. Closes her eyes and runs through her spiel one last time. Her eyes pop open when her phone rings. She looks down at it. "Jesse," she whispers to Toni, her eyebrows arched in surprise as she answers. "Hello, Jesse."

"Good morning," he says, his voice sounding strained. "You have a few minutes to talk?"

"Yes."

"We need to meet. Can we?"

Teresa's dumbfounded. She can't get her head around this new development.

"Can I get back to you? I'm in the middle of something. Say in an hour?"

"An hour's fine. Just call me on my cell."

"Okay," she says and disconnects. She looks at Toni.

"What did he say?"

"He wants to set up a meeting."

"And?" Toni says.

"You heard. I'll call him back."

"You're gonna meet, right?" Toni says.

"Probably. He sounded weary."

"I told you," Toni says.

"You called that one." Teresa falls back in her chair and closes her eyes. "He's as messed up as me," she says, more to herself than Toni.

* * *

Bird has brought some Jamaican cuisine to the house. They sit at the dining room table and share light conversation while they eat. When the meal's finished, Marcus tells Bird about Missy's revelations.

"Gossip," Bird says.

"What if she's the reason Kathryn left?"

"Gossip," Bird says again.

"Seleste didn't deny it."

"She said it's none of your business either way. And I agree." Bird stands and begins to pace. "Whatever happened between Pops and Seleste has nothing to do with you. Doubt if you even crossed their minds if they decided to do the thing. And if Kathryn knew and was ticked, and since you were still her grandson, why wouldn't she take you, too?" He stops pacing and is standing behind Marcus.

"You tell me." Marcus raises his arms as if in surrender.

"Maybe you were the issue."

"What the hell did I do?" Marcus says and turns to face his friend.

"You were born."

"Make it make sense." Marcus taps his forehead twice.

"Never told you my opinion because you're hypersensitive about Kathryn. But if it's the day of reckoning and you're ready for it, I'm game," Bird says, moving back around to the side of the table opposite Marcus.

"Please no Freud shit," Marcus says.

"Nope. It's Bird shit." They both laugh.

"I'll take that for what it's worth. Let's do this, Doc." Marcus leans back in his chair and clasps his hands together over his head.

"Your understanding is that Kathryn and Pops suspected that your mother was raped. Pops wanted you born and then raised by them. Kathryn didn't. She didn't want you, bro, and resented your old man for bringing you into the world and keeping you front and center in her life. Resentment grew and, if in fact Pops had an affair with Seleste and Kathryn found out, then she used it as an excuse to book."

Bird nods his head, points his finger, then continues, "Their marriage was already in trouble. It was in trouble because of *you*, not Seleste, who, if she did it with Pops, was only a symptom. Who knows what kind of arguments Kathryn and Pops had about you before you were even born." Bird is up and pacing again.

"Somewhere in your subconscious you *know* this. You're logical. Nothing else makes sense. Right?" Marcus lowers his arms and drops his head on the table. Bird comes back around the table to pat his friend's back. "Heavy, I know. It's been my theory for a long time. The Seleste thing doesn't change that."

Marcus raises his head with his chin propped up by the knuckle of his index finger. He stares at Bird, then says, "That may be the case. Kathryn may have left *me*. And maybe I knew it but didn't want to face it. And maybe it's the reason I haven't been obsessed with hearing her explanation or reconnecting with her."

"Should, you know."

"Should what?" Marcus says.

"Hear it from Kathryn."

"That'll be like recovering from a chest wound and asking to have a bullet put through your brain."

Bird sighs and says, "Or discovering that an apology and expression of remorse might heal that wound."

"I doubt she regrets leaving," Marcus says.

"Why wouldn't she?"

"Her reason for leaving hasn't changed. I'm still alive," Marcus counters.

"And she's had years to ponder and regret. With the passage of enough time, people reflect on a lot of things they did and didn't do," Bird tells him. "That's the point you made to me about Malik: that what I do now with some sense of righteousness will come back to haunt me down the road. Right?"

"If that's the case, why hasn't Kathryn reached out to me seeking forgiveness?"

Bird raises his eyebrows. "Or you to her offering forgiveness?"

"I don't see how I benefit at this stage in my life."

"You don't think you loved her?" Bird asks.

The question is unexpected. Marcus shrugs his shoulders. His eyes leave Bird's face and focus on the tabletop. That lowdown blues feeling is back and coursing through his veins as if injected with a hypodermic needle. He raises his head and looks at his friend. "I did," he says.

"Let her off the hook. You told me what I had to do for my son. I'm telling you what you need to do for your grandmother. The one who raised and cared for you."

"After fifteen years, tell her I forgive her?"

"Tell her you want her back in your life," Bird says.

"I don't think I do." Marcus grunts.

"Then tell her you *need* her back in your life. And *that* you do."

"I don't."

Bird chuckles and says, "Mom told me when I was really angry at my dad to forgive him and release the prisoner. And she said that prisoner wasn't my dad but me."

"What is forgiveness exactly?"

"Don't know. I haven't done it yet," Bird says. They both laugh again. "But I think Mom was right. My issues with my dad are affecting my relationship with my son, somehow, and I'm a prisoner until I fix things with my dad."

"Then you first," Marcus says. They both laugh again.

* * *

They're sitting in CEC's executive office. It's nine o'clock at night and Jesse is dressed down for the occasion: pale blue short-sleeved polo shirt, brushed denim jeans, no socks, and white low-cut sneakers. Teresa's surprised. She has never seen him out of a suit in the four years she's known him and believes this change is a tactic but isn't sure to what end. To disarm her into believing this is going to be a friendly chitchat? Then lull her into what? She's clueless about his agenda, and until his call, she'd been prepared to kiss ass. She's not sure she can if Jesse comes at her the wrong way.

"Let me say first," he begins, "that I know you are intelligent, ambitious, straightforward, and passionate. I have always admired you as a person, as a woman, and as a member of our staff. Second, I am a Black man who has never tried to be anything or anyone else. And third, I fought like hell for you in our board meeting to become our next executive. That all being said, I want to apologize and believe you deserve an apology. There was no urgent reason to move ahead with the board meeting or the policy decisions we made in your absence."

He stops and appears to wait for a response. Teresa only nods for him to continue because she has no response. And her own apology has yet to be erected in her mind. She's totally unprepared for his concession speech. But Toni had been on the money about him being regretful. Now Teresa wonders how Toni could be so on point. What had she and Jesse talked about and how responsible was Toni for Jesse's retreat? Has she underestimated Toni's political skills? This possibility impresses her and adds a whole new dimension to Teresa's view of her new friend.

"You should know," Jesse is saying, "I am not your adversary. But I think we do need to air our differences in order for us to avoid any misunderstandings going forward."

"I agree."

"Let me tell you where I stand on the Mary Ann question," he says. "She brought me on the board when my boss ordered me to get more engaged in community activities. He knew Mary Ann, and she got *her* board to add me as a member. I became one of two Black people out of twelve. I didn't agree with the rubber stamp relationship to which the board acquiesced, but I understood it. All of them were her friends or friends of her friends. Or in my case, the subordinate of her friend. But during the past four years, I have become a member on three additional boards, all nonprofits, and I've learned the appropriate roles of both board and management. And what we have at CEC does not reflect those roles." He pauses and appears to wait for a response from Teresa.

"I see," she says and nods for him to continue. He's telling her some things she didn't know and she has nothing to add or contest. Yet.

"Even her anointment of you was not within her responsibilities as management. It's the board's responsibility to recruit executive candidates, interview them, and select our best candidate and hire her or him as the top executive. It's also the board's role to sign off on the new position of vice-president you created but did not get board approval to move forward on. All of this reflects the Mary Ann way of doing business. In my opinion CEC needs a more appropriate board structure and a better system for managing policy, which is one of its major responsibilities." He stops again and appears to wait for her response. When Teresa doesn't respond voluntarily, he says, "Are we on the same page so far?"

Teresa's at a loss for a response that will satisfy her own sense of staying in the game. She's never researched or studied any literature on boards. All she knows is what's she's observed with Mary Ann and *her* board. And the realization in this moment that she's gone to battle on that flimsy premise is disheartening. That she's risked her job based on that flimsy premise is humbling. And that she has to kiss ass because of that flimsy premise is repentance. She says to Jesse while trying to look confident and sound strong, "So what exactly are your ideas for board reform?"

Jesse is gracious and merely repeats what he's already said. She again nods but has no input or feedback. She only wants to get out of here with her job. And after a few more repetitions of his compliments and his mea culpas, she has her job back. She is far less jubilant this time than when she got the job the first time. There are no negotiations this time around. This is her comeuppance and deservedly so. And there's no confusion in her mind that Jesse is a force she'll have to reckon with in the days and years to come as she watches him stroll out of her office.

* * *

"Well?" Toni walks in and slides onto one of the guest chairs.

"As if you don't know. Good eavesdropping job this time. I didn't hear a thing," Teresa says and laughs. "Officially for the record, I'm back."

They both jump up, erase the short distance between them, and embrace. They stay glued together for several seconds before Teresa steps back and looks into Toni's eyes and says, "How much of this is your doing?"

"Beg your pardon?" Toni says, her suppressed grin still evident.

"That man was not the Jesse I expected. You had nothing to do with that?"

"All I did was let him know I wasn't available and he had to make some serious decisions."

She pulls Toni back in for a second hug. Her tears bubble up from deep within, then spill over and down Teresa's cheeks. She doesn't feel embarrassed but rather a sense of relief, then joy. "Let's go to my place and grab some champagne on the way," she says.

"Sounds good to me, girlfriend," Toni replies, "but can we go to my place? Please. I want you to see it. Oh, and then we can work on your boyfriend problems."

Twenty-Eight

"I've thought about your take on Kathryn's reasons for leaving," Marcus says. "I remember some things she said to me. Some things my grandfather said to me. Some things they said to each other that I overheard. It's like figuring out a mystery that I never knew was a mystery. You might be right."

"Might be?" Bird says.

"Family stuff is messy. Complicated."

"Sure is," Bird says.

"That's why I've wanted to keep it simple. I didn't know and I didn't care. She left, it hurt, and I buried it with indifference." Marcus stands and peers out at the lake.

"Avoidance. That's you. I'm different. I dwell."

"Before capitulating in full surrender," Marcus says.

"Sometimes."

"All the time from my vantage point." Marcus smirks.

"It's my marriage you're referencing. But my family's no picnic either, and there were things I had to handle. I kept you in the dark about that."

"Like what?" Marcus asks.

"Like my parents divorcing."

"I know about that," Marcus says.

"About the divorce but not all the conflict that came with it. And now we're a family of two tribes. Me and Mom and the other tribe," Bird says and laughs. "Joyce and Janelle will always be daddy's girls. Not outright warfare between the tribes. The truce is fragile. Always in danger of collapsing. I dwell on it."

"Dwell how?"

Bird sits back in his aluminum-framed chair with its green and white canvas. He crosses his legs and one of his open-back sandals falls off an ashy foot. "I blame Dad," he says. "And Joyce and Janelle for not blaming Dad. He broke up the family."

"Who does Milly blame?"

"Mom says there's enough blame to go around. For all of us. I asked her how can the kids be blamed for their parents' divorce. Get this. She said it is because they are often the reason for the marriage in the first place. She looked me dead in the eye and laughed. Was not funny." But Bird chuckles after he says this.

"No family reunions on holidays I take it?" Marcus says.

"At Mom's, the two tribes but no Dad. But at Dad's, I'm a no-show along with Mom. His second family, I'm not up for that. Besides, it would be a slap in Mom's face."

"The son sides with the mom and the daughters side with the dad. There's some real psychology going on there." Marcus grimaces. "Making kids choose sides is the epitome of failure by parents. It's a no-win situation for the kids."

Marcus turns to look north toward the Loop. They're on the balcony of Bird's Hyde Park condo on the twentieth floor. It's in an upscale high-rise building and has a good view of downtown and the lake. Looking north toward the Loop, skyscrapers light up the night sky.

Marcus sighs with a deep appreciation for having grown up in Chicago in a well-off family despite being the Black stereotypical parentless child raised by grandparents. His trip to Hannibal and getting a real sense of Teresa's challenges growing up was just further evidence of the privileged life he had growing up. Bird's childhood wasn't that bad either.

"Man, we need to stop whining," Marcus says. "Our lives were never as bad as they could have been."

"I keep telling you that. You're a trust fund baby."

"And you were raised in an intact family. It's not always about money where kids are concerned." Marcus shakes his head from side to side, emphasizing the point.

"Says the man who didn't have to work for his," Bird says, shaking his head up and down to emphasize his point. "Money makes all your problems easier to survive."

"I guess you're right about that. Makes me respect how tough Teresa *had* to become to get where she is today."

"Too tough for you, huh?" Bird says.

"Maybe. Maybe not."

"Is this woman going the way of the Dodo bird like Ana? You followed this one all the way to Missouri when you wouldn't go up to Milwaukee to rendezvous with your Brazilian lover, so can you really drop this one so easy? You went to Hannibal, bro. I think you're into Teresa more than you were Ana. What are you going to do?" Bird reaches in the cooler and pulls out another light beer for Marcus.

"The ball's in her court," Marcus says.

"And if she passes it to you?"

"I duck and let it go out of bounds," Marcus says, then shrugs.

"And if she passes it to another player?"

Marcus hesitates before saying, "By another player, you mean?"

"She has options, my man," Bird says, "including me."

Marcus laughs, but agrees that Teresa probably has a lot of options out here. "Food for thought," he tells Bird, and takes a swig of his beer.

* * *

They're in Toni's apartment in Hyde Park. It's a spacious two-bedroom tucked in the southeast corner of a courtway apartment complex. Teresa is doing a walk-through, while Toni's on the phone with her mother. Toni's place is as neat as her office and very girly. Pink, yellow, and green colors dominate the walls. Teresa makes her way back to the living room, where four chairs fill the space: two burgundy armchairs, a burgundy recliner and a burgundy round chair.

A side table sits on the right side of each armchair. No sofa but a short, wide stylish wooden coffee table sits in the center square created by the chairs. Toni's second bedroom has been converted into a home office, where she has gone to talk. Teresa takes the round chair and sinks into its circular bottom until her feet come off the floor. She's tired emotionally and physically.

Teresa knows her return to the office tomorrow will cause a minor stir. She won't do a memo or have a meeting to address the events surrounding her abrupt departure from the office and her sudden return three days later. She's going to take a page from Mary Ann's playbook. She really wants to go home and go to bed, but Toni insists on celebrating. Toni has, Teresa now believes, rescued her from, probably, the worst decision of her life. *Can Toni work a second miracle with my love life? If only,* Teresa thinks.

Toni's carrying two glasses of champagne when she returns to the living room and sets one next to each of the armchairs. "How are you going to resolve your impasse with your mother?" Toni asks and plops down in one of the armchairs.

Teresa struggles off the round chair, reluctant to leave its sleep-inducing comfort and walks over to the other armchair and plops down, then picks up her glass of champagne. "There's no impasse. We're done. Ours is a relationship that can't be salvaged. I'm tired of trying."

"She's seriously sick with cancer," Toni says.

"I'll do my part. Visit each month or sooner, depending. Help out financially but I'm done hoping for a miracle."

"Me and my mother have our problems too, but I have to keep trying."

Teresa looks at Toni, wonders what kind of problems and realizes she knows little about Toni's personal life and has been indifferent to it. Until now. "You have a momma?" Teresa says, unable to contain her sense of guilt about her past relations with her protégé.

"Ever since I was born," Toni responds.

"Why have you kept your personal life so secretive?" Teresa knows this disingenuous apology will work with Toni.

"I try, obviously not always successfully, to keep business and personal separate." Toni grimaces.

Teresa smiles, mostly because she reads Toni so well, then says, "So what kind of problems do you and Momma have?"

"She has always believed the world is flat. Me, I've always argued that it's a triangle." Toni laughs, then takes a quick sip from her glass. "It got intense after my marriage. And it got worse after I divorced him."

"Married? And divorced?" Teresa leans in Toni's direction, glass poised for another sip, maybe a gulp.

"Yup. My parents have been married for thirty years. Not always happily but they stayed together. They dated for three years before they married. She thinks I play at life. Majoring in liberal arts. Not getting a professional graduate degree. I think she's trying to make her life choices work in her own head, and my choices grate against her delusions."

"How long were you married?"

"Nine months. I was pregnant but I never told my family. I had a miscarriage and realized I didn't want to be with him like that. We'd only known each other for three months before I messed up."

"How old were you?" Teresa's even more stunned by this revelation.

"Sophomore year of college. Found out I was pregnant and scared to death. I told him we needed to get married before I told my parents. He was as dumb as me. So we got married but held off telling my parents about the pregnancy. Thank God we did."

"We have more in common than I could have imagined," Teresa says.

Toni sets her glass down on the side table and turns to face Teresa.

"Really? Spill the beans."

"I was going into my sophomore year of high school. He was a senior and going to college. We hung out for a while. Did it a few times. And I got knocked up. Told him. He told his parents. His parents told my momma. They worked out some kind of deal. I was forced to abort the fetus. That's what his momma called it. And, oh yeah. He was a white boy."

Toni reaches for her glass, takes a huge gulp, sets the glass back down, and, eyes reflecting surprise, stares at Teresa, who's sipping from her own glass and staring back at Toni. Seconds pass. "Yeah," Teresa says after the long pause, "I know. A white boy."

"Having sex in high school."

"Oh, yeah. That too," Teresa says.

* * *

"I'm not sure what we're doing," Marcus says, explaining to Bird his concerns about his relationship with Teresa.

Bird is nearly prone with his legs stretched out and Marcus sits with his legs crossed. Marcus has indulged his friend and eaten Bird's favorite junk food with gusto: the double cheeseburger and large order of fries. Between them is a wooden table now hosting a half-empty bag of potato chips, soiled wrappings that once contained their burgers and fries, and a plate holding Bird's freshly baked chocolate chip cookies. It has been reduced from eight cookies down to two. The cooler, housing the beer, sits in front of them against the black iron railing with a dozen cans still inside. Both men are sipping beers and munching on the chips.

"Forming a relationship," Bird says.

Marcus looks sideways at his friend and sticks another chip in his mouth. "The mystery is what kind," he mumbles.

"Too early to tell, if you ask me," Bird says.

"Maybe." Marcus tilts his can and takes a quick sip.

"What percentage of your time together is flying high?"

"Eighty, easy. But the nosedives are unnerving." Marcus points his hand upward slowly, then drives it downward.

"The sex?"

"Sixty percent of the high-flying." Marcus nods to emphasize how good the sex is.

"Maybe that scares her. Good sex makes women feel vulnerable. She doesn't want to lose control of her feelings."

Marcus looks at Bird and laughs. "What book have you been reading?"

"An article in the psychology magazine I subscribe to, and a female psychiatrist authored it. She says that today's women want to be independent and don't trust men with their vulnerabilities."

"The reverse is true too. Men have the same concerns."

Marcus gulps rather than sips when he tips his beer again. "True. It's about taking a risk. So you two have to decide if what you see as possibilities are worth the risk of a crash and burn." Bird uses his hand to imitate a plane crashing.

"I've always bailed out way before the catastrophic plane-meets-earth scenario. That's what I'm thinking about now. Is it time to bail?"

"You ever considered you may have bailed too soon a few times? Or is it your intention to never marry? And never father a child?"

"I've seen your movie and it's discouraging," Marcus says.

"I'd do it all over again, knowing what I know now, and it would have a far better ending. Marriage wasn't the problem. It was me and Tonya. Too young for the responsibilities that came as part of the deal. I want to give it another try someday."

"Really?" Marcus says.

"Why not? There are few experiences in life that don't have their ups and downs. Besides, why would I want that *"L"* to be permanent?"

"I could see myself with a son. Or daughter," Marcus says.

"A wife?"

"My kid would need a mother. So I guess," Marcus says, then laughs.

"Say you want to make that move. Ana or Teresa?"

"Not even close. Teresa." Marcus goes to the cooler, pulls out two cans and tosses one to Bird. "I suppose," he says, dropping back into the chair, "that it's time Teresa and I had a real conversation."

"Good. It seems we're making progress. Anything else I can do to straighten out your life?" Bird inhales a cookie, then takes a gulp of beer.

"I think I'm ready to call it a night." Marcus yawns and stands up.

"Like old times," Bird says. "You still can't hang with the big boys."

* * *

"He's gone MIA on me," Teresa says.

"What are you going to do about it?"

The bottle of champagne has been empty for over an hour. Teresa's been energized by their discussion of men. Now Toni has zeroed in on her relationship with Marcus and Teresa feels fully revitalized.

"Isn't that where you come in?"

"Hmm," Toni says. She sits back, lifts her legs, and plants her feet firmly on the edge of the chair's cushion. She sets her glass on the side table, wraps her arms around her legs, and interlocks her fingers. "What are you going to do?" Toni turns her head to face Teresa. "Show up at his place."

"Unannounced?"

"Unannounced," Toni says.

"And get the surprise of my life?" Teresa frowns and shakes her head.

"Get answers. If there's a surprise, that's an answer. If you can locate him, then you two can get some answers. Simple, yes?" Toni winks, then turns to get her glass. "Bold action is required here," Toni says after tipping the glass and draining the last drops. She eases her legs down off the chair and stands. "More bubbly?" she asks.

Teresa stares at Toni, furrows her brow, squints her eyes and ponders. Then nods in the affirmative. When Toni moves over to Teresa's chair and retrieves the other emptied glass, Teresa says,

"I'm not sure what I want. Or what I want from him." She shakes her head from side to side. "That sounds pitiful, doesn't it?"

"To be honest, yep it does." Toni laughs and heads to the kitchen. When Toni returns and hands Teresa the refilled glass, she says,

"You know what you want. You want Marcus Greene. You just don't know what to do with him."

"Brilliant insight." Teresa lifts her glass and points it toward Toni. "You nailed it. What to do with that man?"

"Do you ever want to get married?" Toni asks.

"I've been thinking about it and tried to discuss it with him once."

"How did it go?"

"Because of me it went south pretty quickly." Teresa grimaces.

"If he proposed, what would you say?"

"Honestly, I'm not sure."

"Let's say he proposes to some other woman, what would you say?" Toni lifts her glass and points it toward Teresa. "Honest answer."

"You mean after I shot and stabbed them both?" Teresa laughs, but her heart drops with the idea of Marcus with someone else. Especially Ana.

"Weren't you anxious and excited when Mary Ann just up and made you CEO?" Toni says.

"Yes," Teresa answers softly.

"I think if you give up Marcus, it would be the same as when you quit your job. You'll regret it. Big time. But you know, if you don't want him, can I have him?" Toni raises her eyebrows.

"I see your point."

"So, sister, get it together and go get your man back like you went and got your job back."

"You're right, sister," Teresa says, pursing her lips and lightly shaking her fists.

"That's the fighting spirit," Toni says.

Teresa stops shaking her fists and looks Toni squarely in the eyes. "But what if he doesn't want to be got back?"

"I don't think that's going to happen," Toni says and pats her chest near her heart.

*　*　*

When Fraser called, Marcus told him it was unexpected and that Fraser's invitation to meet to tie up loose ends would be a waste of time. But Marcus agreed to the meeting anyway because Fraser sounded so earnest. It's late morning and the two of them are sitting in a small coffee shop just west of State Street. Fraser's giving Marcus an update on the Womack case. Marcus is focused on the scene framed in the window behind Fraser's head even though nothing noteworthy is happening. Marcus just wants Fraser to know he's uninterested in George's case.

"You're still the counsel of record and you need to know we're not letting you off the case." Fraser sips his unadulterated coffee and tilts his head forward for emphasis.

"For the record, I don't care and I'm sure George doesn't either. It's your case," Marcus says, "and wishing you two the best of luck is all I have to offer now."

"Don't sell yourself short, my friend, you have far more than luck to offer." Fraser chuckles, takes out but does not unwrap a cigar. He slides it into place between his index and middle fingers and begins doing a finger pass roll. Marcus watches with interest as the cigar spins between the showboat's long thin digits. It's a parlor trick Fraser does to disarm his opponents, and it works.

Marcus forces his eyes away from the twirling cigar and up to the performer's face. "You made it sound like you had something to tell me that I needed to know. George's case doesn't live up to the hype."

Fraser continues to keep the cigar flipping between his fingers. He nods and says, "That was just the warmup act. Question: are you still nursing your sore feelings about what may or may not have gone down with the old man and Seleste? It's been a few days, enough time to collect your senses."

Marcus leans back in his chair, looks around the café, and sees a couple of curious onlookers watching the tumbling cigar. He smiles, then says, "It's not keeping me up at night."

"Good. What about Kathryn? She keeping you up at night?" Fraser tosses the cigar in the air, catches it in the palm of his hand and slips it back inside the pocket of his suit jacket. Light applause from the onlookers expressing their appreciation for the brief moment of entertainment. Fraser waves a dismissive hand their way. "Well?"

"I sleep fine. Thanks for your concern." Marcus dips his head to meet his cup of herbal tea halfway.

"I don't think she does," Fraser says, and shakes his head. Marcus raises his head. His brow is carved with a deep crease.

"*Who* doesn't?" he asks, more a challenge than a question.

"Kathryn." Fraser lowers his head to sip from his cup.

"I imagine she's sleeping fine. Why wouldn't she be?"

"That's the main act. I've been talking to Annie Louise." Fraser leans back in his chair and blows out a stream of air that crosses the small table. Marcus feels it as a faint breeze.

"Come again?"

"I decided to talk with Kathryn after this debacle with you and Seleste. Get some clarity on some issues since you weren't going to, my friend."

"You talked with Kathryn?" Marcus squints at Fraser. His leg begins involuntarily bouncing under the table, thankfully out of Fraser's sight.

"I tried but she is indisposed, so I talked with Annie Louise, her first cousin. You know her, right?"

"Yes," Marcus says, unable to fully grasp what Fraser is telling him. "You called Kathryn?"

"Like I said, I tried. Used my private investigator, Ronnie—you know he's good—to track her down. Found out she's institutionalized. Dementia."

Marcus closes his eyes, rubs them gently, then eases them back open. "Dementia? Institutionalized?" is all he can muster to say.

"Shocking, I know. She was so vibrant, but hell, at least she's being looked after pretty well. Annie Louise is handling her affairs. They were living together until Kathryn became impossible to manage. She's been institutionalized for the past year. Doesn't recognize anybody or even know who Annie Louise is. Sounds like she's just a vegetable." Fraser pauses as if waiting for Marcus to speak.

When Marcus closes his eyes again, Fraser continues. "But before Kathryn's mind went haywire, the two of them were like sisters. According to Annie Louise, she and Kathryn had always been so. They both were the only children of brothers. Your great granddad and great granduncle. I think that's how it goes in the family generational hierarchy. Annie Louise had a lot to say about what Kathryn said about her marriage. And you." Fraser pauses again.

Marcus opens his eyes and says, "I'm not sure I want to hear this."

"That's not my concern. You need to hear this," Fraser says. The sternness in his voice surprises Marcus, renders him voiceless. Fraser continues, "According to Annie Louise, Kathryn never loved the old man. Her pregnancy ruined her ambitions and birthed her resentments. She wasn't cut out to be a wife or mother. But your great grandmother, Geneva, wasn't having her daughter get an abortion or become a single parent and taint the family name any more than the pregnancy already had done. Geneva was very religious. Did you know that?" Fraser pauses again and Marcus closes his eyes again.

"No," he tells Fraser, the strain in his voice palpable, "and I guess I never really knew Kathryn, my grandmother and Dad's wife, the woman who didn't want to be either."

"Your great grandfather, Lawrence, was a weak man and caved in to his wife's demands. He loved his daughter, though, and let her come back home after the wife died. Geneva would have never accepted Kathryn getting divorced. Did you know Geneva died shortly before Kathryn left the old man? And you?" Fraser picks up his cup and sips.

"Did Dad know any of this?" Marcus sounds like he's whispering. Like his vocal cords have collapsed.

"According to Annie Louise, he knew Kathryn wanted out. Just didn't know she was going to leave when she did." Fraser spreads his arms wide when he adds, "Probably means the old man had to look elsewhere for pussy. Makes sense, doesn't it?"

Marcus groans. He spreads his own arms wide in imitation of Fraser and says, "Makes perfect sense."

"You're a divorce lawyer; you know shit gets complicated in marriages. You take the side that's paying you and go for the win. On this one, I'd take your old man's side. You?"

Marcus frowns, but it's him performing for Fraser now. A sense of relief has come with Fraser's recap of Annie Louise's tale. He's not sure why but he knows the relief is real. "Dad all the way," he says.

"And George?" Fraser is smiling now.

"I'll give it a second thought," Marcus says.

"And Seleste?"

"She's all yours." Marcus points a finger in Fraser's direction. "Seleste and I aren't the same people we were a few days ago. And neither one of us likes these new versions."

"So your divorce from Seleste is final. You know I have to take her side on this one," Fraser says, then finishes off his coffee and prepares to leave. "Be talking to you soon, Counselor, about old George. Good luck to you and Missy."

"And may the force be with you," Marcus says, then reaches across the table and bumps fists with Fraser.

* * *

Teresa was waiting in his driveway when Marcus got home. Now they're sitting in her car, parked in a spot overlooking the beach and the lake. It's early evening and still light outside. The parking lot's semi-filled and the beach is dotted with strolling couples and women in street clothes watching over children in bathing suits. A few dogs romp through the sand.

"I'm sorry I didn't take your calls or return them," Marcus says.

"I was scared."

Marcus grimaces. "Scared?"

"That you'd had enough of my antics."

"To be honest, I thought I had, too. But that didn't last long, and after I came to my senses, I relied on my stubbornness to make you pay." They both try to laugh.

Teresa caresses his hand, then says, "I paid. To be honest, I cried a little. I felt so sad when I thought it might be over between us."

"I stayed in a funk."

"I'm a handful, I know," Teresa says.

Marcus rubs her cheek. "That you are."

"I can't promise I can fix myself anytime soon." Teresa sighs, then says, "I like us, though."

"I like us too. Most of the time." He glances at her and continues rubbing her cheek.

"I want you to like us all the time," she says.

"I know."

"I know all of our—uh, let's call them stand-offs—have been my fault. Not yours."

"Maybe I've been a little insensitive to your feelings." Marcus moves his hand from her cheek and begins stroking her arm.

"Do you think we can make this work?" Teresa asks, her voice so soft it's barely audible.

"I don't have the kind of track record that says *I* can."

"So. What now?" Teresa says. She reaches for his hand and squeezes.

"I've thought about this. A lot. I think we need to clear the air about some things," he says.

"I'm listening."

"We ask each other the questions we want to ask, and we tell each other the things we need to say. Clear the air and see how we feel afterward," Marcus tells her.

"You first," Teresa says. "It's your idea."

"It's a suggestion. Do you agree?"

"I do, but you still go first." Teresa leans toward him, and they kiss. Long and deep until their heat threatens to detour them away from their decision to clear the air. Teresa slowly pulls away and retreats to her side of the car. "Shoot," she tells him, then closes her eyes.

"Question: do you believe I love you?" he says.

She keeps her eyes closed and answers. "Yes. Do you still love me?" This time she opens her eyes and looks at him.

"Yes. I do." He stares at her. "I do. But it makes me feel vulnerable and I go into protective mode. Can you understand that?"

"Yes."

He pulls her back to him and wraps an arm around her shoulders. Then Marcus says, "That's my issue and mine to handle. I think it's because of Kathryn. I guess I never want to be left hanging emotionally like that again."

"Understandable." Teresa closes her eyes again. "I have trust issues."

"I know."

"I think it's because no one's really been in my corner all my life. At least that's how I've felt."

"You've been your own protector."

"Pretty much," she says.

"So how do we get past ourselves?"

"That's what we're doing now. Right? So can we get rid of Ana?" Teresa shifts her position. She scoots back to her side of the car, puts her back against the door, and drapes her legs across his lap.

"I got in too deep with Ana and broke it off. 'Too deep' means she wanted a connection I couldn't give her." Marcus exhales loudly. "There's no more to it than that."

"Why not?"

"I didn't love her."

"Have you ever loved any of your girlfriends?" Teresa keeps her eyes closed.

"No. Wouldn't let it happen. The feeling I had when Kathryn left us was a feeling I never wanted to have again. When feelings start getting intense, I cut and run."

"Is that why you disappeared on me?" Teresa's eyes are still closed, and her breathing has become labored.

"It didn't work this time. It was too late." Marcus makes a vain attempt to laugh. "I discovered that leaving you wasn't going to be that easy."

Teresa opens her eyes, clears her throat, and says, "I got pregnant and had an abortion while still in high school. I thought I loved the boy and after his parents and Momma joined forces to break us up and force the abortion, I don't think I've ever trusted anyone ever again." She closes her eyes again, inhales deeply, and exhales slowly.

"Momma called me a little whore, and I proceeded to be who she told me I was. Not screwing every boy in town but I did get a reputation. I had three boyfriends after Buddy, the white boy who got me pregnant, and freely had sex with all of them, and they all had big mouths." She keeps her eyes closed but doesn't say anything else.

Marcus rubs her legs and says, "I already knew. Your brother told me."

Teresa slowly opens her eyes, now moist with tears, and says, "You knew?"

"Yes."

"What did you think?" she closes her eyes again, but the tears can't be stopped.

"I didn't take it like a champ."

Teresa's voice cracks when she says, "Thought I was another Ana?"

Marcus swallows. He squeezes her legs. "It was a gut punch. My thoughts were all over the place, but by the time we got back to the motel, I didn't care because I love you."

Teresa cries silently. Marcus watches her a few seconds, then leans back and closes his eyes. Minutes pass. The moon is visible even though the waning sun still sends a few more rays for the remaining die-hard sunbathers.

"You know," Teresa says softly, "I've never felt ashamed. Ever, about any of the choices I've made in my life. Regrets but never shame. But I cared about what you would think about that part of my life if you ever found out." Although her laughter is weak, it is a valiant attempt. "Tommie's an ass."

"I started to punch him in the mouth when he told me. But he'd had six beers by then, so I gave him a pass." His laugh is stronger than hers.

"How do you feel right now?" she asks, wiping at the tears still easing down her cheeks.

"That we should give this our best shot," he says.

"Me too." Her eyes stay closed, but she quits trying to stem the flow of tears.

A nice breeze blows through the open windows along with the mixed sounds of the different species of birds that perch in the swaying branches of trees or dart through the open spaces above the beach. There is even reggae music drifting through from somewhere nearby. Marcus looks down at Teresa and smiles, then reaches over and slides a finger across each cheek, disrupting the glistening wet streams. She opens her eyes and smiles back.

THE END

NEXT UP...

"Richard P. Cannon" is a tale from the short story collection, *In the Kingdoms of Men*, which is Book One of **The Seven Stories Series**. The Seven Stories Series includes two books, each book containing seven stories that chronicle key moments in the lives of ambitious men who succeed and fail in love, work, and family relationships. This excerpt from "Richard P. Cannon" offers readers a peek inside this entertaining and thought-provoking collection of tales.

I

"Richard P. Cannon"

He thinks he's broken-hearted and thinks I can save his marriage. He's a man whose dreams have been realized and his unquestionable success is worn like a kingly crown. Richard P. Cannon, a man who's felt on top of the world, is a confident and self-made man. He earned an MBA from the University of Chicago and owns a chain of laundromats all over the city. He's a man who believes his noteworthy accomplishments, achieved through hard work, sheer determination and perseverance, assure him the respect and admiration he seeks from those closest to him. He's about to learn that living in a man's world doesn't mean he's king. I'm Monroe Grimes the lawyer and my client is a young, black, talented and rich thirty-two-year-old entrepreneur. The two of us, sitting across from each other at my chrome and glass desk, are meeting for the first time. "She doesn't really want a divorce," he says, his distress, unhidden, reveals the struggle he's having processing his situation. "She still loves me, and I still love her. I've been faithful. Been her rock. The man, *she* told me this, that checked all her boxes."

At first, it frustrates me. Richard has convinced himself that he's hurt. He wants to be a victim but he's not. He's a failure. At marriage anyway and he's not used to failing. But marriage is not a business. And most of the people who try it fail. Including me. To get him to a place where he accepts that his marriage is over will take time, and patience. Time, I have plenty of and it's expensive. Patience is the least he deserves for the money he's going to pay, when it's all over, to both Mrs. and me. The system is his adversary and he's going to need every ounce of toughness he possesses.

Richard is a short chubby man with dark skin and soft hands. The Hickey Freeman suit is an extraordinary fit and his manicure is meticulous. Richard's head is bowling ball round. His thinning pelage is cut close but a few bald spots resembling finger holes tell the whole truth. His pencil-thin mustache is neatly trimmed and is the only facial hair on his baby face. Richard's teeth have obviously received the attention of the best orthodontist in the city, and his cologne reminds me of my old man's own woody smell. It creates a kind of connection for me. He is not an unattractive man. According to Richard, his thirty-seven year-old wife is a good-looking woman who is handsomely dark, full-bodied and has beautiful eyes and a winsome smile. She is also a wonder woman in bed. He fell in love, it appears, minutes after his first orgasm with her. Five years later he's still addicted.

Minutes pass before he's ready to discuss his case again. I make sure we discuss our financial arrangements. The retainer is $10,000, my hourly rate is $150 and expenses are billed separately. He doesn't blink so we sign the agreement. They have no children together, but she brought in her five-year-old son for Richard to parent. He loves the kid. Maggie loves the kid. But kids aren't enough to save a marriage. Richard says they've had the normal ups and downs all married couples have but never anything serious. Maggie claims they have irreconcilable differences. He thinks maybe she's just testing him. He told her as much. She dismissed him with a wave of her hand.

He's deep in his denial phase and cannot fathom the notion he might have been taken for a ride. He begins a soliloquy on their first years together. Fairytale stuff. I don't know if he's been taken but somewhere buried deep inside his fragile ego, I do know he knows. Richard Cannon shits cash money and Maggie probably smelled it the moment they met. Luxuriated in it for a half decade before deciding she wants out. Yet he wants to find a way to make her stay. My experienced intuition tells me she won't though. When Richard concludes telling me about their early wonder years as man and wife, I ask several of my standard interview questions.

He tells me he believes Maggie has seen an attorney because she advised him to get one. She told him she wanted a divorce two weeks ago while he was engaged in foreplay one evening. It took him completely by surprise. She gently pushed his hands away, got up, walked out of the room and left him naked sprawled across their bed. He assumed she was still upset from an incident that happened that morning. In order to get ready for the challenges of his intense workday, Richard has a shot of bourbon each morning and had a glass in his hand when their son Hayden walked into the kitchen, saw the glass and like usual asked Richard what he was drinking. "My picker upper," Richard said, giving his routine answer. Hayden as usual asked if he could have a taste. Richard, for some reason he can't really explain, handed the boy the glass and told him to take a sip. Hayden took a swig. Choked and almost past out. Then threw up all over the kitchen. Made Maggie mad.

Richard says Maggie doesn't shout or curse when she's mad. Just says what she has to say in a curt tone while staring you dead in the eyes. Then she walks away. I ask how often has she gotten mad? Once a week? Twice a month? More or less? Richard says about once per week since they married. His wife, he says, has consistently found an opportunity to challenge or chastise or criticize him whether it's been something he did or said or thought. He then reiterates his belief that his and Maggie's rifts are simply routine occurrences for married couples. When I ask if he gets angry with her, he says yes but only in response to her temper tantrums. "Tantrums?" I say. Richard nods.

Maggie, he says, had gone through some rough times before they met. She refuses to discuss her parents. The grandmother who raised her was both religious and strict. Granny wouldn't let her date in high school and made her attend church functions several times a week. She went to an average public high school, then on to city colleges earning a certificate to be a pharmacy technician. Then on to Western Illinois University for a bachelor's degree in Pharmaceutical Sales and Marketing. A long road for her, Richard says, that took her seven years to travel. Then at twenty-five, she started her career with Mercy Pharmaceuticals, fell in love, had a kid at twenty-six and by twenty-eight ended up a single parent. He tries to have patience with her mood swings, he says pointedly, because he understands how traumatizing her life before him has been. I nod to show I'm listening.

Richard's story is far different. Raised by his physician mother in a nice south side neighborhood, he went to a private elementary school and an elite public high school. He earned his bachelor's degree in finance from Howard. The only disruptive time in his life, he says, was when his father died on a ski trip with some buddies when Richard was four. He says he doesn't remember many things about his father but does remember that day. His mother, a frank talking person, told him with very little indirectness that his father killed himself. Such a dumb ass way to leave this world, his mother said as she cradled him in her arms. Richard says that he doesn't recall grieving the way his mother says he did. She told Richard he cried every day for weeks while he stood looking out the window waiting for his father to come home. He still has vivid memories of his dad, Richard says, and still misses him very much. I nod again.

* * *

Richard says he got lucky while working on his MBA. Two blocks from his small one-bedroom apartment in Hyde Park was a well-maintained laundromat that he used regularly. Eventually he met and got into a discussion with the owner, J.D. Turner, a white entrepreneur in his 70's. When Turner learned that Richard was pursuing an MBA at the university, they struck a deal for Richard to become Turner's independent contractor marketing the laundromat's services on campus. Richard worked hard and smart. Turner taught him the ins and outs of the business. Within a year the business ran into financial trouble. Turner talked about finding a partner to infuse some cash. He needed $35,000. When Richard suggested he could be that partner, Turner balked and questioned whether Richard could come up with the money. When Richard assured Turner he could, Turner then tried to persuade Richard to make it a loan.

Richard told Turner that if being black was a disqualifier as a partner, then he, Richard, wasn't qualified to continue bringing in the cash flow from the university crowd. Sixty percent of Turner's business was the result of Richard's efforts, so the two became partners. Once he was a part of management, Richard quickly discovered that Turner used the laundromat's cash mostly for his personal lifestyle, hence the need for a cash infusion. Richard fought Turner for control of the finances of the business often using the threat of leaving and starting his own laundromat nearby. Two years later Richard became the sole owner and paid back his mother the $35,000 loan. That was the inauspicious beginning of what has turned out, Richard says, to be the launch pad for his incredible success.

* * *

This talk of divorce makes Richard feel like he's losing another piece of his heart like when his father died. Then he cries some more. I wind things down. It's been an hour. This has been a fruitful session, mostly for background and to get the money and agreement straight. Now we'll wait to see what Maggie's next move is going to be. I escort Richard to the door and advise him to give Maggie my information to give her lawyer. He looks at me with pain etched deeply across his face and says maybe that won't be necessary. "Maybe," I say, and pat his back as he prepares to leave. "But, regardless," I assure him, "you can handle whatever comes your way. You didn't get rich by accident."

It's been several days since our last meeting and Richard has been served divorce papers. Now he owns his anger. "You know," he tells me, "Maggie says our marriage was a mistake. A fucking mistake." I'm caught off guard a bit. For some reason I didn't expect Richard to use profanity, and use it so well. "She wants me to believe that she believes that we were never in love." He's not suited up today but still well-dressed. Some nice tan loafers adorn his feet. He's wearing a pair of brown dress slacks with a light blue long-sleeved polo shirt that hugs his pudgy midsection. He doesn't sit but roams while he rants. My suite isn't large; three small offices, a reception area, a kitchenette and two restrooms. The view is great though.

A big picture window overlooks Michigan Avenue, Grant Park and Lake Michigan. Richard says, as he paces in front of the window, that he still hopes that he and Maggie can go to counseling and work through this confusion. He stops and stares out the window. He rubs his head repeatedly. Standing next to my desk he looks sideways at me. That's what he wants me to tell her lawyer, he says, marriage counseling. "Is this something Maggie's willing to do?" I ask, knowing the answer is obvious. "That's why her lawyer needs to convince her," he responds.

Her lawyer is Valerie Eastman, a redhead middle-aged woman with light blue eyes. She's all about the fees so if the divorce can be strung out with as much animosity as possible, that's a bigger payday for her. She's not likely to advocate for a quick reconciliation. The divorce case we were lawyering a year ago settled after quite a bit of bloodshed. It should have settled in one month. But Valerie, as I began to understand during our first meeting and came to know without a doubt after several breakfast, lunch and dinner negotiation sessions that followed, was exquisite at turning time into money. It took six months to finalize that divorce and reach a settlement agreement. I don't tell Richard this, just yet. His emotional tenacity is strained to the limit right now.

"I will advise her lawyer accordingly," I say, "and see what happens. Right now, we need a strategy just in case the divorce goes forward." Richard turns to face me, his eyes glaring, his hands pressed together in prayer mode, but he says nothing. Just looks at me or rather, I feel, looks through me before dropping his eyes, turning away and going back to looking out the window. I know what he's going through and not just because I'm a lawyer. I've also had my share of broken marriages; three to be exact. Like him, I was dumbfounded the first time. And like him I was mostly just dumb.

* * *

We see women who don't exist when we emotionally commit. Our blind spot. We take the parts that attracts us and weave them into our fantasies of the ideal partner. The other blind spot for a good guy is his emotional pursuit of becoming the woman's fantasy. We give up our power. Our sense of manliness. We make ourselves too vulnerable. And we lose the ability to listen with more than our ears. We lose our male instincts for survival. Women signal in subtle ways early on whether they hold you in high esteem. After my first marriage failed, I knew something was wrong with me. But it's only after a series of serious emotional ass-whippings that I truly understood. And if it is to happen, it must begin with pain. But, even then, there are no guarantees. I stare at my client's face in profile. It is painted in pain.

Marjorie Jefferson gave me my real lesson. I was twenty when I married her and she was three months past her eighteenth birthday. I was attending DePaul in the city and she was a freshman at the University of Illinois in Urbana. What turned out to be, in hindsight, my intractable insecurity rather than my belief in her misery from being separated from me, sent me helter-skelter down to Urbana one afternoon. We went out for a drive that lasted five hours before I was able to convince her to elope. I had it all planned out. We went to Vegas. A week later and married, we were both back at school. She at hers, me at mine.

I was feeling fine. Then she didn't come back to the city for two weeks and I couldn't reach her. Then she reached me with her petition for an annulment. I was hurt. At least that's what I believed. I blamed her father. I cried and cursed her for days on end although she remained MIA. There were no sightings and no contact as her father continually assured me that it was over because it never happened. He was and still is a lawyer. I hated him and feared him. Over the past twenty-five years I've seldom seen Marjorie since she lives on the west coast, but I've seen her father quite often. I told him several years ago that he inspired me to become a lawyer. He laughed and soon after we worked out a deal involving the case that had brought us together again.

And I came to understand that I was more disappointed in myself than hurt by the loss of Marjorie. I had given up my sense of self to become what I thought she wanted. I became weak. Women despise weak men. I have known of many situations where the men didn't survive, emotionally or mentally, the loss of their fantasies. There have even been a few homicides and suicides as a result. I don't think Richard got to be successful by accident so I'm hopeful that he's strong enough to survive this and get on with his life.

My second wife, Diane, was always telling me that I could be notoriously insensitive at times. Mostly when she and I were out and about perhaps walking arm in arm or hand in hand when some eye candy, as she would say, appeared on the scene. It would be a charming smile with an up and down nod or a slow finger wave or maybe a quick wink, then the eye candy would be gone and the two of us would move on except we didn't, of course. Within five years I was divorced again at thirty. By the end of that marriage, I knew who I was and why it failed. I loved my wife but I loved me more. And when she wanted out, I tried to persuade her to stay but I never begged. When she asked me to move out, the fight was on. Not to stay married but over my property. It ended in a truce of sorts and fairly, by my standards.

* * *

I meet with Valerie for a nice and somewhat expensive lunch to be eventually paid for by my client even though Valerie will front the cost today. She's dressed in a lovely green linen suit with a black silk top. The swells of her small breasts are teasingly visible but not enough to be too distracting.

She says hello in her best business voice which I promptly ignore. "Hey yourself, looking fabulous as always." I add a wink for good measure. It's not a calculated ploy. It's as natural for me as breathing.

Valerie looks me straight in the eyes. "Of course, I am," she says. But she's not really vain or pretentious. She works her image in the manner of a person impressed with her own appearance but she is not that person.

In our first meeting a year ago, she was frank enough to say, when I mentioned her vanity, "This is my better side." And after three hours of negotiating, a bottle of wine and a few more compliments, she said, "You know, Counselor, once inside these clothes you may not be so impressed." "Maybe," I said, "but will I ever be fortunate enough to discover that for myself?" Rolling her eyes was her response and it came with a smile. It began to feel like a date as we discussed politics, crime and the weather. She made constant eye contact and her baby blues were little magnets keeping me attached to her long heart-shaped face. She was and still is a captivating speaker.

"I relish this city, warts and all," she says. Her words slide out in a smooth and polished cadence. Her teeth are small and proportioned and her lips shine with flesh-colored gloss.

"Do you still live in Lincoln Park or did you escape back to the suburbs?" I say.

"The City in a Garden is the only place for me," she says. With that she picks up her glass of craft beer and we toast her life in Lincoln Park. We finish our appetizers and main course then she orders dessert. She leans back, sighs deeply and says, "I guess it's time to go to work. By the way how is Mr. Cannon?"

I say, "Not taking this threat to his family, home and marriage in stride. And he wants things back to normal."

Shaking her bobbed red hair side to side, she asks, "What's his version of normal?" She has the jawline and neck to make the style work.

"Not having two lawyers meeting on his dime discussing his fate, I suppose." My tone is flirtatious.

She nods and laughs. "Well, the Mrs. doesn't believe her life's been normal for some time. She wants normalcy, too." I ask if reconciliation is off the table.

"It's not even a consideration," she says. I ask how much she wants. "What's fair," she says.

I look over her head, out from the corner in the back of the restaurant where we are sitting, and take in the busy scene. The tables have filled. I focus on those twosomes that appear to be couples. Some are laughing and others seem enmeshed in intimate conversations. But not the couple across from us. They are headed our way, and from their body language, it will be sooner rather than later. They stare into their plates, eat slowly and are obviously avoiding eye contact with each other. Her meal is a big salad bowl and his is a steak and baked potato. I catch Valerie's eye and nod in the couple's direction. Valerie looks at them then back at me and raises an eyebrow.

"They want different things for their lives," she says.

I look back over at the couple and say, "Just because they want different meals?"

"I'm talking about our clients," she says, and gives her come-hither smile again.

"Why is she so adamant?" I take a sip from my glass, then smile back.

"The marriage was a mistake." Valerie says this with the conviction of someone who has borne witness to the marital discord we are discussing.

"A five-year mistake?" I raise my eyebrows.

"She tried to make it work," my counterpart assures me. "She is tired of parenting two kids when she only had the one."

"What are the going rates for nannies?" I ask. Valerie laughs again. I laugh too.

"How angry is he?" she asks just before sliding a forkful of cake into her mouth. She chews eagerly. Bashful she's not.

"Hurt," I tell her. "He honestly doesn't know why she's so pissed."

"She's not pissed," Valerie says, fork poised to unload another piece of cake. "Mrs. Cannon is determined. For her it's over. Didn't work out. Not her first one, you know." She slides the velvet red cake deep inside her mouth and moans.

"But it's his first time," I tell her.

"Oh right," she says, "he's a virgin." I nod. She lifts another piece onto her fork. I'm sipping wine for my dessert.

"What about their son?" I ask, sipping then savoring my dessert as the cool sweet taste of fermented grapes fills my mouth before cascading down my throat. "What will be the psychological effects on the kid after two divorces?"

Valerie sets down her fork next to a single remaining slice of cake, clasps her hands to make a base to support her chin. "I wonder, too," she says. "The Mrs. is very aware of the potential negative effects on Hayden but she just doesn't want to stay any longer."

"What is her real problem with Richard?" I say.

She trains her blue eyes on my brown ones. "She doesn't like your client." Valerie tells me this using her matter-of-fact tone.

"What does that even mean?" I say.

"For women, it's a deal-killer," she says, then polishes off that last piece of cake.

* * *

My third wife, Phyllis, divorced me because, she said, I worked too much, paid her too little attention, and expected her to always be on call for sex. True on all counts. But she knew who I was well before we married. Phyllis said she had hoped I would change. I said I had no reason to change. Because she was a stay at home mom Phyllis said she felt unappreciated. The world didn't respect what she was doing and neither did I. She might have a point, I told myself then, so I told her I would do better. She said it was too late. Given what Valerie has just told me about Maggie, I don't think my wife liked me anymore and, in her mind, she was already gone. But I also realize my wife's requirements for me to meet her expectations meant I had to give up the ones I had for myself. Déjà vu all over again. The woman I had fallen in love with, married and had two children with was a figment of my imagination. And to her, in the beginning, I had the makings of a knight in shining armor. Because of these misplaced expectations, our marriage was doomed from the start and probably so is my client's.

* * *

Richard arrives for what is now our sixth meeting far more casually dressed than he was in our previous sessions. The marital discord is wearing him down. His eyes have dulled and his shoulders now sag. "She did love me," he says, standing at the window staring out at the lake. I wait to begin discussing the sticky issues that come with divorce. "And I still love her," he continues. "Enough I guess to give her what she wants." He is worth ten million dollars. Valerie has sent me the wife's settlement proposal. Maggie wants half. I wonder what he thinks he's hearing at home.

"Have you and Maggie discussed settlement terms?" He turns to face me as I sit at my desk, leaning back in my chair that rests against the same window he's probably had fleeting thoughts of jumping out of to stop the pain. That was the same mentality I had when my first marriage failed to materialize. His has been in effect for five years. He's understandably distraught.

"No," he says. "She says that is what you lawyers are being paid to do." I ask him what he thinks is fair. He asks me what I think is fair. He didn't do a pre-nuptial agreement. I ask him if he thinks half his net worth is fair. Richard turns slowly and deliberately to face me. "She is asking for half my money?" he says. "More like demanding it," I say. "Think that's fair?"

He drops into the seat across the desk from me. We lawyers may facilitate the discussion of money but the parties must do their own negotiations. "I don't think so," he says after several seconds have passed.

"How much do you think is fair?" I say. Richard looks bewildered and I understand why. I felt the same way when dividing the assets became a reality in my second divorce. I did a prenup for my third one. And Richard has far more at stake than I ever had. How do you price partnership roles in a marriage? You can't and when you must, an emotional firestorm inevitably ensues.

"Not half," he whispers.

"Why not?" I say. His eyes are smoldering embers when he stares at me. "I had eight million before I ever knew her," he says. "How can she want half of that?"

"So, you believe she should only get half of the remaining two?" I say. Richard winces then looks down when he says, "I will let her have the two. To me that is fair." His voice carries with it a hint of resentment. This will be our counter proposal. And it will not be accepted.

"Richard," I say, "your love is about to be tested."

He smiles a bit, then looks up to face me. "I know," he says.

"Your balls, too," I tell him.

"Yeah?" he says, "Well, like you said before, I did not get rich by accident." Richard stands up, walks back to the window, stares out at the lake and starts whistling.